IN THE WAKE
OF THE RAVAGING FLAMES . . .

She knew where she was, and yet how could it be so changed? She was in that part of her plantation where the sugar cane grew. She shook her head in disbelief. Had the darkness from which she had been running caught up with her and blackened her whole world? Was she to be stripped of everything she possessed? *Non. Non.* Never!

She still had Cher Château. That could not be changed. She would run home and bolt the door. Lock out the black world which was engulfing her!

As Asya ran, her heart pounded more from apprehension than physical exertion. Cher Château would be all right. Nothing could destroy it. Its beauty made it inviolable. It was her home. Nothing could happen to a home. Asya ran faster. The path was sharp with stones, and her feet hurt, but their pain did not register. She must hurry to Cher Château and fight off all it was that endangered it.

ASYA
A WOMAN AND A STORY—TO FIRE
THE PASSIONS AND STIR THE SOUL!

ASYA

ALLISON BAKER

A DELL BOOK

Published by
Dell Publishing Co., Inc.
1 Dag Hammarskjold Plaza
New York, New York 10017

Dell ® TM 681510, Dell Publishing Co., Inc.

ISBN: 0-440-10696-6

Printed in the United States of America
First printing—December 1978

Part One

Chapter One

The waves lapped against the shores of St. Domingue, and the mountains, purple in the distance, dozed like slumbering field hands in a patch of sugar cane. The trade winds floated in from the Caribbean and tousled the leaves in the trees like a mother running her fingers through her child's hair. In the capital city of Cap François, a tropical afternoon sun had baked a somnolence into the narrow streets with their pastel pink and blue buildings. The Creole inhabitants rested in the shuttered coolness of their thick walled homes. It was March of 1791 and not much different from any other March the French colony had known.

Suddenly, a loud crash of thunder ripped through the town. The mountains came awake and appeared ready to pounce angrily upon the surrounding earth. The winds stilled. The leaves in the trees became torpid. The sky blackened as though a genie hand had snuffed out the flame of the sun, and an air of doom hung threateningly over the land. A jagged streak of lightning fractured the heavens and found its target in a tall palm. The tree quivered and, like an amazed giant, loosened its grip on the earth beneath and crashed down upon the small pink house it had always sheltered. From the splintered dwelling came the scream of a terrified woman. Abruptly it died. As if on cue, the heavens opened and rain pounded upon the roofs of the houses with savage vehemence. It thrashed the shutters of every structure in its way, wildly demanding admittance, not as a guest but as a vandal bent on destruction.

Trees, which had stood proudly years before Columbus had come upon the island, were struck down like saplings, and along the walks in the town square, the once tall, aspiring poinsettias lay flat on the cobblestones, their red heads smashed by the pummeling rain. Where the swamps had been green and gentle, they suddenly frothed and swirled until they had whipped themselves up into a chorus of frenzied ghosts dancing crazily toward the unpainted slave cabins on the outskirts of Cap François. They engulfed one of the Negro dwellings in their foamy drapery and mercilessly tossed it high in the air. From the interior of what was once home to a black-skinned family, the body of a child was catapulted into the violent waters and devoured. Capriciously, the waters plucked up another cabin, and the game went on.

In the sugar-cane fields, the slaves, whose black backs had sweated in the heat, lay flat on their stomachs, afraid, forgetting their loathing of the whip, yearning only for survival. But the rains flogged on in their wild rage, seemingly bent on wiping man and his handiwork from the face of St. Domingue.

In the morning, the rain stopped, but an overcast sky glowered down upon the island. The people ventured out of their dwellings and peered about. Great trees, centuries old, lay splintered, their roots torn from the earth and pointing skyward. Broken-down balconies and palm fronds were piled up before the doors of the shops, a tangled wreckage covering the street from curb to curb. Out on the plantations, the cane fields lay ironed to the ground, and the slave cabins were axed into kindling. Here, hopeless wailing floated through the morning air, a dirge to the night's destruction.

Those of St. Domingue who had come safely through the crisis did what man will always do. They took stock of the situation and then began to set life back into its old daily routine. The less fortunate, those who had suffered great personal losses, were dragged along by the energy of their neighbors.

When the storm was only two days past, the Creoles of St. Domingue island turned their attention back to another storm, a storm which had been brewing for years and did not involve the elements. This storm involved two men, Vincent Oge and Jean-Baptiste Chavonne. Together, these men had stirred up more agitation in French St. Domingue than any upheaval from the sky. Their tempestuous blowings had been felt as far east as Paris.

Vincent Oge and Jean-Baptiste Chavonne were mulattoes, each born of a white father and a black slave mother. Years ago, either as a caprice perpetrated upon his white islanders or in a freakish mood of compassion, a French king had granted freedom to all such progeny. Freedom, but no legal status. They were free to own slaves themselves, free to build plantation empires and engage in whatever commerce they could scrounge from the full-blooded Creole, but they had no voice in the government of their native land. As representatives of the thousands of mulattoes who lived on the richest island in the French Empire, Oge and Chavonne had gone to Paris to ask for equal rights with their white landsmen. The French States General, caught up in the cry for freedom for all the oppressed, found the request less complicated than some of the local problems on the agenda, and granted the request.

Vincent Oge and Jean-Baptiste Chavonne returned to their Caribbean island, victorious, but only in the eyes of a power-mad conclave across the sea. The Creoles of St. Domingue, while loyal to their king, refuted the decision of his governing body, apprehended the two mulatto leaders, and sentenced them to death.

The execution was set for March 12, 1791, and the means of death was not unusual: "—whilst alive to have their arms, legs, thighs, spines broken and afterward to be placed on a wheel, their faces toward

9

heaven, there to stay as long as it would please God to preserve their lives: and when dead, their heads to be cut off and exposed on poles."

But two days before the appointed date, the storm had pounded down from the heavens. Many took it as a sign that God was not pleased with man's treatment of his colored children. Nevertheless, when the sun again brought light to the day and man found that he could still be master over his brother, he brushed aside all uneasiness and proceeded with the plans for the execution. A scaffold was erected in the town square so that all might watch the death of the two men who had challenged Creole supremacy.

Only the Negro slaves still thought of the storm as a sign, but their voices had no place in the halls of the lawmakers.

Early in the morning of March 12, a carnival air already permeated Cap François. The Creole planters flocked into town and gathered in the square long before the appointed hour. Shops were closed. Hawkers noisily called out their wares of sweetmeats, rum, and bananas as they moved among the excited spectators. Little dolls, fashioned on sugar-cane sticks, were displayed on stands set up in the shade of the overhanging balconies along the streets—dolls to keep the young children, who had been brought along by their parents, amused until the show began.

However, not all the carriages found their way into the town square. Far out on the Plain du Nord, at the point where the sea road leaves the town road and winds its way along the coast to the dock, a single carriage separated itself from the stream of town-bound traffic and set out on its solitary way toward the sea. It was a golden vehicle, decorated with the blue and white fleur-de-lis of the King of France. Inside, a young girl sat weeping while the man beside her cradled her in his arms.

"It will be only until the baby is born, Celeste," he

said. "Time will pass quickly, and we shall be together again."

"I am afraid, André. I'm so terribly afraid. I know I shall never see you again." The girl opened her handbag and fumbled through the contents. Tears wet her cheeks. She shook her head to clear her vision. The man reached into the handbag and pulled out a lace handkerchief. He daubed her eyes, and then leaned over and tenderly kissed each lid.

On the seat across from the man and the girl, a black woman watched. Her color of skin marked her as a slave, but she bore herself with an air of truculence. Her back, stiff under a faded green dress, defiantly refused to rest against the satin covering of the carriage. Her face was that of an ascetic, long, thin, with hollow cheeks and taut skin. On her left cheek was an ugly pink scar, wide near the mouth and narrowing toward the eye. The gash had caused her upper lip to draw back in a permanent snarl, showing strong white teeth and red gums. The woman sat with her arms folded across her bosom, affecting an air of cold disapproval. Although a battered straw hat decorated with pink grass flowers shaded her eyes, it could not hide the intensity with which she regarded the couple across from her. For all her outward calm, she was inwardly disturbed. The tears which ran down the cheeks of the young girl also wet her own heart, for Celeste was her daughter, and she, Negu, was weeping with her.

Celeste, her own child! Hers! Born of a white father whom Negu had hated, she had grown into a delicate beauty. Her skin was a rich, creamy color, a blending of the two races. Her hair was dark, wiry, but her eyes were a pale green, clear as a translucent lake, with a halo of long black lashes. Celeste's features were as fine as those of the marble statues in the Drapeaux gardens.

Negu looked at her daughter with pride, and, for a moment, the features of the Negress softened. But just

11

as suddenly, the anger flared up again as she thought of the man who sat next to Celeste and who would soon be the father of her grandchild.

André Drapeaux was in his forties, though he did not look it. His brown wavy hair was still thick, and when the sun shone upon it, it gleamed like bronze. André was a short man, but his shoulders were broad and his stomach not yet paunched like those of other men his age. He had a round face and smiling gray eyes which gave him a cherubic look. His skin, while fair, was ruddied by constant exposure to the sun. If color had been any criterion of an owner's interests in his fields of tobacco and sugar cane, André might have been taken for the most devoted planter on the island. However, Celeste's lover left the financial well-being of his properties to his overseers and agents. His only interest in the land lay in hunting for mementoes from the days when Christopher Columbus had settled his men on St. Domingue. André spent weeks in his library going over old maps in an effort to locate possible sites of buried Spanish treasure. Celeste had accompanied him on many of his trips into the interior of the island. Upon her return, she was always dreamy-eyed and silent, as though the places she had just visited were too overwhelmingly sublime to discuss even with her mother.

Negu was mystified by her daughter's abstraction. To be sure, M. Drapeaux was a great talker, closing his mouth only to draw on his big-bowled pipe or to drain his wineglass. He was conversant in all subjects, from how to smoke a ham to what happened to the Ten Commandments after Moses had broken them. But even in the tavern of the Hôtel de la Couronne, where André went daily for his game of billiards, he gave others little opportunity to enter into the conversation. His discourses droned on and on, as though he were personally responsible for the enlightenment of his listeners.

This condescending manner of her master's revulsed Negu, but it was the very trait that seemed to endear him to Celeste. And Negu had no doubt that her daughter's quiet, gentle manner of listening, the way her green eyes looked up at him adoringly whenever he expounded his theories, had been what most attracted him to her. Celeste was a silent audience who flattered by never contending.

Negu would not interfere in her daughter's happiness. If M. Drapeaux was her choice for a lover, Negu would abide by it. What she would not abide by was André's negligence in providing for his mistress.

It was a common occurrence in St. Domingue for a Creole master to take a black or mulatto mistress, and for the mistress to provide him with a child. But Mme. Drapeaux, though she cared little for her husband, was a jealous wife. She resented the hold that the beautiful Celeste seemed to have over her husband. When Celeste was in her fifth month of pregnancy, and André had gone alone to St. Marc to follow a lead on a Spanish halberd, Mme. Drapeaux sent two of her field supervisors to Celeste's quarters. Without regard to her sex or condition, they had fiendishly bound her wrists with a rough rope, by which they dragged her along the rough path to the center of the slave quarters. There, she was tied to a stake, stripped naked, and given twenty lashes. Negu could still hear the hateful voices spitting out the count like enraged animals. Negu would have flung herself upon her daughter's tormentors and shredded them to pieces with her bare hands, but others held her back, cautioning, "Wait. You can do nothing."

Afterward, it was Negu who carried her daughter into the nearest slave shack and bathed away the blood from the golden skin. It was Negu who hunted in the woods for the herbs to make a poultice that would shut the wide gashes from the whip. As she administered to Celeste, she did not cry. Somewhere inside her a fountain of sorrow overflowed, and as it spread through her breast, it sopped up the pain and in its place left hatred.

She knew what she must do. The Creole could strip

13

the slave of all he possessed, even his own flesh, but he could never confiscate that knowledge which the slave's African heritage had bequeathed him. There was one weapon which she knew how to use. Voodoo! Like a tiger crouched in readiness in the shadow of a tree, Negu waited for the day when she would bring destruction to André Drapeaux and his wife. But she would be less merciful than the tiger that strikes once and kills. Death was too final a blow. She would arrange a living sacrifice to her hatred, a sacrifice that was paid, day after day, year after year.

Negu studied the man across from her. The hypocrite! He was all gentleness as he cradled Celeste's body against his breast. Why not! Hadn't he managed the problem well? When the white physician who had come to examine Celeste had told him she would have difficulty bearing the child, he had arranged to ship her off to France. There she was to be placed in the care of Soeur Benedicta at the hospital of the Sacre-Coeur in Chalon-sur-Marne. His own mother had suffered complications before his birth and he himself had been safely delivered by the renowned nun who was, by now, in her seventies. Shipping Celeste far, far away was the easy solution to André's problems!

The golden carriage slowed to a stop. It had arrived at the dock. Negu thrust open the door and slipped out. Subserviently, she waited as André stepped down from the carriage and turned to help Celeste alight. Despite his officious manner, André was tender in his handling of his mistress. He ran his fingers caressingly about her neck until they touched her chin. Tilting her face up to him, André kissed Celeste on the mouth. Then with both hands, he carefully brushed the black hair back from her temples, while he studied her face. She looked back at him in faith and love. Negu envied them. Her own white lover had not been so tender.

André spoke quietly. "Good-bye, my love. I shall be here when you return."

Celeste's eyes widened. Apprehension came into her

face. She pushed André away and stared at him. As though seeing something frightening, visible only to herself, Celeste cried, "No! No! Suppose I don't return. Who will look after you?"

Startled, André reached out for her, but she ran from him to her mother. Hysterically, she grabbed Negu's shoulders. "Mama, Mama! I'm so afraid. If I shouldn't come back, look after André for me. Promise. Promise that nothing will harm him. Nothing, ever."

Negu's mind darted off to the hills beyond the Plain du Nord. She thought about the secret meetings of the desperate slaves. But the child could not know. She could not possibly know. Yet, the wild fright in Celeste's voice, the frenzied hands digging into her flesh through her dress, told Negu that the girl had some premonition of the rebellion to come.

Her hesitation was noted by Celeste, for she stepped back and looked hard at her mother. Even though her voice was shaky, she spoke with determination: "I shall not go, Mama, unless you promise before God and Dambolla to look after André. You must promise, Mama!"

It had been an effort for Celeste to speak so forcibly, and her strength left just as quickly as it had been summoned. Helpless, whimpering, she lay her head against Negu's breast and sobbed, "Promise, Mama. Promise."

"Celeste," André said, putting his hands on the girl's shoulders, and trying to draw her to himself, "I'm a strong man. Nothing can harm me." He seemed amused, as by the carryings-on of an unreasonable child, and it irked Negu. She drew in a deep breath. Her voice was firm and reassuring when she spoke. "Celeste, I promise to look after André and all that is yours while you are gone." Negu groped for the edge of her skirt with one hand as the other lovingly pulled Celeste's face back from her breast. She wiped the tears away from those beloved green eyes. Negu coaxed, "Smile, dear, so that I who love you so much

15

will carry the image of a happy daughter until you return."

Her words brought a chameleon change to Celeste's face. It was the face of a little child, trusting, believing what has been promised it. Lovingly, Celeste put her arms about the older woman's neck and whispered, "I love you."

Negu knew then that she would do everything in her power to keep her promise to Celeste. She turned her daughter toward André and said quietly, trying to keep the tremor out of her voice, "This is your moment, your last moment together."

With that she walked from the pier.

Chapter Two

Negu walked toward Cap François. Although the dock and the warehouses were on the outskirts of the city, far from the town square, she could hear the carnival shouts of the spectators. White, of course. Who else would dare call out in jubilation during the day? Only at night, in the protective woods, would a black raise his voice, for the woods blanketed a black man's lamentation of his sufferings, his call to his beloved. A black man did love. A black man hurt and a black man cried out in pain. The whites did not believe this. They thought him a slave, one who was only made to serve. One who was less than a dog because he did not whine for a pat on the head. But at night a black man and a forest could merge; under cover of darkness, and in company with his brothers, a black man could plot retribution against those who wronged him. Negu knew these nights. It was like shouting to a confessor, not of one's sins but of the ways in which one had been sinned against. The whites called it voodooism. Little did they know it was not a religion. It was a meeting of exultation, of stimulation—an arousal to action. The night was not far off when the whites would pay. Did they in their smug way think that the merciless execution of Chavonne and Oge could frighten the blacks who died each day on the rack of degradation?

Slaves were living, feeling—human. The whites had Christianized them without letting them live as Christians. They had told them of a God of goodness and then withheld that God's goodness from them. If it was

17

so about God, and the blacks believed it to be so, then the black man would have to help himself to God's gifts for all his children.

Negu began to shudder. The cacophony of voices in the distance grated against her ears and she knew that the execution was well underway. The men on the rack, strong though their intent, must have cried out in pain and derisive jeers interspersed the shouts of the merrymakers. Pain. That was what the mob had come to watch. Negu winced at the thought and hastened her step.

Soon she arrived at one of the less affluent business sections. Here, the shops were closed, since both merchant and patron had convivially gone off to the square. The lancet arches made by the entranceways of the shops stood like immobile guards along the vacant streets. At the end of the thoroughfare was a narrow path which led along the edge of swampland and then turned abruptly into the woods. Here, undisturbed by the vacillating crowd, she could begin to plot her revenge. As she walked along, her thoughts centered on Mme. Drapeaux, André's wife.

"Wife?" Negu shrugged her shoulders. A wife was of small concern in St. Domingue when a white planter loved a mulatto girl. French law decreed that no white man on the island could have intercourse with a black slave girl, but who among the inhabitants was hypocritical enough to enforce the law? The lawmakers themselves had mistresses with black blood. It was as natural as the sun in the sky, as the cane in the fields, as the altar in the church.

For the black concubine, it was a happy arrangement so long as the attachment continued. Negu herself had been taken young, at the age of fifteen. The fact that her master was past sixty did not concern her. He had after all, set her up in her own quarters across from the opera house in Cap François. A carriage, jewels, servants had been hers. M. Matraux had even taught her to read and write. They were a game to him, those lessons. No other man of his acquaintance had an educated black mistress. Most blacks spoke patois, but Negu's master had taught her the French of the Queen's court in Paris. His favorite book was Rabelais' third volume of *Pantagruel*. Often in the evening, as Negu read aloud to M. Matraux, he chuckled and bent over to give her a proprietary pat on the rump to show his approval. It wasn't long before M. Matraux became more interested in Negu's rump than in her well-accented reading of Rabelais.

At first, she enjoyed her role as mistress to such an eminent planter as M. Matraux. But after her first pleasure had worn off, Negu grew bored. There were long hours, sometimes days, when she was left alone to amuse herself. It was during one of these periods of ennui that her interest came to nest upon one of Matraux's slaves. He was the messenger who brought delicacies from the Matraux kitchens and cellars to her apartment. He was tall, lithe, and young, and they fell in love. Negu was too naive to hide her clandestine affair with the youthful slave, and M. Matraux learned of her unfaithfulness. Furious, he had the burly foreman of his field slaves drive her through the streets of Cap François and then out to the plantation in a dung cart. Then she was roughly picked up and hurled into the pigsty.

"Get to your feet, you filthy lover of swine!" he had jeered. She tried to stand in the mud of the sty and he laughed in derision, "Can't tell one pig from the other. But this new one doesn't grunt. Come, grunt so the others will know that their sow has come home."

Negu had begun to cry, but Monsieur cracked a horsewhip across her face, and in her pain all she remembered was the grunt of the pigs at her feet, as she tried to emulate their sounds.

"That's better," Monsieur shouted. "Now there's no difference."

He grabbed her hair and jerked her face toward the barn. "We treat our pigs well here. We provide entertainment for their amusement. Look, my prize sow, I've planned this one especially for you."

M. Matraux slapped her cheek with the handle of his whip and she turned her eyes toward the barn. What she saw made her freeze. Ahead, with his arms outstretched, stood her lover, naked, his hands fastened by nails to the barn.

"I thought you might recognize him better without his clothes." M. Matraux gave a vicious laugh and called to his gorilla-like foreman, "Begin, Gumbo!" The huge executioner, machete in hand, approached the nailed figure and began to slash him wildly about the head and face. As Negu watched the butchery, nausea overcame her, and she vomited down the front of Monsieur's white shirt.

He roared with laughter. "You don't like our little show?" he asked. "We've only begun. Wait until you see the next act. That's where we reach the climax of the performance." Again, that fiendish laughter.

Negu tried to turn away but he clutched her hair so tightly that she could not shut her eyes. She saw Gumbo raise his machete.

"Step aside, Gumbo," ordered Monsieur. "Let the little sow get a full view."

It was only then that Negu became aware of his diabolical intent. As the black gorilla's machete descended, she knew that it was the end of all physical love for the man nailed to the side of the barn. Negu fainted.

That night, M. Matraux died. He suffered a heart attack after sunset and was dead before his physician could be summoned. Negu wept, not because she mourned his passing, but because his death had been too merciful. It had cheated her of revenge.

Shortly afterward, Negu was sold to the Drapeaux plantation where she gave birth to Celeste. M. Drapeaux had been studying in France at the time and, soon after his return, married Adele Devezé, daughter of a wealthy slave trader. Compared to the other Creole girls, the new Mme. Drapeaux was lacking in cultural refinements, but she was coquettish and beautiful and came to her husband with a generous dowry, generous even by affluent Creole standards. Adele Devezé, had not been well received by the more socially prominent womenfolk of Cap François due to the source of her father's income. The Devezé family was nouveau riche and not of sufficient background to fraternize with the great on the island.

However, marriage into one of Cap François' best families changed the complexion of Adele Deveze's social status. At parties she served the best wines imported from the vineyards of France, and she acquired a bright feather in her cap when she hired the king's chef away from His Majesty at Versailles. The Drapeaux name and the Devezé money were wedded into a glorious social marriage.

But André had other tastes. He preferred a more intellectual life. While in Paris he had studied at the Sorbonne, where he acquired a leaning toward philosophy and history. Adele's parties bored him. His student days had taught him to weigh, to criticize the life about him. By thirty, he had examined his present life, very closely and he found both it and Adele wanting.

He was going into his thirty-fifth year when Negu approached him and asked if she might borrow some of the books from his library. He was amazed.

"Do you read?" he inquired in disbelief. "I had no idea that any of my servants had learning."

"*Oui*, monsieur," Negu answered. "I read quite well. But the books I would borrow are not for me. They are for my daughter, Celeste. I am teaching her."

This was a new area of interest for André. It was decided, by M. Drapeaux, of course, that he would select the books, Negu could teach them, and he, André, would test the student.

It was then that Negu began to hate him. All she had intended was to expose her daughter to the pleasure of good reading. Drapeaux was turning it into another exercise for his own self-aggrandizement. Stories came back to her of her master's braggadocio tavern ramblings of how he was educating a mulatto girl, a most attractive one to boot, daughter of one of his slaves. Negu had visions of his right eyelid dropping in a knowing wink when he said "attractive." She could see him toying with the stem of his wineglass as he casually mentioned the books Celeste was reading. Negu was furious. Her daughter was not to be a topic for tavern discussion! The patronizing manner in which he spoke of his alms to the church, his interest in his slave's child, impressed Negu as the boasting of a hypocrite. He wanted the world to regard him as a grand gentleman, who was above the mercenary accumulation of worldly goods. And why not? Why should André concern himself with the filthy franc? Had not his father and his wife's father amply filled the family coffers?!

Negu roused herself from her recollections and thought once again of the future. Revenge must now be her stimulus, and the luxury of hating M. Drapeaux would have to wait for a later time. Revenge! Revenge! Negu's heart sang out in incantation. Her feet, as she placed one before the other, knelled the intonation with a steady beat. Revenge! Revenge! Mme. Drapeaux! Revenge! Revenge!

The path grew darker as the trees became thicker. Negu welcomed the shadows. It was the earth's way of sheltering her from the glare of the white man. The earth enveloped her and seemed to say, "Come, and be a part of me. As I understand the sun and the shade and the rain, so I know you, my sister. I shelter you, the black race, even as I shelter the bird and the squirrel. We are as one. As the sun crosses the sky each day, so do I embrace you and announce that all men, even those who are white, must obey nature's law. If you do wrong, so you must pay."

The woodland path turned and the trees now grew closer together. They looked like dark sentinels who had sidled up to each other to form a black wall of

22

bark. The rays of the sun skipped only upon the tops of the tallest trees and then, like well-trained children, sent back their warm smiles to the orblike parent who had sired them. Negu slowed down. She smelled a sweetness in the air. It seemed as if it came from a rose that had given out one last fragrance before it dropped its petals.

An eerie spirituality took hold in Negu's breast and swelled until it permeated her whole being. She sped forward again. She was like a spirit flowing through its own abode, arrogant with the knowledge of its limitless powers to shape destiny.

Negu came to the outskirts of Joswee's hounfort, and there she stopped. The hounfort was built as any other grass-and-mud hut in the woods about Cap François. It was circular with three long poles protruding through the opening in the center of the roof. There, however, the comparison ended. As the church in the square thrusts its steeple skyward to hold aloft a cross for all to recognize the House of God, so did Joswee's temple carry its trademark. At the end of each pole was mounted the skull of an animal—a cat, a pig, a horse. While no sun came through the thick branches of the trees overhead, rains had buffed the skulls, and they stood out sharply white against the dark shadows surrounding them.

Negu's heart leaped with delight as she looked upon the skulls. Had she been able to, she would have reached up and embraced them, for they were the insignia of the gods, the loas. They proclaimed that here was the abode of the voodoo spirits. Here Joswee, the high priest, tended their house and saw to it that the black man's wishes and needs were conveyed to the gods.

A white circle of chicken bones, polished by time, separated the brown grass structure from the dark green of the surrounding forest. These were the charms, the wanga, the sacramentals which warded off the evil spirits. Across the doorway to the temple hung

23

a dense curtain of long, thin, dried strands of sheep in-
testines. No evil loa, bent on mischief, would dare part
these strands and enter the sacred temple, there to
undo the blessings of the benevolent gods. The mimbon trees on either side of the entranceway were
decked with the symbols of the gods. There were the
crutch for Antibon-Legba, a powerful black whip for
Petro-loa, Papa Sobo's long-stemmed pipe, a necklace
of cocomacque beans for Ersulie, the beard of a goat
entwined about one of the branches as a homage to
Ogoun. Clay jugs of jean-jean, the delicacy made from
wild mushrooms, had been set about on the limbs of
the trees as a homage to Maîtresse. On the ground
about the trunks, small vigil lights, stolen from plantation chapels, tried to pierce the shadows with their tiny
flames. Among the exposed roots of the trees lay other
gifts to the gods from the faithful: bunches of white
grapes; oranges, skinned and ready for eating; chickens, still feathered, hanging grotesquely upside down
with their necks twisted, their eyes popping out in
amazement at the constant traffic of flies. Negu's nostrils widened from the smell of the decayed flesh of the
fowls. She raised her head and sucked in the odor, not
with repugnance but with joy. In exultation, she leaped
across the protective circle of chicken bones and
through the doorway of the temple.

Once inside, Negu hurried to the altar which had
been built about the center poles of the hut. There, a
tall vigil light burned with a flickering red flame. That
meant Joswee was close by.

"Joswee! Joswee!" Negu called. In her impatience to
be about her business, she could not wait for his answer and cried out, "Joswee! Where are you? I need
you."

A figure, so tall that it could have been a magic
genie, rose from behind the altar. "Have patience,
Negu. I am here."

Negu turned toward the voice. Gone was her impatience. Calmness, engendered by the feeling of power,

returned. The high priest was her power and he would help. Negu stretched tall as she looked up at Joswee. Added to his great height, the red silken turban about his head gave the appearance of a giant. Negu's eyes lingered on the turban. The fabric had come from Paris and had once been part of a dress belonging to Mme. Drapeaux. She had worn the dress to a ball and had come home quite drunk. Negu had helped put her mistress to bed. When Negu left Madame's bedroom early that morning, the red dress left with her. Later, when sobriety had returned and her mistress inquired about the whereabouts of the dress, Negu acted surprised.

"But, madame," she explained, "you wore no dress when you returned."

In her bewilderment, the mistress of the house must have thought it the better part of discretion to make no further inquiry.

Negu laughed as she remembered the pilferage.

"You are in a happy mood this afternoon," Joswee said as he came around to her side. His voice was soft to her ears, and yet it carried a rich huskiness. It spoke as though its owner had known all the sorrow of his people, as indeed he must have, for so many came to Joswee for help. The light from the altar danced like twin flames in the houngan's large black eyes. It flitted over his face, highlighting the deformed nose, making it look like two noses. It whisked its red reflections across his glistening teeth when he smiled, but their brightness only served to accent the two black caverns on either side of his mouth where teeth were missing.

"I am glad you are here." Negu knelt and kissed his hand.

"Come, come. Stand up and tell me why you have come. You are so excited that you are trembling." Joswee took Negu's wrists in his large hands and gently, for one so big, raised her to her feet.

"Celeste is gone. She is gone, Joswee. They are sending her to France to have the baby. I shall never see her again." As she spoke, waves of anger rose again in her breast.

"So," Joswee nodded his head, mulling over this information.

"Yes. Gone! André Drapeaux would have everyone think he has sent her to France, because he is so solicitous of her welfare. Bah!" Negu turned her head and spat upon the ground as though with this gesture she might rid herself of the revulsive image of a kindly André. "He is solicitous only of himself. It is a nuisance for a man's black mistress to die bearing his bastard right on his own plantation. But with an ocean between—" Negu shrugged her shoulders and tossed her head. "Who knows? It's all out of sight and neatly taken care of, and everyone will soon forget, including André."

Joswee placed his hands on Negu's shoulders and turned her face upward so that she could look into the almost bottomless depths of his black, black eyes. There she saw resolution as firm as her own. "Except you and me," said the rich steady voice which matched his intent gaze. "We will never forget. I will help you, Negu." Then Joswee turned from her and quietly left the temple.

Negu waited. She was calm now, icily calm. The play, her play, was about to begin. For years she had stored away in her heart those feelings of hatred, of wanting desperately to hit back. She had so often experienced those emotions that now when the curtain parted and she, cast as the leading character, strode out upon the stage, she knew her lines well. Unafraid, she would go through with her role until its deathly end.

Joswee returned carrying two flaming torches. Their dancing fires heightened the red of his turban, and polished his twin noses with their reflection. In the smoke from the flaming pitch fires which began to shroud his head, the high priest resembled an eerie satanic incarnation. He placed one of the torches in Negu's right

26

hand. With a shout of joy, she held it in front of her to light the way. She and Joswee were united in this mystic ceremony. Hell had come to earth and blessed them with powers of evil, not to do evil, but to avenge it.

Swaying from side to side, they began to walk toward the back of the hounfort, chanting Amens as they moved. Through the smoke and the fire, a crude altar of unpainted wood slowly became visible. A jar of sand stood on either side, and into these the high priest and his priestess planted their torches. The smoke began to rise like incense and billow about a square golden object elevated above the middle of the altar. Then the smoke, like an unearthly backdrop, circled behind the golden object, and the light from the pitch fires revealed the picture of a Madonna, enclosed in a wide frame of solid gold. At the moment the picture shone forth, Negu and Joswee dropped to their knees and stretched their arms toward the Virgin and Child.

Then, in the same tempo in which they had chanted the Amens, the two sang out the words of the Ave Maria. When they came to the end, they crossed their hands over their breasts, bowed their heads, and repeated the prayer from that position. Upon finishing this second Hail Mary, they again stretched out their hands to the Madonna, but this time, they recited the Apostles' Creed. At its conclusion, they bowed their heads and repeated it from this second position.

As the singsong homage continued through the Lord's Prayer, the Litany of the Saints, and the Angelus, Negu could hardly control the hysterical excitement that was mounting within. This was the first step in carrying out her vengeance upon Mme. Drapeaux. God in Heaven must be placated. His Mother and His friends, the saints, must not be jealous that she did not come to them for help. They were too big. The little gods, the loas, the friends of the black man, had more time to listen. Perhaps later, the little laos would tell the big God the Father about what they and Joswee and she had done. She looked at the golden Madonna.

The Virgin Mother looked serene and happy with the Babe on her lap, just as she herself had been when Celeste was that age. Now, happiness for Negu lay only in revenge.

With the completion of the second chanting of the Angelus, Negu and Joswee rose to their feet. They removed the pitch torches from the jars of sand and moved on to the center altar. Now the fire from the torches leaped higher, casting their illuminating caresses over two skulls, one on either side of the altar. Negu was home. Here were her friends. She and Joswee stuck the pitch brands into the holes at the top of the skulls, walked to the middle of the altar, and, crossing their hands upon their breasts, bowed.

A picture began to appear. At first it was indiscernible, but as the flames competed with one another in their efforts to reach new heights, they revealed a face. It was an old, old man with flowing white hair. His skin was dark, dark like Joswee's and Negu's.

"Dambolla! Dambolla!" Joswee and Negu shouted in unison. Then they dropped to their knees and stretched their arms outward as if to embrace him. They threw back their heads and called out in joyous song, "Fiolé opor Dambolla! Dambolla! wé dopo Fiolé oh!"

And Negu knew suddenly what she must do. The juice of the poisonous dumb cane! That would be the first of her vengeance! It constricted the throat and caused the saliva to run out of the side of the mouth and eruptions to form on the skin. Negu laughed. How could a man want to kiss a woman when the saliva ran from the side of her mouth. She laughed again. Joswee turned to look at her. Judging from his picture above the altar, she had the feeling that Dambolla was also staring in amazement.

"Dambolla. Wé dopo Fiolé opor Dambolla." But Negu's mind ran on. The image of the helpless woman caused her to sit back on her heels, put her hands to her cheeks, and laugh and laugh.

28

"Negu!" Joswee called out sternly.

"Dambolla. Wé dopo Fiolé opor Dambolla." To compensate for her naughtiness, Negu shouted her homage, but her thoughts refused to be tamed. She thought of ground-up horse's tail dropped into a cheese. It was a mixture that caused violent pains in the stomach, so violent that the sufferer must moan out her distress Then it gave the urge to sleep with a man. But when a woman cannot speak and cannot move, how can she make known her desire?

Negu's imagination ran on. Now that she had the power, one malady after the other would she inflict upon her enemy, Mme. Drapeaux. Death must be slow. So long as Celeste was away, just that long would Mme. Drapeaux lay dying.

Chapter Three

Mère Magdelaine stood by the window in her office and looked out. It was only the middle of the afternoon, but the gently falling rain was already washing away the color of the day and fading it to a pewter gray. The September morning had begun with bright sunshine and capricious winds, a morning that teased one into believing winter was far away. Quietly, a few drops of rain fell, and the sun seemed to beg pardon for its audacity and ebbed in retreat. The rain came faster, but still softly.

Mère Magdelaine was depressed. She always felt this way when one of her girls was giving birth to an illegitimate child. She felt about as useless as a stone in the road when the river rises and floods the land. How could one stone hold back the forces of an aroused nature? Just so, how could she, one mother superior of one hospital of the Sisters of the Sacre-Coeur, stem the waywardness of man? But her work was not to stem the flood but to soothe and repair after the ravages of the tide.

Celeste. Gentle Celeste. Mère Magdelaine's heart seemed to sink and drown in the tears of its own weeping over Celeste. Celeste, who had come from the colonies in hope for herself and her child. Sent by André Drapeaux, who knew nothing about birth except that it was the natural result of an implantation. Yet even his great wealth could not buy knowledge which man has not yet received from the Lord. A broken blossom does not bear fruit, and yet, Soeur Benedicta meant to try to save Celeste. She was already well into her seventies. The Lord had given her both a long life and great knowledge. Through her midwifery, the name of the Hospital of the Sacre-Coeur at Chalon-sur-Marne had spread throughout Europe. The hopeless, the frightened, the mighty, the lowly, the slut and the marchioness, they had all come to Soeur Benedicta. Some paid in the thousands of francs that others might pay only with their gratitude. To Soeur Benedicta it mattered not at all who paid in prayer and who in money; Sacre-Coeur was a maternity hospital and concerned only with the safe arrival of another of God's souls.

Celeste was one of those whose donation was high. Not that the sisters had set a price. It was André Drapeaux who had been generous. Perhaps he had thought the more he paid, the greater the miracle heaven could perform. But what were francs to Heaven, to Heaven that valued only man's soul! Francs were for the easing of poverty and the burdens of one's fellow man, not for bribing God to revoke His punishments.

"Oh, Lord," Mère Magdelaine prayed, "please send us a few little saints, not only saints for the poor, but some for the rich. They need your help, too, so that they may realize their wealth and power are given to them to share with others."

She reached for her rosary, which hung at her side, and walked slowly over to the statue of the Sacred Heart on its wooden pedestal. A red vigil light burned at Christ's feet, and its little flame in the darkening afternoon flickered timidly. Mère Magdelaine blessed herself and knelt on the floor before the statue. There is much to be done in this world, she thought. So much wrong to be righted, so much love to be shared, instead of anger. God in His compassion will have to step in. All I know how to do is run a hospital. If I do that well, then the Lord will have more time for those who are so helpless. She looked up at the sacred face and pleaded, "Please, God, if those who need Your help

31

are forgetting to ask You for it, then I'm asking You for them. I'll do all I can in the hospital, and You do what is needed elsewhere." Then, in a low voice she began her beads.

Mère Magdelaine did not notice that the room was already dark until a cry of "La Mère! La Mère! Mère Magdelaine!" came from the doorway. She turned in the direction of the voice. Soeur Denise, Soeur Benedicta's young assistant-in-training, stood outlined by the light in the hallway.

"Qu'est-ce que c'est?" In moments of stress, Mère Magdelaine kept her voice low.

"It's Celeste. Soeur Benedicta sent me to tell you she's—she's—" The nun began to cry uncontrollably. "She's dead! Oh, Mère, she was so sweet and I loved her. Why did God have to let this happen?" she sobbed. "All the wicked girls in the world! Why couldn't He have taken one of them?" Her voice had risen hysterically.

Mère Magdelaine rose and walked across the room to the young sister. It was difficult to be calm when she too felt like crying out against this injustice. But she kept herself steady, her voice low.

"And her baby? Is it dead too?"

Soeur Denise paused in her weeping. She spoke slowly as if it were an effort to reorder her straying thoughts. "No. The child is living, but it is very weak. So very weak that I know—I know—" Soeur Denise put her hands over her eyes to shut out whatever image her mind had created. "I know the baby will die too." Her voice became louder, hysterical. "It isn't right. It is wrong! Wrong!"

Mère Magdelaine grabbed her by the shoulders and shook her, but Soeur Denise's body was already shaking so wildly that the superior's attempt to calm her down had little effect. The older woman did something which she would later have to relate to her confessor. She slapped Soeur Denise across the face. She slapped

32

her so hard that the nun fell to the floor with the force of the blow.

Soeur Denise looked up in bewilderment, then slowly put her hand to her cheek. In a hesitant, disbelieving voice, she accused, "You struck me."

"Oui. I did," the older woman snapped. "Stand up!" Inwardly Mère Magdelaine was quivering. At times like this, it was hard to be a superior instead of a sympathetic friend. Soeur Denise rose slowly to her feet. She looked dejected and hurt.

"Soeur Denise . . ." Mère Magdelaine paused, then stood and waited without expression until the young nun raised her head and looked at her.

"Soeur Denise, we never question the ways of the Lord. We take vows of complete obedience to His will. Even though He has the whole universe to watch over, He never loses sight of one small soul. All His ways have a purpose. He is not wasteful with life as man is. He called Celeste, because that is in His order of things. He has a reason. Maybe someday He will reveal it to us.

"We here at the hospital are dedicated to His service. There are moments for compassion and moments for action. Right now it is action. If you are ever going to learn everything that Soeur Benedicta wants to teach you about midwifery, you had better hasten in and help with that infant. Save your tears for those times when there is nothing else to do. *Allez!"*

Mère Magdelaine watched the nun swallow twice before her lips moved and a small voice whispered, *"Oui, Mère."* Then she turned and started down the hallway. The superior stood in the doorway of her office and watched the small figure, which was beginning to hurry now. That meant that Soeur Denise was gaining control of herself. Suddenly Mère Magdelaine felt weak. Disciplinary measures took so much out of her. It would be a relief if superiors could scream and indulge in hysteria too. In a moment, when her heart stopped its fluttering and the blood slowed down in her veins, she would go to Celeste and kiss her farewell. But for the moment she sat down by the window to steady herself.

The rain was still falling. It made soothing sounds if one took time to listen. Its patter had a steadying effect, not unlike prayer or faith, and it refreshed. As she listened, Mère Magdelaine became conscious of other sounds, sounds made by carriage wheels rolling up the muddy approach to the hospital door. The carriage came fast. Perhaps it was another patient who had waited too long.

Mère Magdelaine breathed deeply in an effort to calm herself. Before she could move, the mother superior heard heavy footsteps rushing up the front steps two at a time, and then the bell rang wildly as though whoever pulled at the cord would rip it out. No one had ever before demanded admittance so noisily. Mère Magdelaine lifted one of the lanterns from its hook on the wall and hurried down the hall. Celeste was gone and already the Lord must be sending another soul for Soeur Benedicta to help into the world. The frantic summoning of the bell urged her on.

Curious, and now in full control of herself, Mère Magdelaine unbolted the door. As she lifted the latch, the person on the other side gave a mighty push, and the nun had to leap out of the way to avoid being knocked to the floor. Startled, Mère Magdelaine held the light high as she peered out to see who this impetuous caller might be. At the same time, the short, stocky figure of a man dressed in coachman's clothing whirled around and back down the steps to the carriage. Before he reached it, the door opened and the light from the mother superior's lantern revealed the folds of a woman's skirt spilling out onto the road as she stepped out. Mère Magdelaine heard the coachman say in a distressed tone, "*Nein, nein.* Don't try to walk, my lady. I will carry you." He spoke in German.

The woman began to sob, "Oh, Butte, you made it.

You made it! He did not catch us." She answered the coachman in the same language.

He was graceful for one so stocky. Quickly he lifted the woman in his arms and started up the steps with her, her heavy satin skirts trailing down onto the wet flagstones. Mère Magdelaine hurried toward them. With the lantern still in one hand, she raised the woman's skirts with the other so that they would not tangle between the man's legs and cause him to stumble.

In this manner, she led the way down the hall and into the bedroom directly across from her office, kept in readiness for just such an emergency. As she and the man placed the woman on the bed, someone held a light over them, and Mère Magdelaine knew without looking that it was Soeur Denise. In the illumination, the superior noted that the woman was so heavily wrapped that one could tell nothing about her state of pregnancy. But the hood of her cloak had fallen back, showing the face of a girl of about seventeen. Her eyes pleading with the nun, her face wet with tears, she was sobbing, "Save my baby. Don't let him kill her."

Soothingly, Mère Magdelaine answered in German, "No one can harm you here, *mein Liebchen.* Now, now, let us take off these wet clothes, and everything will soon be all right."

Mère Magdelaine hurriedly began to unwrap the cloak. The sooner the girl realized something helpful was being done, the sooner she might forget her fears. Suddenly the superior stopped in her ministrations as her hands came upon a small bundle, wrapped in a white blanket, which the girl held tightly against her breast. Firmly, but gently, she disengaged the young mother's hands from the bundle and pulled back the blanket. She looked down upon the face of a newborn baby. Its face was so blue, Mère Magdelaine would have thought it already dead, but for the small, faint wheezings which sounded in the little chest.

35

"When was this baby born?" she asked as she lifted the bundle from its mother's arms.

"This noon," the girl on the bed answered in the voice of one who is exhausted by the fight, and now wants someone else to take over.

Turning toward Soeur Denise, Mère Magdelaine spoke in what she hoped was a casual tone. "Give the lantern to this man here." She nodded toward the coachman. "Butte, I believe is his name. And you take the baby to Soeur Benedicta. She will want to examine it." She looked frantically at the young nun. Soeur Denise must have seen the urgency in her eyes, for she was gone in an instant.

Turning to Butte, Mère Magdelaine said, "Would you put the lantern on the table there and wait in the hall for me. I will want to talk with you later."

Noiselessly the coachman left the room. The mother superior turned to the young girl on the bed. "Now, my dear, I shall make you more comfortable. Suppose we take off your clothes." She spoke as one dealing with a sick child. "Oh, I see you are already in your nightdress. Well, let's take it off anyway. I'll put a flannel one on you. You will be warmer that way." The nun went to the chest of drawers from which she took an emergency-room gown and two woolen blankets. She was thankful that through the years Soeur Benedicta had insisted on such preparedness, for the patient was shaking with cold.

Having made the girl as comfortable as she could, Mère Magdelaine sat by the bed and gently caressed her cheek.

"What is your name, my dear?" she asked gently.

With her body shaking from both cold and weeping, the young mother paused a moment before she answered, "Sophia."

"Sophia," repeated the nun. "That's a lovely name. I have never known anyone with that name. It is not a French name, is it?"

The body of the girl was quieting now, and she

spoke with somewhat less effort. "No, I'm from Germany."

"Well," said the mother superior, "that's a beautiful country. Once when I was a little girl, my father took me to Bavaria. I remember the Black Forest. Never, never had I seen so many big trees. Do you live there?"

"No, *Mutter*." Sophia's voice still shook, but from weakness now, not tears. "I was never outside Hesse before."

Mère Magdelaine had an odd feeling of urgency. She must know more about these lives which had so abruptly thrust themselves into her care. At this moment, Soeur Denise came into the room with a pail of water and some towels.

"Soeur Benedicta ordered cold applications until she is free to see the patient," Soeur Denise explained.

As soon as Sophia caught sight of Soeur Denise, she began to cry. "My baby. What have you done with my little girl? You are the one who took her away, aren't you?"

"*Oui*. Soeur Benedicta is looking after her," the nun explained.

"Is something the matter? Is she going to die?" The patient's voice rose, betraying her fear. "Maybe it might be better if she did die. Then at least he would not be able to get her."

Mère Magdelaine looked inquiringly at Soeur Denise, as if to ask whether the child were still alive, but the young nun answered with an almost imperceptible shrug. The superior's heart sank. That meant the baby's condition was still uncertain. "Oh, Lord, don't let her die," she prayed, then remembered it was not for her to decide. "Lord, not my will, but Thine."

Perhaps, thought Mère Magdelaine, it might be well to talk with the coachman. "Soeur Denise will look after you, Sophia. I shall be right back."

She started toward the door, but the girl's frightened screaming brought her back. Sophia had thrown off the covers and was getting out of bed as she shouted, "He'll be here any minute, *Mutter*. Any minute now. He'll kill my baby as surely as he did her father. He's crazy!"

"No one would dare come in here and kill one of our babies, *mein kleines Mädchen*. This is a place to give life, not take it. I won't let any harm come to your little baby," Mère Magdelaine soothed. She gently put her arms about the distraught mother and laid her back on the bed. The girl had straight blond hair, and as it spread across the pillow, in the light of the lantern, it shone like the gold in the new monstrance. The nun touched it, and it was soft and silky.

"Mutter! Mutter!" Sophia clutched wildly at the nun's hands. "Promise my brother won't harm her. Promise to protect her. If you save her from my brother, I'll be your benefactress. I'll give you anything you need in this hospital. Just don't let him harm my baby." Her voice rose to a shout as she finished. "Help me!" All her anguish and need were in the last words. "Help me!" Sophia collapsed into deep sobs.

"Sophia," Mère Magdelaine said firmly, "I promised to help you. Trust me." She took one of the towels from Soeur Denise, who was standing by the side of the bed, and wiped the perspiration from the girl's face. Poor thing. So frightened. "Now let Soeur Denise take care of you or you will not be well enough for us to bring your daughter back to you. Remember, we must take care of the mother too."

Whether Sophia believed her or was too exhausted to fight any longer, Mère Magdelaine did not know, but the girl lay still, with her eyes closed, and submitted to Soeur Denise's ministrations.

The superior hurried out of the room and closed the door. In the hall she found Butte, standing with hat in hand, by the front entrance, as if he were guarding the door. His feet firmly planted, the short, hard-looking figure was at attention, ready for action in the defense of his mistress.

"Butte, I don't think we have to be on the alert for an attack," Mère Magdelaine said. "Come into my office and tell me about it."

"No, *Mutter*." Butte's voice was most definite. "Her Highness is right. Her brother is crazy. He's a killer. He'll bring harm to the baby. He said so."

"Her Highness?" Mère Magdelaine was startled.

"Duchess Sophia, sister of Actah, Duke of Hesse."

"Even a duke doesn't have the right to play God," she snapped in indignation.

"No, but he wanted to marry her to the King of Prussia . . ."

"And she had other ideas?"

"Yes, *Mutter*."

"Who is the father of the child, Butte?"

The coachman looked penetratingly at Mère Magdelaine and said nothing. He studied her face as though questioning her right to know.

"How shall I know on whose side I must fight if you do not tell me the facts?" she asked. "Furthermore, we must put the baby's parentage in our records. No one but the mother superior of this hospital ever sees those records. It's quite safe, Butte, to tell me everything. I will then know better what to do."

In a cold, almost vengeful tone, the man spoke, and his eyes, while they were on Mère Magdelaine's face, were seeing something far away. "I drove her to meet him. I carried messages for her, and I'm glad. It was the only happiness she ever knew, and if her brother comes, I shall kill him, for I hated him for his meanness to her.

"It was while he was away on one of his trips to Africa that she met Orlando," the voice went on like the steady toneless sound of a death knell. "He was a Spanish musician. Always, he was happy and sang and laughed. It was he who taught the duchess to smile and be gay like young girls should. He wanted her to marry him and go off to Spain, but she was afraid. The duke had betrothed her to the King of Prussia, a man as cold and as ambitious as himself." Butte seemed to spit upon each of the last words as they left his mouth.

"Why didn't she marry Orlando and be happy?" asked the superior.

"She has been afraid of her brother all her life! How could she suddenly stop fearing him?" he said with understanding in his voice. "And if you are in love, you don't want to bring harm to the one you love."

Mère Magdelaine nodded. "Yes, Butte, go on."

"Well, when Sophia learned she was going to have a baby, she moved to the summer home to wait for her child to be born. The duchess didn't expect her brother home so soon from his voyage, but he returned unexpectedly. He seemed frantic, desperate, a wild man. Everything in Hesse must be put in order, since when he next left for Africa, he planned never to return home again. His sister must marry the King of Prussia at once."

"Then he learned about Sophia and Orlando. The poor man never had a chance. I was at the summer house with the duchess when word came that her brother had killed him, run him through with his sword. That was why the baby was born this noon. The shock was too much for the duchess. Word came that Actah was on his way out to kill the baby. For their safety, I brought the duchess and her daughter to you. I could have killed Actah at the summer house, but it is better that I kill him here. At least, he will have you to pray for his black soul. In Hesse, he would have had only the curses of his people to hurry him into Hell."

"They would hang you for his murder. Is it worth the price, Butte?"

"Ja. Is worth it." His voice was certain. "I don't want any harm to come to my lady or her baby."

"No harm will come to them, Butte. Here, we are dedicated to saving life. In this hospital no one but the Lord has the power to say who will stay and who must leave this earth."

40

"But, *Mutter*," Butte looked at her as though she hadn't understood what he was saying, "you are only women. You must have been in here away from the world for too long. You can't fight a crazy man and his sword with a rosary and your blessings."

"My son, there are more peaceable methods of winning a war."

"*Nein, Mutter, nein.* I beg your pardon if you think I speak in insolence to you, but shut away here from the world, you think that God takes care of everything. You have no idea how hard people on the outside work to help Him run the world. Sometimes we need action besides prayer."

"Butte," Mère Magdelaine drew herself to her tallest height and spoke in the voice of one who gives an order and expects instant obedience. "Butte, your horse needs attention. Take it around to the back where there is a stable. Feed it and give it a rubdown. I'll wait here for the Duke of Hesse. I promise you—and mark my words, nuns don't break promises—I promise I shall send for you before the duke can do any harm to either the baby or the duchess. If we need a protector, I would much rather have you alive than dead, for I have an idea that Actah will kill you on sight. Dead you can be of no assistance to us." The man hesitated. In an urgent voice, the superior ordered, "Hurry! Hurry, before it is too late. The duchess has had enough grief without losing you too." She opened the front door and was relieved when the coachman put on his hat and hurried down the front steps.

Mère Magdelaine closed the door. She leaned against it and waited until she heard the horse slosh through the mud on its way to the stable. Then, with a sigh, she walked down the hall. Now, for Soeur Benedicta and the babies and Celeste. The best way to wait for a storm is to carry on with the labors of one's daily routine.

But Mère Magdelaine was only a few moments with

Soeur Benedicta when suddenly, through the quietness of the hospital, the bell sounded. At the same time, fists beat on the door like the hoofs of a horse in a mad race. Mère Magdelaine hurried to answer lest one of the younger nuns should arrive first and be frightened. She put her hand on the latch, took a deep breath. The storm had come quickly! She opened the door.

For all Butte's talk, Mère Magdelaine had expected to see a grizzly giant, but instead she looked down upon a short, slender man. The lamp in her hand showed he had a beard, but his eyes were shadowed by the brim of his hat.

"Yes?" she asked, as though it was not unusual to be so noisily summoned.

"I have come to see my sister, the Duchess of Hesse. Have you got her here?" he asked arrogantly.

"She is with us." The superior opened wide the door. "Will you come in, please?"

The intruder was taken aback. He had obviously girded himself to battle his way in, but he met no enemy. Then quickly, like a puffed-up little rooster strutting about on its skinny legs, the duke stepped across the threshold. Leaning back on his heels, he threw up his head and laughed in derision, "So, my slut of a sister has decided to stop running and take her punishment."

"Here, we have no traffic with punishment. That is the Lord's business," Mère Magdelaine answered in what she hoped was a calm voice, for her knees had now given up their shaking. They no longer seemed part of her. She hoped her legs might manage without them.

"For me the Lord is too slow," he sneered. "I can't wait a generation for Him to make up His mind. I'll take care of my world and let Him look after Heaven." Mère Magdelaine was reminded of Nero watching the Christians being devoured by the lions. "God," she prayed inaudibly, "help me with this wild animal."

"And where do you have my little sister hidden?" he

42

taunted. He had cornered his quarry and was savoring the anticipation of the kill. No hurry now.

Suddenly the door of the emergency room opened and Soeur Denise, bucket in hand, stepped out into the hall. She glanced at Mère Magdelaine and put her finger to her lips. Sophia was evidently quieted.

"Oh, so that is where you have my baby sister," he accused with an edge of mockery in his voice. "I guess you didn't have time to hide her. I got here faster than you expected. It wasn't hard to know where to come to. Your convent is better known than you may have thought."

With his hat still pulled far down over his eyes, he gave a quick low bow, snapped upright, and strutted down the hall toward the emergency-room door.

His quick brusque movements had sharpened Mère Magdelaine's alertness. Fright had left her. Amazed at her own coolness, she hurried down the hall after him. She too was ready for battle.

Already he had opened the door. "Well, Sophia, I've come," Mère Magdelaine heard him say before she could get to the room. His voice was low, but it carried like the roll of drums foretelling execution.

Like the blast of a firing squad, Sophia's scream broke through the quiet of the hospital. "Mother! Mother!" it crescendoed wildly. "Mother! Help! Help!"

The superior ran to her. "I'm here, Sophia. I'm here," she spoke quickly. "Quiet. I'll help you. I promise."

Duke Actah's laugh rang out mirthlessly, shrilly. "You two women against me! Ha! The idea of it!"

It was one of the few times in her life that Mère Magdelaine became enraged. This laughing little monster was no human being. He had no place with God's children. In this shadowy bedchamber, he was Satan in a damnation scene, and she hated him for the evil he was. "You have seen your sister. Will you go now?" she asked in a furious voice.

He stopped laughing. He drew himself up to his full

short height and, like a king speaking to a menial, he announced, "I will go, but I will take the baby with me."

"No! No!" Sophia sat up in bed, despair in her voice. "Don't let him have her." She grabbed Mère Magdelaine's arm and held on tightly, digging her nails though the cloth of the habit, almost as though the tighter she clung the less likely was Actah to get the baby away from her. "He'll kill her. He'll kill her," she sobbed, and the light from the lantern showed the tears wetting her face.

"That's right. I'm going to kill her. The King of Prussia has no need of a bastard in his wedding bed," the duke announced matter-of-factly.

Sophia wept against Mère Magdelaine's breast. The fierceness was gone from her. Weakness had seen to that. Her sobbing was that of a soul without hope.

Looking firmly toward the duke, Mère Magdelaine announced, "I am determined you shall not have the baby. If you persist in such murderous intent, I shall be forced to call the gendarmes."

This statement delighted Actah. The laugh he emitted was one of real mirth. Was the man insane?

"*Mutter*, you are a humorous woman." He toyed with the words as though the battle was his, and he could afford to be indulgent with the vanquished. "Have you kept your nose so stuck in this hospital that you do not know there is a revolution in France? Who are the police now? Heads are rolling in Paris. Who then would concern himself with the loss of one bastard infant?" Suddenly he sobered. His voice was a thin blade of steel, small, but sharp. "Enough of this nonsense," he said. "Where is the baby?"

"I don't propose to hand her over to you." Now hers was the voice of steel. The heartbreaking sobbing of the girl at her breast gave her the determination to fight this man.

A quietness came over Actah, an ominous quiet. He reached up and removed his hat. Slowly he walked over to Mère Magdelaine and stood before her. "Look upon my face. Look closely and then tell me what you see."

Mère Magdelaine did not flinch. It had been years since she had beheld such a sight and that during her novitiate days in a mission hospital in Egypt. The brows above the cold gray eyes, the hair on the top of the head were but mangy spots of brown in a sea of rotting flesh. The eyes were bulging, jaundiced. It was only by examining the lower part of the face that one realized that this was the countenance of a man. The whole effect was ghoulish.

"Perhaps you are not aware of what disease I am bringing into your hospital?" he asked insolently.

"Yes. I am familiar with leprosy," she stated matter-of-factly.

"Look, Sister," he flung out the words arrogantly, "either you get me my sister's baby or I go through this hospital and rub my face against every baby and mother you have in here. I'll infect your whole hospital and don't give me that 'Lord will protect us' stuff! You've been in this business long enough not to expect miracles with leprosy."

"Oh, Mother, don't give her to him. Rather let her die of leprosy than by his hand. It would be kinder." Even as she pled, Mère Magdelaine heard the despair in Sophia's voice.

The superior brushed back the golden hair from the damp brow. "If ever you had faith, use it now, my dear," she soothed.

"Do I get the bastard brat, or don't I?" Impatience had leapt into Actah's tone.

"I shall secure you the infant." Mère Magdelaine knew it was useless to put him off any longer. She nodded to Soeur Denise, scared and huddled in the doorway, to tend to the duchess. Sophia was limp, almost to the point of shock, as Mère Magdelaine laid her head upon the pillow.

The bantam devil leered up at her. His eyes were

45

amused with the scene about him. "Get to it, old woman. There's much to be done and you're wasting my time."

Yes, she would make haste, the sooner to be finished with this heartbreaking evening. Her mind was made up. Her decision must be the right one in the eyes of Heaven.

With all the dignity she could muster, Mère Magdelaine left the room. Surely the Lord could see she had no other recourse. It meant the best solution for the greater number. So sure was she of having chosen the correct path in this dilemma that she stuck out her chin in defiance in the event the Lord challenged her decision. Moving with cool deliberation, the mother superior walked to the nursery. Soeur Benedicta had just finished her ministering to the infant that lay on the table before her. So tiny. Had the Lord thought this small bit of humanity might combat a world of selfish demigods? She wrapped the child in the white blanket brought from the House of Hesse. To Soeur Benedicta, who watched without moving, she gave a slight shrug as if to say, "What else can I do?"

Mère Magdelaine hurried down the cold hallway and into the emergency room. Walking up to Actah, she said, "I have brought you the baby."

From the bed came the piteous weeping of the young mother. The duke held out his hands to take his niece, but the nun spoke. "Before you leave you should know something." Gently, she turned back the blanket. The infant was still, and the eyes were closed. Actah glanced up at the mother superior, a perplexed look in his ghoulish eyes.

Mère Magdelaine nodded. "Yes. The child is dead. The Lord saved you from a second murder this day." The cry which came from the bed was like the final wail of a departing spirit, as it leaves its mortal body.

A fiendish laugh came from the man. "Your great God need not have bothered. I could have done the job as well." He reached for the baby. "I'll take her. I don't trust you religious with your miracles and witch-craft. I'll make sure she gets buried."

With that, he snatched the child from the nun's arms and stalked out the door, his satanic laugh shattering the stillness of the hospital. Beelzebub was returning to Hell, triumphant.

Chapter Four

In all these months, no word had come from Chalon-sur-Marne. Not once had M. Drapeaux written to his mistress across the ocean, but Negu supposed it was just as well. He would have no doubt related to her in his letter all of the details of his unhappy wife's death. He would have explained that a violent stomachache had led to a slow paralysis that had drawn up one leg until she could only get about with the aid of a slave and a crutch, and then how one day a fall from the bedroom balcony put her out of her misery. Better that Celeste did not receive such a letter.

Since August, however, his letters might have been of a different tone. Boukmann had struck. Since then, Monsieur was too nervous to take pen in hand, to sit in one spot long enough to write a message. Perhaps, thought Negu, it was better that way. Celeste would have wept had she known what was happening in her homeland. She would have lived in fear lest her André be struck down by one of the murderous maroons. Right now, Negu was happy to have her daughter safe in the care of the nuns, away from that renegade Boukmann, a runaway slave who had led violent uprisings against the Creole masters. His revolt, bloody and merciless as it was, had left the land Celeste loved in stinking decay.

The slaves had not learned their lesson from the executions of Chavonne and Oge. They did not bow down their heads, cease their mumblings, and sing out, "The Master is my God. His will be done." The smold-

erings of hate, the bitterness engendered by beholding
the dignity of man and never being allowed to walk in
it—these irritants had been building up for too long,
and now, like a boil which has run its course, they had
come to a head. The brutal murder of their champions
in the town square was the signal to begin, not end,
their battle for freedom.

All they had needed was a leader like Boukmann—a
fearless, cunning, hulking man. Neither whip nor fire
had been able to make him renounce the powerful
desire in his blood to run again in freedom as had his
African forefathers. All this past summer, the slaves,
under cover of night, had crept noiselessly into the
woods to listen to Boukmann's exhortations. They
came from kilometers away, swiftly, for slavery could
not diminish the strength and speed of the savage runner. The drums called through the night. First was the
small sound of the boulatier, summoning, in a hushed,
almost secretive voice, to the rendezvous. Next came
the stronger drums, the damning ones. Always, the call
came on a moonless night when the mountains and the
forests and the slave quarters were blended into one
eerie black world. At the first sound of the drum,
candles were snuffed, fires smothered in the shacks of
the slaves so no informer could betray who went and
who stayed.

The Creoles called it a voodoo sex orgy, and they
stayed inside their high-ceilinged mansions where the
candles burned bright in crystal chandeliers and the
French wines warmed the blood and made them feel
secure and nurtured. They told tales, all hearsay, of
what happened when the natives answered the call of
the drums, for not a Creole amongst them had ever
been a witness to such a gathering. They spoke of
"permitting" the slaves these "nightly prowlings," as
they referred to them, and then commented as to how
worn out, but well behaved, their black chattel would
be the next morning.

Death struck St. Domingue on a moonless night

in August. The wind, stirred by a growing faraway hurricane, rustled the leaves, betraying the trees in their hiding places in the shadows. The blacks, fleet and silent, moved through those shadows to the trysting place in the hills. Sporadically, the beat of the drums came through the dark. First, the timid surreptitious note, followed by a bolder call. Another tossed along the message in a cockier tone and others joined in loud answer.

Far back from the road a fire started in a clearing in the woods. It beckoned the Africans as the flame does the moth. Each brought with him an unlit torch and a weapon for warfare: the long pronged pitchfork from the stable; the sharp-edged machete that mowed down the sugar cane; the long-handled axe that felled the mahogany trees. Scimiter-shaped knives, whose sharpness was demonstrated by the ease with which they severed the jugular vein of the pig, were pilfered from the butchering sheds. Cudgels, sledgehammers, spikes. Man and his armament assembled about the fire, wildly eager for the order that would start their demonstration in the name of independence.

The fire roared as it devoured firewood. When the flames had leaped so high in their arrogance that they seemed to taunt Heaven; when the drums, numerous as the crickets sounding from their unseen haunts in the bush, had built up into one mighty tidal wave of sound which rolled up to beat against the black floor of God's Paradise overhead; when the faces of the slaves crouched about the fire were as many as the sands on the beach, only then did the drums slow into a recessional and fade away, like an intruder slinking into the night. Silence! The silence of impending evil!

Now came one voice, at first faint as a baby's whimper. Gradually, others joined, whispering a singsong chant, lapping like little waves of sound against the black beach of night. Again, the drums awoke, timidly speaking as little demon voices urging the chanters to more vehement song. They joined forces and together

50

rose in more assertive tones. Higher and higher grew the voices of man and drum. With their volume came courage. The chanters rose up from their crouched positions and raised their arms skyward, hands reaching up to clutch the night itself and pull it smashing down to the dirt underfoot. Like a crash of thunder, the voice of a master drum rolled out, rumbling over the heads of the black assembly and vibrating away through the woods. At the same time, a figure leaped toward the roaring flames. It was a young girl, tall, naked, with well-sculptured limbs. She stood before the chanters, brandishing a club from which a rooster dangled, bound by its legs. The girl's body was covered with a thick grease, which ran in rivulets in the cleft between her breasts and over her stomach. Her hair was wound tightly around the sides of her head, giving the effect of a large nest resting on top. It was Desaix, one of Joswee's young houncis. To her was entrusted the wearing of a sacred snake, Dambolla's disguise when he came to visit his suppliants upon the earth.

As Desaix lifted the club high all suddenly froze. Drums and voices ceased abruptly. The chanters stood motionless like macabre spooks from an underworld of the damned. The fire held center stage, as its red fangs darted high into the night. Desaix was a glowing statue whose greased body mirrored the glow of the flames. Only the rooster, hanging by its feet, dared to stir. It raised its head, cocking it from side to side, as it stared at the fire with its beady little eyes.

Now the lights and shadows, brushing over the scene, caught a new movement. A small, weaving black head slowly rose from out of the hairy nest on the top of Desaix's head. Little eyes, polished by the fire's light, glittered menacingly. The mouth opened in a wide yawn and flauntingly shot out fangs of fire. The serpent slowly raised itself high upon its throne and truculently surveyed its assembled subjects. Then, gracefully it arched itself out over Desaix's face, hung

51

suspended there a moment, then placed its head cozily alongside her nose. With its tail still curled inside the nest of the hounci's hair, the snake relaxed in contentment. Truly, Desaix was the beloved of Dambolla.

From somewhere in the shadows, a boulatier began to beat. The snake raised its head in a listening attitude. It seemed charmed by the call, for its head weaved about in a rhythmic pattern. At this moment, the rooster crowed. The snake stopped its motion and stared in affront at this infidel who had dared desecrate the mood of the blessed. The black head of the serpent stretched out toward the sinning fowl, when another drum injected its voice. This call was hurried, insistent. The snake paused to listen. Another boulatier spoke, softly, with the message of sadness, hopelessness. The snake turned away, dismissing the fowl. Slowly, almost imperceptibly, it began to descend the body of the high priestess. It flowed down between her naked breasts and curled around a thigh to her back and slithered down between her buttocks. It was a long snake with the tail only leaving the nest when its head had already reached the calf of her leg. The drums called in low, pleading, piteous voices, and the snake was responding. Dambolla had heard his people.

When the serpent disappeared into the shadows where the drums had beckoned, Desaix let out a scream. A scream as shrill, and wild, and bloodcurdling as all the outraged demons of Hell must have made when the Lord had flung them from Paradise forever. With a quick motion, the hounci grabbed the rooster and ripped him from the club. She clutched his head in one of her large hands and in one quick snap decapitated the fowl. Blood geysered up, but before it could fall upon the ground, Desaix threw back her head, opened her mouth to let it pour down her throat. So fast did the blood jet out that it came out of the sides of her mouth, ran down her cheeks and chin, and flowed like a bright red sea over her body. The slaves fell to their knees and clasped their hands in prayer.

Another figure sprang from the shadows. It was Joswee, fully clothed. He still wore his red turban, but now it was decorated with a circlet of rooster feathers. In his hands he carried a wide wooden bowl. Falling on his knees before his high priestess, he shouted, "Dambolla, wé dopo Fiolé opor Dambolla!" and held up the bowl.

Desaix removed the headless rooster from her mouth and held it over the bowl so that it might catch the blood as it poured from the fowl. A single drum began to sound. At first it came quickly, in time with the flow of blood. As the blood decreased in volume, so did the drum until it became a slow beat counting out each red drop from bird to bowl. When drum and blood were scarcely perceptible, Desaix turned abruptly and flung the carcass of the rooster far out into the shadows in the direction the snake had gone. Dambolla was giving his blood, even to the last drop, for his people who had come to him for help. The priestess again faced Joswee and took the bowl of blood from him. Slowly she raised it above her head and began to sway rhythmically from side to side. The blazing fire was reflected on her bloody breasts and belly and its shadows flickered over the bowl as if impatient to possess its contents.

Again the drums took up their call. At first, the only ones heard were those in the circle of shadows just outside the fire, but their urgency soon brought answers from more distant drums. These, in turn, were joined by those far away from the Plain du Nord, out to the horizon of mountains against the black sky. They were a plague of sound: ominous, relentless, funereal. It was Death on its march and it would not be turned back.

Desaix moved toward the fire with the drums counting out each step. When she had drawn so close that it would seem that the flames would truly envelope and consume her, Desaix slowly turned the bowl and poured its contents into the flames. The fire hissed

53

back in protest, and little black clouds of smoke rose from the spot where the blood had fallen. It was the signal.

The slaves leaped to their feet and began to scream furiously. At the same time the drums beat out in wild rage, each striving to outshout the other, in a savage summons to violence. Desaix whirled like a dervish about the fire where all could see her and be contaminated by her frenzy. The slaves tore the clothes from their bodies, thus stripping themselves of every vestige of civilization. Urged on by the mad call of the drums, the natives shrilled and whirled as though sound and motion had met in an uncontrollable spasm in each black body. Without a pause in her pagan dance, Desaix grabbed a torch from one of the slaves and plunged it into the fire. Then she held it up high for all to see. Banshee cries poured out from each throat as the natives surged toward the fire where they lit their torches. Desaix, glowing like a red ghoul in the light of the flames, was already running madly toward the Plain du Nord. Boukmann, a black bear of a man, naked and with a small pointed head, began trumpeting like a wild animal on a charge and beckoned his fellow blacks to follow.

Propelled by the hysterical beat of the drums, caught up in the tide of madness, the slaves went screaming after their leader. Enraged, embittered, insane, they were devils now who had knocked down the ramparts of Hell and had fallen as a scourge upon the earth that it might wither and die in their hate.

The burning torches were giant fireflies flickering in the darkness as they spread out over the Plain du Nord. Here were the lovely estates of the Creoles. The Creoles, who ate and drank and laughed in their big, cool houses, and said this was their due for they were white. The Creole, who could maim or wipe out a black man's life if he dared to attempt to leave the animal world to which he had been relegated. The black man had watched and had learned. Learned how to

54

maim and wipe out life too, and this night he would show how well he remembered the lesson.

The howling natives hurried through the night, back to their own plantations where they would strike the first blows for freedom. The slave quarters on the outskirts of each estate were the first to be fired. Next, the doors of the stables and barns were tightly closed and the torch applied. The cries of the animals and fowl, at first low surprised rumblings, then mad pleas for survival filled the night air. Like so many suns, the flames of the holocausts lit up the sky and earth, making it easier for the slaves to move swiftly toward the planters' homes. The firing of the slave quarters and the outbuildings served only to whet their appetites. It was the white family in his mansion that was the *pièce de résistance*. As the rebels approached each house, shots rang out, but they were useless against the rolling momentum of an insane mob. A few slaves fell, and they were soon trampled underfoot by their confederates who came after.

With axe and cudgel and pick and torch, the vandals entered the hitherto holy house of the owner. Screaming madly, they came through hacked-down doors and broken windows. They splintered the shiny mahogany furniture, slashed down the crystal chandeliers, and broke harpischords in two with one vicious blow of a cudgel. Whole cupboards of china were upset, and the upsetters roared in fanatic delight at the crashing sounds. Figurines, pictures, lamps—all were smashed by the devastating plague. Their possessions having been destroyed, it was then time for the white masters to meet their death. Gathering momentum from its own violence, savagery mounted the stairway, cutting away the balustrades as it did so. Like pigs rooting in the sty, the savages mauled everything in their path as they searched for the white families. And they found them, each individual quaking in his own hideaway. Only the infant, used to love, looked up and smiled when a drawer in a bedchamber was pulled out and his shelter revealed. A blood-curdling cry of victory filled the house as a black hand savagely jerked the baby out of his blanket, severed the legs with his machete, and flung him in a bloody arc against the opposite wall of the room.

Spurred on by their first feat of murder, the slaves sought other victims and found them. Through the houses came the sounds of wild terror, followed by the thud of a blow, and then the moaning cries of men and women whose pain was too great to bear. Blood rushed along the hallways and down the stairs as if a dam had burst. This was freedom!

Chapter Five

Although Negu had not partaken in the voodoo ceremony and the subsequent slaughter that August night, she knew all that had occurred. What the other slaves on the Drapeaux plantation had not reported to her, Joswee and Desaix had. Over two hundred fifty plantations had been wiped off the Plain du Nord in one single night of terror.

Remnants of the Assembly, frightened by the empty chairs of its slain members, ordered out the army; but how could an army, whose sole activity had long been no more than the execution of political insurgents, track down the maroons in their hiding places in the mountains?

Whole families of planters left their homes and sought refuge in the city until the uprising was quelled. As long as Boukmann, the guerrilla leader, was free, white life was unsafe outside the city of Cap François.

But Negu was not concerned about the safety of the white life on the Drapeaux plantation. That was *hers* to snuff out—or prolong—as she willed. Boukmann had been so informed. Boukmann was her brother. And even though Negu knew he was more beast than human in his passion for hate and murder, it was that very passion that made him understand her own hate for André Drapeaux.

Negu was also aware that, in time, Boukmann could no longer protect the plantation. With the runaway slaves already baptized in one orgy of blood, they would soon shake off *all* restraints rejecting any leader who might hamper this newfound freedom. For that time, Negu must be prepared. She promised she would look after André and his possessions.

Already it was several months since Boukmann had led his murderous band in its attempt to wipe out all Frenchmen in St. Domingue. Negu knew that they would strike again soon, for it is not by inactivity that a man keeps his leadership. Every day she listened for the messages of the drums. And late one afternoon in November, she heard them. This was the night, they told her.

Shadows were falling as she made her way to the Drapeaux house. She entered the kitchen and found the cook, Evadne, rolling out sheets of pastry dough, listening all the while to the message of the drums. Evadne looked up when Negu came through the door and her eyes were big and questioning. Then the cook looked toward her husband. Nassy, in his emerald-green butler's uniform, was wiping a wineglass, but his unseeing eyes were focused on some scene in his mind. All the while, he leaned sideways toward the window, listening to the sounds of the night.

Evadne rolled her eyes back to Negu and in a hushed voice asked, "Should we leave now?"

Negu shook her head. "No, not yet. Wait until I have seen M. Drapeaux. Where is he?"

Evadne's mouth dropped open, but she made no sound. She just stared with that bug-eyed look.

Negu left the kitchen to find Monsieur by herself. She would try the library first. The door was closed and she knocked. As she waited for an answer she thought of the irony of the situation. She, who was offering life, must come humbly before the man who would otherwise be doomed. Negu shrugged. Her life had been without gratitude. Why look for it now?

When there was no answer, Negu turned the knob and slowly opened the door. André was standing by his escritoire holding a partially emptied decanter of brandy in one hand and a glass to his mouth with the other. Negu knocked on the door frame. With a convulsive jerk, André whirled around, at the same time dropping the glass and bottle to the tile floor. The sound of the crashing glass was followed by an oath from André.

Then he shouted at Negu, "Damn you, Nigger! Quit sneaking up on me like that." He pointed to the floor. "Clean up this mess," he ordered, and walked to the cabinet for another bottle of brandy.

Negu stood in the doorway, making no attempt to move. She clamped her teeth so tightly she wished André were between them so she could chew him to shreds.

André turned from the cabinet, pouring his brandy with a shaking hand as he came across the room. He stopped abruptly when his feet crunched some of the broken glass. For a moment he stared at the floor as if trying to determine why the glass was there. Then slowly he turned toward Negu and asked in an irritated voice, "Why aren't you cleaning this up? Are you getting too mighty to sweep a floor?"

In a cold voice, Negu answered, "Have you forgotten, M. Drapeaux, that this 'nigger' is the grandmother of your unborn child?"

The look of dismissal which André flung in her direction before he turned away, fanned the fire of hate for him which Negu had banked inside her breast. It was all there again, raging up into her throat so that she had to swallow hard to push it back down that she might breathe again.

André gulped another glass of brandy and walked toward the window. As he studied the darkness of the sky, he remarked casually, "By the way, I heard from the nuns in Chalon-sur-Marne today. Celeste died in childbirth." Then as an afterthought, he added, "Too bad. I shall miss her."

Negu froze. All feeling collapsed within her. Only her lip, where the scar pulled it back from the gum, quivered and would not be controlled. Suddenly, life was empty. Even hatred lost its appeal. Slowly her mind began to grope. There was something she should know. She remembered. In a husky voice she asked, "The baby—does it live?"

"Yes, yes," he replied impatiently. "It's a girl. Asya. Asya is her name."

Suddenly Negu was alive again. Here was something to live for. Someone to care for. Asya. A beautiful name. The sudden resurgence of life in her cold body fired Negu with the need for action. She strode over to André who was standing by the window and spun him around to face her. She knew what she must now do.

"What else did the nun write?" the woman's voice whipped out.

Ignoring her, André drained his glass in one swallow. For a moment he stood motionless and then he began to weave. In disgust he hurled the empty brandy glass to the floor. "Damn those drums, Negu!" he shouted. "What are they saying?"

"What other news did Mère Magdelaine write in her letter?" Negu asked again in a cold voice.

"At a time like this you want to talk about *babies!*" He lurched toward Negu, grabbed her roughly by the shoulders, and tried to shake her, but the terror within him robbed him of his strength. Instead, he clutched at the woman for support. He brought his face close to hers and asked in a low, almost confidential tone, "Negu, what do the drums mean tonight?"

The woman shrugged. "It's another voodoo meeting, I suppose."

André shook his head in an effort to comprehend. "No," he said. "No, it's more than that." He dropped his hands from her shoulders and stood listening. He spoke in a hesitant whisper, "Only once did I ever hear them so loud and so many. It was—" His voice trailed off and his eyes grew wide with fear.

Negu lowered her voice and in a sinister tone finished for him, "—in August, perhaps."

With a moan, André clutched his hair with both

hands. "Yes, yes. That's it. Are they coming again? Tonight? Here?"

"You expect me to know all that?" she asked, fixing him with her eyes.

"Yes!" he shouted out. "Yes. You know everything that goes on around here. You're a voodoo witch." He pounded at her with his fists. Screaming out with pent-up fear, he demanded, "What do they say, Negu? Tell me."

Negu's voice came out like slaps on his face. "Boukmann is calling to his maroons and any others who want to fight for freedom. Tonight they come this way. Now it is *your* turn. And your neighbors'."

André went white. He stumbled to the window, listened to the now wild dissonance of the drums, and turned back toward Negu. "What shall I *do*? They'll get me if I stay here. I *must* get to town. That's it. I *must* ride to Cap François." In his fear, he was talking to himself.

Negu strode toward M. Drapeaux and slapped him hard across the face. With that first blow she knew André was hers to forever manage as she chose.

He looked at her wild-eyed. Then he found his voice. "Negu!" he said in a tone of hurt surprise.

"I had to do that," she answered. "You were becoming witless. Listen to me. There's not much time. Listen closely."

André seemed to have forgotten the drums while she spoke.

"Your stable and field servants are all gone to the woods to hide. They heard what the drums say. They're afraid Boukmann's men might think they're on your side and kill them. Only the house slaves are here and they'll leave as soon as I tell them. You haven't time to get into town anymore. If you go out of this house they'll surely find you and hack you to pieces, slowly, so you don't spoil their fun by dying too soon."

André moaned. He looked furtively over either

shoulder to see if someone might already be sneaking up on him from behind.

"You won't be safe at a neighbor's. You can't be sure which of the homes they'll pick, and once they get into a house you're doomed. You know that. The bullets of all of you put together are not enough to shoot down the slaves, so many will there be."

For a moment André stood transfixed by terror, bloodshot eyes staring out from his white face. He hunched over, his hands clawing at his throat, pulling away whatever in his mind's eye was cutting off his breath. His head shook in disbelief. "No, no! Not here! Not me! I've been good to my slaves." His voice quivered. Tears flowed down his cheeks. "I've been *real* good to my slaves. Say I've been good to my slaves, Negu. I *have*, haven't I?" He turned to Negu and nodded his head for her to agree. "Say I have, Negu. *Say* it. They wouldn't hurt *me*, would they?"

Negu was exasperated. "You don't seem to understand, M. Drapeaux, that those are not just *your* slaves out there in the hills. They are *everybody*'s slaves, and they want their freedom. The only way they know how to get it is to kill. They are afraid of nothing. Nothing, but one thing!"

Several times André swallowed and wet his lips before he could gasp, "Tell me. What is it? What is it?"

Negu remained silent. Was he ready? She did not want to argue, lest he slip out of her hands.

The drums took over, a hurricane of sound, lashing the earth. André began to sob. He grabbed Negu by the arms. "Negu, what is it? Tell me. I'll do anything. I'll set you free. I'll do anything. I've always been good to you."

Negu looked at him scornfully. She hated a slobbering man. "What would I do with freedom *now?*"

"All right. Anything you want. Anything. I swear to God. Anything. Don't forget, I'm your grandchild's father. Remember, you even said so. Her father. You wouldn't want anything to happen to Asya's papa, would you? *Would* you? Help me, Negu!"

He had played right into her hands. Now she would have her triumph. "That's right. You're her papa. I will save you. The voodoo gods started this revolution and only a voodoo god can keep them away from this plantation."

"How? How? Quick. Do something before it's too late. Quick."

"Every slave is afraid of the curse of the black horse. I must have your Arab stallion. I have to kill it, for the curse won't work with another."

The drums were now mounting to hysteria. "Yes. Yes. Hurry, hurry. Anything. Go *now*." He tried to push her toward the door, but Negu held back.

"One other thing."

"Yes?" André was already nodding his head in agreement.

"About Asya. You must adopt her legally. I don't like my grandchild being a bastard." With a sly smile she asked, "Do you, Monsieur *Papa?*"

"No, no," he shook his head quickly and just as quickly went back to nodding it. "Yes, yes. Whatever you say. Yes. No. Whatever you want, but hurry!"

Negu walked over to the escritoire and dipped a pen into the inkwell, at the same time pulling a parchment toward her. "What are you *doing?*" M. Drapeaux's voice was bordering on hysteria.

"I'm writing up your agreement to adopt Celeste's child. Tomorrow you may forget."

"Don't take time to do that. I gave you my promise," he screamed. "I'll adopt her. I won't forget."

But Negu wrote on, with André all the while pounding the desk and shouting, "I tell you I *won't* forget. I'll *do* it. Those drums! They're coming! They'll be here. I'll *do* it. Hear those drums. They'll be here! Hurry! *Mon Dieu,* Negu, hurry!"

When Negu finished her writing, she handed him the pen. "Sign your name."

He looked at her crazily. "Right here," she snapped. "You're wasting time."

Hurriedly, André scratched his name and then fell sobbing to his knees beside the desk, leaning his forehead against the edge of the top. His arms hung down dejectedly at his sides. He was crying as Negu left the library, "Oh, God, save me. Save me. I don't want to die—not that way."

The drums had reached their highest pitch, telling her that she had no more time, but Negu was prepared. She hurried through the kitchen where Evadne and Nassy, stiffened by terror, gazed at her like two zombies.

"It's all right," she called. "You will be safe. The horse's head will protect you."

Quickly she grabbed a torch from the wall beside the hearth and plunged it into the fire. Holding it before her, she ran out the door. No sooner had she stepped onto the stone courtyard than a giant shadow emerged from the dark. "Here I am," a man's voice called.

"Joswee," the woman said, "I am all set. You have Javan's head?" She held up the torch and in its light saw the severed head of the horse which the high priest carried upside down so as to keep its blood from spilling out upon the ground.

"*Oui*," he answered. "The other torches are already down by the gate. You walk in front with the light and we'll cut across the hibiscus garden. It will be shorter that way. We haven't much time."

The urgency of the drums gave speed to their legs and Joswee and his hounci arrived at the front entrance of the Drapeaux plantation as scattered torches were already appearing over the ridge of the distant mountain. Boukmann's second raid had begun.

While Joswee mounted the head of the Arab stallion on one of the gate posts, Negu stuck a lit torch on top of each paling of the iron gate. Then she untied a bag which Joswee had carried attached to his belt and took out a black powder. Carefully, she sprinkled a little of it on each of the burning torches, causing them to blaze with a brilliant green light and reveal the black head of Javan, eyes shining like two glassy balls. The gatepost, wetted by rivulets of blood flowing down from the severed head of the horse, glistened an eerie red. The light could be seen for kilometers around. Every African would know that this abode was under the protection of the horse's head. No black man would dare risk its curse.

With the head firmly implanted on top of the gatepost, Joswee attached two cauldrons of smoldering goat-manure cakes below and to either side of the wanga. The heat would slowly burn the skin and flesh from the skull of the horse, and the wind would carry the stench over the valley. It was the god's message to all men. The Drapeaux plantation was sacred.

While Joswee attended the torches, adding more powder when the green fire began to fade, Negu hurried to the stable. Here she went to the empty stall which had once housed M. Drapeaux's prize stallion. She played her torch around until its light fell upon a large unpainted box in the corner. She tiptoed over to the box and then slowly, so as to make no sudden noise, dropped to her knees. With one hand she caressed the lid, chanting at the same time, "Dambolla! Dambolla! Dambolla!"

She paused and placed her ear against the box, listening. Again, in a persuasive, luring tone, she sang, "Dambolla! Dambolla! Dambolla!"

In a steady, monotonous rhythm, like the roll of a quiet drum, she tapped her fingers against the side of the box. She might have been gently waking a child.

Soon, Negu's fingertips felt a stirring within the box. Still on her knees, she rocked back and forth, crooning in a sweet husky voice:

Ya fafa Gaaza
La rosée fait bro-dé toup tempso po par lévé

65

La rosée fait bro-dé toup tempso po par lévé
gaint nain oh!
gaint nain oh!

At the end of the song, Negu slowly drew the wooden peg from the lock on the box and carefully raised the lid. Without peering inside she laid her hand along the edge, letting it rest there. Soon she heard the slow movement of a heavy body bestirring itself. Now its cold head discovered her hand and nudged it several times as though trying to dislodge it. When she felt a slimy weight crawl slowly up her arm to her shoulder, she knew that her hand had been recognized. Negu relaxed, but held her body very still. Long ago she had learned that a taut muscle frightened Dambolla. He must know that she was his friend. That her spirit was united with his. She turned her head and gazed into the beady eyes of a rattlesnake, polished a fiery red in the light from the torch she carried in her free hand. For a moment, snake and priestess looked steadily into each other's eyes, and their spirits became entwined as one. Negu's soul thrilled as the snake darted its tongue about her face, caressingly, possessively. With her surrender to her god, she, Negu, was the powerful one. Dambolla would deny his favorite nothing.

Lulled by affection for this woman, the snake began to nuzzle its head under her chin. Then slowly, in an almost cuddling motion, it wrapped its heavy body about her neck, and Negu could almost hear a sigh as it settled there in contentment.

In a flowing motion so as not to disturb the snake, Negu rose to her feet and backed out of the stall. Without changing her pace, she turned and left the stable. Outside, she paused while she played the flame of the torch about the courtyard. At last she saw what she was looking for and walked toward a black mound that shone in the light of the flame. It was the headless body of Javan, an island in a dark red sea of blood. In the same flowing motion, Negu waded into the horse's blood and encircled its body three times. Then she wiped her bare feet on its rump. Dambolla had now seen her disdain for all things cherished by André Drapeaux. Any old nag would have done for the head of the sacred horse before the house, but she intended to deprive Monsieur of his most treasured possessions, one by one!

In a feeling of elation, Negu swiftly glided toward the kitchen doorway. While the snake was heavy about her neck, the priestess was lightfooted in her joy, a strengthening joy which made the godlike reptile easy to carry.

She called out, "Open! Evadne! Nassy! Open. Quick."

She waited. Negu could visualize those two bewildered blacks, afraid to open the door, and yet equally afraid not to. From the window they would have seen her coming across the courtyard in the light of the torch and there was no mistaking what rested about her neck. Dambolla in the highest earthly form, Dambolla, the largest serpent in St. Domingue! She alone in all the island could summon him in this, his most powerful form. To her, he came, to her alone.

The door creaked. One round eye peered out. "Yes?" its owner asked.

"Open the door wide," Negu ordered. "Dambolla has a message for you both."

"A message? Is that all? Just a message?"

Negu did not bother to answer. One does not argue with frightened ones.

Slowly the door opened wide and Nassy, with Evadne cowering behind him, stepped out.

Negu spoke, "You have seen the horse's head upon the gate."

"Yes. Yes." Two heads nodded quickly.

"You have seen Dambolla with me on this land this night."

Evadne and Nassy stared at the snake, too frightened to speak.

67

"You will tell everyone how this snake and I are as one. Whoever brings harm on this land, so long as that horse's head remains before this house, whoever touches that head, will die. Dambolla will strike him dead." At this moment, the serpent raised its head and began to weave toward the cook and her husband.

They screamed, then said, "We do like you say. We do just like you say." They screamed again and vanished into the darkness beyond the kitchen.

Negu smiled and her lip, where she bore the scar, quivered. She spoke softly to the serpent as she caressed its head with her free hand, "You and I, Dambolla. We shall avenge Celeste's death. You and I together."

Chapter Six

Count Etienne de Vastey Grenier, graduate of St. Cyr, nephew to the King of Prussia, lieutenant to Napoleon Bonaparte, whistled as he strolled along the Via Calazzi. The gentle evening breezes brushed against his face, and he threw back his head, the better to wallow in the pleasure of their touch. Capricious, warming, they reminded him of Maria. Maria, who had been snug here in Mantua while he and the rest of the French army followed Napoleon across the Alps and into Italy. Remembering, he could still feel the icy grip of the cold on his spine and, for a moment, he thought he saw the frost of his breath in the night air. But it was only the moon, and he whistled to it, man to man, sharing secrets. Tonight he would see Maria.

The thought of her made his heart skip and his feet dance. She was a slender pixie who looked up at a man and laughed in delight over what her dark sloe eyes beheld. She knew how to lower those long black lashes just enough to hide the boldness in her eyes, and still let little flashes of promise escape. At the same time, her small, even white teeth sparkled in a smile, and her faint dimples intrigued a man only to disappear a moment later.

Maria, who was still in her teens, had more freedom than most Italian wives. The Duke of Mantua, her husband, was in his seventies. Perhaps, when a man reaches such ancient age he is more concerned about a night's rest than the entertainment of a young wife. Etienne visualized the old duke, tucked into his great bed,

69

his nightcap pulled down to his nose, lulled to sleep by the warmth of the goat's milk he always drank before the drapes were drawn. How sad to be old!

Etienne walked faster. Maria was waiting for him. The thought was exhilarating. He looked up at the moon and had the urge to reach out and touch it, so close did it seem. Maria. Maria was strong tonic. Bless that little old husband who no longer cared for tonic!

Count Grenier turned the corner. Down the street he saw the lights on either side of the entrance to the palace of the Duke. The wind had now come up, and the lanterns swung back and forth on their chains, merrily beckoning him to enter.

The Duchess of Mantua was standing by the fireplace in her private chambers, as beautiful as he had remembered. Her eyes twinkled from across the room with the promise of happy surprises, surprises for him alone. Walking over to her, he said, "Maria, you are still the most ravishing pixie of all."

He picked her up in his arms and strode to the divan where he sat down, Maria perched upon his lap. "There. That's better," Etienne said. "Your lips are now level with mine."

Putting his arms about her, he kissed Maria hard upon the mouth. Her arms crept about his neck, and her hands pressed against the back of his head, holding him tight. Fire warmed his loins. His hand caressed her satiny cheek, her warm neck, but when it sought the tempting warmth inside her dress, Maria quickly grabbed his hair and snapped his head backward. At the same time, she sank her sharp teeth into his exploring hand.

Etienne leaped to his feet, dumping the duchess on the floor as he did so. "Damn you!" he shouted. "What kind of a game is this you are playing?"

Maria looked up at him coyly, her eyes amused. "You're a cocky soldier, Captain Grenier, who likes all the girls and thinks all the girls *love* him."

Etienne did not know whether to shake the little

demon or gather her up in his arms. "Don't they?" he asked in mock surprise.

Maria's eyes followed his handsome form as he walked toward the table where several bottles of wine and two glasses had been placed.

"Poor girls," he teased. "They're not as lucky as you." When he had filled both glasses with bubbling liquid, Etienne offered one to Maria. Raising the other, he said, "A toast to you, my dear. The fortunate duchess. The one who has to put up with me."

Slowly, he drained the glass while looking across the room at her with amused eyes. When he had finished, Maria raised her glass. "And now *my* toast," she said. "To the most egotistical, self-centered, cockiest man in the army!"

"Amen," Etienne nodded in agreement as he watched her drink the wine. Then he refilled the glasses, drew a chair close to the table, and sat down. "Here, *cherie*." He patted his lap. "Come here beside me and be comfortable. No more games, eh?"

Languidly Maria sauntered over to him. Slightly raising the front of her skirt, she made a stiff curtsey. "Yes, your Majesty," she said in a mocking voice. "Just as you wish, your Majesty."

"*Cherie*, how about a truce?" Etienne reached out, caught Maria by the waist, and pulled her down gently upon his lap. Grinning now, she put her arms about his neck and snuggled cozily against him.

"Tell me now," he whispered softly. "Why so frisky tonight, *cherie*? Is there something wrong?"

"*Non*." She shook her head slowly. "Well, not exactly." Her face was serious. "Etienne, I'm going to have a baby."

"What?" Etienne threw back his head and laughed. As his chair shook with the convulsions of his merriment, Maria drew herself up in indignation.

"Why is that so funny?"

"It's just—well, your husband is a wonder. Why, he's a credit to the male race."

71

Maria did not move, only sat with lips pursed. Then she said, "No, Etienne. My husband has nothing to do with this."

"What!" The captain looked at her in amazement. Then he picked up the glass she had placed on the table. "I had better fortify myself with another drink."

Maria slid off his lap and strolled toward the fireplace. "No, Etienne. You don't understand. When I mentioned that I was going to have a baby, I did not mean that I am *now* pregnant. I meant that I intend to have a baby at a future date."

Pursing his lips and nodding his head as though thoroughly digesting this new piece of news, Etienne said, "That's nice, but where do I fit in? I've been out of Italy for a while and am a little behind in what might be fashionable these days? Since you have discarded your husband as a candidate to sire your child, who *is* the lucky man?"

"Napoleon." Maria turned and faced Etienne. Her chin jutted out in a show of defiance.

Etienne paused in his drinking and stared across the room at her. Gesturing with his glass, he toasted, "To Napoleon," and drank.

"Is that all you have to say?" she sounded bewildered.

"Why should *I* be upset if your own husband is unconcerned?"

"Don't you like me?"

He leaned back in his chair and laughed. "Females. They're delightful. No wonder I love them." Then he looked toward Maria, who seemed mystified by his outburst. "I like you now while you have a husband, and I'll still like you, Maria, while you love Napoleon. I'll always like you."

"But I don't want you to like me anymore," she answered quickly. "Napoleon would object."

"And why should Napoleon care? He has Josephine. All of France knows how madly in love with her he is. Even you must know that."

"Yes." She was pouting, but suddenly she clenched her little fists and flung back her head, ready for battle. "She doesn't deserve him. She's just a tramp."

"Maria!" Etienne pretended to be shocked. "Careful of your language."

"Well, she is. Just a tramp. I'm no saint either, but I'm not breaking a wonderful man's heart. He's begged her to come to him. He's asked her to meet him in Vienna, in Egypt, in Rome. The last time he was in Mantua, they were married less than a year. Would she come to be with him while he headquartered here? No. She was too busy back in Paris with Talleyrand and the other stay-at-homes who didn't have enough nerve and courage to fight on a battlefield. She revels in all the reflected fame and glory that surrounds Napoleon's wife, and yet she only plays at being a wife. Once she came to him here in Italy, but only after he sent his brother to bring her."

"How do you know all this?" Etienne was amazed.

"Oh," she said coquettishly, "perhaps because I am an Italian. All Italians know everything about everybody's love affairs. We're a romantic race. Love is our soul, our pleasure, our business."

"Then your husband knows all about your philanderings after he retires for the night?"

Maria shrugged. "I don't know. I suppose so. It makes no difference to him what I do as long as I am happy doing it."

Etienne whistled softly. "A remarkable man. Most understanding."

"Yes, he is most understanding," she agreed. "He realizes that he is older than my grandfather. Imagine my husband being older than my father's father."

"*Cherie*, why didn't you pick a younger man to be your husband?"

"Pick?" she asked in a surprised tone. "*Pick* a husband? What girl chooses her own husband? Parents do that. It's their duty to provide a man who can afford their daughter. It is only after a girl has the protection of a husband that she is free to select a lover. It carries more respect and prestige that way. My husband understands."

"Couldn't your parents have found you a rich and understanding husband who was a little younger?"

Maria cocked her head in unconcern. "I suppose so," she said, "but I liked the duke. We are very companionable and have much in common."

"What could a young girl who enjoys playing the coquette have in common with an old man whose interest is his health?"

"Italy," she announced and stuck out her chin defiantly. "We both love our country. We're patriots, Italian patriots." She turned and faced him. "We have no dreams of world conquest like you French who send your armies into Egypt and have your eyes on India. You've taken Germany, conquered Austria, and now we are under your French heel. We Italians are not ambitious for an empire. Our own country is enough empire. The duke, my husband, had long planned to unite all the city-states of Italy. Even as a little girl in my father's house, I used to hear him speak lovingly of his country, of his hopes for it. I grew up wanting Italy strong and united. That was the feeling which drew the duke and me together. Many marriages are not as fortunate as ours. They do not have the common ground which my husband and I have between us. We both wanted the best for Italy."

"And you are willing," Etienne interrupted, "to have a child by Napoleon. This would be the cudgel you could hold over his head to get what you and your husband want from him?" Sarcasm had crept into his voice.

"You misunderstand, Count," she answered in a reproving tone. "Having a child was not in my original plans. True, I began with the idea of playing the coquette with Napoleon to get what I wished for my country. The duke was proud of me. I was the only faithless wife who would take a lover for patriotic reasons." Maria lifted her head and looked smugly down her nose at Etienne.

"Go on," he urged. "I'm listening." He reached for the wine bottle and poured them both another drink.

Maria turned to face the fireplace. Her voice was low now, and the count had to listen closely. "You see, I had never before met anyone like Napoleon," she began. "At home, I saw only my brother's young friends. They seemed scatterbrained with their talk of women. Scarcely a whisker between them and they prattled on about women. Not girls. That wouldn't have sounded so ridiculous. But these adolescent men of the world, these dandies about town referred to their conquests of *women*. All that boundless energy going to waste prowling the streets by night in their search for excitement. When the real excitement could have been in tracking down the traitors from Austria. They knew the number of petticoats of every barmaid in the city, but what would have been more daring was to have learned the number of troops Vienna was infiltrating through our countryside."

Her voice was getting stronger and the words were coming faster. "Oh, these university-educated boys had great minds for retaining bawdy stories and recalling ribald songs. And splendid were their accomplishments. Many could drink a cask of wine in one evening and then show off by dancing the tarantella with some unwashed wench. Have you ever heard a braggadocio recount the tales of his bravery? Do you know some of the magnificent feats of these strong, fearless men of nineteen, twenty? They know how to fall upon the lamplighter as he goes about the dark streets at night doing his work and beat him up. One old man! They are not afraid of one old man! It only takes five to almost kill him. Aren't they brave?

"And the sword," she continued. She was now standing firmly in front of the fire looking into it as if what she was recounting was all pictured in flames. "The sword. They are wonderful duelists. As they

75

stumble on their drunken way home from the taverns in the early hours they go after the little old ladies who are on their way to morning Mass. They prick them in the seat with their blades. Oh, it's hilarious to see them jump. Fun? If you've never seen it, you must try it sometime. You'll die laughing at the way the old women hop up and down while their rosaries rattle and they scream out."

She turned quickly toward him. "I know what I'm saying. I was only a child, but my brother and his friends had to brag in front of me. It was important to their ego that they brag before everyone, even a little sister. That was my introduction to young men. Not a word about the wonderful ideas a mind might entertain. Not a word of what a young man could do to help Italy. Let the soldiers and old men be the patriots. Let *them* be the fools."

"Perhaps the parents were to blame," Etienne suggested.

"Of course they were, and that includes my papa. 'It is the way with youth,' he excused when some poor devil complained about the brutality of my brother and his friends. 'What can we *do* about it? It is the nature of a boy.'" Maria mimicked. "'He is like a bird who must flap his wings and make a big blow and shake out all the dead feathers before he takes flight.' Then he would always offer the complainant some money. 'Here, my good fellow, take these lire. They will help you forget.'"

"And your brother was never punished?"

"Never! Papa always thought his behavior amusing. 'The little devil,' he used to say lovingly. 'What a scrapper.' Once, a man threw the money back at Papa and spit at his feet. Papa was angry and wanted to have the man arrested but couldn't find him. That is what I could never understand. Papa is a smart man, and yet he has never realized that a human being outside his own affluent class has thoughts and feelings too. The fisherman out there on the river, the tailor in his shop, the bootmaker's apprentice who works only for his daily ration of bread and wine. All these people have minds which dare to entertain ideas about freedom to walk safely on the streets; to have enough to eat too; to be dry when it rains; to live without forever groveling in the gutter."

Etienne looked at her admiringly. "For a woman, you have done a goodly amount of thinking."

"Women think too, in case you males were not aware of it," she flung at him angrily.

"I suspected they did, but I had never encountered that species before." He chuckled.

Ignoring him, Maria continued, "I married the duke. I was fed up with the boredom and frustration I knew at home. I wanted to be doing something. Our country was falling apart, and those who had the education and position to strengthen it were selfishly concerned only with the comfort of their own hides. Everyone else be damned!"

"Maria!" he shouted in surprise.

"Well," she pouted, before answering defiantly, "I mean it." Her voice changed. Tenderly she said, "And then I met Napoleon." She paused, seemingly dwelling on the memory of that wonderful occasion. "I had planned to wangle out of him everything good that I could for Italy. I know I am beautiful and men desire me. I would use what nature had bestowed upon me in behalf of my country. I would give to Italy the gifts I had bought from Napoleon with my body. The duke and I were to be two happy patriots!"

Maria laughed delightedly. "But the joke was on me. A happy joke. I fell in love with Napoleon. For the first time in my life I know what it is to want to fall down and worship a man, but I love him. I love him," her voice sang.

Etienne was startled. "Maria, you're out of your head. Half the women of Europe and Egypt are swooning over Napoleon. He's fame. He's the victor, the hero. He performs miracles on the battlefield and

77

conquers as surely at the council table. But, to be in love with the cocky little fellow—"

"Little?" she queried. "Cocky? I hadn't noticed. He is so tall that I look up at him and want to fall down and adore him. And never could he be cocky. He is a god who walks firmly, for he has earned the right to possess the earth."

Etienne whistled. "Listen to her, will you! Maria, you are raving like a schoolgirl with a crush. Come to your senses."

She turned on him angrily. "*You're* the schoolboy. You are as impossible as my brother and his friends. You, who have been with him every day in battle, at Marengo, at Malta, at Alexandria. You, who have seen his brilliance and leadership. You know of the good he has done. Corsica, where he was born, was enslaved by France and he set it free. In France, a bloodthirsty mob was guillotining the country's finest minds, and Napoleon made it the most powerful country in Europe today. He did not waste his youth in the tavern. He had ideals. He used his time to study and to plan how best to build a great Europe. And when he frees a country from the slavery and sloth of its dissolute rulers, he does not kill and pillage. He is kind to the people. He knows what is good for them whether they agree with him or not. I know of many instances where he has been merciful to the guilty."

"Like when?" Etienne asked.

Fired with zeal, she rushed on. "The Prince of Hatzfeld," she announced in a smug tone. "Napoleon had possession of letters, written by the prince himself, proving that he plotted to overthrow Napoleon, and when the princess pleaded for mercy for her husband, Napoleon gave her the papers and told her to tear up the evidence. That proves he has the soul of a god."

"Rubbish. Pure propaganda." Etienne was unimpressed. "The Hatzfeld family is a powerful one. If Hatzfeld is executed, the whole family is against Napoleon. Hatzfeld is released, forgiven. Napoleon has a powerful ally."

"You are too cynical," she accused.

"All right. I'm cynical, but," he asked, "what is to become of your beloved Italy in this grandiose scheme of your little Corsican god? You said yourself that Napoleon plans to rule Europe, Asia, everything he can get his hands on."

"That's the point. He will make each country a separate state of the French Empire. But each country will be united under one head. Each country will be allowed to rule itself under a set of good laws which he will set up for the benefit of that individual country or state. Thus, Italy will be united too. It will be strong in a Europe of strong states. It will be on an equal footing with Germany, Austria, and Russia too. We will no longer be the bone which every dog that comes along takes a bite out of. We too shall have national pride." Maria looked at him from the side of those sloe eyes as if daring him to discount the truth of what she had said.

"You're a lovely dreamer. I suppose the Duke of Mantua will be the titular head of Italy as a consolation for losing you?" he asked, smiling at her indulgently. She was so sure of herself, so unaware of the greed which prompts a man's struggle for power. And yet, who knew? Napoleon had a tender spot in his nature for women, beautiful women.

The corners of Maria's mouth quivered and she broke into a smile. Her dimples peeped out and the impish light danced in her eyes. "The duke would like that. I shall ask Napoleon about it when the time comes. But first, I must make him love me, for I already love him so madly. That is why I shall have his baby. Then he will know I love him and he will forget about Josephine. I love him, I respect him, revere him, honor him, admire him. Everything it is possible for a woman to be to a man I shall be to him with all the health and energy and mind I possess. To be with

79

Napoleon is to be in Paradise, and I intend to make him feel the same about me."

Etienne applauded.

Maria looked offended. "You're laughing at me."

Etienne said nothing. He reached for the wine decanter and slowly filled his glass. Standing up, he raised it to the girl by the fireplace. "To Italy. May she appreciate my sacrifice." There was an edge in his voice.

When he had drained the glass, Etienne placed it quietly upon the table. Turning, he walked from the room.

Chapter Seven

In March of 1802, the night before the signing of the Treaty of Amiens, Napoleon Bonaparte stood before a group of his chosen officers and announced, "Both the savage and the civilized man need a lord and master, a magician who will hold the imagination, impose strict discipline, bind man in chains, so that he may not be out of season. Obedience is man's destiny; he deserves nothing better, and he has no rights."

With the signing of the treaty, Europe belonged to the First Consul of France. Egypt was already his, the vantage point he needed from which to attack India and wrestle it away from England. And after that—the rest of Asia. To complete his plan, England must be invaded and stripped of military might.

Then, with his European house in order, he was free to turn his attention to the United States. With his far-seeing mind, Napoleon realized he needed a toehold in the New World—an unwanted Caribbean island which no New World country would suspect as a military base. St. Domingue was the perfect island. According to the tales of slaughter and destruction, St. Domingue was a doomed land, torn by slave rebellion. What government would want it?

The cocky little corporal, who had already conceived the image of himself as a world ruler, devised a daring plan by which he might acquire both mighty England and lowly St. Domingue in the same strategy. Napoleon would send his brother-in-law, General Leclerc, with the French fleet and ten thousand soldiers to capture St. Domingue. Lord Nelson, sensing the attack, would follow Leclerc across the Atlantic. Having taken the island, Leclerc would secretly hurry back to blockade Brest, while the Grand Army, already waiting at Boulogne, would have three days to invade England. But Napoleon underestimated Nelson. The British admiral did not fall for the ruse, and Leclerc sailed towards the Caribbean alone.

While Napoleon dreamed his dreams of world rule, there were others, too, who lusted for power. One of these was Toussaint L'Ouverture, President of St. Domingue. Born a slave on the Breda plantation, Toussaint had early shown signs of such great intelligence that his owner had him educated. With this advantage, when the revolution came L'Ouverture worked himself up through the chaos to become the first president of St. Domingue. At once, he set about to bring order and prosperity to the island. He gave the plantations back to the original owners, that is, to all those who were still alive and had returned at his promise of protection. The slaves were urged to go back to their former masters, but now they would be referred to as "cultivators" and receive a percentage of the profits from their labors. L'Ouverture urged that the island be replanted and rebuilt, and that foreign businessmen be encouraged to invest in its economic recovery.

But the black subjects did not cooperate. They had finally won their freedom and now refused to work. Freedom meant sitting in the sun. Freedom meant following one's own inclination, whether it be to steal or to sleep or to spit. Freedom meant living like the birds or the fish or the snakes. To fly or swim or strike at will.

Toussaint, who had made himself a father figure for his people, found a scapegoat to carry out the unpopular task of persuading the new citizens to return to work. Jean Jacques Dessalines was the former slave of a black man. He was referred to as The Mad Tiger. A huge, pinheaded, slobbering gorilla with long, thick arms, Dessalines could clutch a man in his bare hands and squeeze him until the life ran out of him. His methods of returning his fellow men to work were ruthless, but effective. Those who didn't return, died. It was that simple. Some he burned alive and others he buried in sand up to the head and poured molten wax into their ears. One of his favorite means of obtaining cooperation was to have a laggard worker placed across two wooden saw horses and sawn in half. In this manner, ten thousand former slaves were slaughtered.

Dessalines' brutal methods soon had most of the workers back on the job, and prosperity began to return on the island. For his efforts, he was made governor of the southern part of St. Domingue, the part with the greatest concentration of mulattoes. The Mad Tiger hated white blood and seemed to have an uncanny ability to smell out even the smallest amount of it in the citizens he was sent to govern. His idea of the duty of his political office was the extermination of whites and mulattoes. His fervor in this activity did not even wane when Toussaint L'Ouverture sent him the admonition, "I asked you to prune the tree, not uproot it."

In the northern section of the island, which included the seaport and capital city of Cap François, Toussaint established another of his aides, Henri Christophe, as governor. Before the revolt, Christophe had been a waiter and chalker in the Hôtel de la Couronne, owned by a freed slave. By saving his tips, Henri bought his freedom from his black master and later married his employer's daughter.

The Hôtel de la Couronne had been a popular tavern, one which many men of the former Creole aristocracy had frequented for billiards and rum. By observing them, Henri had learned to conduct himself in a gentlemanly fashion. Tall of stature, soft-spoken, thoughtful, M. Christophe looked well suited to his role as a leader of the new republic.

This was St. Domingue at the time Napoleon

dispatched the impressive French fleet and ten thousand soldiers under the leadership of the great General Leclerc to take possession of the island. On board the main ship with Leclerc were President L'Ouverture's two young sons. They had been studying in France for the past two years, and, as a show of goodwill, Napoleon had granted them a vacation from their studies so that they might visit their father. Also on board was General Leclerc's new bride, Pauline, Napoleon's eighteen-year-old sister, who had come with her ball gowns, pet poodles, and flirtatious ladies-in-waiting to set up court in this tropical land.

The dazzling array of French power and finery sailed boldly into the harbor of Cap François and demanded the surrender of the island. But while the crowned heads of Europe had bowed before the First Consul, the illiterate, kinky-headed rulers of St. Domingue did not know that they were expected to fall in obeisance when Napoleon so ordered.

"I have no authority to hand St. Domingue over to you," Christophe replied to Leclerc's order for the capitulation of the island.

"You are in charge here, are you not?" Leclerc inquired.

"*Non*, monsieur. I am only the governor. You must speak to the president, M. L'Ouverture."

"And where may I find him?"

Christophe shook his head. "I do not know. He is attending to some business in the central part of the island and did not say when he would return."

"Can you not get a message to him?" Leclerc was exasperated. Never before had he had any trouble arranging a meeting with the head of a country for the purpose of discussing terms of surrender.

"I could try, Sir, but the interior is very mountainous, and it is not always possible to find him. He is well acquainted with the countryside and I am not."

"I'll give you three days to bring M. L'Ouverture to

me," Leclerc declared, "and if not, I shall put my troops ashore and take the city."

In three days, Christophe returned and in his soft, unruffled voice reported that he had looked everywhere but had been unable to reach Toussaint L'Ouverture.

Leclerc was indignant. This was ridiculous. The great army in all its splendor marching forth to battle a ghost! Under the circumstances, Leclerc took the only peaceable course left open to him. He sent his terms to Toussaint through Christophe. He explained that the French had come to help their country, to improve it, to raise the citizens' standard of living. Along with Christophe, he dispatched L'Ouverture's sons in hopes that they might persuade their father to trust the French.

By the end of the week, there was no reply. Both message and sons had been as completely absorbed as salt in a water jar. Leclerc, still in control of his overly aggravated disposition, drove up to the governor's palace in Cap François and confronted Henri Christophe.

"Where is my answer from M. Toussaint?" he demanded in a stern voice.

Christophe gazed at him slowly and in his serene way, inquired, "Did you not receive word from him?"

"I did not!"

The governor shook his head. "I guess he has no word to send you."

Leclerc was dumbfounded over the ease with which the new leaders of St. Domingue ignored his presence. He spoke in a cold firm voice: "Governor Christophe, I am asking you for the last time to peaceably turn the city over to me."

"Sorry, M. General, but I cannot do it. The president has not issued an order to that effect."

Leclerc delivered an ultimatum: "I will give you two days in which to procure that order. If I do not have it by the day after tomorrow, I shall forcibly take the city."

"I wouldn't advise that, General Leclerc," Christophe cautioned in a quiet voice.

The Frenchman stiffened at the rebuff. "And why not?" he asked with hauteur. "What is to prevent my coming ashore? You surely cannot stop me."

"There will be no town. I shall burn it," Henri said simply.

"That's the risk I must take," was the crisp answer. The general left the palace.

No message came from the island. Just before the dawn of the second day, as the troops were preparing to disembark, the dark sky of night suddenly blazed with a hundred fires of a stubborn city that chose self-destruction to surrender. Leclerc shook his head over the waste, and Pauline wept. She had heard of the loveliness of the governor's palace and had seen herself enthroned there as its mistress.

"Why did they burn their beautiful city?" she wailed. "The French would never burn Paris, *ever*."

"Because the black man did not build Cap François as the French did Paris," her husband answered. "It came of a culture not their own. Having contributed nothing to it, they do not mind returning it to nothing."

The death of the city, together with the presence of the invading troops, brought submission. Toussaint, given amnesty, came down from the mountains and accepted the French as the lawful rulers. He was offered a job in the newly formed cabinet, but he declined, pleading age and weariness. He preferred to retire to his plantation, but would be available to provide counsel should the need arise.

Because they had fought hard for their people, Dessalines and Christophe were given positions of seeming importance in Leclerc's military organization. They were to gather up the arms from all the natives on the island and store them in the French armory in Cap François. It was the obvious occupation for the two leaders, since who among the French could ferret out the guns concealed in villages, swamps, under stalks of sugar cane? Who else knew how to contact the maroons in their hiding places in the mountains and persuade them to turn over their guns?

The two former aides to Toussaint did a thorough job of collecting thousands of guns and storing them in various hiding places throughout the island. Dessalines and Christophe had promised Leclerc that as soon as all the weapons were retrieved they would bring the entire armament in to Cap François. As the days passed, it seemed to Leclerc that the men were stalling, but he did not press the matter. The brother-in-law of Napoleon had other problems of reconstruction that demanded his immediate attention.

The worst problem was the loss of life among the French soldiers. Natives raided the barracks by night and killed the men as they slept. Thousands were slaughtered by guerrillas in the mountains. Hundreds of others fell ill of various tropical diseases and died.

Back in Paris, the First Consul was very angry. It was already nine months since Leclerc had sailed to take this small island for France. Instead of hurrying back to blockade England, Leclerc kept calling for more men. By now thirty-six thousand soldiers had been dispatched to St. Domingue, and still came the cry for reinforcements. Nine months fiddled away in an unsuccessful attempt to wrestle one little piece of ravaged land from a bunch of savages. Napoleon would wait no longer. From the reports received from Leclerc, he planned a course of action.

First, Toussaint L'Ouverture must be removed permanently from the island. So long as the former president remained on St. Domingue, the natives would carry the hope of rising up again under his leadership. With the old leader gone, rebellion would die. It must be done quietly so that no accusing finger could point to the abductors.

Jean Jacques Dessalines must also be eliminated. His former record of savagery was a menace to Napoleonic plans. He was capable of dropping his civilized pose at anytime to go storming off to the mountains and whip up a native army. Napoleon believed in aborting the embryo before it matured.

But he needed a native leader. One who could be depended upon to be loyal to France while the French army was occupied elsewhere. Henri Christophe, whose loyalty to his superior had never wavered, even in the face of Leclerc and his display of military strength, might be the man Napoleon needed. But, the First Consul had to be sure. He would assign someone to find out more about this unlettered native patriot. This man who had the nerve to stand up to one of France's greatest generals.

Napoleon called for Lieutenant Etienne Grenier, the young officer whose audacious exploits had recently come to his attention. When the young man was before him, he explained the mission. "M. Christophe is the man I have selected in my mind to be the native administrator of St. Domingue. You are to make his acquaintance. Learn what goes on inside the man's head and where his sympathies lie. Can we trust him beyond a doubt or will he turn traitor when we are in an all-out war with the States."

"If I may, sir, what about Petion?" Grenier suggested. "He was educated here in France and might be more inclined to cooperate with your plans."

"I know the mulatto bastard. I made a point to meet him during his studies here. He is a fool! A fanatic about democracy. Probably carried away by the fervor he witnessed here in Paris during the Revolution. Petion was a great aid to Toussaint while he was president, but the man is too unselfish for leadership. Too weak for my purpose."

"I see, sir," repied Etienne. He had learned that although Napoleon welcomed intelligent suggestions, one must never question him twice.

Napoleon continued, "Tell General Leclerc that you are bringing an additional nine thousand soldiers, which—" the First Consul pounded the desk to emphasize each word—"which will make forty-five thousand soldiers I have supplied him to take one damn little island, and he hasn't secured it *yet*. Not *one* soldier more will he get! The *Freire* sails for Cap François tomorrow at seven hundred hours, Grenier. Immediately before sailing, you will receive sealed orders for General Leclerc. They are to be placed directly into his hands by you. Good luck, Grenier." Napoleon stood up in dismissal, but the officer before him did not move.

"Have I not made myself clear?"

"Sir, I am a cuirassier of heavy cavalry, and you have assigned me to espionage in which I have no expertise."

Napoleon laughed, but to the ears of the young officer, it sounded more like a sneer. "Lieutenant, it has been brought to my attention that you have expertise in many more activities than the military. It is never my intention to discourage the ambitions of an officer. However, to lessen the trauma of the transfer, you are promoted to the rank of captain. That should stimulate your 'expertise' in this new venture."

The first man of France sat down and gave his attention to the papers on his desk. The face of the young officer betrayed no emotion, but his eyes narrowed as though taking the measure of the game before the kill. Then he gave a rigid salute and turned on his heel. Before he reached the door, Napoleon called out, "Take care of yourself, Captain, while in St. Domingue. General Leclerc is forever complaining about his soldiers falling ill. If they left the women alone, they would not contract those 'tropical' diseases. A woman can change a man's destiny, as well you know." And, as well *you* know, thought Etienne.

At dawn the next day, Captain Grenier sailed westward on the *Freire*. For two months, he was buffeted by the winds and the waves until he felt like dice shaken before the cast. But the water calmed as they neared the end of the voyage, and when Grenier first saw the island of St. Domingue, a curtain of mist, like a frothy white shroud, hung over its mountains. As they came closer, the mist cleared, and Captain Etienne Grenier raised his spyglass. On the outskirts of what must have once been a city, he could see skeletal structures, black and charred, standing like a huge, crazily angled iron fence against a backdrop of purple mountains. Along the waterfront and stretching back for some distance, new buildings had already been erected.

So this was the land that was thwarting the great Napoleon's dream of world conquest. Count Grenier wondered if the arrogant English would ever know that their country had been saved from invasion through the stubbornness of one tiny island. He felt a kinship with little St. Domingue. Leaning on the railing of the *Freire*, the officer watched it grow larger, as the billowing sails carried the frigate into Cap François.

Chapter Eight

Etienne Grenier saw President Toussaint L'Ouverture
but once. That was at Belle Fleur, General Leclerc's
palace on the outskirts of Cap François. Pauline, Leclerc's young bride, was entertaining all the island's
white Frenchmen of any importance at a dinner party
shortly after Etienne's arrival. The drum and bugle
corps had been asked to present a concert, after which
there would be dancing. Eteinne had looked forward to
meeting the female population of the court as had all
the other officers.

This dinner was Mme. Leclerc's first social affair,
and she was as rapturous and self-important as a child
at her First Communion feast. It was her day. Pauline,
unlike her brother, Napoleon, was blond as a Nordic,
and on this island of blacks where one almost forgot
there *was* a white race out of uniform, she was as welcome as a light in a window on a dark street. Like the
other Bonapartes, she was short with a tendency to
plumpness, but at her young age, the pounds were
properly distributed so as to give a voluptuous effect.
In the unlikely event that one might overlook her feminine attractions, Pauline's décolletage was so extreme
that the beholder was loath to turn his eyes away lest
he miss the exact moment her neckline might lose it
restraint.

When Etienne Greneir was introduced to the first
lady of St. Domingue, he bowed over her hand, and as
he did so Pauline moved so close to him that he inadvertently brushed her bosom as he straightened up. She

shyly dropped her eyes and curtseyed. Then she gazed up at him with guileless blue eyes and said in a breathy, intimate voice, "Monsieur Captain is most welcome to my house. He is most welcome *any* time." She emitted a delighted giggle, then, remembering her place, curtseyed again and strolled off on the arm of her husband.

Watching the handsome couple as they walked toward an arriving guest, Etienne thought he detected a stiffness in Leclerc's manner that he had not noticed before. Etienne knew that Leclerc, a true product of the military life, was more concerned with the science of attack and the mathematics of battle positions than with parties and social frivolity. Still, tonight he seemed particularly restrained. The general, having let his wife be spirited off to dance with his adjutant, now hovered near the doorway as if in expectation of another guest. At the same time, his eyes darted about the room, seemingly counting off those who had already arrived. Whom, wondered Etienne, was he looking for? It seemed to young Grenier that everyone was there!

There was General Rochambeau, standing with a fresh glass of whiskey in hand. Etienne had been repelled when he first met the man two weeks ago, and his distrust of him had not been resolved on subsequent occasions. Rochambeau had a long hollow-cheeked face with a thin pinched nose that gave him an air of frigidity. He had small eyes, deeply set under bushy eyebrows which forever hid in shadow any thoughts which might betray the man within. His high forehead was extended by a receding hairline, and his upright military bearing made him even more aloof. Etienne was not a religious man, but if ever he thought of Lucifer again, it would be in the image of General Rochambeau.

Philippe Duponceau, adjutant general to Leclerc, was playing the gallant to Leclerc's wife. Having finished his dance with Pauline, he had raised his glass in a toast, and from where he stood, Captain Grenier heard him say, "To the loveliest Bonaparte of them all."

Etienne enjoyed Philippe. He was well past thirty, but his easy laugh and debonair manner made him forever youthful. In the middle of his forehead, his black curly hair formed a widow's peak, and upon his arrival Etienne had been warned by one of the other officers not to make any humorous remarks about this caprice of nature. It was a Duponceau family trait, and Philippe was proud of it. His sister, who had been born without this mark of beauty envied him its possession. In any case, Etienne had no intention of ribbing Duponceau. The adjutant general was a slight man, but very fast with his fists.

Philippe loved girls, *all* girls, and all girls returned his affection. He toasted each one with some epithet that he had undoubtedly used before on some other lady, yet each adored him because he made her laugh and feel popular. Even a prim, elderly woman in gray, a chaperone to some young lady, smiled indulgently at Philippe when he winked at her. Certainly it was a gay night for everyone. People drank and talked and forgot their cares. They had long been overworked and overstrained, and a party was just the remedy for their sagging spirits.

At last the guest for whom General Leclerc had been waiting arrived. There was a stir in the crowd and someone beside Grenier whispered, "Toussaint L'Ouverture." In what seemed more relief than pleasure, the host hurried toward him. Pauline hastened to her husband's side and, in a posture of dignity, curtseyed in welcome to the distinguished guest. She was delighted to receive such an important visitor at her very first social affair.

Toussaint stood before this group of unfamiliar faces and smiled warmly. His political partisanship of the past had been a nuisance. Now, at last, it had been surmounted, and they were all friends. The former president was a short, rather slight man, but the brilliant glow of candles from the crystal chandeliers polished his ebony face and gave him a spiritual cast. From where he stood, Grenier could not hear what the former president of St. Domingue was saying to his hostess. However, it was obvious that Pauline was saying all the proper, complimentary words of welcome, for her husband stood by, a pleased smile on his face, as he permitted his wife to handle the conversation.

Etienne deemed it most generous of Leclerc to give such a genuinely warm welcome to their former black foe. Toussaint had evidently been asked to the party as a friend, a neighbor, a free man, an equal. Now there surely could be no doubt in the mind of L'Ouverture that he was wanted.

Having permitted Pauline time enough for her pretty speeches, Leclerc put his arm on Toussaint's elbow and began to guide him about the room. With an air of great pride, he introduced him to the guests. When Grenier was presented, he looked down into warm brown eyes, and liked the man at once.

"Captain Grenier arrived from France only two weeks ago," General Leclerc explained.

"Then you must have passed my two sons at sea," the older man said.

"They are going back to France?" Etienne asked.

"Oui, they are returning to school at St. Quentin. This is a new country and education is not what it should be. It is the best heritage I can leave them."

"You are very far-seeing, M. L'Ouverture. Your sons are most fortunate to have such a father."

Leclerc beamed at Etienne in approval and then said to Toussaint, "You must meet some of the other members of my staff so that you will begin to feel more at home among us." The general led his distinguished guest toward several of the minor officers and their wives.

For a moment Etienne had the feeling that he was a character in a play. He had spoken his few lines on cue, and the two leads had gone on to enact the rolls in which they were cast. But he dismissed the thought when Philippe Duponceau came toward him with a glass of wine. "Have a drink," he urged. "It whets the appetite for both girls and food, and we have plenty of both here. Why so serious?"

Etienne wondered about that too. "I must be slipping," he said to his fellow officer. "You're right. I need a drink." He took the wineglass and emptied it.

"That's better," Philippe said. "You look less like a schoolmaster. Now for the girls." He looked about the room. "I see just the one. That redhead talking with Mme. Leclerc. How about engaging our hostess's attention while I spirit her shapely friend off to some obscure corner?"

"That's not very flattering to our hostess. Why don't you take *her* off to a corner?"

"Pauline? She giggles too much. I've had her in a corner before."

"Excuse me, sir," Etienne mocked. "I should have known. You're one of those philanthropists who is fond of *all* the ladies. I'll help you out by bombarding the attentions of our hostess."

"Save your ammunition," his fellow officer advised. "That camp has few ramifications in defense. Falls quickly." Philippe strolled toward Pauline and her friend of the auburn tresses and Etienne followed. He would keep his serious thoughts for another day. This was a party, after all.

Pauline and her companion brightened considerably as Etienne and Philippe approached. "Here come the handsomest men on the island," their hostess effervesced.

"And where should the handomest men be?" Philippe asked, "but with the two most beautiful women?"

Pauline tossed her head. "Captain Grenier has been here but two weeks. He has not had sufficient time to make a survey of the female populace. He cannot be so quick to agree with you."

"Madame need not concern herself," Etienne said.

"I assure you that after a serious study of every female in the vicinity, I shall arrive at the same conclusion as General Duponceau."

A waiter came by with a tray of filled wineglasses, and Captain Grenier reached for one. Raising it toward Pauline, he turned the glass as though musing upon its beauty, and said, "Wine in crystal is like loveliness in a woman. Sparkling, stimulating, and tempting. To our hostess, the headiest wine of them all." As he drank, Philippe slipped off with the redhead. Pauline swelled with pleasure, a rather precarious reaction, since her décolletage had already demonstrated a tendency to slip from its assignment.

"You are most gallant," she cooed.

But they had hardly begun to converse when the call came for dinner. Grenier, happy to be relieved of his duty, escorted his young hostess to the elegant table and seated her next to her husband, the general. Then he took his own seat farther down and discovered, much to his amusement, that his dinner partner was none other than the charming redhead Philippe had had his eye on. She proved to be a disarming young woman, bubbling with laughter and willing to prattle on happily about anything. Her name, Etienne learned, was Mlle. Freneau, but, by the end of dinner, she insisted that he call her Malvina.

"Is it true Etienne," she asked, spooning a second helping of dessert, "that during the night when our soldiers are asleep zombies come down from the mountains and steal their guns, leaving rattlesnakes instead, and the snakes poison our men? Is it true?"

"Quite. There are vicious snakes around here," Etienne said, knowing only of one soldier who had been bitten and he by a harmless garter snake. "Snakes here run to twenty feet long," he teased.

"Really!" Malvina's green eyes grew large. "That big! How awful!"

She was silent for a moment as she considered a monster of such magnitude. But only for a moment.

"And they say the negros over here know how to handle these snakes. They can hypnotize them and get them to do whatever they want."

"That's true. They're bosom friends."

Malvina looked up at him, her eyes twinkling. "You are making fun of me."

"I wouldn't dare."

With an air of repressed excitement, Malvina leaned close to Etienne and whispered, "Pauline and I figured a new game we can play. Don't tell anyone, but I think it could be fun to get one of these rattlesnakes—dead, of course—and scare some of the girls around here. I can hear them screaming already. It might also be a laugh to frighten some of the servants who work in the palace. One of them said that snakes are sacred. The longest rattler of all is owned by a black witch on some plantation a short distance from Cap François. Its body is what the spirit of some god uses when he goes about in disguise to see how people are behaving."

Etienne's brows shot up in surprise.

"That's what she said. Some god. They've got some really strange ways, those black folks." She lowered her voice. "There's lots we don't know about them."

She glanced over at Toussaint at the head of the table, then turned back to Etienne. "See that little old black man up there beside our host? You might think he's just a poor Negro, but he really is wealthy. I guess anyone who makes himself the boss of a country is rich. If General Leclerc succeeds on this island, Pauline will find herself married to a rich man."

"General Leclerc is a military man," Etienne defended, "and will always receive a salary, nothing more."

Malvina patted Etienne on the knee. "That's all right. You men must stick together. Did you know," she chattered on in a whisper, "that L'Ouverture gave Duc René Dubois a large sum of money to look after his sons? He went back on the ship with the two L'Ouverture boys and promised to place them in the academy at St. Quentin, and supply all their needs while they are in France getting an education. Their father entrusted enough money to Duc Dubois to enable those boys to live like kings for years. So you see, that old black man really is rich. Probably has a mine hidden on his farm and has everyone thinking he's just a poor peasant."

Etienne heard only a part of this last story of Malvina's, for the mention of Duc Dubois had startled him. He knew Dubois to be a notorious gambler and con artist. Years ago, in order to pay off gambling debts, the duc had dissipated his young sister's inheritance and then mortgaged the Dubois family château in Chambourg. Duc Dubois was a charming man, with beautiful manners and a boyish smile. His sincere demeanor had fooled many into trusting him. But time and again, the rascal had broken hearts and bank accounts. Grenier was deeply sorry that the old man had fallen prey to him. That money would never be spent on L'Ouverture's sons.

"Malvina, who gave you this information?" he asked.

"René himself."

"Perhaps he lied."

"He showed me the money. I didn't know there *was* that much money in the world!"

Etienne moaned. It must be so. Duc Dubois never had any money except what he swindled. If there had been games of chance on any scale in Cap François, every soldier would have known about it. He could not have won it at cards.

"If you don't believe me, look at this." Malvina thrust an arm under his nose and displayed a solid gold bracelet laid with pieces of Chinese jade. These were encircled with diamonds. It looked like a piece of jewelery one might find in the museums of Italy, the type Napoleon was always purloining for the Louvre in Paris. Etienne whistled.

"Didn't it bother your conscience to let Duc Dubois spend money on you which belonged to two young schoolboys?"

98

"Of course not. You sound like an old fuddy-duddy. One of the former Creole planters came back and needed money to rebuild his plantation. René bought the bracelet. War is like that. Winner take all. Duc Dubois said it was only right that he spend some of the old duck's money on this bracelet. He called it a handling charge." Malvina sounded very smug.

"A handling charge on M. L'Ouverture or you?"

Mlle. Freneau arched her eyebrows. Slowly she leaned close to Etienne and, with her lips brushing his ear, she whispered, "Wouldn't *you* like to know?"

But even the generous flirtations of Mlle. Freneau could not take Etienne's mind off those children. He had not met the lads himself, but General Leclerc had told him what fine boys they were, smart and sturdy. What would become of them once Dubois no longer had to keep up his pretense?

When dinner was finished and everyone had risen from the table, General Leclerc came to Etienne and said, "Captain, will you assist Mme. Leclerc in taking care of the guests? I have a short meeting arranged with M. L'Ouverture. It is of great importance that we attend to a certain matter tonight. I have asked Rochambeau and Duponceau to join me and our guest of honor. We shall conclude our business by the time the concert is finished. Then we shall join you."

This request from his superior greatly disappointed Etienne, for he had hoped to be present at such a meeting. Leclerc must have noticed, for he added, "Tomorrow I shall give you a full account of the meeting. Someone must take care of the ladies after all," he said jokingly, but his face belied his tone. He looked taut, like a soldier for whom the battle is about to begin.

Pauline came running up to Etienne, and taking both his hands in hers pulled him excitedly toward the salon. "Dear Captain, what fun!" she said with her characteristic ebullience. "My husband tells me you will be our host while he dispatches some boring emergency of state. Isn't it wonderful? We can hold hands during the concert. It is quite correct for the host and hostess to do so."

"You have a generous husband who permits so lovely a wife to hold hands with a potential rival." Etienne gave her an admiring look.

"M. Captain is very chivalrous. He has made the evening the most enjoyable since we landed on this decadent island." Pauline sent him a sidelong glance. "I hope General Leclerc asks me to give another party."

"Your husband *requested* this affair?"

"Oui, and he requested something else." Pauline reached up and, pulling his head down to where she could whisper into his ear, said, "He also asked me to invite M. L'Ouverture and to be especially gracious to him. I shouldn't be telling you all this, but well, we're all in the army together."

Pauline removed her hands from his head and, looking pertly up at him, inquired, "I played my part well, didn't I?"

"My dear, you were a most captivating hostess. I'm sure your husband was very proud."

Pauline pulled his arm through hers and held it so close to her bosom that he could feel her heart beating. "Liar!" she teased, looking up at him. "My husband never notices anything I do. Not anything," she repeated, invitation in her voice. "Now, shall we take our guests into the salon, dear host? With you to hold my hand, I don't think I shall mind this concert after all."

As she led the way into the large, chair-filled salon, Pauline became a pouty little girl again when she complained, "General Leclerc insisted upon a fife and drum corps. He said it would be a pleasant way to relax before dancing. Who *needs* to relax before dancing? He can't get the army out of his system. Even when I'm giving a party he has to drag in something military."

Etienne chuckled at this remark, and Pauline gurgled on.

"It was bad enough to invite a noisy fife and drum

corps to a concert, but he insisted it start exactly at ten-thirty and play until he sends word for it to stop. By then, everyone will have a headache and go home." She brightened. "But *you* will stay on, won't you? Promise."

"Indeed I shall, dear Madame. Nothing could drag me away." Pauline gave a satisfied smile and leaned against him. The concert began.

Pauline was right. It was a noisy affair. Too much sound to be contained within one room, even a room with many windows. Inadvertently, Etienne glanced toward the long windows. A French private stood before each one. The shutters were closed. Strange! Especially since privates never attended officers' social affairs.

The corps droned on, drumming and blowing from one number to the next without pause. It reminded the Count Etienne de Vastey Grenier of the carnivals in Europe where the dentist arrived with his musicians. Their job was to blast away so the crowd could not hear the patient's screams while his tooth was pulled. Odd, that his mind should conjure up such a comparison!

Whether it was his own imagination or really fact, Etienne was no longer sure, but the corps grew louder and louder until notes seemed to beat in through each ear and meet with a strident bang in the middle of his head. Would the program never come to its close? Surely there were more pleasurable methods of entertaining one's guests than subjecting them to a prolonged ear-beating! And suppose an emergency occurred on the island. All the officers and dignitaries were in this house. Who could hear a courier's knock on the gate or his call for help!

Etienne froze. Why had the thought not occurred to him sooner? This was the perfect setup for *just* such an occasion. But what? Why? Suddenly he knew. He wanted to leap from his chair and run to the room where the conference was taking place. The secret lay

there, of that Etienne was sure. This whole evening
had been a camouflage for some political maneuver.
Etienne was furious. His insides were about to explode
at any moment but he had to contain his impatience
and remain quietly seated beside Pauline. If it had not
been for those years of military discipline, Captain
Grenier might have rushed from the salon, seeking ad-
mission to the conference room.

As it was, he sat in what he hoped was a listening
attitude, just like the other puppets about him in
Leclerc's drama. A good officer carries out orders no
matter how mysterious the assignment.

At last, the concert was over. What Etienne had endured for an eternity had in reality taken only forty-
five minutes. The large double doors were opened into
the hallway and Rochambeau and Philippe walked in.
The guards about the windows came to attention, and
as though on cue, the musicians let their music die
away. Applause, more from relief than appreciation,
finished the concert.

But where were General Leclerc and his guest,
Toussaint? Why had they remained in the conference
room? Etienne saw a house servant with a tray of wine
and glasses walk down the hallway toward the study.
Captain Grenier rebuked himself. He was wasting the
entire evening entertaining foolish suspicions, acting
like a jealous wife. A roomful of beautiful women and
he was conjuring fantasies about two older men who
merely preferred a companionable glass of wine to ex-
changing meaningless amenities with a group of par-
tygoers. He would put this nonsense out of his head, at
once. Turning to Pauline, he asked, "And now, my
lovely hostess, shall we dance?"

He held out his arm to Pauline and they started
toward the ballroom, where the musicians, real musicians this time, were already assembled. Sounds of in-
struments tuning up could be heard in the salon. When
they reached the hallway, General Rochambeau stepped

before them. He bowed to Pauline and said, "I hope my dear lady will pardon the intrusion."

Turning to Etienne, he delivered an order in that cold condescending voice which he reserved for the men below his rank: "You are to report to General Leclerc in his study. At once!" His black eyes staring out from under his heavy eyebrows told nothing, as usual, but his lip curled back in scorn.

Etienne bowed to Pauline. "Excuse me, Madame." As he walked toward the study, he heard Rochambeau say in that oily voice he reserved for beautiful women: "If Madame will permit, I shall be delighted to open the ball with her."

Outside Leclerc's study, Captain Grenier paused a moment, unconsciously drawing himself to attention before knocking upon the door.

From inside a weary voice said, "Enter."

Etienne turned the knob and stepped into the room. General Leclerc was slouched in his chair, his legs outstretched, his feet resting on the polished tabletop before him. His eyes stared fixedly through the open French window into the darkness beyond. Two glasses and a wine bottle, untouched, stood on a tray on the table. Captain Grenier waited at attention, quiet, afraid to breathe deeply lest the sound add to the weariness of the man before him.

At last, the older man raised his head and let out a deep sigh. With his eyes still staring into the darkness beyond the window, he said, "He's gone."

Etienne had the feeling that the general spoke more to himself than to any listener. "He's gone," he repeated in the same tired voice, "and I am Judas."

His head began to nod in agreement with himself. "I am Judas. I too know his despair. Judas and I, two of a kind."

By now General Leclerc's head was automatically going up and down as evenly, as methodically, as the pendulum on a clock. "I and Judas. Traitors." The head agreeing. "We both betrayed a good friend."

"General Leclerc," Captain Grenier stepped before his commander, "you sent for me." The presence of the younger man must have broken the spell of whatever mesmerized him beyond the window, for he slowly turned his eyes up to Etienne's face and was visibly struggling to bring himself back into the room.

Looking directly at the young captain, he said once again in a low voice, "He's gone."

"Who is gone, sir?"

Slowly, the general lifted his heels from the table, grasped the arms of his chair, and like an old man pushed himself to his feet. He walked over to the wine bottle and filled both glasses. Handing one to Etienne, Leclerc raised the other in salute toward the window and toasted, "Toussaint L'Ouverture is gone. Let us drink to him." With that, he drank slowly, almost reverently, as if at a religious ritual.

The wine must have been the tonic Leclerc needed, for when he had placed his empty glass on the table, he drew himself up to his usual military posture and said with more life, "Turn, Captain, and see for yourself." He pointed out the window. "You brought the sealed order. Now you can write in your report that it has been carried out."

Now it was the younger officer's turn to walk toward the window. The night was very black, the kind of blackness the sky wears before it hangs out a late moon. The window faced upon the sea, and out there, sliding toward the horizon, was the *Freier*. There could be no mistake, for Etienne could clearly discern its length by the distance between the lights from stem to stern. Baffled, he turned toward the older man.

"General Leclerc, are you telling me that M. L'Ouverture is on that ship now? Sailing for France?"

"An astute observation." Etienne noted a trace of mockery in the voice. "Very astute, my bright young man. Napoleon should be very pleased with our performances, yours and mine. You brought the order for the abduction of Toussaint and his immediate shipment to France, and I sent him over on the return voyage of the very same ship which carried you and your damn order. We shall be promoted for the efficiency with which we executed this crafty bit of chicanery. You and I, that is. Let us drink to the prospects of our golden future!"

Refilling the glasses, the general handed one to his junior officer and raising the other, he said, "Napoleon wanted it done quietly, unobtrusively. No one will ever know that we are the culprits who removed their sainted leader from these black savages. Fight fire with fire, they always say. We had to have years of training to know how to do it. It takes generations of civilization and schooling to act like a savage and sneak away their little god, but we did it, didn't we, Grenier? Come, let us drink to our cleverness." He raised his glass to his lips, his eyes on the captain. Grenier did not move.

"Drink," the general barked. "It is an order!"

The two men stared at each other, their eyes locked in a duel. Etienne's hand slowly opened, and he let the glass slip from his grasp and crash to the tile floor. He regarded the older man defiantly. "There is nothing in the code which commands a man to drink with his superior officer."

Leclerc's eyes wavered in retreat and studied Etienne closely. After a moment he placed his glass untouched on the tray. Quietly, he said, "I have ordered men to be shot. They had broken a rule and knew me to be just. It was all in line with being a soldier. Man learns how to wipe out the lives of his fellows; how to play God; reshape the world; how to die. All this I can do—coldly, effortlessly, proudly. That is my duty, my profession. But to hold out my hand in friendship and then to betray that trust, this shames me. After tonight, I can never hold my head so high again." Slowly, like a flag slipping to half-mast, he bowed his head in dejection.

Etienne was angry. Angry that he had become en-
meshed in this treachery. Angry with himself. Yet, his
heart went out to the older man before him. "You but
carried out your orders, sir."

With his arms hanging limply at his sides as though
they were too heavy to lift, Leclerc walked out upon
the balcony. He lifted his head and said like one passing sentence, "A man who has been raised in honor,
who has enjoyed honor, who knows pride in honor,
never lowers himself by besmirching that honor."

He drew in a deep breath so that he might receive
sustenance to continue. "If a man is stripped of all
medals, all insigniae, all rank, and retains his honor, he
stands tall forever. His is the highest decoration of all."
His voice became a whisper. "The most important one,
I have lost forever."

The captain walked up to the older man and stood
behind him. He wanted to place a hand on his shoulder, if only to let him know that he understood, but it
seemed like such a futile gesture. Instead he said, "Sir,
I wish I had lost the order at sea." To himself he
sounded juvenile.

Leclerc turned around and faced Grenier. A small
sad smile flickered on his lips, the smile one uses when
addressing a child in time of grief. "Son," he said,
"don't blame yourself. You are too young to know how
to outwit an old veteran like Napoleon. You are
handed a paper, you listen to orders, you carry them
out. If you protest or defect, you are shot and another
man does your work."

"The same is true for you," Etienne answered. "You
are a soldier and must obey orders."

The general shook his head. "Not so blindly. I am
older. There could have been other ways."

"Such as?"

"Procrastination. Refusal. A man cannot blindly
deny responsibility for the actions he takes—even if he
is simply obeying the orders of his superiors. Someone

has to rise up and speak for justice, else how do we get justice? If I am shot, I die for a purpose. Perhaps my death will inflame someone else to echo the cry for justice. But I die in honor. As it is, who will ever remember Leclerc, or if one does, it will be as a Judas, a Brutus. Toussaint L'Ouverture? His name will inspire freedom forever." General Leclerc picked up his wineglass. Hesitantly, he turned it in his hand while he said in a musing voice, "Do you know what he said when the soldiers came into the room and placed the chains about his wrist and started to lead him away? I shall never forget. Never. He allowed the guard to lead him out the window and onto the balcony, and when he approached the stairway he held back. The soldiers did not try to stop him. They recognized his greatness. He turned to look at me, and his voice was calm and certain. I thought of a black god on Judgment Day. 'You think to kill me, but it is only my body that will die. My spirit is planted deep on this island, deep, like the roots of the cocoamaque. It nourishes underground and strengthens and one day will sprout up, and its branches will grow to such great measure as to spread their shadow over all of St. Domingue. My people will be free. All you who oppose that freedom will die.'"

General Leclerc straightened to attention and raised his glass toward the sea. "Humbly I salute you, Toussaint L'Ouverture."

Slowly, as if reviewing the image of the man while he savored the wine, the military general of the island drained his glass. When finished, he held it against his chest, as he gazed out toward the sea. Captain Grenier waited until the reverie was ended.

In the voice of one whose mind is not on the occasion at hand, General Leclerc said, "He placed a curse upon me, a deserved one."

Etienne glanced sharply at his host. In the shadow of the balcony, he looked gaunt, his face drawn, his attitude tense. "You are tired, sir. It has been a hard

107

day, and one a lesser man could not survive." To his own ears, his words were barely adequate.

Leclerc remained standing, holding the glass at his chest as one might his hat while the coffin of a friend is lowered into the grave.

Chapter Nine

That was Pauline Leclerc's first and last state party. Yellow fever struck the island. General Leclerc issued orders that no one was to travel between Cap François and Belle Fleur. The women were to remain at the palace, and he set a guard about the grounds to see that his wife's merry friends did not go adventuring into the town. As for the men under his command, any soldier attempting to sneak into the palace, even though it be to see his wife, was subject to hospital duty. To most men this was a worse threat than the firing squad, for the disease was highly contagious and meant a slow death. The general applied the same restriction to himself: He stayed with his men at the barracks.

The disease was an unseen enemy, and even the bravest of men were badly scared. The natives claimed that with their little black god, L'Ouverture, gone from the scene, evil spirits had boldly infiltrated the island and were gleefully devouring his abductors. It was the Curse coming to their aid.

With the uncanny intuition of jungle folk, the natives, while they were unaware of the details, knew the French were responsible for the disappearance of their adored leader. For years, yellow fever had not plagued the island, and that it should hit with such fury at this time was a sign that Petro Loa was indignant. He was a violent, forceful, malignant god, and could be summoned by the crack of a whip. After his disappearance, Toussaint's riding crop was found on the beach near the French palace, a sure sign that their leader had sought heavenly assistance for his people before he was spirited away. Toussaint was their true president and would never abandon them.

The soldiers themselves began to believe in the voodoo curse. At night, the drums rolled with a menacing tone, which conjured up a picture of doom creeping in like a black spirit with blood-red eyes, steadily, relentlessly, marking his victim for death. Over the beat of the drums rose the eerie voices of the natives, wailing out their grief for Toussaint. Even the moon hid its shining face, and each night appeared to be blacker. The islanders claimed that the rada loa, the gentler spirits, had hung the crêpe of a black cloud over the moon, as a sign that the heavens were in mourning. And always the next day, several hundred more soldiers were stricken with the fever.

General Leclerc was baffled. Never before had any disease cut down so many of his men. Dysentery, smallpox, measles, yes, but never this hopeless, wanton slaughter. It had come so fast and killed so quickly that it was a few weeks before the medics realized that no one recovered. First were the petechiae, or what appeared to be mosquito bites. These came and went with pains in head and limbs, followed by chills and fever.

At first, the soldiers were loath to report to the dispensary, especially when they found urination painful, for many feared it was the result of a night spent with an infected whore. After all, a man had to take what was at hand, and the black women of Cap François were agreeable. In a few days, the men recovered and they laughed at their stupid fears, seeking out the taverns again and rebuilding their bravado with rum and women.

Then, without warning, the fever returned and with it the headache, parched throat, and nausea. The eyes grew bloodshot and the men grumbled, "The damn rum! I'd better cut down."

But there was no next time. Quickly the fever moved on to ravage the body. When the skin turned yellow, and the victim lost control of his bowels and bladder, he became frantic for a physician. Too weak to walk, he was carried to the hospital where he was placed in a row of cots, now one of many frightened yellow-skinned boys.

The beds were not occupied long by the same patient. Progress toward death went fast. The fever and the hemorrhaging and the abdominal pains converged at once upon the victim. He vomited black blood and the pain of the effort was so excruciating that he called to God for merciful death, and even as he called, his tongue turned brown and speech was thick from his great thirst. The last stage was swift, twelve hours, but to the sufferer each second was eternity. Then came the relief of stupor and finally death.

Nor did death close the book on man's call to his brothers for attention. The stench from the deceased's body immediately filled the hospital ward, sickening even the black orderlies whose vomit spewed over the earthen floor and mixed with the vomit of the patients who were not yet so fortunate as to have passed on. At first, a corpse was allowed the dignity of its own grave. Soon, however, the deaths were so numerous, hundreds each day, and one day over a thousand, that huge pits were dug and the bodies were tossed in like weeds on the compost pile. They were heavily covered with carbolic acid and lime, to hasten their decomposition. Finally the earth was shoveled over all, covering forever the remains of men's lives.

At night, a vapor rose up from the spot and it looked to the soldiers like the buried dead had come out of their graves and bunched together in a macabre death dance, wavering upward in rhythm to those persistent faraway drums. Beating, beating interminably, like doom approaching.

The men of the army were forbidden the town, but it was a senseless order. Who wanted to wander away from the comfort of being with his countrymen! And yet, as each soldier waited for the plague to strike, he

111

gradually withdrew from his fellow men. Who knew which of his companions might be the one to pass the curse on? Soon the soldiers took to regarding each other with suspicion, as if an unexposed enemy lay in their midst.

The officers had difficulty commanding obedience from the men, for those who had not died from the yellow fever seemed to already be dead from fear. To get the work done, it was necessary to pay the natives to bury the dead and to act as orderlies in the hospitals. There were always plenty of natives willing to work, and they gathered each morning around the administration office, waiting to be hired. It was not that the blacks were industrious or anxious to be of help to the stricken army. They came into the hospitals with an air of pleasure over seeing the anguish of the white invaders and buried the dead as casually as a dog covers its bone. The black man was immune to yellow fever.

"They are counting us off until we're all gone," one of the soldiers remarked.

"At this rate, they won't have much longer to count," someone answered.

To add to General Leclerc's troubles, there were uprisings in the mountains. He sent out company after company of soldiers to hunt down the guerrillas, but his men, dispirited by the plague and handicapped by officers who knew nothing about tracking the enemy in the jungle, fell into ambush and were wiped out.

In Cap François, the natives sneaked into the barracks at night and knifed the soldiers as they slept. Guards were simply no match for the jungle stealth of the black. Soon hospitals were filled to overflowing and many men died for lack of medical attention. Doctors died too and soon only the privates who had been drafted to assist the physicians were left to minister to the sick.

General Leclerc became frantic. Through infection, warfare, and disease, he had lost over twenty-five thousand men since his arrival on the island. The strain was telling on him. He looked as cadaverous as the yellow fever victims.

"You must take care of yourself, General," Etienne Grenier cautioned one day when he was assisting his superior in plans, not of colonization, but of survival. "If you should become ill, the men would lose heart."

"Rubbish," Leclerc tossed aside the suggestion. "They always have Rochambeau, Duponceau, and if I might say so, a very good officer in you, Grenier."

Etienne did not answer. How could one give advice to an old warhorse like the general.

And then all at once, there was no Duponceau.

Philippe had been away from the administration office for two days, and when he returned it was only with the greatest effort that he could give his attention to the duties at hand. Gone was his jaunty spirit, submerged under an air of *laissez-faire*.

Etienne, noticing Duponceau's sickly appearance, suggested, "Go to the dispensary. Perhaps the alchemist can mix you a potion and if you go to bed the rest of the day, you will feel better."

Philippe did not answer, only shook his head and went on with the reading of the report on the desk before him. Rochambeau, who had been standing by the window with some papers in his hand, turned and, after fastening those impenetrable eyes of his upon the younger officer, remarked, "If you're getting the damn fever, get down to the pesthouse with the other victims. Don't vomit your black insides around here."

A sudden air of tension hit the office. Grenier, without looking in his direction, could see General Leclerc's back stiffen in anger. On many occasions, Rochambeau had made the general angry, but this time Etienne thought he had reached the limit of his patience. The chief of staff spoke to Philippe in a voice of studied control, "General Duponceau, if you wish, you may be excused from your duties for the rest of the day."

Philippe shook his head. "Thank you, sir. If I feel the need, I shall do so." He took a fresh sheet of paper and began to write.

Rochambeau tossed his head arrogantly and, reaching for his pipe, told the room in general, "I'm only thinking of the success of our venture here in St. Domingue. Who would take charge of the men if something should happen to us officers?"

"The women!" Leclerc snapped.

A scraping sound came from Duponceau's desk as he pushed back his chair. He picked up the sheet of paper on which he was writing and walked quickly from the room.

"Touchy fellow," Rochambeau commented as Philippe closed the office door.

Again that stiffening of the chief's back, but Leclerc said nothing, seemingly engrossed in the report on the desk before him. From the corner of his eye, however, Etienne noticed that he never turned the page, merely sat there, tense and quiet. He himself could not concentrate on the statistics of the losses the army had suffered and the circumstances surrounding those losses which he was compiling for forwarding to Napoleon on the next boat to leave Cap François. The only sound was that made by Rochambeau when he knocked the bowl of his pipe against the spittoon on the floor by his chair.

Suddenly, the silence was broken.

"Rochambeau!" It was the voice of Leclerc cracking out like a blast of thunder on a too still afternoon. The vehemence of his tone startled Etienne. He had never known his commanding officer to speak so angrily to anyone.

Rochambeau must have been surprised too. For a moment his face lost its arrogance, and he looked bewildered, but only for that one fleeting moment. Immediately, his chin shot up, his lip curled, and his eyes narrowed. Rochambeau was ready for combat.

"Were you speaking to me, sir?" he asked coldly.

"You are the only Rochambeau in the room, aren't you?" His voice seethed with anger. Rochambeau deigned to rise from his chair and walked, still cockily, to the desk of his superior.

"You wish to speak to me about something?" he asked disdainfully.

Anger rose up inside Etienne's breast as he watched the scene. Leclerc was a military leader of renown. His honor and age, if nothing else, demanded respect. Someday he hoped to have the satisfaction of bashing in Rochambeau's insolent face.

"No, I don't wish to, but I have to," Leclerc whipped out. "Last night we lost over three hundred men. Killed in ambush. I want those guerrillas stopped, cleaned out. Since the men can't seem to defend themselves, I want you to show them how. You're tough, aren't you?" Etienne thought he detected a sneer on his general's lips. "*You* show them how. Take a whole battalion up into the hills and finish them off. Is that clear? And another thing," he hissed, "find out how the guerrillas got those guns."

"I'll tell you how." Rochambeau's voice now matched Leclerc's in its anger. "You took those two damn niggers, Christophe and Dessalines, and made them officers, *that's* how. They relieved all the natives of any armament in their possession, as ordered, and supposedly hid it in some remote mountain hideaway. But where? Nobody *knows* where—nobody, that is, except those two same commendable officers." Rochambeau answered, paused and then added, "sir," as one might toss a sou at the feet of a vermin-infested beggar.

Leclerc rose to his feet. In anger he shouted, "Why have you not seen *before* this that those guns were brought into the armory? Already it has cost the lives of hundreds of our men."

"I have ordered and ordered your chosen black leaders to get the hell out into the woods and bring those muskets in, but each time they say they are trying to round up enough carts to haul them in. Now they tell me there *are* enough carts, but they're all tied up with carrying our dead soldiers to the grave. If I had my way, I'd bury those two traitors *with* the fever corpses, ALIVE!"

Leclerc stared at his second-in-command for a long time and when he spoke, it was in a voice of deathlike quiet: "Take a battalion and get those guns. At once."

Rochambeau must have recognized that he had pushed his general too far, for his voice was respectful when he asked, "And where, sir, shall I store them? The armory has been taken over by the medical staff."

"Build another one." The same ominous tone.

"Yes, sir." Rochambeau turned and as he walked from the room, Etienne saw a look of hatred on his face. He felt sorry for the men of the battalion he would lead that day.

When the door had closed, General Leclerc dropped into his chair. He picked up a sheaf of papers from his desk, and his hands were trembling. His face was whiter than his beard and sweat poured down his forehead.

Captain Grenier hurried to his side. "Can I help, sir?" Perhaps some coffee or brandy?"

The general nodded. With great effort he whispered, "Brandy."

Etienne procured it from the cupboard and, pouring a glass, handed it to Leclerc. The man was shaking too much to take it and Grenier held it to his mouth while he drank. He looked cold, for his lips had faded to the same whiteness as his face. Finally, Etienne saw some color returning to his cheeks. He tilted the glass to give him another sip, and the general reached up and placed his cold hands over Etienne's.

"Thank you, Captain. I am much better now." Leclerc spoke very quietly as he set the glass down upon his desk. Then he turned and faced the window, a sign to the captain that no further assistance was needed.

For the remainder of the afternoon Etienne busied himself with his overdue report to Napoleon. When he was just finishing the last page, a knock came on the office door.

"Come in," Leclerc ordered curtly. He, too, had been preparing important business.

The door opened slowly, and a frightened-looking private entered. He looked warily at the general and then sidled up to Etienne's desk, saying as he did so, "I have a message for you, Captain Grenier." The man must have been running, for he panted as he spoke. He looked over at Leclerc as if he were unsure of the proper protocol in the presence of so great an officer. Then he continued, "It is an emergency, General Duponceau. He's asking for you."

Etienne's heart almost stopped beating. A foreboding hand had touched it. "Where is he?"

"He's in the hospital, sir. They brought him in a while ago, and he keeps calling for you. He has the fever."

The captain rose from his chair. A chill crept through his body. "I'll come at once. Which hospital is he in?"

"The one that used to be the armory, beside the swamp near the dock."

"You'll do no such thing!" It was General Leclerc speaking, and his voice was brusque and definite.

To the bewildered messenger he shouted, "Get out of here!" The fellow, frightened, ran from the room, forgetting to close the door.

"Shut the door!" Leclerc screamed after him, but he never returned. The general strode over and slammed the door. Then he whirled around to Etienne.

"You damn fool! You go into that hospital, you'll die of the plague!"

"Is that so bad?" Etienne was cold with anger, the kind of anger that sharpens the mind and readies one for battle. He faced the general in defiance.

117

"You are an officer," Leclerc continued. "You are of value and not dispensable. The men, yes. There are always plenty of privates, but a commissioned officer cannot be sacrificed so casually."

"And what sets me apart from those other poor devils? The worms don't know the difference between a captain's uniform or a private's, in the grave. They digest one as easily as the other."

Leclerc turned gray. The combativeness went out of him and he fumbled his way to his desk and let himself wearily down on the chair. "You are young and idealistic," he spoke with sadness. "You see your fellow men die and you want to help. Why endanger yourself? Of what use is a martyred saint? Have you forgotten the years of training the army has favored you with, your years of study at St. Cyr to mould you into something of value to your country. You are better than the peasant who knows only how to carry a gun. All men are *not* of equal importance."

"That is only because man makes it that way. Am I better than other men because I am an officer and can point out to them the road they must travel to die, and, in this land, to die like dogs. Am I so far above them that I should turn my head away from a friend who calls to me in death? Should I tremble and hide lest death touch me too? You yourself said that man cannot excuse his cowardice by whimpering he had to follow orders. Leaders are not always right about their orders.. Those are your own words, General!"

Etienne picked up his hat and without looking back at Leclerc walked from the room, quietly closing the door behind him.

Outside the administration office, he found Leclerc's landau hitched to the trunk of a mimbon tree. The driver lay stretched out in its shade, snoring away, seemingly unconcerned with the hazards of conquest.

"Some fellows go through life like children without a care," Etienne thought to himself as he untied the reins, "so I shouldn't upset him if I borrow the general's transporation."

With a feeling of urgency, the captain jumped onto the landau and was soon racing out toward the swamp at the edge of Cap François. As he rode he thought of Philippe, the gay dark-haired laughing Philippe, whose zest for life and beauty caused a spring of mirth to bubble up inside the darkest heart. And now the spring was dry and in its place was a stone, weighty and sharp. Even as he called to the horse to hurry, Etienne was depressed. The depression crept into his joints, causing them to ache, and he felt weak and tired. Even the reins in his hand were heavy and his neck wanted to lay down his head. He drew in a deep breath in an effort to throw back his shoulders, but it was a futile gesture. Instead, he wanted to slouch down on the seat and close his eyes and rest. Why could he not be like that irresponsible soldier back there in the dirt beneath the mimbon tree, sleeping until the dangers had passed.

He tried to concentrate on getting more speed from the horse and it did help some. If only he arrived at the hospital before Philippe died. Died? What made him so pessimistic? Being in the hospital did not portend death. Didn't soldiers go to the hospital to recover? Don't fool yourself, Etienne. Don't fool yourself. Nobody recovers from this dread disease.

He whipped the horse furiously.

When Captain Grenier drew up before the armory, he sat in exhaustion for a moment before alighting from the landau. As he waited, he became conscious of a stench in the air and his stomach began to rise in objection. Now his head was spinning. It must be from the sun. The white building kept sliding around, at the same time hurling a fiendish glare into his eyes, and he shut them. Even so, that damn armory kept going around like a carousel. The only way he could make it stop was to go inside the building. With a great effort at maintaining his balance, so that he walked with the studied movement of a drunk, Etienne stepped from the landau and walked into the makeshift hospital.

At first, it was dark after the brilliant sunlight and he could not see; then the coolness of the interior refreshed him and he felt steadier. But the stench inside was stronger and he involuntarily put his hand to his nose.

"Take a few deep whiffs and get it over with," a voice said, "after that you get used to it. Can't fight it."

Etienne's eyes were getting accustomed to the darkness, and he saw a soldier standing behind a desk, his arm raised in salute.

Having recognized him, Grenier asked, "What the devil is that odor?"

The man behind the desk shrugged. "It always stinks like hell around a hospital. Pardon the language, Captain, but that's the way it is in one of these butcher shops. When the surgeon chops off a leg or an arm, it's got to pus for a long time, until the patient dies, or heals up. The same with machete cuts or powder wounds. Hospitals are all like this," he finished matter-of-factly.

Philippe Duponceau in all this. The shining, scrubbed, polished Philippe. The fastidious officer. Again that feeling of urgency.

"I received word that General Duponceau is here. Where can I find him?" The weakness had left Etienne, and he felt strong enough to carry his fellow officer out in his arms if necessary.

"General Duponceau is in the plague ward. Too bad. Always liked the fellow. No laugh in him now anymore," the guard answered with no more feeling than if he were on duty outside a pigsty.

"And where is the plague ward?"

The man jerked a thumb toward a closed door. "Through here. This is where all the shot-up and cut-up cases are. It's a little crowded but keep on walking on down to the end of the room and go through the door down there. That's where the pesthouse is. Be

120

sure to shut the door after you go in, because the men get mad as hell if anyone leaves it open. They might not have all their parts, but what they have they want to keep the plague from getting."

He opened the door for the captain. "Give my regards to the general," he said. "Tell him I'm real sorry he caught the fever."

Grenier looked at the soldier's face. The eyes looked at him with compassion. "You'll see, sir. It's real rough."

Captain Grenier stepped into the ward and then stood still. As he looked about he had the feeling that he had walked into a huge hamper of death. A receptacle where Death had gathered together all the last, agonizing remnants of a pitiful humanity and was pressing out each writhing life in its bony claw.

At first, Etienne could only make out a confusion of bodies. The walls of the armory were high with small windowlike openings near the ceiling which permitted little light to enter and, from the heat and stench, obviously little air. The floor was littered with sick men sprawled on straw, like animals in a stable, who either lay churning in agony or quiet in coma. Down the middle of the room and along the walls was a higher elevation of bodies crowded onto cots. He shook his head in disbelief. Two or three patients occupied each cot, arms, feet, face entwined until surely an occupant could not discern his parts from those of his bedfellows'. Some lay naked while others clutched at filthy-looking rags which kept slipping from the shivering bodies they were supposed to warm.

Etienne felt a tug at his pants. He looked down on a young boy lying on the floor, his army boots still on his feet. His one arm was wrapped up to the elbow in a dirty bloodstained bandage, which had once been part of his shirt. The upper part of the arm was swollen as big as a melon.

"Don't let them cut off my arm. Please don't let them cut off my arm," he sobbed. "I'd rather die."

121

His eyes were crazed with fever as they pleaded with Etienne, but they suddenly filled with stark terror and the boy turned his head apprehensively to gaze off at something nearby. His shoulders came up in fright and he screamed, "No, no! God, no!" He put his good hand across his mouth in an effort to be brave. It was a pathetically skinny hand.

Etienne turned to see what the boy was looking at. Nausea engulfed him and he wanted to vomit. His stomach was empty and only fluid came up in the back of his throat.

Two men lay on a small straw-covered cot. One wore only his underdrawers. He was curled in a ball with his feet drawn up until his knees were under his chin, and his bare arms were clasped about his legs. So badly did he shiver with the chills that the entire bed hopped. "I'm so cold. I'm so cold," he kept saying as he tried to nuzzle his back up against his bed partner in an attempt to gain comfort from the other's body heat. "Won't somebody get me a feather tick, a blanket? Even a rag," he ended in a wail.

The man beside him lay with his eyes shut, his face tense with suffering. His one leg had been amputated above the ankle and the open stump extended over the bottom of the cot so as to allow the pus from the infection to drain down into a pail on the floor. The container was filled with the yellow matter and had begun to spill onto the floor and flow into the bedding of the patients lying nearby. A black swarm of flies was hovering over the stump, buzzing out invitations for others to join. Only the most forward settled on the open infection since the leg was in constant motion from the man with the chills who uncontrollably shook the whole bed.

Etienne took off his coat, and walking over to the pair on the cot, covered the shaking man. The amputee beside him opened his eyes, and taking in what Etienne had done, he said with great effort, "*Merci.* Now I hope to God he stops shaking the bed."

Etienne started down the long room. Compassion, nausea, and anger churned in his breast, leaving the rest of him weak. History recorded only the wealth of a colony, not the price of its acquisition. Who back home, when he boasted of victory, ever spoke of this rabble in the infirmary?

By the time Etienne came to a single cot on which a black native was sprawled out in rapturous slumber, he was seething. There was a demijohn on the floor beside him and the odor of rum and sweat from the inebriated orderly mingled with the smells from the other human discharges. On the floor beside him lay a young boy, red with fever. His parched lips had split, and the blood attracted flies, which clung to his mouth in a black circle.

"Water. Water," the boy begged. "Won't somebody give me some water?"

Etienne reached down and, grabbing the sleeping orderly by his kinky hair, dragged him to his feet. The man opened his eyes in bewilderment. "Is something the matter?" he asked, looking up at the captain. "Did I done something wrong?"

Etienne, with his hand still clutching the native's hair, twisted his head toward where the boy lay moaning on the floor.

"How can you sleep with this boy beside you crying out for your help?"

"Oh, I can sleep easy," the man answered, his amazement now leaving his face. "That noise don't bother me none, General. Some of the other patients can yell louder than him, but I'm used to it and I never hear it when I take my little naps."

The captain released his grip on the orderly's hair. He raised his foot and kicked him in the stomach, sending him smashing back onto the cot. Then, grabbing him by the belt of his pants, he brought him up to his feet and yelled into his face, "Get this lad some water and everybody else around here who needs some. We may not have bandages, but water we have plenty of."

"Yes, General. Yes, sir. Right away!" the native started to walk toward a water keg in the corner of the room, but he stopped when Etienne barked after him, "Come back here first."

"Yes, General. You bet, General."

Etienne removed his white shirt and tossed it at the orderly. "Use this for bandage. When I come back, I don't want to see any of the men with flies on open cuts. You understand?"

"Oh, yes, sir." The man was regarding the shirt with a speculative eye.

"Oh, no you don't." The captain pulled the shirt from the drunk's hand. "Don't get any ideas about that." He began to tear the garment into small pieces which he dropped upon the empty bed by which he stood. "There are your bandages, ready for use."

"But I didn't say nothing. I was just going to get the water like you told me to, and then come back and do all the—"

"Shut up! You planned to keep the shirt for yourself as soon as I was gone. Now get going, and if I ever catch you sleeping on the job again, I'll kick your black ass all the way from here to the swamps."

The man's eyes grew big with fright. He turned and ran toward the water keg. Etienne stooped down, and carefully picking up the feverish boy from the floor, placed him on the cot vacated by the drunken orderly. "Here's your water, soldier," he said. The orderly had returned and was dipping a gourd into the bucket he carried. Etienne glared at him and said nothing.

"You see, General. When you come back I have everything in good shape here. I do just like you tell me."

Etienne walked toward the door. He had almost forgotten why he was here. Philippe. Again that feeling of haste. He opened the door and stepped into the next room.

At first Etienne could not see what was before him,

for so powerful was the new stench that greeted him, he involuntarily closed his eyes as though by doing so he could shut himself off from it. His stomach rose up to vomit out in protest and he opened his eyes to see where he might relieve it. But again there was no food to emit. Only a thick fluid came up into his throat and out through his nose with a burning sensation.

Etienne stared about. It was a bare room, lacking in any furniture, but when he looked down, the agony of what he saw tore at his heart. A tightly woven carpet of bodies covered the floor. Bodies of soldiers, either nude or in various stages of undress, lay there so thickly entangled that Etienne could not discern whether they rested upon straw, the earthen floor, or one another. Some stirred faintly. Others lay still, either in stupor or death. As Etienne stood there in horror, not knowing which way to cross the room, as there was no path among the patients, he heard only a few moans and the buzzing of the flies swarming over the prone men like little black clouds.

"This is the plague house, and it ain't healthy for a white man to come tromping through," a voice said.

Over against the wall was a tall husky Negro, bare to the waist, his shoulders glistening with sweat. He shook his head in disapproval and, waving his arm to indicate the soldiers lying on the floor, he asked, "Do you want to look like these boys?"

The officer gazed back at the victims. What kind of a disease was this which caused man to rot while he still lived? The bodies were emaciated, the life-producing fluids draining away through all of nature's outlets, leaving only these rotting remains. Some were yellow in color. These still moved. One of the men half rose on his elbow and began to retch out a black-looking blood that spilled upon the stomach of the boy beside him. The boy never moved. He was a ghastly gray in color. The whole room smelled like a graveyard whose tombs had been opened, and this stench was only heightened by its mixture with the odor of excrement from the uncared-for patients in the room.

Etienne turned toward the Negro and asked angrily, "Why haven't these men been kept clean?"

"My helper and me, we do the best we can. As soon as we pick out the dead ones each day and throw them on the wagon to be hauled to the burial, we wash up the floor. But we got to get rid of the dead ones first or we can't see the floor. 'Tis a bad evil which hit the white man." He shook his head over the enormity of it all. "They die faster than we can dig the hole to put them in."

As he spoke he stooped down, and picking up a bare body from the floor, he flung it over his shoulder. Then he groped through an assortment of patients at his feet, pulled one out by the arm, and tossed it over his other shoulder. With his great strength he handled the dead like so many sacks of coffee lying on the dock, waiting to be hauled away.

"I'm looking for General Duponceau. Where is he?"

"I don't know." His answer came so fast that Etienne was certain it was his habitual reply to every white man's question.

"I want to know where General Duponceau is lying," Etienne snapped authoritatively.

"Oh, you mean he's in *here*." The Negro was truly uncertain now, playing for time.

"Yes, he's here, and don't pretend you don't know where," Etienne shouted. "You probably had your eye on his medals as soon as he came in, planning to steal them when he shut his eyes. Now, where is he?"

"Oh, oh, *that* one." The Negro's voice faltered and his eyes roamed about the room. He raised his big hand and pointed to a far corner. "I think he's the one up against the wall." The disposer of the dead hurried from the door, ending the inquisition.

Carefully, Etienne stepped across the prostrate bodies and made his way toward his friend. He hoped to God he was still alive.

Chapter Ten

Like the others, Philippe was lying on the earth floor, his face turned to the wall. So still was he that Etienne would have thought him dead were it not for his yellow color. Etienne knelt beside the general and, slipping his arm under Philippe's shoulders, raised his head and pillowed it on his lap. The sick man opened his bloodshot eyes and gazed up at Etienne. A flicker of recognition appeared and Philippe tried to speak, but his tongue was too thick to form words.

Etienne looked about for the water bucket. He spied it a distance to his right in the midst of some fever patients. One man had his arm around the pail in a possessive gesture. Gently, the captain laid Philippe back upon the floor and, then stepping gingerly over the sick men about him, he carefully picked up the bucket. The man whose arm had encircled it opened his eyes. They were bloodshot and full of agony. He tried to speak, but either he was too weak or his lips too parched, for his mouth did not open.

Etienne stooped down, and holding the man's head with one hand, he dipped the ladle into the bucket with the other and then held it to his mouth. Scarcely had it wet the lips when the feverish patient recoiled as in nausea and turned his face away.

The captain carried the water pail over to Philippe, and when he put the ladle to his mouth, Etienne noticed that the tongue was brown and dry, like baked clay lining the bottom of a dried-up stream. The general drank thirstily and when he had finished, he looked gratefully up at Etienne and said, *"Merci."*

He spoke with difficulty, as if he had to force his heavy tongue to move, but he spoke. Etienne had not come too late.

"I thought the fever couldn't catch up with a general," Philippe said feebly, and the light of a smile tried to break through the misery in his reddened eyes. The bravado of the man had not been completely beaten down.

"Especially a general whom no girl could catch up with," Etienne teased, but his heart was heavy, and he could have wept at how a disease could raze the magnificent structure of a human body, and yet permit it to breathe amidst the destruction.

With great effort, Philippe spoke again: "A girl. That's what I want to talk about."

"The same Philippe. No use wasting my sympathy on you, old boy. Instead of thinking about making a good confession, you have your mind on girls. If we were allowed off the base, you'd be wanting me to set up a date for tonight." The captain's jaunty words belied his grief.

"Thanks for trying, but I hope, by tonight, to have a date with an angel."

"I wonder if the Lord lets you pick. If He does, will it be a blonde or redhead?"

"A blonde." When Philippe closed his eyes in weariness, his mouth lost its tenseness as though its owner might have forgotten his pains in the remembrance of happier times. "A blonde," he said again. "She was blond."

"Who, Philippe?" Etienne felt he was intruding upon a dream, but he feared Philippe might slip away forever, and he was loath to let him go.

"Claudine, the girl I love," the man answered quietly. He was more relaxed now and seemed at peace. For a wild moment, Etienne dared hope the fever might be leaving, but he knew it was only that—a wild foolish moment.

In an effort to prolong his friend's mood, Etienne asked, "Is she very beautiful?"

"Like an angel. In face and in heart." He took a deep breath and opening his eyes he looked up at Etienne. The vision had vanished and the pain was back in his face. "I must hurry to tell you. I haven't much time."

Feebly he reached inside his crumpled jacket, and withdrew a letter. His hand shook and the letter slipped from his fingers and lay on his stomach. His voice was scarcely audible as he said, "She loved God more than me. She entered the convent. Each year on my birthday she sends me a bouquet, a spiritual bouquet. A novena she's made to St. Martha. A novena to take care of me and give me what I need most. Poor St. Martha. How could she grant that request? What I needed most was Claudine." He could no longer move his dried-clay tongue, and the voice stopped. Etienne held a ladle of water to Philippe's lips and he drank only a few drops before his face contorted in nausea and pain.

His breath began to come quickly, hurrying in a final burst before it quit his body. Philippe spoke again, all the while gasping for every word. "This year Claudine will not know where to send my gift. I will be gone."

His hand caressed the envelope upon his stomach. Etienne had to lean over to hear, he spoke so quietly now. "I have written her my last letter and am sending my last gift, my Croix de Guerre. I want you to make sure she gets them."

Etienne laid his hand over that of the sick man. "She will get them. I promise you. She will get them."

The hand under his relaxed. The captain looked at Philippe's face. His eyes were closed but his mouth was open to suck in one more breath. If it entered, what did it matter? Philippe was dead.

Etienne sat as he was, with his friend's body cradled

in his arms. So this was death. Death, which takes away life, not only from the dead, but from the living left behind. The captain felt a great weight descend upon him and set upon his heart.

He put his arms about Philippe and held him in a farewell embrace. As he knelt upon the floor in his own private wake, his eyes strayed to the envelope. In an effort to relieve the tightness in his throat, he read the address aloud, "Soeur Denise, Hospice Sacre-Coeur, Chalon-sur-Marne." He pressed Philippe to his breast. Somehow he had the feeling that if he held him so for a while, Soeur Denise, Claudine, might feel Philippe's soul brush by on its way to eternity.

Slowly something began to penetrate his consciousness. It had been there for a while, but Etienne had not been aware of it until it overwhelmed him. The stench. It reached his nose, burning it with its fumes. It was the vapor of death, rising from the body of his friend like the exhumation of a thousand graves at once.

Etienne looked at the man he held. His face and hands were already gray. The plague was an evil from Hell. Not content with taking the soul of the man, it lingered to desiccate his body. It left nothing behind to weep over. Philippe was gone, soul, and now body.

Etienne laid him on the floor, and picking up the envelope for Claudine, he stuffed it into his pocket. Before he stood up, Etienne brushed the general's hair back from his forehead with his hand. All that now remained which resembled Philippe was his widow's peak.

The malodorous fumes from the pesthouse so enveloped Etienne as he made his way to the door that he staggered like a drunken seaman. Breathing was painful and each time he gasped for air he feared his convulsive stomach would eject itself through his throat. His heart pummeled his chest in a wild effort to be freed from its imprisoning cavity, and his eyes retreated behind a blur. His body was no longer his to command. Each part had become a separate rebel with a mind of its own, fighting for its right to be released into the fresh air.

He heard moaning as he went by. Perhaps in his blind stumbling he had trampled some of the dying upon the floor, but he could not help himself. If he did not soon get some pure air, he too would fall among them, there to be lost forever.

Etienne fell as he reached the doorway. He would have lain there had not strong arms picked him up and seated him on a bench with his back against the wall.

It was a big black orderly from the pesthouse. He was shaking his head while his eyes examined Etienne. "You're a goner, too, General. Just ain't gonna be no white folks left on this land."

With a foreboding fear, Etienne slowly looked down at his arms and then at his chest and stomach. They were there. The purplish eruptions. It was death's own coat-of-arms welcoming him into its family. For Etienne, the hope of life vanished. At that moment, a cannon roared in the distance. But there was no quickening inside the captain's breast, no exhilarating response as he used to feel when a battle was on. This cannon was not shooting at a mortal enemy. It was attacking an invisible one which surrounded the army. One of the sergeants had claimed that the noise and smoke would sweep the disease from the air just as it had helped in the plague in Marseille in the last century. The sergeant was wrong. Nothing could help. The big black was right. They would all be wiped out, every last Frenchman.

Etienne looked down at his hands. Were they already yellow or was it only the sun which made them look that color?

"You want I should help you inside where you can lay down?" the big orderly asked.

Etienne cringed at the thought and did not answer. He only shook his head.

"Just like you want it, General. You might as well sit out here a spell. It's pretty crowded in there. Later, if you can't make it inside, I'll drag you in. Don't worry. I'll find you a good spot too."

Etienne tried to answer, but his throat was parched, and his tongue cleaved to the roof of his mouth. All he could do was sit, the weight of his body too much to move. He was abandoned. Doomed. Other soldiers would march on, plant the French flag in other countries, wear well-pressed uniforms, and be cheered. They would make love to new mistresses in silk dresses in cool villas. Were people really still dancing the minuet back in his homeland? Were parties still being held and Frenchmen laughing and drinking wine and helping themselves to pastries and stuffed hare? Didn't anyone wonder about the soldiers in St. Domingue who were rotting into extinction?

Suddenly a determination born of his revulsion rose up inside him. He would not pass to his death through the hell in that pesthouse. Hell was *after* death. Even the wild animals of the forest had the privilege of lying down on the cool earth and dying in the clean air. The Lord had created him above the animals. Then why should he die with less dignity?

Etienne stood up, but he almost fell back upon the bench with the pain which suddenly seemed to bludgeon his head. He leaned against the wall of the armory until he could keep his balance, his eyes squeezed shut in a vain effort to ward off the agony. When his body had measured the pain and accepted it as its own, Etienne opened his eyes. The world was but black silhouettes. His vision cleared, and he saw the swamps with the ocean beyond. Moving slowly, so as not to upset the pain from its balance inside his head, Etienne began to walk. The sun. The sun had never been so hot. Had it moved down from its place in the sky to swallow him in its fiery maw? He burned, but when he looked down upon his skin, he was not in flames. It must be those purplish pimples that fired his body so. The pain grew. It spread from his head, down his back, and weighted his arms so that they hung limply at his sides. His groins felt pierced by daggers, severing control of his legs, and he fell to the ground.

Slowly he managed to push himself to his knees. He looked up at the sun. It was still in the sky. His mind cleared, and he knew the fire was being enkindled in his own body. The fever. The damned fever! If he could get to the water, he would throw his body into the sea, and it could do with it what it would.

Slowly he crawled on hands and knees. He trusted it was in the direction of the swamps, for it was too painful to even lift his head to see where he was headed. Some unknown saint must have guided his efforts out of pity, for Etienne found himself at the edge of the swamp. The tide was up and there was water. Blessed water. With a final effort, he dragged himself forward and lay his cheek in the cool wetness.

"Merciful God, *merci,*" he prayed.

There he lay, content for the moment that relief had come to one part of him. Soon, however, his whole body clamored for the refreshing coolness. He was heavy, and his arms had no strength to move his weight. He rolled himself over until his body dropped into the murky water of the swamp. There he lay on his back with only his face above the water, his arms outstretched to embrace the refreshing wetness. He did not know nor care if the mud beneath him might part and absorb him into its depths. His fevered body was cooled and the swamp grass, stirred by the breezes, fanned his upturned face. He dozed.

He dreamed he was drowning, that water was stinging his nose and he could not breathe. Suddenly he awakened, and found it was no dream. The tide was rising! He forced himself up and struggled out upon higher ground, lying down amidst the dry palmetto. Immediately, the sun burned down upon him, stirring up the fever and the pain again. Would it not be better to throw himself back into the swamp and let its waters engulf him forever in their coolness? He half rose on an elbow and gazed at this possible escape from torture. He shook his head. He was no coward. He would die like the others. Still a soldier.

With great effort, he rose to his feet and looked about. His vision was blurred and he shook his head to clear it. He saw a path and his feet fumbled their way to it. He was very unsteady, but pleased that he was still upright.

As he trudged along, the sun baked him with its hot flames, encouraging the fever within. The earth kept rising, and it was only by firmly planting one foot in front of the other that he was able to hold it at a distance. Once it did get past his defense, coming up quickly to hammer his head. He lay there on the path, wondering if it was worth getting up again.

Then all at once he was no longer hot. Etienne rolled over to look at the sun. It was gone. A black cloud had blotted it from the sky. The wind started to sweep viciously across the earth and the sky, dark and frowning, complained in loud roars of thunder.

Etienne watched, fascinated. It was like the start of a battle. Heaven was gathering its forces to attack the earth. The flashes of lightning, the noise of the thunder, they were the cannons of the sky, the heavy ammunition. Black clouds of reinforcements hurtled in and sent a fusillade of rain down upon the enemy earth. Etienne felt its force upon his face and chest, like wet buckshot, but it was cold and welcome, driving the fever from his body. He laughed out loud. And Napoleon thought he was the mastermind of the battlefield!

Etienne shut his eyes and sighed. He was tired. The beating of the rain upon his body had chilled him. He sat up. He must find shelter. His hands and arms were shaking so much that they were of little use in pushing him to his feet, and several times he fell on his face in the mud before he finally stood up. He looked about. Which way to go? Some distance ahead were woods, looking black in the darkening day. He headed for them.

The woods were thick, but even so, the wind blew

with such force that it parted the branches of the tall trees so that the sky could spit its cold rain down upon Etienne. His chest tightened, and breathing was difficult. His groins ached, and yet he doggedly forced himself to move onward.

Long after sensitivity had departed from his body and the power to think had gone from his mind, Etienne walked. He was a mechanical man, without will or intent, moving only until the key should unwind. Was he dying? Was this the way the spirit separated itself from the body? No oblivion? Only this slow transition?

And then he came to a clearing. The wind had settled down and the rain became a steady pelting of the earth. He paused to look about in the gathering gloom. Before him was a native hut, but larger than the usual type. As his eye took in its measure, he was startled to see three skulls above the roof. It was then that he noticed the stench of the place, the same smell he had been running away from, the odor of rotting flesh. Was this what death was? Was this where one suffered until purged of his sins and readied for Heaven? Was Purgatory made not of fire, but of rain and chilling cold? Was it a place where you inhaled the stink of your own decaying body until the Lord sent for you?

He looked about. Bones of all sizes littered the ground. Littered? No, they seemed to be in a circle formation about the hut. Perhaps this was where man left his body forever, and his spirit stepped into Heaven through the doorway of the grass hut. He moved toward the entrance. The wind blew across his face, depositing odorous feathers on his wet nose and lips as it went by. He wiped them off with his hand, but the rotten taste had gotten into his mouth and he gagged.

His legs were no longer his to control. He lurched toward the door of the hut. It gave way, and he stumbled through, falling on the floor within. He was conscious of sudden warmth and he gave a deep sigh of relief. Painfully, he raised himself on an elbow and looked about. The tiny room was bathed in a reddish glow. The light source seemed to be a large candle set upon what looked like an altar. As Etienne watched the candle, a tall figure slowly took shape. It was a man. He grew taller and taller like no man Etienne had ever seen. He had two noses and wore a high turban.

Oh, God! There was a devil after all! He, Etienne Grenier, had merited Hell!

Despair clutched his breast, as the floor of Hell rose up and hit him in the face.

Chapter Eleven

The quiet fall of rain on a thatched roof called to Etienne from far off. Its steady rhythm was a lullaby, and he dozed off again, warm and snug. Later, someone held his head and he drank a sweet liquid, but his eyes were too heavy with sleep to look up to see who it was. The rain still fell. Again he slept.

For some while now, something had been calling to him through his unconsciousness. It gnawed and tugged, beckoning to him through the snugness of oblivion. Even before he opened his eyes, he wondered what was disturbing him. He lay still, his body in lassitude, but his mind trying to stir. What was it that called to him? He listened. The rain had stopped. Now he knew. It was the quiet that disturbed him. He opened his eyes.

There was a rustling. Was it a voice or just a breeze in some nearby tree? He tried to think, but no thought came. There was that sound again. It said, "Good morning, Monsieur."

Etienne turned his head. A Negress sat beside him, a Negress with a long pink scar on an embittered face. She appeared to be snarling at him. Had he displeased her? He looked up at her eyes. They were warm with sympathy. He shut his eyes and shook his head. Funny-looking woman. He would sleep again. That way he would not have to wonder who she was.

He heard footsteps and whispers, but he kept his eyes shut. He was too tired to bother with people. He wanted the rain and the oblivion.

137

A strong arm slipped under his shoulders, and he was lifted into a sitting position. Etienne opened his eyes.

A Negro with two noses was holding him upright. Etienne wanted to feel his own face to see if it too was distorted, but his hand was too heavy to move.

"Drink this, Monsieur," the Negress spoke. "It will bring your strength back." She held a gourd to his lips and he drank. The liquid burned, and he wanted to push it away, but he was too weak.

The strong arms laid him back upon the bed. The drink kindled a fire in his stomach, and it spread through his body. He wanted to go to sleep, but the fire inside would not let him slip off.

"Come, Monsieur," the woman's voice said soothingly. "You must try to get up."

Etienne lay still, pretending not to hear.

"You have been asleep a long time," the voice continued. He did not want to get up, but he was hot and threw off the covers.

"That is better. Your body is impatient to be up. Come, Joswee will help you."

Etienne opened his eyes. All thought of sleep was now gone. The fire had reached his head, stimulating him to movement. He wanted to be up. The Negro with the split nose was helping him out of bed. This must be Joswee, who was setting him up on his feet. He would have fallen back upon the bed had not the Negro supported him, for his feet felt pierced with needles.

"My feet. Someone left a pincushion on the floor," Etienne protested.

The Negress laughed companionably. "Your feet are wakening up. They slept too."

Etienne smiled. Her voice cajoled as though he were a little boy and she his mother. He looked at her as she sat by the bed. She had intelligent, luminous eyes, which regarded him with sympathy. She looked like a witch with that scar, but he felt drawn to her.

138

"Who are you?" he asked.

"Negu." She stood up. "And now it's time for you to go back to bed. You have done enough for today. Joswee," she called to the Negro, "help him off his pincushion."

Again on his back, Etienne laughed up at the Negress. "You're the boss around here, are you?"

"You have no idea what good care she takes of everyone," Joswee answered for her.

"Does she look after you too?" he asked. "You look big enough to take care of a regiment."

Joswee chuckled. "Big and little, she has her way with all of us. She is like the mama in a household."

"Mama Negu," Etienne said. "I shall call you Mama Negu. I like having you take care of me too." He was drowsy. It would be good to sleep again.

To Etienne, the days that followed were all alike. He must have been sick, so Mama Negu maintained, and Joswee corroborated everything she said. But Etienne had no memory of life before Negu and Joswee. Life had begun with the rain and the awakening in bed here in Joswee's living quarters and from that time on, he was concerned only with growing stronger each day.

"You must get strong, strong like you have never been before," Negu always said. "There is much work for you to do."

But she never spoke of the nature of this work and Etienne had no interest in inquiring when all this would happen. He lived in the present, one day at a time. Mama Negu was often away for long periods, but Etienne never asked what she did in her absence. Whatever transpired, he accepted without curiosity. He lived with Joswee at the hounfort, and joined the houngan in farm work.

Behind the voodoo temple was a large field of sugar cane, where Etienne learned to use the machete. At first, he could work for only short periods of time, and his hands blistered. Joswee looked at them and shook his head.

"You have never done hard work with your hands. That is not good for any man no matter what is the color of his skin or the size of his purse." Then, he pierced the blisters with a thorn and rubbed dirt from the cane field into the raw wounds.

Handing the machete back to Etienne, the tall Negro said, "We will cut a while longer. That will toughen your hands."

Each day, Etienne grew stronger and his body luxuriated in his returning health. "You will soon be well enough," Joswee encouraged, but well enough for what, Etienne did not care.

"You must be like this jasmine," Negu told him one day as she pointed to the red flower. "Enjoy the sun and the rain, eat of what the earth provides and grow."

"But the flower grows up and I grow out," Etienne teased.

"The more difficult for anyone to pluck you," she cautioned.

Etienne tossed back his head and laughed at the mental picture of himself being snapped at the stem like a jasmine. Reaching out, he took the Negress's face between his hands. "Mama Negu, you fuss over me like a well-paid mistress. I like it." He leaned down and kissed her on the tip of her nose. He was content.

A few things puzzled Etienne, but not for long, since his mind rejected all problems. However, there was the night Joswee took him into the voodoo temple and the red light, flickering across the priest's face, stirred some long-forgotten memory. Somewhere before, he had seen that face. "Have I known you for long?" he inquired of the high priest. "Only for as long as I have known you," was the answer. Etienne looked about and his eyes fell upon a picture of a mother and child, a picture framed in gold which stood on the altar. The woman and her babe looked familiar.

"Who are they?" Etienne asked. "I should know them."

"Oh, that's Mary and Jesus," Joswee answered in a

matter-of-fact voice, which implied that everyone knew them. Etienne dismissed the incident, but that same night Negu came with a small jug of a sweet, red liquid and insisted he drink it. She waited beside him until he had done so.

Besides Joswee and Negu, Etienne saw only one other person, a voluptuous Negress named Desaix. Each day she came carrying a hamper of baked goods on top of her head. Meringues, tarts, bread.

"You must be a witch's apprentice to conjure up such pastries out here in the woods," Etienne joked, but Desaix's only comment was a giggle. After depositing the food on a table, she disappeared into a cane-stalk enclosure behind the hounfort.

"What does she do there all the time?" Etienne asked Joswee one day.

"Looks after her pets."

"Why does she hide them? Let's visit them." Etienne started in the direction of the stockade, but Joswee put a restraining hand on his arm.

"Only Desaix goes to her pets. They are snakes, rattlers. They listen only to her because she is a high priestess and snakes are the earthly form of Dambolla. The larger the snake, the greater the power of the high priestess."

"Sounds spooky to me," Etienne commented.

"Spooks have their purposes too. Don't ever underestimate other people's whimsies, for often they exist out of necessity."

For his evening meal that day, Etienne had a clear broth, and Joswee did not eat at all. "Is this all I get?" he asked. "Desaix was here today with her hamper of pastries. Where did you hide them? At least, could I have one to dip in the broth?"

Joswee shook his head. "It is good for you to be hungry tonight. Tomorrow you will want a big breakfast, and your stomach will be ready for it."

The next morning, Etienne awakened long before sunrise. He was more aware of Joswee's snoring than

141

ever before, although it had accompanied all his sleeping hours since the two had been together. He lay quietly on his bed of straw, remembering that it had not always been such a hard bed on which his body used to rest. There had been soft mattresses and silken feather ticks. Thick bolsters to pillow his head. But the bed was comfortable, and his body had grown used to it. A soldier learns to sleep anywhere, even a captain.

A captain! Remembrance began to surge into Etienne's mind like water rushing in when the dike gives. The worried face of Leclerc. The insolent hauteur of Rochambeau. And Philippe. God, no! Philippe dead. Now it all came back. The plague! He was sure he still smelled the stench of the pesthouse, and he sat up abruptly as if by doing so he could pull himself away from its nauseating reach. The puzzle of his past was jumping into a sequenced picture. Now he recalled his fumbling through the storm for a place to die and his blacking out in the red light of the hounfort when Joswee had appeared like a genie from the underworld.

It all came back. He had had yellow fever and yet he had lived. He leaped from the bed and groped for the tinder box. When he had lit a candle he examined his skin. The purple petechiae had disappeared. He, a white man, had lived through the plague.

"Joswee!" he shouted. "Joswee, wake up!" He wanted to share his elation.

The snoring stopped. The black shadow of Joswee rose up from his pile of straw on the floor in the corner and he came toward Etienne. "I know, I know," he chuckled. "You discovered you're alive. You are like the Resurrection on Easter Sunday. Hallelujah!"

Then he shook his red-turbaned head and scolded, "But it took you so long to rise up from the dead, Etienne. The Lord did it in three days, and you needed two months."

The high priest's eyes danced with merriment in the light from the candle. "You are teasing," Etienne said in disbelief.

142

"Look at yourself, man. You had the plague when you came. Now you are healthy and strong. Have you ever felt better? It takes time."

"My God!" Etienne suddenly felt weak. "Two months! General Leclerc will have me shot. He'll think I deserted."

"I wouldn't worry about your boss none if I was you," Joswee said in his soothing voice, a voice which had the effect of dispelling all care. "General Leclerc is dead."

"Dead!" Etienne suddenly feld cold. He realized he was naked, and going over to the bed, he picked up the cover and wrapped it about himself. He was shaking so hard that he had to sit down. Leclerc dead! Then a horrible thought presented itself. Rochambeau!

"Joswee, who's in charge of the army now? Did Rochambeau die too?"

"No. Too bad. The storm came and blew the plague away before it got that no-account man. Too bad. I guess," he added in a matter-of-fact tone, "if a man is born to hang, he'll never drown. Too bad." He shook his head in disapproval of the course of events.

Etienne was uneasy. "How are things going with the army?"

"It seems like with that new general spreading his hate all over the place, things are bad. But with you well again maybe you can change things before it is too late." With the last, an ominous note had crept into the high priest's voice.

A feeling of urgency permeated Etienne. The sun was now up and he should hasten into Cap François.

"Take things easy," Joswee cautioned. "Don't go barging like a barking pup before it knows how big is the thing that made the noise. We'll have a good breakfast. A nice friendly breakfast and talk things over. You think smarter after eating."

Etienne reached for his trousers. "Don't bother none with those britches," Joswee said. "You can't go back to the army in rags. We'll find something better for you

143

to wear." Taking down the piece of burlap he always placed across the doorway to keep the evil spirits out at night, Joswee stepped out into the sunlight. He built a fire. "You have to shave," he explained. "You can't go into town looking like a billy goat. I'll have some hot water ready in a jiffy. Meanwhile, I'll cut your hair so you look like a gentleman officer again." Indicating a tree stump, he said, "Sit down. We'll get this all done before breakfast."

While submitting to Joswee's tonsorial ministrations, Etienne heard voices down the path which came from the woods. Negu and Desaix. While it was still early in the morning, the two women sounded cheerful and happy, as though they had been up for hours, warming up to this conviviality.

The women came into the clearing, each balancing a hamper on her head. Over her arm, Negu carried something protected by a white sheet.

"Good morning, ladies," Etienne called. "What's the idea of intruding into a man's toilette?"

Desaix went into the hut, but Negu strolled over to the men. "It's about time you had a toilette," she snapped at Etienne, but her eyes were soft and pleased as she surveyed Joswee's handiwork. "You might be a handsome man at that after Joswee uncovers you from behind all those whiskers," she observed. Turning to the high priest, she said, "When you're finished, the breakfast will be ready."

And what a breakfast. They ate outside, he and Joswee, while the women served. Etienne felt like the dissolute Henry the Eighth when Negu produced a Liebfraumilch from her hamper. There were stewed mango fruits, chicken buried in a cream sauce topped with truffles, hominy grits, ochre cooked with side pork, eclairs stuffed with rum custard, Brie cheese, coffee with brandy.

"Now keep eating," Negu urged. "It may be a long time before you get another meal like this."

"I *can't* eat that much," Etienne protested.

144

"Try. Always stuff when you have it. You never can tell about the next meal."

Etienne looked at her admiringly. "Negu, how did you come by this food out here in the woods?"

She shrugged as though the explanation were a simple one. "Monsieur, my master has nothing to do but eat. He takes too much and grows fat. I thought it might be neighborly of him to send some down for you."

Etienne raised his wineglass and toasted, "To Monsieur, your master. Convey him my appreciation when he rises."

Negu laughed and refilled the glass.

Negu and Joswee had thought of everything. When breakfast was completed they brought him his clothes. They were what Negu had concealed under the sheet she had carried over her arm. It was his own uniform, cleaned and pressed, complete with captain's rank insignia.

"Wherever did you get it?" he asked, looking from one to the other.

Joswee shrugged. "We have friends."

Etienne shook his head in amazement. "I never knew anyone who had such opportune friends as the two of you."

"We wanted to bring you a general's uniform, but it was too small."

Etienne laughed at their audacity. "That was thoughtful of you, but the sudden promotion might have gone to my head. In this uniform I feel more at ease. Besides, General Rochambeau might not have understood and been envious of my swift advancement." He chuckled to himself as he buckled his belt.

Suddenly he remembered something. He searched the trouser pockets. Where could it be?

"Are you looking for the letter you had when you came here?" Negu asked.

"Yes. A very important one. I was to post it for a friend."

"It has already been done," she answered simply. "We did not know whether you would live or die and it seemed like a poor time to ask you about it. I gave it to an English merchantman who was sailing for Jamaica. The mails from St. Domingue are not trustworthy at this time."

Etienne gave a long whistle of relief. "Thank God you found it." He put his arms about Negu. "Thank God for you and," looking toward the tall Negro, "Joswee too."

"Give thanks to Him for Negu," Joswee said. "It was her idea. We never saved a white man before from the plague. Never wanted to. Wasn't sure how to, but Negu wanted we should try."

Etienne's eyes sought Negu. *"Why* did you want to?" he asked. "You did not know me. Why was I the fortunate one to be saved?"

Negu rubbed her chin with her hand and looked up at the sky. "It was the address on the letter."

"The address? You know someone at that address?"

"Yes," Negu nodded. "M. Drapeaux, my master, has a—" she hesitated, groping for the right word "—a ward at Chalon-sur-Marne. Soeur Denise has been very kind to Asya. Asya is the ward. If someone wrote a letter to that nun, I wanted her to have it."

"But where do I come in?"

Negu answered, "You could have been a friend or a relative. I was not certain, but when you had a connection with Soeur Denise, you deserved my help, for the house of Drapeaux owes her much."

Her words were like a benediction upon him. Soeur Denise and Negu between them had made a miracle happen. The spiritual bouquet of St. Martha had blessed him instead of Philippe. Looking into Negu's eyes, he said, "I owe something for my return to life. As yet, I do not know what, but someday I shall repay my debt. That I promise you, Negu, and I bind that promise with my life, the life you saved for me." He

146

put his arms about the priestess and clasped her to his chest.

For a moment, Negu relaxed against him. Then as though embarrassed by his tenderness, she pushed him away. "Life is cheap here," she said lightly. "You'll do me more good by holding onto your life. Now get along with you and give Rochambeau a hand with the army. You didn't get all that soldier training just to stand around in the woods and hug an old black slave."

"Desaix will show you the way out of the woods," Joswee said. "She knows the safest paths to take."

"Safest?" Etienne was puzzled.

In his slow voice, Joswee explained, "Things are a little stirred up in town. Rochambeau isn't too popular since most of us don't particularly like the way he is running things around here. A white man walking alone might just come to a little harm even though he is a captain. Some of the boys don't read those insigniae so well. But don't worry," his tone assured Etienne, "Desaix here has friends. No one will touch you while you are under her protection."

Etienne shook his head in admiration. "You black folks really have a world of your own. Do you also have some secret code by which you keep in touch with each other?"

"We manage to get along." Joswee's tone dismissed the subject. He held out his hand and Etienne clasped it. Neither man spoke. Words seemed futile.

Chapter Twelve

Etienne followed Desaix as she led him out of the woods. He had to chuckle to himself. Count Grenier, a graduate of St. Cyr, captain in the great French Army, aide to Napoleon, was dependent upon an illiterate Negress to take him to his post in town. He had learned much through books and training, but when it came to the elemental requisites of life like finding one's way out of the forest, he was an untutored babe.

Desaix was interesting to follow. It was the way she used her hips. Some girls flung them out insolently as they walked along, but not Desaix. Her well-rounded hips flowed smoothly in a wide arc from side to side, moving in a sensuous rhythm. Her lack of undergarments was betrayed by the way her full red skirt outlined her limbs and buttocks. She carried her head high, not in arrogance but like a queen who stretches tall the better to drink in the sight of her kingdom. As her arms swung freely forward and backward her breasts rose upward like a ship with a full wind in its sails. Desaix was built for sleeping with. It was difficult to walk behind her and keep one's mind on warlike activities.

"Desaix," he called to the girl ahead of him, "do you mind if I walk beside you. It gets lonesome back here by myself."

She stopped and, tilting her head, looked back at him coquettishly. Her full lips were in a half smile indicating she was aware of what he could have been thinking. "The path is narrow," she said in a hushed

148

voice. It was the first time Etienne had heard her speak. Always before it had been that same feminine giggle.

He came up beside her. "So, you do talk," he commented. "Good. We can converse together."

"Converse?" she queried. "You call it converse?"

"Yes, converse. Talk," he assured her. "That's all." He took her arm as they walked along the path.

"Do you realize this is the first time I've seen you without a hamper of food on your head?" he asked. Turning, he scrutinized her face. "Not bad. Not bad."

Desaix tossed her head. "I have my man. He says 'not bad' too," she announced smugly.

"Oh, I catch on," Etienne laughed. "Hands off. Tell me, who is this fortunate man?"

She looked up at him with a pleased look. "I gits myself the fightingest man in St. Domingue," she purred. "The Tiger himself, General Jean Jacques Dessalines."

A whistle escaped the captain's lips. "So, already he is a general. Did Napoleon or Rochambeau give this promotion?"

Desaix shrugged one shoulder and let it drop in a gesture of dismissal. "Who cares about outsiders? His own nigger soldiers call him General, and that's gooder than a medal from a stranger."

"Where is your General Dessalines, Desaix?"

She looked at him archly. "General Rochambeau is askin' the same thing, and he's puttin' hisself to a lot of trouble to find out."

"Like what?"

Desaix pursed her lips and said nothing.

"So, now you can't talk, eh? I have to find out for myself."

"You'll find out easy enough. It ain't hard to see what that devil is up to."

"Careful, Desaix, it's my superior officer you're speaking about," he teased, but her lip curled in scorn. The spirit of gaiety vanished. Her face looked evil. Disdainfully she tossed her head and walked in front of him.

For some time, they went in silence, each occupied with his own thoughts. At last, Etienne stopped and turned the girl toward himself. "Something serious is going on in Cap François," he said, "and I want to know before I get there. If I am informed, I can be of more help."

Desaix looked at him, and yet her black eyes were not seeing the man before her but seemingly staring at another scene, one of horror. Suddenly she put her hands over her face.

"Oh, General," her voice broke, and she sobbed, "it is horrible. Even I, I who cares nothin' 'bout men except what they pays me, can't stand by and do nothing. Help us, help us!" She fell against his breast and threw her arms about his neck. "Help us, help us!"

Etienne put his arms around her and waited until she had quieted. Then he unclasped her hands from behind his neck and pushed her from himself. "That was a good act, Desaix. I'd like to know what it's all about."

"No, no, you don't understand." Her voice carried despair. Tears flowed down her cheeks. "I ain't play-actin'. Horrible things is goin' on in town. Rochambeau, he try to wipe all black men off the earth. It's awful!" Her words erupted in hysteria.

Grabbing her by the shoulders, Etienne shook the girl. "Quiet down and tell me what goes on," he ordered.

"You see for yourself I don't lie. You kin go down to the harbor and find out. Every day Rochambeau drowns so many us black folks that the merchants complain the bodies clutter up the harbor and they can't git their boats in."

"Desaix, the truth!" he demanded.

"By Jesus, by God, by Holy Maria, by Dambolla, I swear I tell the truth." She shrieked and sobbed at the same time.

"Then why doesn't your General Dessalines come to their aid? Don't he and Christophe still have the guns hidden in the mountains?"

"*Oui, oui,* they want to help, but their men are afraid because of the dogs."

"D-o-g-s?" Etienne dragged out the word in disbelief. "Dogs, you say. Your men are brave. Why should they be afraid of dogs?"

Sniffing quietly, Desaix picked up her skirt and blew her nose. Etienne had been right. She wore no undergarments.

Brusquely, he pulled the skirt from her hand and it fell down into place. "You're a big girl now," he snapped. "Keep your skirt down."

With fists clenched and eyes flashing out venom, Desaix jumped away from him. "You stupid Frenchman. I tell you about the dogs. Your big, mighty Rochambeau, he bring in hundreds of wild dogs from Cuba. He sets them out through the hills to smell down the black man and tear them to pieces. Dogs don't care none whether they're men or kids. We all stinks the same. Has you ever seen a kid with its guts spilled in the dirt? Still moanin' while its legs is gittin' chewed? Has you ever seen your brother held to the ground by a savage animal while his nose is bitten off? What does you think I's talkin' about, lap dogs? Them is man-eatin' dogs, and the men has a right to be afraid.

"But don't you worry none. Dessalines, he soon comes down, and so will Christophe, and enough men to pay back gut for gut, nose for nose to the Frenchmen. My people are dumb 'bout army fightin', but any jungle man can kill and don't mind dyin' when he does it."

Desaix came up close and spat in his face. Before he could grab her, she jumped back. "Thanks for your help. You kin kiss my black ass." She whirled about, flipped up her skirt and stuck out her bare buttocks. In a flash she was gone.

Etienne shook his head in disbelief. Was the girl lying? Rochambeau was without morals, but civilized. Such vicious slaughter went back to the Roman arena. And yet . . . He was thinking of that cruel face with impenetrable shadows for eyes. The disdaining pitiless voice as it had spoken to Philippe. An urgency rose within him, and he began to run.

Etienne had no recollection of where the hounfort had been in relation to Cap François, but it was still early in the morning and if he kept the sun on his right, the ocean should be straight before him. The trees were thick and tangled and yet paths snaked everywhere through the woods. Etienne ran quickly, always hoping that around the next curve might be the sea. What he would do when he arrived at the post, Etienne had not the slightest idea. All he knew was that he must get there.

Abruptly the trees stopped, and Etienne came out by the swampland which fringed the shore. Far ahead he could see a French frigate in the harbor. Staying to the higher, dry ground, Etienne hurried toward the ship. Now he could see much activity, people moving about on board and crowds standing on the wharf. He had to take the road which ran along the edge of town, for the tide was high, and the water was deep in the grass. As he hurried along toward the wharf, chafing at having to take the longer way, the moaning of the wind in his ears became louder. Or was it the wind? He was puzzled for a moment. Then suddenly he knew. Oh God, no. It could not be. But it was. It was all there for him to hear. The whines, the sobs, the screams of hysteria; the cries of a frightened mob calling out in anguish or denunciation. Etienne began to run, for if he did not hurry he would be too late. For what? He did not know.

Captain Grenier came to the dock and stopped. Except for the French soldiers in charge, the place was alive with slaves, hundreds of them. So many that one could not see the boards on which their black feet stood. And then Etienne saw the reason for their cries.

Each was shackled to the others by heavy irons about his ankles. They were pushed into lines by the soldiers who cracked black snakelike whips across their faces.

"What goes on here?" Captain Grenier shouted at the sergeant in charge, one whom the officers had always referred to as "Pinhead."

At the sound of his voice, the cacophony surrounding Etienne quieted, but only for a second. Then it rose about him like a hell of sound. "Help us. Save us. They're killing us. We've done nothing. God help us. I don't wanna die like that." The cries barraged him like a cannon shooting out its fodder. Despite the beating of the whips against their faces, the natives surged about Etienne, their last hope. "Help us, help us!" they shouted, their breath blowing into his face, their saliva wetting it from the vehemence of their call. Some fell down on their knees to appeal and those behind pushed forward, stumbling over them.

"Get back," Etienne ordered. His voice was more effective than the whips, and while they did not recede, they quieted. "Now, what's this all about? What have these men done?" he snapped at Pinhead.

The sergeant's birdlike eyes opened wide in his small but elongated face, and thin lips barely moved as they let pass a deep bass voice, a voice which seemed to grate up from the bowels of the earth. "They're black, ain't they? That's enough reason to drown 'em."

Etienne looked at the man. The little head on a fat body made Etienne think of a duckpin atop a barrel and he wanted to knock it off. It was a waste of time to talk with one who has an empty sack for a mind.

With great control, Etienne demanded, "Sergeant, where is General Rochambeau?"

"Aboard ship, watching the entertainment. That's what it is when you're brass. You get a good seat for the show."

Etienne grabbed the whip from the sergeant's hand and flung it upon the gangplank of the ship. "No more beating of the prisoners," he commanded in a voice near to fury. "I'll be back with further orders."

As he ran up the gangplank he heard Pinhead grumble, "The damn nigger lover, does he want I should rock-a-bye them!"

No sooner had Etienne reached the deck than what had been a low rumbling of protesting voices from the other side of the ship suddenly became a wave of sound screaming up to the heavens. He ran to starboard. What he saw there froze his body so that he no longer was capable of movement. He was just in time to see death from the gangplank. In time to see the last of the bodies of the black men, shackled each to the other at the ankles, silhouetted against the sky like blackbirds crazily flailing their wings to stay aloft, and then suddenly dragged down by the weight of the men before them, their screams instantly smothered by the sea below.

In his frozen stupor, he saw a corporal, a tall skinny fellow, walk up to the side of the ship and look over the railing to observe the result of his work. In his hand he held a heavy cudgel, red with blood. Etienne breathed again and each breath brought anger. He strode up to the corporal, who turned around at the same time. Seeing the captain, he said as he saluted, "Good morning, sir. Sorry you missed the fun. I just sent forty of the black niggers to hell. Stick around and I'll have another batch ready before—"

"Where's General Rochambeau?" Etienne had the urge to spit on the beaked nose sticking out of the skinny face before him.

The corporal blinked. The question did not seem to penetrate. "Where's Rochambeau?" Etienne shouted.

"Oh." Still blinking in that bewildered way, the man answered, "I'm not sure, but I think he is in the captain's cabin. The captain went ashore, but he left his bottles behind." Whereupon he gave a knowing wink with a buzzard-like eye.

154

"Stop these executions until I return," Etienne ordered.

"Sure, sure, I'll hold up the show until you get back," he said good-naturedly.

Etienne hurried toward the captain's quarters. This was the *Freire* on which he had come to St. Domingue and Etienne lost no time in finding his way. The haste which had driven him most of the morning was now so strong that he could have walked through walls to save time. He found the door he wanted. Turning the knob, Etienne walked in.

"And when do you enter without knocking?" a voice snapped out like a hand across the mouth. It was Rochambeau sitting at the table, a decanter of wine before him, a half-filled goblet leaving his lips. The insolent set of those bony shoulders was recognizable anywhere.

Etienne did not answer. His eyes were two vials of hate pouring their venom upon the back of the commanding officer. Slowly Rochambeau turned his head. "Oh, so it's you," he sneered. "The deserter has come back."

"I did not desert," Etienne denied. His voice sounded cold even to his own ears. "If you had bothered to inquire, you would have known that."

Rochambeau slowly drained his wineglass. Then in a voice which clearly betrayed his boredom with the moment, he drawled, "I was not sufficiently interested to be concerned with your whereabouts. They were of little importance to me." With an exaggerated flourish he slowly lifted the bottle and studied its contents in the light from the window. "A remarkable claret," he said.

"Are you drunk?" the captain accused, as he walked to the table and stood beside the general.

With a show of great forbearance and restraint, Rochambeau carefully put down the bottle. In a tone that he might use in speaking to an exasperating child, the general said, "Young man, I am merely enjoying myself. And *now*," he said, "let us discuss your impudence in entering my room without knocking."

"Your harangue on conduct becoming an officer can wait," Etienne shot out. "What I am interested in is conduct becoming a man. Why are you having those men murdered?"

"Men?" Slowly, disdainfully, General Rochambeau turned his head, and his gaze, starting at Etienne's feet, wandered up his frame, almost to his face. But Etienne never got to look into those black cavernous eyes, for Rochambeau shifted his attention back to his glass of claret, dismissing the captain as unworthy of further attention.

"Yes, men." Etienne was infuriated. "They are black, but they are men."

The officer at the table threw back his head and gave a derisive laugh. "My dear boy," he explained in a condescending voice, "when one is black, one is not a man. He does not belong to the human race. Like the dogs and the cattle, he is put here to serve us. The cow, the pig—they feed us. The dog is a pet. If the dog goes mad, do you object to shooting him for your own protection? Of course not. Like the dogs, the black men on St. Domingue have become mad and must be removed. Every last one of them. It is cheaper to drown than to shoot them. Our gunpowder must be conserved for a more profitable use. It's as simple as that." He gave a little wave of his hand to indicate the discussion was closed. He put the glass to his lips and drank.

"It's not as simple as that," Etienne shot out, at the same time angrily knocking the glass from the general's hand so that it went flying across the cabin to crash against the wall. "I am the second officer in charge here and I have something to say. I will not stand by and permit human beings, no matter what their color, to be slaughtered by an officer who has lost his mind."

Rochambeau's head shot up. His body bristled with combativeness, then he rose so quickly that his chair tumbled backward. With a clipped, military turn, he faced Etienne. "And what do you propose to do about it?" he asked in a deadly voice.

At last, Etienne saw into those cavernous eyes. They were beady and bright, devoid of emotion. Cold like those of a snake who regards his victim before the strike.

"I propose to take charge here," Etienne snapped. "If you were shot and bleeding to death, I would be forced to take over the command. Right now, you have a hole in your head, and your brains have spilled out. You're through, Rochambeau!"

Rochambeau's eyes became slits in his face. "No young upstart is going to push me around," he answered in a cold, controlled voice. "I intend to do what Leclerc could not—take over this island for France. If I have to kill everyone, black and white, in this damn hellhole, I shall do it even if I am the only one left alive. But take it, I will!"

In silence, the two men regarded each other with venom. At last Rochambeau spoke again, his lips curled in derision, "Or is it that you have found a black bitch to bed with and, like the dog that you are, any female in heat will do?"

It was then that Etienne struck him. All the hate, the revulsion, he had ever felt for the man spilled over as he smashed his fist onto Rochambeau's nose. Not once, but again and again and again. Like a drunken man, Captain Grenier abandoned himself to the exultation he felt each time his fist cracked the face of this creature he despised so much. At last, when all the viciousness inside him had been unleashed, Etienne let the officer drop to the floor. He stood over him and looked down on the unconscious form. Rochambeau's face had become a fountain that spewed its red waters from many faucets. Blood gushed from his ears, his nose, his mouth. Whether Rochambeau lived or not, Grenier had no concern. He wiped the blood from his hand on the tablecloth. Turning his back on the prostrate general, Etienne left the cabin.

Captain Grenier ran up to the deck where he had left the corporal. That starved-looking buzzard of a man had not been idle during Etienne's visit with Rochambeau. He had already brought a group of the manacled natives aboard. With his bloody cudgel he was pummeling them into some semblance of order by the gangplank. "The bastards don't understand about a straight line," he explained to Etienne, while at the same time he cracked one of the prisoners on the knees and roared, "Stand up. Don't you know what your damn black feet are for?"

Fear had completely taken over the black bodies of the prisoners. With all control gone, their heads nodded senselessly and their mouths hung limply open. Saliva spilled down over their chins in a white foam, and their hands quivered as with palsy. In their fright, their legs kept collapsing, and the corporal, even with the assistance of his soldiers, could not keep them upright. It was life, life of no more value than an anthill about to be wiped off the deck and destroyed in the sea.

Etienne was mad as hell and as his anger grew, he knew precisely what he must do. Turning to the corporal, he shouted, "I have just come from General Rochambeau. The orders have been changed. He has work for these men. Remove their chains."

The buzzard eyes stared uncomprehendingly. "But the fun. You didn't see any of the fun."

Etienne regarded him with loathing. "Remove their irons at once," he snapped.

With a show of surliness, the soldiers began to take off the chains. When they were done, Etienne ordered the prisoners to follow him. Still bunched together in fear, they followed him from the ship like a black cloud.

When the captain and his band of natives stepped down to the dock with its hundreds of whining, cursing, writhing prisoners, a stunned silence hit the air. Man had given himself up to despair, and suddenly along came hope. Etienne could feel the white eyes bulging out from black faces, miserable eyes, looking toward him with wistful expectancy. It was not that he could really see them. Their piteous appeal was something he could sense in the air.

He let his voice boom out so all could hear and know that help had come. "Sergeant Pinhead, remove the irons from these men!"

The little head bobbed on the barrel-chested body. From deep down inside him came the cavernous voice: "Pinhead? You call me Pinhead?" Some of the privates began to snicker.

"I don't care what the devil your name is." By now, Captain Grenier was a cresting tidal wave which could not be stopped. "Unshackle these men!"

The sergeant's thin line of a mouth almost disappeared as defiance spread over his little face. "I will not!" He spat out each word in that heavy voice. "I take orders from Rochambeau."

The tidal wave swelled up, and Captain Grenier pounced upon the barrel with the duckpin head. Raising it high in the air, Etienne hurled it so that it crashed against the side of the ship. A sound as from an oversized bellows hit the air. Etienne turned toward the other soldiers. "General Rochambeau won't be giving orders for a while. Get the irons off these men, NOW!"

There was an immediate scurrying of the soldiers, followed by the clanging of chains. They rattled them needlessly, but it was their way of showing how quickly they were carrying out orders. As they worked, Etienne stood on top of the anchor hold, the better to dominate the scene. There he waited, fierce and immobile, his fists clenched in a show of readiness, prepared to deal with the least sign of disobedience. Even after all the prisoners were freed, Captain Grenier did not move. He glowered down upon each man before him, until in either bewilderment or uneasiness, both black and white stood at attention, waiting for his next move.

The captain spoke in a clipped, military voice that brooked no interference: "All you prisoners will come with me to the mountain beyond the Plain du Nord. I have work for you to do, and if you do it well, I promise that you will never again find yourselves in chains." A murmur began to hum through the crowd assembled before him. Etienne raised his hand in a quick gesture for silence and hurriedly continued: "You soldiers of France, count and stack all these irons on the side of the wharf. If any of you leave before the job is finished, you will find we still have use for them."

Etienne jumped down from the anchor hold and strode across the dock. The natives stepped aside to let him pass through them and then they closed ranks and followed silently behind. As the captain reached the street which ran through the town and out to the plain, the tidal wave inside him spent itself. Etienne had no idea where to take these men after he did reach the plain, but he would worry about that later.

With an air of bravado which he no longer felt, Etienne led his black army through the town square and toward the church. He saw the big crucifix of the outdoor shrine in the side yard. A woman was kneeling before the cross, her arms stretched sideways, her head flung back, in an attitude of dedication.

The captain began to run. It had to be Desaix. What other black woman had the courage or brazenness to flaunt herself in Cap François during Rochambeau's reign of terror and yet seek the protective immunity of the church grounds.

When he came to the crucifix, he called, "Desaix, cut the playacting. It's Captain Grenier." He felt gay, heady with success. Now he knew the course to take. At sight of the girl, he had cast the die.

"God is sure goin' to be mad at the way you interrupt my prayers," a reproving voice answered. Desaix lowered her arms and rolled her head toward him. He noticed that her eyes were laughing.

"So, you didn't run away after all," Etienne said.

"Desaix never goes far from men's goings-on. What you want with me now?"

"Take these men to Dessalines, Desaix. I have brought him volunteers." He pointed toward the ragged army which stood out on the street watching.

"And you?" Still on her knees before the crucifix, she cocked her head coquettishly.

"I? I am coming too."

Chapter Thirteen

At Negu's insistence for his safety, André Drapeaux had fled to Jamaica, where he lived for fifteen years. But now, under the iron fist of Henri Christophe, the new president, St. Domingue at last knew peace and order, and M. Drapeaux returned to the easy life of his plantation.

Negu was not happy. M. Drapeaux was seeing too much of that Rowbottom woman. Eloise Rowbottom was the daughter of an English businessman, who, like many of his countrymen, had come to the new republic to build his fortune.

The plantation owner was forever inviting Mlle. Eloise and her father out for dinner; for a view of the magnolias at the height of their bloom; or for chocolate on the terrace after a trip to the stable to inspect the new colt. The Rowbottom creature was beginning to act as though what she saw belonged to her. Negu saw that appraising look in the young woman's eyes as she glanced about whatever room in the house she was in. A true merchantman's daughter, evaluating the cost of the crystal chandelier, the Italian paintings, the glided chair.

André. That fool. Did he think a beautiful young girl gave a fat old man starry-eyed glances because she found him attractive? Knowing André, he probably did. He was too self-centered to even suspect that his material goods could possibly overshadow his worldly charm in the heart of this delicate female. Hah, thought Negu. Mlle. Rowbottom was about as delicate as a tiger's whisker.

Negu's worst fears were realized. André gave a dinner to celebrate Mlle. Eloise's eighteenth birthday. All the affluent English business people of the town were invited along with some of the older French families who had returned to claim their plantations. The way Monsieur was carrying on during the preparations, the Negress was certain that something more than a birthday celebration was afoot.

A ball was planned with musicians brought in from Jamaica to play for the dancers. Wine kegs, which had lain buried under cobwebs since before the '91 revolt, were dusted off and tapped for the gala occasion. It took Nassy a whole week to wash the eight crystal chandeliers in the ballroom of the house and fit them with sixteen hundred candles. Polishing and shining the wall candelabra consumed another two days.

Groundsmen came in with buckets of heavy cream which they poured over the ballroom floor and then rubbed in until the surface was as shiny and slippery as a wet stone. Only when Monsieur himself had tested it with a solo gavotte was the floor pronounced ready for the dance.

The ass, Negu thought as she came into the room in time to see Drapeaux execute a few swooping terpsichorean feats, whistling a melody all the while.

The night of the party, Negu was everywhere. Not since the days of Mme. Drapeaux had the villa shone so brightly or sounded so gay. Torches were set up along the circular driveway to welcome the guests as they drove up in their carriages. From an upstairs window Negu looked out to admire the illumination, and she saw Javan's skull, polished white through the years, reflecting back the rays of fire.

It's almost like a family seal before the gate, she thought approvingly.

However, Mlle. Rowbottom did not regard the grotesque image so favorably. She and her father were the first arrivals, and even as André bent over her hand in welcome, she said in a pleading voice, "Oh, André everything is so wonderful, and then I look at that spooky skeleton out by the gate and it scares me. Take it down."

Negu, who was standing in the nearby doorway giving the salon a last-minute inspection, wanted to spit in that baby-doll face. The English girl was assuming the airs of a mistress. How dare she presume to take charge. She, who was young enough to remember the time when she still wore wet pants.

"Eloise, *ma cherie*, it's only the whimsy of one of the servants. You have to indulge them. It keeps these niggers happy. Don't worry your golden head about it."

"Please," she pouted. "With those fires around it, that Nagshead looks like some spook from out of the grave, grinning at you to remind you that your turn is coming too. Please, it is my birthday. Take it down."

"Of course, *ma cherie*, at once." He beckoned with his fat finger to Nassy, who hurried over. "Take Javan's head from the gatepost," he ordered with the aplomb of a king announcing a decree. "Its presence disturbs our guest." Then Drapeaux gazed fatuously down into Eloise's rapturous face. "Tonight you are *queen*," he said.

Looking most distressed, Nassy hurried over to the doorway from where Negu had witnessed the little scene. "What shall I do?" he asked.

"Nothing," she replied. "Just go about some other business."

"But what shall I do if they inquire if I removed the head?"

"Tell them you did."

"But," the Negro gave her a perplexed look, "but if they look out they'll *see* it's still there."

"Yes," Negu said slyly. "They will, won't they."

With that she returned to the dining room to finish her final preparations.

ASYA

The guests began to arrive and from then on Negu
was so busy overseeing all the behind-the-scenes activities necessary for an entertainment in the grand manner that she did not hear the announcement M.
Rowbottom made at the conclusion of dinner. Later,
one of the young pantry maids told her the news.

"Ain't it romantic?" she cooed. "There's goin' to be
a weddin'."

At the words, a chill went through Negu's body. The
cream pitcher she was carrying suddenly became heavy
and she had to grip the handle firmly so that it did not
fall to the floor. "Whose?" she asked in a dead voice,
although she knew before the answer came.

"M. Drapeaux and Mlle. Rowbottom. Her papa just
announced it in the dinin' room. She's so pretty," the
young maid sighed, "just like an angel."

At that point, Evadne came in from the outside
kitchen and added her comments to the conversation.
" 'Bout time that man got hisself a wife and took to
stayin' home. Ah's glad she is young. Sure glad. We
needs lots of babies here to fill this big house."

Negu was no longer listening. Suddenly the handle
snapped in her hand and the porcelain cream pitcher
smashed on the stone floor. Negu was numb. For a
moment she stared at the puddle of spilled cream.
Then she turned stiffly on her heel and walked from
the room.

Negu did not know where she walked. Her feet held
her will and where they took her, she went. Past the
outside kitchen. She saw the fires from the hearth
leaping up, shooting their light through the open windows. They were real, but she was not. She was of the
world, and yet she was not of it. She was cold. Since
she was not alive, the fires did not warm her. She was
a spirit and the wind blew through her.

She could not stop. Her feet were possessed and
they carried her away. Down past the lane of Negro
shacks she came upon a big fire. Men and women were
gathered around it, singing and clapping their hands,

165

but no one noticed her. She stepped close to try to warm her hands. The smell of burning hair, the hair on her arms, reached her nostrils, but her hands were still cold. Why was everyone so happy, she wondered. But her lips were paralyzed, and she could not move them to ask. Still, her feet urged her to move on.

The path was dark now. She could not see. Had she no eyes, or was it a black night? Her feet knew the way and she could not hold back or they would go alone without her, and she would be lost. Was this death? Somewhere she had heard about the Valley of the Shadow. Was this it? Was she a spirit hurrying on to join the dead? If so, she must hurry. Celeste would be there.

Suddenly her feet stopped. Several yards ahead of her was a large structure that she did not recognize. Was it the mansion of the dead? Her feet carried her forward and through an unseen doorway into the blackness within. There was something familiar. She sniffed. Her nose, at least, was working. What was this smell? It was familiar, if only her head would tell her. It knew. Why did it not inform her?

Then, out of the darkness, a whinny came. Now she remembered. It was hay she smelled. She was in a stable. Her stable. Her feet kept walking. They carried her past several stalls and abandoned her at the last one. While she stood there, wondering how to move without feet, she heard a light rustle toward the back of the stall. It was so faint that she wondered if she might have imagined it. There it was again. A slight scraping against something wooden.

She remembered now. It was Dambolla. Her beloved Dambolla calling to her. It was he who had summoned her here. She ran forward and fell on her knees by the box. "My darling, my darling," she cried. "You knew I needed you."

Tears came up from her heart, tearing her breast with their vehemence before they spilled out of her eyes. She let her head fall upon the top of the box and

166

her face lay in a pool of tears. Her body shook and she abandoned it to her weeping.

At last, weak and depressed from her outburst and needing to touch something living, Negu raised the lid of the box and reached inside. At once she felt the cold head of the snake nudging against her hand. It was trying to comfort her, to let her know that it was her friend.

"You still have me," it seemed to say, as it began to wrap itself around her arm. "Don't despair. There must be something I can do."

"No, my friend," Negu sobbed, it is hopeless. He will marry that young witch and her brats will claim the Drapeaux inheritance." Her shoulders shook with grief, and her head fell forward on her bosom.

The serpent tapped her ear with its head as if to reassure her. She reached up and stroked the snake. Half-sobbing, half-talking, Negu told him of her hopelessness.

"It's no use, my friend," she shook her head, "it's no use. While Monsieur adopted her on paper, Asya will never get this land. What chance would a nigger woman's grandchild have in court against a white man's legal white offspring? There is no hope. No hope."

Her voice was a chant, reciting the litany of her woes, and her tears trickled down her cheeks as she continued, "How many years have I waited? Fifteen? Sixteen? So long have I kept my promise to Celeste. So long I have watched over the father of her child. Would not Dessalines have killed him as he killed all white planters who stayed, had I not warned him to go to Jamaica? It would have been better had he stayed. He would be dead now, and Asya could have come home to her own land. Now is the time for Monsieur to send for his daughter. Instead, he talks of a new bride. Negu will never see her granddaughter. Never. Never." Her mournful tones faded away. "Never."

So engrossed was she in her misery that Negu was

167

only half conscious of the snake which had been lying immobile against her shoulder. Only when it put its head down the neck of her blouse and slithered down her back did she come from her reverie. Its cold body sent a chill through her and she shivered. It was Dambolla's way of shaking her in reproof, to rouse her to some action.

"No, no, my dear, I can't let you," Negu denied the thoughts the serpent had implanted in her mind. "No. No." Her voice was sharp and quick, trying to wipe out the thought before it formed. "No. Celeste would never forgive me. No." She unbuttoned the front of her blouse and the snake, slithering down her back and across her ribs, came up between her bare breasts until its head was level with her mouth. Its tongue stroked the deformity of her scarred lip, chiding her for her humanity in the face of the inhumanity she had known.

Lovingly, Negu took the head of the snake between her hands and held it against her cheek. As one might reason with a child, she said, "I know you want to help, Dambolla. You could kill him. It might look like an accident. A poisonous snakebite. It could be blamed on someone's carelessness that you got out of your box. But it won't do, my friend. I cannot kill him. Celeste loved him. I promised to look after all that was hers. I must keep my promise."

The head of the snake was cool against her cheek, and somehow comforting. In the darkness of the familiar stable Negu relaxed. Slowly she started to sway, forward and backward, at the same time, crooning, "La rosée afait brope tou temps soleil tar bele. La rosée fait bro—"

The song was from her people, and as she sang her spirit joined with the souls of all those who, through the ages, had spun out their miseries in this same dirge. The motion and the beat began to soothe her sad heart. "La rosée afait brope tou semps tar bele."

When at last she felt whole again, she stopped singing. She sat in silence, her mind at work. What if an accident should befall Mlle. Rowbottom? Would not the danger be temporarily removed. Of course, there was always the risk of some other young girl winning Monsieur's fancy. She, Negu, was growing older, and with her own death, there would no longer be anyone to watch over Aysa's inheritance. But what could she do?

Hugging Dambolla's head against her cheek, she whispered "I don't want to die before I have lived," my friend. Tell me what I must do."

Suddenly she knew. Why had she not thought of it long ago? Asya could have been with her by now. And Celeste could not accuse her mother of breaking her promise. Had she herself not died and yet lived tonight? It was painless.

Negu laughed. She was free and young again. Not an old hag of more than fifty, aged with hate and despair, but more like a mademoiselle of fifteen. Gay and laughing, for life was good, and wonderful things were going to happen. She placed the reptile against her bare bosom and crossing her arms, she pressed it to her. "Dambolla! Dambolla!" she called out with a resounding joy. "I have won! Asya is coming home. Did you hear?" Raising her voice, she shouted her jubilation up through the rafters and the roof, and to the world. "Celeste's child is coming home. Home. To here. We have won, we have won!"

She let go a wild laughter, and to her own ears it was the clapper hitting the sides of the bell as it proclaimed some joyous feast day. "I have won!"

Her first exultation having been spent, Negu quickly returned the serpent to its box. "Rest, my pet." She spoke to the snake like a mother who must put her child to bed and be about her tasks. With a last perfunctory pat on the cold head, she lowered the heavy lid and hurried from the stable. Although she could have found her way through the blackest of nights, the sky had now hung out its moon lamp and was lighting her way to the hounfort—the hounfort and Joswee. Negu began to run.

So involved was Negu in laying her plans with Joswee that it was noon of the day after the great party when she returned to the Drapeaux plantation. André had risen late and was having breakfast in, of all places, his library. Suddenly realizing that she had not eaten since the day before, Negu went to the outside kitchen. Evadne was eating a mess of black-eyed peas and collards flavored with side pork. The aroma appealed to her too long empty stomach and she sat down to join the cook. As she ate, she glanced about the one-room building. While it was old and the stone walls were cracked, they were thick and kept out the tropical heat. It was the kitchen of a great house. Copper pans flashed brightly from the walls where they hung. Heavy black iron pots stood piled by the huge fireplace. Through the open doorway, Negu could see the great boiler leaning against the smokehouse. A smokehouse with big black hams hanging from its rafters—enough to feed all of Cap François. She was content, and the lunch sat well. A great house is not defined by its parlor, but by its kitchen. Negu nodded her approval. This was a house of abundance, and soon it would belong to Asya.

"Why is Monsieur eating in the library?" she asked Evadne by way of making conversation. It was well to make conversation with the cook, for she and her husband, Nassy, kept informed on all goings-on in the vicinity. Much easier gathering the gossip at the font of all knowledge than assembling it bit by bit from various informants.

"Bizness, I s'pose." She shrugged a plump shoulder. Evadne had put on weight through the years. A sign of a good cook. A skinny one is afraid to use butter and lacks skill in rolling out a rich pastry. Not Evadne. She would be fine for Asya.

Negu brought her thoughts back to the conversation at hand. "Is someone with Monsieur?" she asked.

"Oh, dint you know? M. Rowbottom come by early this morning. Thought he owned the place by how he insisted the master git up. But," and Evadne rolled her eyes and held out her hands in a hopeless gesture, "you know how Monsieur likes keepin' to his bed late after he's been winin' some the night before. The master, he niver stirred till 'most noon. No 'mount of nudgin' kin budge him none till he's done got all his sleep in." She giggled. "Like tryin' to waken up a rock." As an after-thought she added, "A buzzin' rock."

"I wonder," Negu asked thoughtfully, "what was so urgent that the business couldn't wait."

"I dunno." The cook's face lighted up. "Here come my man now. We soon find out," she announced as Nassy came into the kitchen. "Sit down," she spoke in a bossy tone while pushing a mug of coffee toward her husband. "If you're finished totin' victuals to the master and his soon-to-be kinfolk, tell us what the 'mergency meetin' was about."

With an air of importance, the butler raised the large mug to his mouth and slowly drank the coffee without stopping once for breath.

Crossing her arms over her ample bosom, Evadne leaned back in her chair and watched her spouse with admiration. When he set down the empty mug, she said, "Ya still kin do it. After all these years, ya still got the air to swaller the whole cup."

Nassy wiped his mouth with the back of his hand. "Yeah," he agreed. "Sure kin. It's 'cause I don't waste my breath none gossipin' like some females I know." With that he cocked a big eye knowingly at his wife.

"You sure better had kept some breath left inside ready to go fur yuh, 'cause me and Negu wanna know what's transpirin' back in that there liberry." With that she reached across the table for the earthenware pitcher of hot coffee and menacingly moved it in the direction of his head.

171

Nassy raised his hand in defense. "Now, Woman, you knows I's only kiddin'. I aim to tell yuh. You just gotta learn to sit on your temper as good like you sit down on your fat ass."

"Yuh let my fat ass out of the conv'sation," his wife warned, "and tell us what them big ears larned inside that liberry."

"Wal," the butler drawled, "M. Rowbottom bein' the biznessman what he is, he come 'round 'bout bizness."

Evadne reached for the pitcher, whereupon her spouse hurried to add, "Bizness 'bout the weddin'."

"Yeah," Evadne encouraged. "Negu and me here, we'uns impatient. We knows natcherly the talk is bein' 'bout the comin' nuptials. What else is there for a man to talk 'bout whin his only chile is plannin' on takin' her a husband? Git goin'. What he say?"

"Woman, I keep tryin' to tell you, but you keep buttin' in with that flappin' tongue of yours. If you shut your mouth for a minute I'll pass on ev'rything I heared."

Evadne pursed her lips and glared at her husband. "Git to the point," she ordered. "I's listenin'."

"Wal," the butler began in a slow voice, "seems like M. Rowbottom has a bad heart. In the 'citement of givin' 'way his only chile, he might, just might, so he admits, pass on to his 'ternal reward. So it will give him great peace of mind to have M'sieur make up his will, leavin' all his worldly goods to Mlle. Rowbottom."

The sound of a low cry caused Nassy to turn to Negu. "Ah don' blame yuh none for bein' surprised. Ah 'most dropped my tray of Evadne's beaten biscuits whin I heared the talk. The gintleman sure got hisself a passel of brass. Askin' for the worldly goods afore the preacher dun spoke the words."

Finding her voice, Negu asked, "What did the master answer to that?"

"Oh, him. He say how sorry he is to larn 'bout that no-'count heart, and if it make his father-law to feel

172

gladder, then he do like he say right 'way. Then he start tellin' him how to take good care of his heart so he can live a long time to see his chillun's chillun like it say in the Bible. Tha's what they talk 'bout when I leave 'em. The chillun's chillun."

"Did they have to shut themselves up in the privacy of the library to discuss that?" Negu asked icily.

Evadne leaned across to Negu and whispered huskily, "I guess he don' wan' no one to know how money-grabbin' he is. It don' look so good to want the money 'fore it's legal to have it."

Negu's whole body was tensed. There was something she had to know at once. "Nassy, when did the master plan to see his barrister?"

"M. Rowbottom want he should go right 'way today, but the master think they kin wait till the morrow. He says he is still in a romantic feelin' after the party and he don' want to bother none with legal paper stuff yit. I see M'sieur don' like it none, but I guess he know he done purty good to git the master to see bizness things his way. What with his health bein' poorly and all, he say all right, tomorrow, but not a day later."

At his words, the rigidness went from Negu's body. A warm feeling glowed within. She was thinking, *Tomorrow.* A short titter came from her lips. Then another. Her companions looked at her in wonder. Like a spring, she began to bubble up with happiness, and then let it out in laughter. She laughed and laughed until the sound of her gaiety filled the old stone kitchen. And when she had laughed until her breath was almost gone and tears wet her cheeks, Negu picked up her skirt and wiped her face, mumbling into the folds as she did so, "Tomorrow? We shall see." If Evadne and Nassy heard, she did not care.

Toward sunset, the sky blackened away its usual brilliance in the west, casting a foreboding darkness over the earth. The wind rose, and by nightfall, both the inside and outside shutters of the Drapeaux house

173

had been securely fastened. The wind rattled and hammered against them like an enraged beast blindly hurling itself against the sides of its cage, and when they held firm against its vehemence, it came swooping down the chimneys howling its protestations. Nassy closed the dampers, but the wind whined and sobbed out its defeat in the flues.

Negu sat in the serving pantry, putting the silver flatware back into the heavy wooden chests. It took a long time to get a house back to order after a big party, but she didn't mind the work. She lovingly polished each piece with a soft clean cloth until it was a mirror throwing back the reflection of the dancing candle on the table. This was all Asya's. As she worked, Negu hummed. All Asya's.

Evadne and Nassy sat watching her. They had offered to help, but she refused. They could not know how she felt about the silver. It must be perfect. Not the shadow of one fingerprint when Asya came to claim her heritage.

After a while, she asked the couple, "Why do you stay here? Your work is done." She wanted to be alone with her thoughts. Somehow it brought Asya closer by just thinking about her granddaughter and her delight when she would see silver.

In a quiet voice, Evadne answered, "We'uns scared. The more folks what sit together on a night like this, the better it be."

"Nonsense," Negu rebuked. "It's only a storm. It will pass."

"Ah hope so," the cook answered in a morbid tone, "but the loas sure peeved about somethin' tonight. Old Petro Loa is crackin' his whip till all the dead folk in the ground is moanin' how it hurts."

Nassy slowly nodded his head in agreement. "Jist like yah say. The dead is really howlin' tonight. That whip, it stings good."

At this point, the door opened, and Cilla came into the room. She was Evadne and Nassy's fifteen-year-old daughter. Her father was training her to be a parlor maid.

"You git all dem candles snuffed out already?" Nassy inquired in amazement. "Gal, you work fast like dat, and I soon lose my job."

"No, M. Drapeaux, he call me," the girl answered. "He's fixin' to git hisself early to bed, and he wants a bottle of claret brought up."

"All right. Why dint yah say so? I'll fetch it 'mediately." The butler rose to his feet and started toward the wine cabinet.

"No," Cilla shook her head. "He don't want yah should bring it. He 'specially said for me to git it. Also *two* glasses." Her brown eyes had a look of apprehension.

Nassy whirled around and stared disbelievingly at his daughter. Negu glanced at the girl and then gave her attention back to the silver. Furiously she rubbed the knife in her hand. Inwardly, she seethed. The nerve of him. Trying to bed with a child. Poor frightened Cilla. She was a skinny little bird, ready to fly off in any direction at the thought of doing something nice for anyone. A fragile doll meant to be more than a bedfellow for a sweaty old man to froth over. Negu loved Cilla. Everyone did.

"Chile," her father roared as he found his voice, "*I'll* take the wine bottle and two glasses. Big glasses, and him and me will drink together, and I'll tell him my little girl ain't no whore." Nassy's thin chest bloated with ire and his eyes looked like two black shots aimed to fire.

The girl shook with fear. "Please don't. M'sieur will git angry, and make you and Mama work out in the fields."

"We ain't slaves no more," Evadne shouted as she commandeered the conversation. In indignation, she slowly heaved her bulky body to her feet. "We's our own country now and we got our own nigger leader. If we'uns don't like where we work, we quit. Your papa will carry the wine up to his fat maj'sty and if he had any guts he'd hand it to him with a good whack on the head. And you, young lady," she addressed her daughter like a general pronouncing doom at a court-martial, "you hie yourself to your bed, and if I iver catch you so much as walkin' in the same room as Master Drapeaux, I'll take the strap to your little behind."

It was then that the sound came. It came from outside the kitchen door, but they could all hear it from where they were gathered in the pantry. Quietly, and unmoving, they listened. There it was again. A small wail trying to give birth to a sound. At first it was muted, but it kept trying until it grew stronger and finally forced it way into the ears of the listeners. Was it the wind shut out, sobbing its grief through the cracks of the door? Or was it the loas of the dead, blowing breath for the mourners to use at the wake?

A footstep sounded outside the door. As light a step as only a spirit might let fall, but it was enough to break the spell on the listeners.

"Mama," Cilla cried, "I'm afraid." She threw her thin arms about her mother's neck and pulled herself close against the enfolding bosom.

Evadne sat down and drew her daughter up on her lap. The hands that patted the girl's back were shaking.

"I ain't goin' nowhere," Nassy said as he walked toward the table. His figure had quickly lost its former air of bravado, and his chest was sunken more than usual. His knees were trembling when he sat down, and he leaned closer to the candle for its warmth.

"I ain't goin' nowhere," he repeated. "Ah's just settin' here. Tha's one of them loa spirits out huntin' for a man to die. and I don' aim to git caught."

Negu returned to her polishing. Lovely silver. Soon it would all be Asya's. Her lips did not move, but there was humming in her breast.

The next morning, André Drapeaux did not keep his promise to M. Rowbottom to visit his solicitor. He was ill. By early afternoon, he was dead. The physician, called in too late, ascertained that it must have been the heart since Monsieur was of an age when overexertion could be taxing, and as he recalled, the recent ball had been a stimulating affair. However, he philosophized, it was the right time to go, when one was in a happy state. With that remark, and an aside to Negu to say he would send the deceased's dimensions to the coffinmaker, he departed.

Since the weather was hot and the coffin was completed, Monsieur was buried the next day. Mlle. Eloise did not come to pay her last respects to her late fiancé. M. Rowbottom, who came with a group of businessmen from Cap François, mentioned that his daughter had become hysterical when she learned of her loss and had to be quieted with drugs.

Humph, thought Negu when she heard. She's bemoaning the loss to her purse, not to her heart.

That same evening, although the weather was still hot and there was no breeze, Negu ordered all the shutters of the great house to be closed. "It is so that his spirit, if it returns, cannot come in to haunt us," she explained.

She went to the library where Nassy had carried the six large requiem candlesticks after the funeral. She wanted to shine them and wrap them well, for now they too belonged to Asya. They were of solid gold and were used only when a member of the Drapeaux family passed away. It would be nice, she thought longingly, if niggers could have golden candlesticks at their funerals too. It lent a prosperous note to the corpse.

The house was quiet, and it was easy to hear the call when it came from the night. The shutters were closed, but the plea reached Negu's ears as she sat on the floor working with the candlesticks.

"Help. Help. Come help me." It was a struggling cry, the kind one tries to make during a nightmare and cannot quite get out.

Negu sat unmoved, listening to the call. The distressed crier was walking slowly. She could hear his voice as he came up the carriage drive toward the front door. "Help. Help. Save me."

Joswee had wasted no time. She wondered whose body now lay in the Drapeaux mausoleum in the tomb which would eventually be marked as André's. Probably some diseased field hand who had never known the touch of a silk pillow beneath his head. She laughed noiselessly. Mme. Drapeaux would surely be indignant over lying for all eternity by the side of a black man.

She wondered if Joswee and his fellow hounci had to hit Monsieur very hard on the head to awaken him from his induced sleep. She hoped he had a bump from the blow, but she doubted it. Joswee knew how to do his job. He would have given just the right tap, enough to keep the victim conscious but not alert enough to try to fight. He must also be able to make the slow walk from the graveyard to the house. So far so good.

Suddenly, the woman heard light footsteps running toward the front door of the house. Quickly, she jumped to her feet and ran into the hall. All her work would be futile if the victim was admitted to his home again. It was Cilla trying to unbolt the door.

"There's some poor man outside calling for help. Can't you hear him, Negu? Help me with this door and we'll bring him in."

The woman reached out and, with a quick blow of her hand, slapped the girl to the floor. "Don't open that door," she ordered.

In bewilderment, Cilla looked up at Negu. No black person had ever struck her before.

"That is the ghost of the master who calls," the older woman explained. "He is lonesome and wants company. The first human he sees he will take to the grave with him." She held out her hand and pulled the girl to her feet. "I'm sorry I had to hit you, *cherie,* but I did it for your own good. Now run to your mama and

178

stay with her until his spirit has gone back to the tomb."

Cilla let out a hysterical yell. Placing her hands across her mouth to hold back her fright, she tore off toward the rear of the house.

When the girl had gone, Negu stood by the door. The voice was now receding down the other side of the drive and out onto the road. It was necessary for M. Drapeaux to pass his home for the last time on his way to the hounfort, else, so the laos decreed, he would be restored to life one day and return to claim his possessions.

As the cry faded away, Negu knew it would be a while before the procession of the man and his accompaning hounci from the grave reached the hounfort. There Joswee would be waiting with the potion. A potion which he alone knew how to concoct. It was the one secret the medicine man had not shared with her.

"It is too great a knowledge to place in the hands of a woman," he had said. "To know how to raise a man up from his coffin, to make him walk and work for you, and yet be dead, is a dangerous magic. A woman is a creature of whimsy or fancy emotion. It is better I keep some of my art for myself."

Often, however, he had permitted her to watch him at work and now she knew what was awaiting Monsieur. The fire would be burning high before the altar in the voodoo temple. Black shadows would leap about the walls of the hounfort, made not by the flames but cast by the gods who had come dancing to the ceremony. Tired by his long walk from the family burial plot and frightened in his semiconscious state, Drapeaux would be half dragged to the flames by the lesser hounci. Tears would probably flow down those fat cheeks, tears of weakness, of hopelessness. His last earthly emotion. Then a cut would be made on the left temple, after which he would fall to the earthen floor. At first, the open cut would reject the potion, and blood and brew would mix on the side of the man's

179

head. But soon it would take effect, sapping the mind and the will with its wetness. M. Drapeaux would cease to moan, and his tears would stop, for those are the reactions of the living.

For the rest of the night, he would lie dormant on the floor until the fire died and the shadows no longer played about the walls. This would mean the gods had departed and taken with them the soul of André Drapeaux.

In the morning Joswee would have another zombie for hire.

Chapter Fourteen

For Asya Drapeaux the Hospice of the Sacre-Coeur was home. The white-robed sisters were her family, and Asya was happy. Asya had no knowledge of life outside the walls of the hospital. She expected that she too would grow up and one day become a nun who took care of babies and their mothers.

Each morning as she prayed, "Dear Angel of God, my Guardian Dear, to whom God's love commits me here, ever this day be at my side; to light, to guard, to rule and to guide," she saw her own angel in the form of the Queen of Prussia: beautiful, blond, in silken robes; eyes smiling down in love; and arms out to ward off danger. The queen must surely have been God's gift to the hospital, thought Asya, because the nuns of the Sacre-Coeur closed all their prayers and chants with words of thanksgiving for her, their patroness.

It was true, that the nuns at Sacre-Coeur owed the queen a great debt of gratitude. She had built them a large new wing which the nuns referred to as Queen Sophia's Ward. And she had given them donations for all their babies. Several times a year the queen would arrive for a visit. All work and prayer would cease until she had been properly greeted. She would throw her arms about Mère Magdelaine, and they would cry together. Asya had never understood why they wept when they were all so happy, but Mère Denise explained that real happiness touched the heart and that was where tears started. Then they would laugh together, and the visitor would kiss all the old nuns and meet the new ones. Asya was happy to be included in the class of old regulars since she was hugged and kissed too. The queen always smelled so very good—like guardian angels should.

The queen's carriage was driven by an old man, whose head was as shiny and bald as the big newel post in the entrance hall and who appeared just as sturdy. His name was Butte. Since both he and Asya were outsiders, being neither infants nor women, they were drawn together. He began to bring her little toys which he himself carved from wood: a bossy-looking hen; a silly goose; a shaggy dog with its mouth wide open in a bark. To look at them made Asya laugh. She loved each of them equally. The queen also brought her gifts, but they were beautiful expensive dolls, much better for sitting on a shelf in her bedroom. Butte's presents were for everyday playing.

Butte told her stories, wonderful stories about shipwrecks on the Rhine, and goddesses flying through the sky, and a beautiful mermaid with golden hair. And about the time the Devil washed his feet in the well in the village square and the water turned black. His stories were much better than the ones the nuns told about Jesus cleaning up the floor in the carpenter shop for his poor tired old father or about Jeanne D'Arc seeing visions and saving France. How could one have fun, wearing old armor and sleeping on the ground!

The last time Butte drove the queen to the hospital of the Sacre-Coeur, he brought Asya a beautiful necklace of black roses. The wood had come from the Black Forest, and each rose was no larger than the tip of her finger. He had carved each flower by hand and joined them together with a silver thread. "For you to remember me by when you are a beautiful *fräulein*, and I am no longer here. I made one for the queen when she was *mein kleines Mädchen*, and now I have made one for you. You are the only two little girls I have ever known."

182

That was the last gift Asya received from Butte. He died before the queen made her next visit.

One day toward the end of Asya's thirteenth summer Mère Magdelaine sent for her and told her she must go away to school. Asya did not want to leave the hospital. She could not understand why she could not remain there forever. She knew all the prayers by heart and most of the Bible from hearing it read so often. Why should she have to learn to read and write and speak many languages? One could deliver babies without knowing anything about books. However, early one fall morning, the Queen of Prussia came with her new, austere-looking coachman and drove Asya to what seemed like the end of the world.

"This is a very fine boarding school," the queen explained. "You must be educated. You can't grow up like a peasant."

"Why not?" Asya cried. She loved her patron, the queen, but missed Soeur Denise and the other nuns almost as soon as the carriage had departed. "I want to go home," she wailed. "I want to go home."

Queen Sophia stroked her black hair. "You'll love the idea of school once you get used to it," she said softly. "School is the place for fine young ladies, Asya. Don't you want to be a fine lady?"

But Asya only wept louder and buried her head in the fur-lined corner of the carriage. And soon her sobs were drowned out by the thundering of horses' hoofs as the carriage picked up speed, carrying her farther and farther away from the hospital she knew as home.

After a while she lifted her head and, looking at the queen, sobbed, "Mère Denise was wrong. When tears start in the heart it isn't from happiness. It's from hurt, 'cause my heart hurts."

Although her eyes were so swollen that she could scarcely open them, Asya saw the queen burst into tears. Taken by surprise, she momentarily forgot her own grief. She moved close and asked, "Why do you cry? You are a queen and queens don't have hurts, just happiness."

Queen Sophia put her arms about Asya and the two wept together until Asya fell asleep on her shoulder. She did not awaken until they had arrived at the boarding school. A sleepy-eyed Asya made no effort to protest further. Turning her cheek for Queen Sophia's farewell kiss, she hugged the grand lady and then, without emotion, watched her drive away.

With a sigh, Asya turned to follow the strange nun who was leading her to her room. She did not like the new nun. She was not going to like any of the soeurs whom she passed in the hall. They wore ugly habits with stiff white collars. They did not want little girls putting their arms about their necks, not like Mère Denise whose neck was easily available for hugging. She was not going to like anything here. She would not open a book. Eventually they would have to send her home.

Contrary to her determination, Asya did open her books. The world of knowledge fascinated her and was a refuge from her homesickness. In addition, buried in her schoolbooks, Asya was able to remain apart from the other young ladies at the school. They all seemed so strange to her and she was afraid of them. One little girl frightened her more than the others. Her name was Eleanore. Eleanore had long, silky blond hair, a pert turned-up nose, and china-blue eyes. She was popular with the other students and traveled surrounded by them, resembling a queen bee and her hive. One day, Eleanore and her cohorts could stand Asya's aloof attitude no longer and they descended upon her.

"Are you a princess?" Eleanore asked.

"No. I'm Asya. Just Asya."

"I'm a princess," Eleanore told her and stuck her flip little nose higher in the air. "I'm a princess of the House of Ludwig."

Asya studied Eleanore in surprise. To her a princess was a beautiful young lady with a jeweled tiara on her head who rode in a golden barouche to great balls in a big warm castle on the Rhine. Not a schoolgirl, dressed in a brown uniform and long winter underwear, pretty though she might be.

"My friends here are all of the nobility too," Eleanore informed in a haughty tone. "Gretchen is going to be a queen when she is eighteen. Martha is a duchess, and her uncle is a close friend to Napoleon. Stephanie is a cousin to the handsome Czar Alexander of Russia and she already has her own castle. Everyone here is an aristocrat. If you're not, how did you get into our school?"

Asya had never given any thought to her acceptance into this institution of learning. Nor would she have divulged that information to her inquisitor had she known how she had arrived there. Instead, she looked Eleanore directly in the eyes and snapped, "It's none of your business."

Eleanore gave a nasty laugh as she turned to her companions. "Oh, girls," she said, "she must be an orphan who doesn't know any better. She's so vulgar. I saw who brought her here. It was the Queen of Prussia, and you know how she's always being charitable to paupers. Why, just look at her," Eleanore rambled on. "She is made funny. Her skin is too dark and she has black hair, the same color as the ebony table in the visitor's salon. Who ever heard of hair the color of furniture! And as if that wasn't odd enough, her eyes are so light! Gray-blue eyes look good on a redhead, but not on her! She's like a mongrel dog, made up of something from everything! And perhaps if she lost some of that plumpness, she might have some semblance of a figure." With that, the girl gave Asya a hard slap across the stomach, causing her breath to be expelled in an explosive sound. The other girls burst into laughter and Asya felt like a court clown.

It was simply too much for her. A feeling of intense hatred surged up inside Asya, unlike any other she had ever known. Before she could think, she raised her hand and slapped Eleanore hard across the mouth. Then, unable to curb her fury, she pulled Eleanore's hair and slapped that stuck-up nose with all the force she could gather. The attack turned into a free-for-all, as Asya felt hands tearing at her own hair and pummeling her face. She was thrown to the floor and drowned in kicks from hard school shoes. She was scratched and bitten, but she flailed out with fists and feet. If she was hurt she was too angry to feel pain.

At last the bodies were thrust aside, and Asya found herself pinioned firmly on the floor. She looked up to find four nuns clutching angrily at each of her limbs. Their appearance startled her. The beautifully starched ruffled collars were squashed, bloody scratches lacerated their faces, and their headpieces were knocked off, revealing shaved heads. One nun had a bleeding ear. It could have been bitten. The other girls had fled, leaving Asya alone to face the condemning court.

"You will get up, Asya," a cold voice ordered. It was the superior, Mère Aurelia. "Go to your room."

Asya fled, thankful that she had not been punished before the enemy. That humiliation she could not have borne.

Later, back in her room, Asya examined her eyes in the mirror. Eleanore was right. They did not match the rest of her. She was like that dog with the strange eyes. The kind you could see through. What was it called? A Weimaraner. I don't care if I am funny-looking, she consoled herself. I'm rich. I'll buy boatloads of silks and have more clothes than any princess. I'll hire an army of servants and boss them around. Someday. I shall be the richest woman in St. Domingue!

Mère Aurelia never asked the cause of the altercation, but later that afternoon she summoned both girls to her office and spoke sternly to them.

"Young ladies do not fight. They respect one another's mind and person. If one finds herself in disagreement with another's attitude, she does not show her disapproval by indulging in street brawling. The

Lord Jesus," she paused to bow her head in reverence at the mention of the Holy Name, "set us all an example of forbearance by his suffering on the way to Calvary. So that you may have time to reflect on the lesson He gave all mankind, you will both rise at five each morning and report to the chapel. There you will recite the Way of the Cross aloud together. You will repeat the service each evening after supper and then come directly to my office for your evening studies. This routine will continue until I deem a change is warranted. Good night." She looked each girl in the eye and added in a scathing voice, "*Ladies.*"

With those words, Asya felt the warm flush of shame in her cheeks. She had been more humbled than if Mère Aurelia had given her a tongue-lashing before the entire student body.

For the first week, the girls recited the prescribed prayers like two wooden puppets. After the service, they walked stiffly down to the mother superior's office and sat there, ignored and lifeless, except to turn the pages in their school texts. Asya felt only cold resentment for the girl. Eleanore must have been experiencing the same feeling, for at the beginning of the second week of the sentence, she whispered from behind her school book, "It was all your fault. You had no business slapping my face."

"You shouldn't have talked to me like that," Asya said in a low voice without looking up from her work. It was the first they had spoken to each other since that awful day. After a few minutes of silence, Eleanore whispered again, "You punched my nose hard. It still hurts."

"Good." Asya kept her voice low so as not to bring one of the nuns running into the office. "Maybe you'll learn to keep it out of other people's business."

"I hate you."

Asya did not answer. Somehow vindictiveness lost its savor when one had to battle in whispers.

Several nights later, a storm rose while the two girls

sat alone in the superior's office. Lightning danced mockingly past the window, and thunder blasted menacingly in the sky. The rain threw itself in torrents against the glass as it tried to crash its way in. Neither girl could study.

"I don't know why we have to sit in this spooky old office every night just because we had a fight," Eleanore grumbled.

"I don't either," Asya agreed. She sat very still, for she had the feeling that if she did not move the storm could not touch her.

"I'm afraid." Eleanore was close to tears.

"So am I, but I won't let them know it. They would think it served us right for fighting. I'll bet they're scared too."

"I can just see them lighting all the blessed candles in the school to keep away the lightning," Eleanore said scornfully.

"Everybody's probably gathered in the chapel praying for the Lord to spare His wrath."

"They didn't bring us a blessed candle. I guess they think we deserve His wrath."

"Probably forgot about us," Asya stated in a matter-of-fact voice. Talking released the tension the storm had built up in her.

"Or if they do think of us at all, they probably feel we deserve to sit here all scared and frightened by ourselves."

"I'm not scared. I'll show them. I'm not afraid at all." Asya closed her schoolbook. "I'm not going to study. I'm going to watch the storm." She walked to the window. Meeting the storm face to face removed some of its fearsomeness. Watching the rain was actually fascinating. This was spring, and all the storm really did was wash away the ugliness of winter from the earth. It was God's scrub brush. So engrossed had she become in the tumultuous world outside the window that she momentarily forgot about her fellow culprit until Eleanore stood beside her and said, "It *is* much

188

better looking at the storm than cringing away from it, isn't it?"

The girls watched until the storm spent itself and the rain fell with a steady, monotonous hum. Only then did they become aware that the hostility between them had dissolved. Eleanore was the first to speak. "I don't know why those old nuns have to get so incensed simply because we were having a little fight."

"I don't either," Asya agreed. "That was our business. I don't know why outsiders have to butt in. They had no idea what it was all about. We can settle our own affairs our own way."

"You're a good fighter, Asya."

Asya giggled. "So are you. I'll bet that's the most excitement those old nuns have had around here for years."

Eleanore snickered. "Didn't Soeur Susanne look funny with her shaved head and her banged-up ear? Did you bite it?"

"No. I thought you did." Asya giggled softly.

"I'm sorry about the name-calling, Asya," whispered Eleanore. "I guess I did sound pretty nasty."

"I didn't have to be so secretive about myself. I could have told you that my parents came from French St. Domingue."

"French St. Domingue!" Eleanore gasped. "Napoleon's Josephine comes from somewhere near there. I hear Mama talk about her. She's so beautiful and popular. She's a Creole. Maybe you'll grow up to be like her and marry a world conqueror."

"I hope so," said Asya. And even as she answered her new friend she could feel beauty sprout out about her like roots from an old potato.

Chapter Fifteen

After their long penance was over, Asya and Eleanore became friends. As the years passed, they were practically inseparable and one hardly ever saw one without the other by her side.

One afternoon, the day before Asya's fifteenth birthday, Eleanore pranced excitedly into her friend's room, holding a pale-blue envelope high in the air. "Asya," she squealed delightedly. "You shall never guess the news!"

Asya, sprawled across her bed where she was completely engrossed in a homework assignment, looked up impatiently. "What is it, Eleanore?"

"I've just received a letter from my mother, and she's invited you to our home for the Christmas holiday! Isn't that grand? Oh, you *will* come, won't you?"

For a second, a pained expression crossed Asya's face. Christmas! Each year it had become more unbearable. The other girls all had homes to go to, while Asya had to spend her holiday in the cold dark school whose only concession to the season was a crib in the chapel and three Masses a day instead of one. At Christmastime, home was the place to be, and Asya was always reminded of the fact that she didn't have one.

"Asya! You *will* come, say you will!"

"Yes, Eleanore," Asya smiled. "Of course, I shall."

"Oh, just think how much fun we shall have!" Eleanore babbled on excitedly. "And, Asya, you know what else Mother says in her letter? She says that

Creoles have always been the richest people in the world. They were at one time even richer than queens and princesses! Imagine! But that is, of course, providing they still have their plantations." She paused for a moment. "Does your father still have his?"

Asya had no idea what M. Drapeaux owned. All she knew was that a man from an island on the other side of the world sent money to Mère Magdelaine for her support. They said the money came from her father. Her going to live with him was just something that would eventually happen. Like the end of the world. No one gave much concern as to when it might occur. Not wanting to disappoint Eleanore, she answered, "Why, of course. And someday I shall go and live on it."

As Christmas approached, Asya began to worry slightly about her trip to Eleanore's home. Eleanore had always bragged about their great wealth, and Asya was afraid that she had neither the manners nor the proper clothes to wear.

"Oh, pooh! You are probably richer than we are, Asya. And, anyway, it is time you became accustomed to these things. Perhaps my brother will teach you what it means to be a young lady," said Eleanore, a twinkle in her eye.

At the mention of Kaspar, Eleanore's brother, Asya grew pale. She knew nothing about boys and she was, she had to admit, afraid of them. "What do I say to him, Eleanore? I know so little about boys. I've never met any."

"Then it's about time you did! Kaspar will give you a real education. Or would you rather become a nun and wear a plain black habit all your life and never know what you're missing?"

Eleanore made the monastic life sound like a real threat to happiness. "No, no. I suppose you're right."

But, from the very beginning, the long weekend at the House of Ludwig was a fiasco. Kaspar had brought a friend home for the holidays, with whom Eleanore became immediately enchanted. Eleanore spent so much time with the young man that Asya was left pretty much on her own. No one seemed to have much time for the young guest. No one, that is, except for Kaspar, who followed her around like a puppy.

From the moment she had met Kaspar, Asya did not like him. The way his eyes rolled over her body made her feel like one of Mère Denise's unclothed infants during a physical examination. Then one afternoon everything quickly came to a head. Wanting to get away by herself for a while, Asya had slipped into the library. It was while she was on tiptoe, reaching up for a book, that she suddenly felt someone's hands on her breasts. It was Kaspar. He was behind her, his lips on the back of her neck. She tried to free herself from his grasp, but he held her firmly.

"Don't be frightened." His breath was hot on her skin as he spoke, and between each word his wet tongue stroked the flesh of her neck. "I'm not clumsy. I know how."

His one hand began to unbutton the top of her dress and she screamed.

"Shut up," he hissed. "Do you want someone to hear us and spoil our fun?"

"Let me go. Let me go!" She reached up over her head and pulled his hair hard with both her hands, but instead of releasing her, he sank his teeth into her neck. The more she pulled, the harder he bit. At the same time, her breasts hurt from his tight grasp. Frustrated, she quickly grabbed one of his hands in both hers and managed to move it close enough to her mouth to give him a vicious bite. He was taken by surprise and relaxed his grip on her as he let out a roar of pain. She jumped free and ran toward the door. Before she could reach it, the door opened and Eleanore's mother walked in.

"What's going on in here?" she demanded indignantly, her eyes condemning without trial as they took in Asya's appearance.

Asya began to cry. It was all so hopeless.

"What's happened to your hair?" his mother asked Kaspar. "And your hand? It's red. I think an explanation is due your mother, and—" turning her eyes back to Asya, "your hostess."

Asya looked at her interrogator, but could not find her voice. With tears of humiliation running down her cheeks, all Asya could do was stand there and button her dress.

"Son," Eleanore's mother said gently, "you will tell me, won't you, dear?"

"Of course, *Mutter*. While I hate to, it is your right to know what type of guest we have in our home."

Asya's tears stopped. She watched as Kaspar walked slowly up to his mother, his head shaking in disapproval.

"It's too bad about some of the students they admit to that school Sis goes to. Poor unsuspecting Eleanore. She's so naive, too."

"Whatever do you mean?" His mother's voice rose in alarm.

"I'm talking about our *dear* little houseguest," Kaspar answered. "She made advances to me. Wher-*ever* do those little convent schoolgirls learn so much, Mutter? I think you should have a talk with her."

"*I* made advances to you?" Asya found her voice again. "You liar!"

Kaspar sneered, "Don't try to defend yourself." Then he lifted his wounded hand. "See, *Mutter*," he explained, "look what she did to my hand when I told her to lay off."

"Oh, my poor little boy." The queen was horrified. "We have a wild animal in the house." She picked up his hand and held it against her cheek. Turning to Asya she asked, "How could you abuse our hospitality in such a wanton manner? How *could* you?"

"He's lying. I tell you, he's lying!" Asya pleaded.

In a voice trembling with rage, her hostess screeched out, "My son does not lie. He does not lie to his own mother." She hugged her son closer to her bosom. "Young lady, go to your room. I will see what is to be done about this deplorable situation." She was visibly trying to control her emotions. While the queen's cold eyes were still upon Asya, Kaspar slipped his hand around his mother's back and dangled something in Asya's direction. She gasped. It was her black necklace. Asya's hand flew to her neck. It was bare. Kaspar had somehow stolen Butte's gift.

"That's mine!" she yelled, starting toward him. "Give it to me."

The queen stepped in front of her. "Have you lost your mind. I told you to go to your room."

"Kaspar has my necklace, and I want it," she sobbed. "It belongs to me. He can't have it."

The queen turned to Kaspar, who had quickly put his hand with the necklace into his pocket and was now staring at his mother with childlike innocence. "I don't know what she's talking about, *Mutter*. I think the girl is a little addled in the head. I have nothing of hers. See for yourself." Whereupon he stretched out both hands. "See, I have nothing."

"It's in his pocket," Asya shouted. "I saw him put it in his pocket. Look there and you will see for yourself."

The queen drew herself up haughtily. "I would not insult my own son by doubting his word. He has nothing of yours."

The injustice of it all caused an explosive feeling in Asya's breast. She tore past the woman, and taking the boy by surprise, flung herself upon him. The impact threw him to the floor, and she tore with her nails at his face as though she would rip it apart. "I want my necklace. I want my necklace. You stole it. I want it!" she shouted through tears. "Give it to me!"

The strength of her fury was not enough against Kaspar, and he knocked her from him, crashing her head against the terrazzo floor. She remembered nothing until a severe headache awakened her later in her room. That same day, a servant packed her few belongings. She was sent back to school. No one came to tell her good-bye.

Later, when Eleanore returned to school she came to Asya's room. "What a stinking fuss about nothing that silly mama of mine made. To listen to her rave one would think that only animals should know about mating. 'That dear, sweet innocent Kaspar,' she always says." Eleanore's tone grew insipid as she imitated her mother's voice. " 'I wish the bold girls would leave the dear boy alone.' Hell! He's been chasing girls so long that I think the kid was born for it!"

Asya shivered in revulsion. "He is like an animal."

"He is, isn't he?" Eleanore laughed. "But that's my big brother. That's the way he is. Can't do anything about it. It's his way of having fun. You should have cooperated. You have to learn sometime, and the nuns can't teach you as well as Kaspar can. It was your big opportunity. You should see the nice gifts he hands out to the girls who please him."

Asya burst into tears, burying her head in her pillow. "I wonder who shall receive the necklace he stole from me," she sobbed.

"Oh, for Christ's sake." Eleanore was exasperated. "If you miss that damn necklace so much, here, take my bracelet. My mother gave it to me for Christmas." She held out a circlet of rubies.

Asya shook her head.

"There's more where this came from. Keep it." Eleanore took Asya's hand and placed the jewelry in it, but Asya flung the bracelet to the floor.

"Fool!" Eleanore said in derision. "Everybody does it. Silly little girls like you end up unwanted spinsters." Stooping, she picked up the bracelet and scornfully left the room.

Asya was relieved at the close of the school term. Now she could return to the hospital. She could share her pain with Mère Denise. But when she arrived she was disappointed to learn that both Mère Denise and Mère Magdelaine were away in Rome on official business. There was no one to whom she could confide her hurt.

And then, swiftly, suddenly, came the turning point in Asya's life. The morning after her return to the hospital, as she sat feeling lonely and sorry for herself, her solicitor arrived at the hospital. In an urgent voice, he told Soeur Brigitte, acting head of the hospital, that Asya must leave immediately for St. Domingue. It was time for her to journey there to claim her inheritance. There was no time to lose, for if she did not go at once, she would be in some danger of losing everything.

Soeur Brigitte was in a quandary. Should she let Asya go? What would Mère Magdelaine do in her place? Finally, she gave in to the blustery determination of the lawyer. She sent Asya packing.

Asya accepted the decision bravely, almost anxious to turn this corner in her life. She had felt an urgency burning within her for some time. It was the tug of the future. It was her destiny calling to her. Whatever it might be, she would face it.

Before her departure, Asya went to Mère Denise's office. She wished there could be a miracle and she might find the nun sitting at her desk. But the chair was empty. Her eyes roamed over the office, and Asya recalled little happenings from her happy, protected past. The closet where Mère Denise kept the records of all the babies born in the hospital. Only Mère Denise and Mère Magdelaine were permitted to see what was written in the big books. No one else. The closet was never locked, for no one would break the trust placed in her. The hard wooden chair by the desk was strong enough to hold a white-robed nun and a little girl on her lap. There, Mère Denise had told her stories. About what? She could not remember now, but they were always beautiful. Asya used to think everyone loved each other until she went to school and learned about hate. She wanted to tell Mère Denise all about her hatred and have the nun change it back to love, but her one friend was gone, and Asya, beneath her brave front, was bewildered and scared. She knew she was rich and rich people were supposed to be happy. But somehow she did not feel very happy. Her eyes fell upon the statue of St. Martha in a niche in the wall. St. Martha was Mère Denise's favorite saint.

"I like her," the nun used to say. "She's a sensible saint. She didn't believe in merely talking about goodness, but she went ahead and did something about it. While Maria sat and visited with the Lord, Martha shined up the house until it looked good for their guest. After Maria had made Him hungry with all her talk, Martha had fixed something for Him to eat."

"I thought in the Bible Jesus said that Maria had chosen the better thing to do," Asya had argued.

"He ate the dinner, didn't He?" Mère Denise asked. That had terminated the discussion.

Asya studied the statue. The face was plain. In one hand she held a pitcher and her sleeves were rolled up, indicating she was in the midst of some household chore. Always, Mère Denise had kept a candle burning at the feet of the saint. Without the light now, the room felt cold and forsaken, like the chapel on Good Friday after the Blessed Sacrament was carried out.

Asya lit a candle and placed it in the red glass holder before the saint. She watched as the flame flickered and swayed like a babe awkwardly trying to stand upright. Then it burned with a warm glow, steady, bright, ever reaching upward like the spirit of Mère Denise.

Asya's heart ached for a word from someone who loved her. She was leaving her home with no more fanfare of farewell than was accorded one of the cows from the Sacre-Coeur farm when it was full grown for market. She wept and a tear dropped upon the candle, causing it to flicker wildly.

It seemed to be shaking its head at her and saying,

"No, no, no. Don't cry, my darling," just as Mère Denise would have done.

Asya rubbed her eyes on the sleeves of her dress. Still sobbing, she prayed, "Little candle, burn so long as you can, for when you have died out, so will my childhood be gone. Just as then there will be darkness in this room, so will my heart feel cold, and I will have grown up."

Through her tears, she looked at the face of St. Martha, softer now in the light of the candle. "Watch over her, St. Martha, watch over Mère Denise." Again she wiped her tears on her sleeve. "Don't bother about me. I will take care of myself from now on. I will take care of Asya."

Slowly she turned her back on the glowing statue and walked from the room, leaving the candle to flicker on into the night.

Part Two

Chapter Sixteen

St. Domingue had not always been so named. Long before Columbus came to the island, when the peaceful Caribs inhabited the land, it was called Haiti. The Carib word for mountainous, reaching toward the sky.

Slavery in the New World began on this once-lovely island. The greedy Spanish were the first to import the black man from Africa to do the heavy work of searching out the gold they were certain must be there. Their handling of the human cargo was inhumane. Naked, shackled together in irons, the slaves were so thickly crowded on shelves in the windowless holds of the ships which carried them to Haiti that when one man urinated, he wet those beside him. So close above their heads was the next shelf of miserable prisoners that no one could sit up. Nor move so much as to lean on an elbow, for there was no room between him and the next man.

When the sea was rough, the chattel was not taken out on deck for its daily airing. Some were helplessly suffocated by their fellow wretches, and often it was days before the corpse was removed.

On calm days or nights, one could hear the banshee moaning of the heartbroken, the homesick; the crying for loved ones never to be seen again.

But the mad search uncovered no gold, and the Spanish turned the slave to the fields. Then the great plantations began. When the soil became more valuable than gold, the French sailed in and, after bathing the rich land in black and Spanish blood, claimed the island for France. They called it St. Domingue. Next the English, looking over the waters from Jamaica, took note of how great an asset such productive soil could be to the coffers of the king, and they came by to forcibly discuss the idea with the French governor. After wiping out all French residents, the English won the discussion. A bloody business, but the King of England was pleased!

So it went, country after country, each claiming the island for its own. Finally, France recaptured the western half and Spain the eastern half. For years they lived side by side, ignoring one another as if a wide sea lay between. The French built great plantations from the harvests the soil yielded. They produced tobacco, mahogany, and, above all, sugar cane, which the New England traders took home to be made into rum. Soon the French colony was so affluent that to be "rich as a Creole" became the continental measuring stick of wealth.

And then the black man rose up against the French, claiming the land on which he had toiled in slavery as his in freedom. Dessalines, the Old Tiger, holed up in the mountains. His followers were ready to slaughter or be slaughtered in the fight for the possession of their own country, but Dessalines was sharp enough to realize that he would have difficulty combating a white man's army. His knowledge was that of the jungle, his specialty a quiet emergence from the forests at night to deal death with the machete. Although he had the firearms and the gunpowder that he and Christophe had collected from their own men and never turned in to Leclere, he did not have military knowledge.

He was pleased, therefore, when Captain Etienne Grenier, arriving with Desaix and the new recruits, offered to make soldiers out of the ragged maroons. For months he watched as Captain Grenier stayed in the mountains with the guerrillas, training them in the military art.

202

Their desire for freedom made them quick learners. Just as the black army was ready to come down from its stronghold in the mountains to drive the French off the land, one of their spies spotted the approaching English fleet from Jamaica. Etienne sent a note to the flagship by native swimmer. It was a request for the Britishers to bottle up the French frigates in the harbor while Dessalines and his army, under the generalship of the former French cuirassier of the heavy cavalry attacked by land. The British, ever delighted to do a bad turn to their perpetual enemy, cooperated and the French were beaten.

Etienne was with Dessalines aboard the English frigate when the Tiger roared out his terms of peace to the defeated Rochambeau. The once proud and haughty Frenchman stood on the deck, staring vacantly out to sea. His aquiline nose now spread across the center of his face in a mound of bumps like a flabby bag of pebbles. Where the front teeth were missing, the upper lip had already folded under, giving Rochambeau the appearance of a senile old man. The general would forever carry the mark of his beating.

When he saw his former captain in the company of the new conqueror of St. Domingue, Rochambeau spat out, "Traitor!" However, with his front teeth missing, the epithet came out as "Twaitor," adding a ludicrous touch to his downfall.

It was after he had placed his mark on the papers of surrender that Dessalines picked up the French flag which lay on the table between him and the French general. Holding it under Rochambeau's mangled nose, he tore the white strip from between the blue and the red and flung it into his adversary's face. "Never!" he shouted, "never will white man rule this land again. From now on, it belong to nobody but us blacks!" Then he added, "And us's name is Haiti."

A short time later, Etienne left the island. The war was over and his side had won from a military standpoint. Dessalines no longer needed him. Dessalines needed no one. He was top man. He strutted about, pounded his chest, and shouted, "I am de chief. I led yous to win. Nobody tells de chief how he runs de tribe."

Rising from field hand to "chief" was a monumental step for Dessalines. Knowing nothing about statesmanship, he started his reign by summoning the people together in the center of Cap François that they might hear of his benevolence. He announced that now would follow another golden age like that when the great Toussaint L'Ouverture was president. Like Toussaint, he forgave the whites all their crimes against the blacks. All whites could return and claim their former lands. The black man was not too proud to do business with his former enemy. From now on there would be peace and prosperity for all! He thrust a black fist skyward and, opening his cavernous mouth, roared, "Hail Freedom!" The mob shouted back, "Hail Freedom! Hail Dessalines!"

But with the advent of freedom, order and work disappeared. The slave became the sloth. Freedom meant no more work. Freedom meant dancing and drinking and lovemaking during the cool night and sleeping by day in the shadow of the cabin. Freedom meant insolence, street brawling, rebuffing Dambolla, for who needed spiritual assistance when all the world was there for the taking. As the wild animal in the wood, man was beholden to no one.

Dessalines' idea of being a leader was to enjoy the best of everything in the land. That meant residing in a palace, so he ordered one built.

"Who will pay for it?" asked one of his aides. "You have no income, no money from taxes."

"Nobody collects money from de chief," was Dessalines' simple answer. "Everybody pays him."

There were plenty of advisers willing to tell Dessalines how to run the new government. For answer, he told them to follow their own advice, but in the meantime they had better keep him supplied with all the luxuries he demanded. As a result, the government officials became little war lords who usurped the former plantations and forced the natives to work them.

In a short while, Dessalines proclaimed himself emperor. He wore a differently colored waistcoat for each meal. In his satin britches and yellow coat he resembled a dressed-up gorilla as he pointed and toed through the gavotte on his short stocky legs. The height of his buffoonery was the importation of a music teacher from France to instruct him in the art of playing the harp. But his bumbling fingers ripped the strings and in his frustration he smashed the harp and likely would have done the same to his instructor's head, had not the young man sought refuge in Spanish St. Domingue along with one of the Tiger's more comely mistresses.

Meanwhile the subjects became more and more intolerant of their foolish leader and finally, one day Dessalines was assassinated. His dismembered body was dumped in a bloody pile in the town square and there left to rot. It was the people's monument to the man who had brought them freedom. The liberator who did not know how to live in liberty.

Without delay, Henri Christophe announced himself as president of all Haiti. Petion, the mulatto leader of the southern part of the island, contested Henri's right to the supreme office as a violation of the new constitution. Christophe gathered an army to march southward and permanently silence the voice of the protestor, so that he might claim the whole country for himself.

However, the self-proclaimed president overestimated his own military prowess. When the long and bloody battle was over, Petion had lost many men, but still retained sovereignty in south Haiti. Having used up his financial resources, Christophe withdrew from further aggression and was content to keep the northern half of the country for his own.

During all those years of political unrest in Haiti, Captain Etienne Grenier was in Philadelphia, amassing a fortune in the shipping and import business. His various ships' captains kept him informed of the tumultuous affairs of the little island. When Grenier learned that Henri Christophe was the new president, he sent a gift of a shipload of wheat to the impoverished country together with the offer to buy up the mahogany trees which grew wild upon the land.

President Christophe's reply included not only the assurance of Grenier's sole rights to the mahogany trade, but a request for his return as his personal advisor. At the same time Grenier received a letter from his Aunt Sophia, wife of King Frederick of Prussia. He had written to her a request for knowledge of the whereabouts of Toussaint L'Ouverture's two sons.

Sophia's letter brought bad news. Toussaint's sons were dead. Their one-time guardian, the Duc Dubois, was conducting himself in so flagrant a display of wealth that all Paris was agog with gossip as to its source. She was long in answering, for it was only with great difficulty, she wrote, that she was able to trace the whereabouts of the L'Ouverture boys. They had been placed in a public orphanage by the duke, where they died of starvation. She had tried to locate their bodies so as to give them a resting place such as all loving parents wish for their sons, but they had been buried in potter's field, and there was no possibility of identification. The only consolation she could hold out was that the father, who had died of consumption shortly after his arrival and imprisonment in France, died believing his sons were well cared for.

The letter angered Etienne. Was this then Toussaint's reward for a life given over to struggling for the freedom of his fellow slaves? Death for him and his sons!

Philadelphia was suddenly staid. Suffocating! An old man's realm of security. Haiti. The thought of that Caribbean island in its poverty and its ineptitude stirred an excitement in Etienne. He knew what he wanted to do. He would accept Henri Christophe's offer.

Captain Grenier sold his business and sailed south, stopping briefly on the island of Jamaica, where he deposited the profits from the sale in a reliable English bank. Embarking at Kingston, he sailed for Haiti.

Chapter Seventeen

Acting as adviser to Henri Christophe turned out to be more exhilarating to Etienne Grenier than sitting in a shipping office in Philadelphia charting the voyages of merchantmen. Enterprising businessmen from many countries streamed into Cap François with offers of financial help, which in reality were guises for bleeding the new nation of its natural resources. Christophe had a native intuition for penetrating their pretenses. Untutored he might be, but he drove a hard bargain, and every contract was signed only after it was drawn up to the new president's highly profitable favor. As far as Christophe was concerned, there was no need for an agreement on paper, for the Negro stood on his word. However, if Haiti was eventually to be accorded an equal dignity with the nations of the world, then Haiti must do business as the nations of the world. It was Etienne's task to read all legal contracts, to point out loopholes whose wordiness disguised their true meaning before Christophe affixed his X to the paper.

Christophe badly needed business, and he freely invited new industries to the island. However, his people could care less and refused to work in the foreigners' shops. The Tiger, Dessalines, and his butchery were of the past. The new man seemed gentle enough. The sun shone, fruit grew on the trees, and the hens in the yard could forage for themselves. Why work?

But Christophe soon lost patience with this attitude. A black nation must show that it too is capable of governing itself. Haiti must be an example for those other black nations who would emerge in the decades to follow. He would not permit countries, governed by whites, to point with ridicule at Haiti as a comic-opera land. People must work. All foreign interests who invested in Haiti were guaranteed labor. To fulfill this promise, Christophe passed a hard law, so hard that the natives at first laughed in disbelief and chortled about the new president showing off. He *was* showing off—his authority. Every man was assigned to a job. Any who refused would be hanged on the site of his employment, there to swing by his neck for ten days while the buzzards fed upon his dead flesh.

After three such examples, a labor shortage no longer existed.

Along with the natives, Etienne was shocked. "Aren't those rather extreme measures?" he inquired of Christophe.

"Naturally. Parasites need extreme measures. One must deal with them in terms they understand," was the quiet answer. "I first gave them the opportunity to work in pride for their new country, but they selfishly thought only of their own lazy bodies and refused."

Etienne shook his head. "I cannot agree with you. They were not too selfish or lazy to fight for their country."

"It is easier for man to fight for his country than to work for it, at least among my people. They are originally of the jungle and fighting is in their blood. Even among the white race, fighting is simple for man to understand. You are an army man. You know that. Men are gathered together, and the leader shows them where to go and how to fight. All his companions are doing the same as he. He does not have to think for himself. The leader sees that he has food and tells him when he may eat, and when he may sleep. A soldier is similar to a puppet. The officer pulls the string and the little wooden head jumps. Right?"

"Your fighters were not soldiers. They were your neighbors who by their own desire banded together to

209

throw out a savage, senseless leader. They were not drafted into the army by a government at war," Etienne flung at him. He was angered by the casual explanation.

"So!" Christophe raised his eyebrows in surprise over his aide's sharp tone. "So, you think each Haitian figured it all out for himself that he would fight for freedom. No, my friend." The president shook his head. "No. He fought because everyone was fighting. In your army, you use the bugle. Here it is the loudest curse which sounds the action to battle. The biggest mouth stands before his fellow men, spits out his hatred of the oppressor, and urges all to riot and rebel. The rousing voice stirs up feelings of nationalism which the listener had never before known he possessed. Now, he too shouts, 'Freedom! I shall die for freedom, but freedom I shall have!' and gives his life for a cause which he himself thinks he has initiated. Poor fellow." Again Christophe shook his head.

"Stupid fellow," he continued. "He is truly a soldier drafted into military service by the voice of the arouser and all the time he thinks it is his own idea. It only takes one to set fire to a plantation and the others must follow suit. They are like a horde of elephants where the leader charges and the others follow, stampeding, trumpeting, crushing life under hoof. Does an elephant know why he charges? Did a soldier in a French army know what his officer's main objective might be? Did he so much as know why he was at war?"

At this point, Christophe got up from his chair and, leaning across his desk, asked, "And who do you think *killed* Dessalines? Who do you think had the courage to fire the shot which wounded the emperor, the sight of whose blood stimulated the pack to pounce upon him and devour his body?"

"It was a lieutenant in Dessalines' own army," Etienne announced.

"Oh, no. Not true. Nor was it I, my friend. The emperor was killed by a quiet little man, so black and skinny that he looked like a spider. A man who never had a thought of his own in his whole dull life and had never done any more for his country than wipe the mud off his lieutenant's boots in preparation for one of Dessalines' eternal parades. A scum of a native who happened to possess a gun just at the moment when his emperor was bellowing at the whole damn rebel mess. A failure, who on his own would forever be a failure. It was this no-account son of a bitch who pulled the trigger, for, cloaked by the surrounding mob, he suddenly was a giant in his own eyes. Man will dare with others that which he is too spineless to do on his own."

"And what did you do with the spineless spider?" Etienne inquired. "Make him a general?"

"I hanged him."

Sarcastically the captain asked, "What! No hero's crown for a man who wiped out a tyrant?"

"The tyrant was law and order. I couldn't have other failures think it heroic to assassinate the next head of a nation, for I am that next leader and I do not aim to let some insignificant bastard, by the mere pressure of a trigger, wipe out my life's work for my country."

"You are most farseeing," Etienne commented drily.

"I know my people. Heretofore, they have lived only as slaves of another's land. Now, the hard lesson of learning how to be a citizen of their own country begins. I will use native methods to educate them, for these they understand. Punishment. Death."

"Brutality does not build a healthy nation."

"Why should I not hang a citizen in time of peace if his refusal to bear his share of the load is to the detriment of his country? Here in Haiti, I cannot win the war against ignorance, sloth, poverty, if all do not march together. Each must work for his new land if he wishes to share in the rewards of liberty." With that, Henri Christophe sat down, his chin stuck out defiantly.

"Pull in your chin, Henri," Etienne laughed. "I'm not going to tangle with you. At least, not right now."

The president leaned back in his chair and sighed. The tension in the room eased. "Thank you, my friend."

"Don't thank me, for I do not agree with you. "I am merely following the advice of a very smart man who once told me not to measure others by my own meterstick."

Christophe nodded in agreement. "Sound advice. He was a very wise fellow."

Etienne chuckled. "He was, sir, and still is. It was Napoleon."

Six months later, Etienne found himself in a maelstrom of activity. He was the president's constant companion. In addition to advice on commercial practices and world markets, Christophe consulted with Etienne about other needs. For his new country he must have a hospital. Did Etienne know where he could get doctors to staff it? Schools. Schools. Above all, schools. Before the buildings were constructed, Christophe established outdoor schools at Port de Paix, Gondives, Milot, St. Marc. The children in the hinterlands must be educated as well as those in the capital city. Roads must be laid out to bring the products of the interior into the city for shipping. Letters had to be written to the capitals of the world requesting recognition of Haiti's independence and asking an exchange of emissaries.

The world. He must know what was happening in the rest of the world if he, Christophe, wished to be a part of it. Long into the night, Etienne read to Henri reports of the goings-on in London, Paris, Rome, and above all, Washington. The United States was Henri's special hope.

Henri Christophe's passionate ambitions for Haiti consumed all his energies and those of the men who worked with him. The long hours began to take their toll on Etienne. One day, when the bright afternoon sunlight was streaming through the president's office windows, Etienne put on his coat and strode out into the fresh air. He took a deep breath. Delightful! A brisk walk would do him good.

Count Grenier strolled along the rue Hilaire and across the town square. The ocean was at his back, for he was deliberately walking away from it and heading toward the woods. The waterfront meant piers and commerce and exports. And he had come out to escape all that. Etienne lifted his head and inhaled deeply. The air came into his chest and wiped away the cobwebs even as an opened window refreshes a house closed up too long. He had forgotten his hat, and the sun bathed his head with its warm benediction while the wind capriciously ruffled his hair. He was free. He belonged to no man.

Reaching the woods, Etienne sat down on a fallen log and rested his back against a tree. He whistled. It was a gay little Italian tune. He thought of Maria. It was the first time since he had come back to Haiti that he had thought about her. In fact, the first time he had thought of any girl. That was being too busy. Must not let that happen again. He gave himself up to whistling. One melody after another. No thinking. Only whistling.

How long he sat there whistling before it happened, Etienne had no idea. All at once he noticed it. When he had first come, it had not been there, but now it was. The shadow across the log. A woman's shadow. Her skirts were tattered, her hair long and uncombed, sticking out grotesquely from her head. A wood nymph? No, more likely a wood witch who had come out to see who dared break the silence of her shadowy lair. Etienne whistled more loudly. The shadow of the woman was as still as those cast by the trunks of the trees in the woods. He stretched his legs and rested his feet on what should be the shadow of her bosom as it lay across the log. The action was as refreshing to him as a flagon of wine, and he switched to a drinking song. His body abandoned itself to his spirit and his spirit merged with the lively wassail tune.

Only after a resurgence of life flowed through his body and he breathed again like a free man with no binding ties, only then did Count Grenier turn his head to look at the substance of the shadow. The whistle on his lips faded, lingered hesitantly for a moment, and died.

He saw a tall woman with a big frame, a frame so emaciated that it was but an arrangement of bones on which to hang the rags that clothed her body. The fleshless arms were but two long canes from which the big hands dangled, hands that seemed big enough to pull the bones from out her shoulders. Her kinky hair reminded him of a tumbleweed which he had once seen back in the States. A tumbleweed dipped in black mire and set atop a head. Her eyes stared down at him. He felt she looked at him only because her eyes were open, and he was there.

It was what Etienne saw in her eyes that wiped the whistle from his lips. Hopelessness. Abject hopelessness. The woman wore the look of one who expects nothing more from life, not even the hope of death.

"Mon Dieu!" Etienne gasped. *"Mon Dieu."* Slowly he got to his feet, slowly, because if he made an abrupt motion, this caricature of a woman might fall apart. Never had he come upon so dissipated a human being. More wraith than mortal.

"Who are you?" he asked, and the concern he felt for her was genuine.

Her head wobbled as if she could not will it to move in any specific direction. Tears filled her eyes, welling up over the hopelessness mirrored there, and spilling down upon sunken cheeks. Her lips trembled as she tried to form the sounds of an answer. At last she managed to stutter out, "You too?"

There was a familiar look in the eyes which now pleaded up at him, begging, as it were, to be recognized. "You too, M. Gen'ral? Nobody knows me no more." With that her head fell forward upon her chest and she began to cry.

M. Gen'ral. Only one woman had ever called him that.

"Desaix," he cried. "Desaix!" Throwing his arms about the bony creature, Etienne hugged her to himself. "You old witch, I never thought to see you again!"

He stood her off and his eyes surveyed the woman before him. "What a sight you are," he said, "but I'm sure glad to see you."

All at once she was blubbering and laughing at the same time, her nose and eyes running wetness over her face. She managed to gasp, "You did know me, M. Gen'ral. You dint forget Desaix."

"Of course not. Wipe your nose and tell me about yourself," he said.

Using her sleeve, or what was left of it in the tattered garment, she dried her face and after emitting a few final sniffles managed to say, "Poor Desaix. Nobody wants Desaix around no more. Poor me." She shook her head in self-pity. "Poor little me."

"Come, come, Desaix," Etienne teased. "Cut out the playacting and tell me what happened. When I left Haiti you were the most important female on the island. You were the Old Tiger's mistress. You had helped fight for freedom. You were somebody famous. What happened?"

She shrugged. "You know how men is. Can't do nothin' about them. The way Dambolla made them. Old Jacques got tired of me. That's all. Just got tired of me."

"He didn't just throw you out penniless?"

"Might say. Just might say. So many beautiful young girls. New faces, new bodies, and him being the emperor. Just too many temptations for him, I guess. He forget about poor old Desaix. Poor Desaix."

"You didn't retire from the battlefield without a

struggle. You're too much of a fighter," he admitted, "to give up easily."

"Oh, no, I didn't go easy. Some fight." Her eyes widened and her voice swelled with an ominous note. "He was mad. I thought he was goin' to chew me up. Never was I so scared from what I done."

Etienne was curious. "What did you do?" he asked.

"Well, he got hisself a whore he dint tire of. I got jealous—jist a little bit. So, I made up me a potion and threw it at her. Dint hurt her much." Desaix added casually, "Only her face. It boiled up like steam from a kettle."

She paused to emit a small giggle. "From den on, to kiss dat slut would be like kissin'· de snout of a swine dat got cooked all night in de stew pot."

"And then what happened?"

She pursed her lips in thought and said slowly, "I took off. I hid in the woods. That was the trouble. A gal can't do business in the woods. It's a place to starve. I growed so skinny. No man wants to bed with a bunch of rattlin' bones."

"But," said Etienne, "Dessalines is dead. What are you afraid of now?"

"Maybe he's dead, but somehow I felt easier when he was livin'." She shook her head. "Oui, much easier. Sure I was mad, but that don't mean I wanted him dead. But they killed him. They killed my Jacques."

Her tears came back again, big ones, sliding down her face. Her lips quivered and she bit them in an effort to hold back the sobs. Etienne put his arms about her and pushed her head down on his shoulder. "Cry, honey. Cry all you want, and then when you feel better, we'll talk."

Etienne had only pity for her. A girl who had once been so warm and spirited, well formed and solid, now whittled down to no more than a skeleton. The deep sobs, which racked her body uncontrollably, poured out of the loneliness she had known for so long. The physical starving she could have endured, but the banishment from others had stifled her soul.

When she had quieted somewhat, Etienne placed his hands on her shoulders and pushed her away. Then he pulled out his shirttails and wiped her face. "It's the only part of me that's dry," he laughed. "Never saw a girl who could squeeze so much water out of two such beautiful black eyes." His words had the desired effect. She giggled.

"Now you feel better," he told her. "It's what you've been needing. A man around to notice you."

She picked up his hand and tenderly placed the palm against her cheek. "You're so good to me. You're the only one who has been kind to Desaix."

"Think nothing of it. I always go around drying the faces of distressed damsels with my shirttails."

Her shoulders shook, but this time with mirth. It was he who became serious. "Desaix," he asked, "why do you stay here in the woods now that the Old Tiger roared his last? What's the matter with moving back to town?"

"It's that old devil. Christophe." Her eyes looked big with fright. "He don't like sluttin' and tha's all I know. He wants everybody should work and I'm not used to a reg'lar job."

"Nonsense. You're a good worker. When we were up in the mountains while the French still occupied the island, you worked hard like a burro. Remember the meals you fixed? Where you pilfered the food, nobody gave a damn, but it was because of you that we didn't starve. I don't know if it was a labor of love for your man or your country, but you worked hard for the cause."

She shrugged her shoulders. "Country and man go together. I pick the man and the country he favors is good enough for me too."

"Spoken like a true patriot."

Suddenly, he had an idea. Taking her by the arm, he

urged her toward the log on which he had been sitting before her arrival. "Sit down, Desaix. Rest that featherweight body of yours while I talk."

Standing over her, he said, "How would you like to work for me?"

She shot to her feet. "You just bought yourself a woman," she cried as she threw her arms about his neck.

"Unwrap those canes from around my throat," he laughed as he pushed her away. "I'm not buying your whoring. It's your cooking I'm interested in. Now sit down and listen."

As she resumed her seat, he continued, "I have a house in town. I need someone to run it for me. That would be your job. Everything. The cooking, buying, washing. Whatever it is a woman does to keep a house going. If you need extra help, you hire it. But no men. Hire only women. You're going respectable now, Desaix."

"Oh no," she said in a definite voice. "No women. I do ev'rythin' myself. I'm not puttin' temptation aroun' a nice man like you. I ain't sharin you with nobody."

"Shut up," he laughed. "This is a respectable proposition. Probably the first one ever offered you."

Suddenly her face clouded. She bit her lower lip and shook her head. "I forgot," she said. "I clean forgot. Maybe I hadn't oughta go?"

Etienne chortled. "Are you playing hard-to-get now, Desaix?"

"Oh, no, M. Gen'ral." She looked up to him and the Frenchman was surprised to see fear in her eyes. "It's Christophe. He don't like me none. He don't like me respectable. He don't like me no-how."

"What put that idea into that kinky head of yours?"

"It's 'cause of him I stayed in the woods so long after they kill my man. I was 'fraid to go to town to work."

"Desaix," his voice was stern, "what else have you done?"

Her lips pressed hard together in a grim line and her eyes narrowed. Then she stuck out her chin and declared, "I tol' him off. I done tol' him off good. He killed my man. It was his fault that old Jacques was murdered."

"Desaix, you're touched in the head. Some little bootblack fired the shot that killed him."

She tossed her head in derision. "That little bootblack was so dumb he couldn't even shit down a hole. It was Christophe, I tell you. It was him what killed Dessalines. It was him what told that no-'count idiot to pull the trigger. It was him what gave him the gun. It was him what put the idea in his head in the firs' place. I know!" Desaix jumped to her feet. Her voice was high and loud with vehemence. "I know. He was jealous. Christophe was always jealous of Jacques from the very beginnin'. I tol' him so after the murder. He dint have the decency to give an emperor a fittin' burial. They left his body on the ground in front of the palace when they was all finished cuttin' it up. Do you know who buried it?"

Etienne shook his head.

"I did. I gathered up his body." Her lips curled. "Did you ever have to gather up the pieces of the body of someone you loved before you could bury him? Did you?"

She wanted no answer, for her voice hurried on. "Whin I put him in the groun', in a hole I dug myself, whin I shovel the last clods of dirt on top I stood there and thought of how hard he fought for his country and of how his country spit on him and revile him and not even bury him. It was then I git to feelin' like a wild animal. I think when Jacques die, his spirit comes into mine to live, 'cause it knows how much I love him. So now, I'm the wild tiger and I hate. I went to the palace to see the great big presiden' sittin' at his fine desk. I git in only 'cause he say all in trouble must come see him. I look like trouble what needs plenty of help, so the guards let me in.

"God, I tol' him. I tol' him 'bout all the trickery he done. I tol' him that he murdered my Jacques. That he plan it all so he could be emperor." By now she was screaming hysterically. Her fists were clenched and she began to beat them against Etienne's chest. "He killed him! Killed him!"

Etienne grabbed her shoulders and shook her vigorously. He shook her so hard that her teeth rattled against each other. "Desaix," he shouted, "shut up. Shut up, I tell you! You're out of your head."

As swiftly as her fury had risen, so did it go. She collapsed against him and he put his arms around her. She did not weep, just lay quietly while he soothingly patted her shoulder. After a while he spoke.

"Brave girl." He put one hand under her chin and tilted up her face. "Brave girl. No tears. That's good. I have no dry shirttails left."

She smiled up at him. "I'm sorry, but I had to tell you. Don't trust that Christophe."

"I trust no one, Desaix. Anyway, I'll be all right with you looking after me. And Christophe won't bother you with me taking care of you. So, that way, we help each other."

She frowned. "Don't laugh at me, but old Jacques has come to stay inside me. Sometime you come home and find a wild animal keepin' your house."

He threw back his head and roared in laughter. "Desaix, you've been in the woods too long. Come, I'll show you where the house is." He put his arm under her elbow and they walked back toward the town together.

Chapter Eighteen

Etienne's hiring of Dessalines' former mistress proved very satisfactory. Not only was Desaix a superb cook, but she was a merry relief from the pressure of his duties as Christophe's adviser. Perhaps it was the privilege of carte-blanche marketing he had allowed her that was putting the flesh back on Desaix's bones, for in the eight months she had been housekeeping for him, she recovered her once magnificent figure. Now, with some hips to flaunt about again, she sashayed about the house like a vulgar favorite in a seraglio. That was one of Desaix's attractions. Her wanton vulgarity. There was no mistaking what she was by the way she eyed a man and impudently walked past him, the rhythmic swaying of her body advertising what she had to offer that he was missing. She dressed modestly, which made her all the more alluring, since the soft folds of her garments intimated the beauty of the body beneath them. She had a sweet soprano voice which she kept to a soft tone as she sang at her work. Her songs were snatches of voodoo love melodies and each night as he entered the house, Etienne stopped to listen. He was glad to be home.

Always Desaix wore large dangling earrings which jingled musically, and when she served him at the table she leaned down close to his ear and shook her head until they tinkled like fairy bells accompanying her song. Etienne took her by the ears, pulled her face close and kissed her lightly on the cheek. "Now," he said, "you're forgiven. You don't have to cavort

around anymore to entice me with your charms. Whatever trouble you got in today, I forgive you."

He knew she was back to her old habits of finding
men irresistible, but if that was what it took to keep his
housekeeper happy, it was no concern of his.

One evening when he arrived home, Desaix's song
had some of the tempo and rigor of a triumphal march,
and he wondered what mouse the overgrown kitten had
caught this time. He decided to ignore her jocund
mood and sat down to dinner as usual. However, when
Desaix entered the room it was as if Cleopatra were
making a grand entrance accompanied by blaring
trumpets. In lieu of trumpets Desaix's voice sang out
loudly somewhere in the upper range.

With this mighty accompaniment, Desaix, holding a
tureen of marmite, paused at the doorway to shake her
head in time with the song. When she had finished with
a mounting crescendo, she cocked her head toward
Etienne to see what effect the performance had upon
her employer. Really it was not the music which concerned her. It was meant merely to call attention to
Desaix's surprise: her new earrings.

The earrings needed no ear-splitting gimmick to be
noticed. Never had Etienne seen such magnificent
emeralds as hung from the ears of his housekeeper.
They were as round and large as biscuits and encircled
with a double row of beautifully cut diamonds. On Desaix, they resembled two flowerpots of green ferns. He
leaned back in his chair, crossed his arms, and gave his
housekeeper a stern look.

"All right, Desaix," he asked, "where did you get
them?"

She pursed her lips and raised her eyebrows naugh-
tily. "Oh, I don't know as I oughta tell yuh. It really
ain't your business."

"Guess not," Etienne answered laconically, and he
lighted his pipe, dismissing the subject.

She moved close to him and stood in silence. Then

she burst out, "Yuh's the most aggravatin' man I know. Ain't yuh's got no cur'osity 'bout nothin'?"

"Should I?" He looked up at her and grinned. After studying both Desaix and the gems for a moment, he answered the question himself. "I have an idea I should. You can sit down beside me and kick off your shoes. You can talk better that way and I won't see those big bare feet of yours hidden under the table."

With a quick movement, Desaix was seated. When he heard her shoes slip from her feet onto the tile floor he knew she was ready to talk.

"Now, *cherie,* let's have the whole story," he encouraged. "Who gave you those crown jewels?"

She raised her chin and announced with great hauteur, "Prophète. None other than Prophète."

Etienne was taken aback. He could not have been more surprised had she named Christophe himself as her generous lover. But *Prophète.* The captain frowned. He did not like the association. Prophète was head of the palace guard, a handsome Dahomey, fluttered and sighed over by all the women of the court.

By most standards, he supposed Prophète was considered an outstanding specimen of male pulchritude. He was tall, flat-bellied, broad-shouldered, and the red Dahomey uniform enhanced his dark skin. His great pride was a long shaggy goatee, which the ladies found irresistible. Many a time Etienne had seen some wily female running her hands through this hirsute adornment, all the while cooing and tittering about its beauty. Rubbish! He himself thought it resembled the filthy beard he had once seen on a bison in a medicine show back in Philadelphia. And the man's eyes. They were red like the eyes of the wild buffalo. The eyes of a wandering beast.

But what Etienne disliked most about Prophète was that the man was utterly without scruples. Etienne had heard tales of great jewel robberies on some of the more affluent plantations. Prophète was always the prime suspect, but the police were never notified, for how could a dutiful wife report to her husband that her lover had stolen her diamonds? He wondered which erring wife was now mourning the loss of her emeralds. He also wondered why Prophète had lavished such an expensive gift on Desaix, when the man could have his pick of any of the well-dowered daughters of the aristocracy.

"Jealous?" Desaix's taunt broke into his thoughts as if she could read them.

"Insanely so," Etienne teased. "I'm going to ask you to make me a wammy so I can put the bastard under my evil spell."

Desaix did not take this retort in the facetious manner Etienne intended. Her face grew thoughtful as she said, "Tha's what I come to talk 'bout. A wanga."

"I'm no medicine man," the captain told her. "You had better see one of your friends who is on more intimate terms with the gods of Haiti."

Desaix shook her head. "Right now I needs a friend what am a friend of a friend of dem gods, and you am it."

"So, those earrings are a bribe and not just payment for benefits received." He reached over and placing his palm under each ear, he lifted the dangling emeralds. "Well, what's it all about?"

The girl gave a deep sigh. It was her preface to a mighty problem. "Do yuh 'member M. Drapeaux what died some months ago? The one what had sich a big, rich plantation?"

"Of course."

"It seems like he don't have no heirs here in Haiti to grab up his worldly goods. It's all very mysterious as to who gits it, but right now, it ain't got no legal owner."

"Yes," Etienne encouraged. "And in some way that is a concern of yours?"

"Not 'xactly, but it does 'cern Prophète. Ev'rybody all knows how pres'dent Christophe makes no mind 'bout his big men in guvamint snitching rich lands whin there ain't no legal owner. Somebody gotta own a plantation, and if no owner come to claim it, it goes to whoever kin grab it first. Or if the rightful owner is laggin' 'bout puttin' in his 'pearance, it's too bad for him that he dint step on it and git there first. Yuh knows 'bout that, don't yuh?"

Etienne nodded. He had never approved Christophe's practice of permitting his top ministers and army men to claim property untenanted by its owners. The president insisted it was a most efficacious method of settling ownership without the delay of legal procedure. The sooner land was worked, the faster jobs were created, and with the jobs came prosperity and taxes. He saw no evil in the practice. What profited the nation had his blessing.

"Well," Desaix continued, "there's that big Drapeaux plantation what ain't got nobody claimin' it right now. Prophète wants it."

"Your boyfriend usually takes what he wants. What's stopping him now?" The captain was disgusted. Reaching for the glass, he drained it. The cognac burned away the bad taste of Desaix's report.

"It ain't so easy," the girl explained. "It's under the protection of the gods."

Etienne chuckled. "So. The great big tough general and lover of women is afraid of the bogeyman."

Desaix's eyes grew large with the seriousness of the situation. "Dis is a big wanga. It's a horse's head. Dat shiny white skel'ton settin' on top of da gatepost sticks fear right into yuh. Anybody what touches dat house dies sure as hell. No, suh," she shook her head in a foreboding manner. "No, suh. Nobody had better touch dat Nagshead but de one what put it dere."

"The solution is simple. Ask the one who put it there to remove it."

Desaix sighed. "It ain't dat easy. Negu don't take kind to nobody askin' her to cart 'way her wanga."

At the mention of the voodoo priestess, Etienne sat up. "Negu. Negu," he shouted the name. "Negu, my old friend. You mean to say that's where she's been all this time, and you never told me."

"I dint think you was int'rested."

"You didn't even think," Etienne corrected. "I'm going out there tomorrow and scare the hell out of her. It'll be great to see Mama Negu again."

The girl brightened. "Das what I want you should do. Go see her. Tell her a friend of yours wants de house, but 'spects her voodoo sign and would she be so good as to please git it off dat post."

"If I know Negu, she'll take that damn head down when she's ready and not before."

"Yeah," his housekeeper agreed. "Yuh could be right. That Negu, she niver says much, but jist goes on a doin' what she 'tended to do all 'long. She's stubborn like a mule. And yit," her face brightened as a hopeful thought struck, "if she don' pay yuh no mind, yuh kin take down de nag's head you'self."

"Oh, so it's all right for *me* to die sure as hell. So *that's* the kind of housekeeper you are. A traitor!"

"No, no, no," Desaix hurried to deny. "It ain't dat. You don't believe in voodoo."

"The wrath of the gods hits believers and nonbelievers alike." He deliberately made his voice sound like a prediction of doom.

She fidgeted uneasily. "It's thisa way. Negu wen' to all dat trouble to save yuh from the plague, an' it ain't likely she'd let Dambolla wipe yuh out now. She got a way wid de gods, so she has. She's pretty 'portant, an' I don' think you gonna die if you secretly snitch away dat wedder-beaten head. Negu, she kinda likes yuh."

"Cut out the sweet talk, Desaix. Save it for Prophète. Tomorrow I'm going out to see Negu. If I think about it, I *might* ask who is the next owner. That is; only if I happen to think about it."

Etienne stood looking up at the skull of Javan atop the gatepost. It was sleek and white like an ivory carving, and it caught the sun's rays and tossed them out in all directions, giving the effect of a shining halo.

Somebody surely lost a good horse, Etienne thought as he admired the wanga. Those voodoo gods play hell with the natives.

He was struck by the immensity of the jaw and teeth. Bared of all flesh, they looked vicious. "I can see how the superstitious Haitians could be intimidated," he said aloud. "Those teeth look capable of chewing up anyone."

He rode his horse up the drive and on around to the rear of the mansion. There he tethered her to a mimbon tree. Giving the mare a pat on the flank, he cautioned, "Watch your step, old girl. You saw what they do with old nags down here."

Walking toward the outside kitchen house, he noticed a woman working in an herb garden. She must not have heard him come, for she was bending over picking plants. She was too plump to be Negu. He strolled toward her, and yet she did not look up. One way to get her attention, he thought, as he raised his hand and gave her a smart smack on the rump.

The woman let out a howl, at the same time throwing up her hands in fright and letting the gathered plants fly in all directions. She turned to face her assailant, her eyes popped in fear.

"Don't let me frighten you," he soothed. "Just wanted you to know I was here."

Still trembling from the suddenness of his introduction, she stood looking up at him and said in a quivering voice, "Dat ain't no way to meet a lady."

"Madame," he removed the straw hat from his head, and with a great flourish gave her a sweeping bow, "I apologize. You are so right."

He replaced his hat and clicked his heels. "I will state my mission," he spoke with mock dignity. "I have come to see Mama Negu, the devil's apprentice. Is she around?"

Warily the woman looked up at him. "I'll fetch her,"

she said and hurried toward the back door of the big house. From her haste, he suspected she was glad to make her escape from a demented stranger.

Slowly he strolled along the same path she had taken, and as he neared the house he heard the woman talking excitedly to someone inside. "I tell yuh, he's the freshest white man I eber knowed. Neber saw me 'fore, and smacks me right on my behint. Sho' is handsome, though." Then, as if suddenly remembering her mission, she said, "He's askin' for yuh like he knew yuh." Her voice grew louder as if it were following someone who was moving away. "Be keerful, now. Don' turn yuh back none to that man."

A figure appeared in the doorway. It was Negu. In a few quick strides, Etienne reached her. Putting his hands on her waist, he swung her out into the sunshine. "Mama Negu!" he shouted. "Mama Negu!"

He put his arms around her, hugging her, as both he and the woman laughed in the joyous excitement of reunion. He held her away from him and looked her over. "The same slim figure," he laughed down at her. "Not an ounce more."

Then he flung her up in the air over his head and shook her as though she were no more than a doll. He was so happy to see her that he had to make some physical movement to release the joy bubbling inside. He set her down. "It surely is good to see you again."

"I knew it was you when Evadne came and told me. It had to be you." She spoke in an excited voice; all the while her hands were shaking as they tried to straighten the kerchief about her head which had become askew during the vigor of Etienne's greeting. "It just had to be you."

When she looked up at him, Etienne saw that her eyes were filling with tears. She tried to blink them back, but they kept escaping down her cheeks. Quickly, for she was embarrassed, Negu wiped them away with the sleeve of her dress and tried to smile, but the scar on her lip quivered.

"Come, come, *ma cherie,*" he cajoled. "What kind of a reception is this? One woman screams at my appearance and the other weeps. Am I so awful a sight?"

She laughed. "Non. Non. It is only that you have made me so happy. I thought you had forgotten me, but I was wrong. You remembered and you have come to see me." The tears came again.

"Darling Mama Negu." He put his arms around her and held her gently against his breast. Laying his cheek against her red-kerchiefed head he said tenderly, "I would have come sooner had I known where you were. I should have inquired. I owe so much to you. Yet it was for that very reason, because I owe you so much, that I did not take time to inquire. I suppose that I thought you knew—that you would know—"

He hesitated and the woman answered. "Yes, I knew. I know you have been busy. You have become a good Haitian.

She jumped out of his arms, and now it was she who held him away from her while she sized him up. "You look good." She nodded her head in appraisal. "Real good. The boy has gone from your face, and in its stead I see a man. A grown man. A man who won't be pushed around. That's good. Christophe needs a few men around. He's got enough overgrown boys hanging about for the pickings they can get."

"Enough about me." He companionably put his arm about her waist. "I've come to hear what's been keeping you busy since I last saw you. Have you been setting the world straight with that black magic of yours?"

She gave him a shrewd look. "Quit trying to pry into my private life. If I tell you everything I know, then you'll be just as smart as I am." She laughed easily, and with her laugh, a spirit of camaraderie united them.

"Come into the house," she invited. "Come in. No, not the back way," she protested as he started toward the kitchen door from which she had come. "You are a guest. We must use the front. We shall have wine to celebrate your return and Evadne will prepare you a lunch like you have not had since you left Paris."

They talked for hours. Rather, Negu talked and Etienne listened. It was as though she had been waiting for a listener to whom she might spill out all that had been stored inside. The sudden death of M. Drapeaux; the big celebration that had taken place before the planter's demise; the thousands of candles burned, the kegs of rare wine consumed, the sugar cooked into the pastries. She did not seem nearly as saddened by the death of her former master as by the huge sums of money that had been spent in his last months.

At length, when she had unwound and he had an opportunity to get in a word, he asked, "Mama Negu, what's all this to you? You seem upset that so much money was spent. But why, *cherie?* The guests had fun. Poor M. Drapeaux was happy before he passed away and the heir will never miss the wine from the cellar. By the way, who is the heir?"

Negu did not answer at once. She rubbed her hand over her mouth, and her eyes took on a contemplative look. She was evidently weighing her answer.

"It's not that I'm curious," he broke into her thoughts, "but you know it's unwise to leave a plantation untenanted by its owner. Already there are those who have an eye on this property."

"Who?" Her voice tore into him. "Who? Who would dare to want this plantation? It *has* an heir! If anyone tries to put his dirty feet on this land, I'll kill him. Who is it?" Her voice spat out the question with a vengeance.

"Prophète," Etienne answered calmly.

"I'll kill him." Her eyes narrowed. He could tell she was already plotting how to do it.

Etienne laughed. "Don't look so ferocious, Mama Negu. Save your voodoo murder weapons for some other time. The man's scared to death of the place. You have that damn skull stuck out in front, and the fellow actually believes in spooks. Wouldn't come near it. The house is safe as long as you have that wammy out there."

She smiled and the scar on her lip gave her a diabolical look.

"However," he continued, "it would be much easier if the heir put in his appearance. It would put an end to all the plots and speculations in town."

Negu frowned. "You're right, and it worries me. The heir is in France, but will be here as soon as word reaches—" she paused "—reaches the new owner."

Captain Grenier had the feeling that she was wrestling with the idea of telling him something more and yet had not made up her mind as to the wisdom of revealing everything to him. "Something's bothering you, Mama Negu. You can trust me, you know. I owe you a favor. Perhaps, I can give you the advantage of my advice which you won't take anyway."

She gave a small mirthless laugh. "I need more than your advice. I'd like to borrow your services."

He whistled. "Sounds interesting."

"The solicitor will send word to me when the heir is due. Captain," her eyes brightened. "Would you be good enough to meet the ship?"

"Why, of course. I'll be right there when it docks and be ready to help the doddering old heir down the gangplank. Who is it? Some forgotten ancient cousin?"

"No," she said quietly, her eyes dancing, challenging him to guess again.

"I'm thinking," he said accusingly, "that you're holding back something interesting about this heir."

"I am. It's a girl. A young girl." Negu threw back her head and laughed. "You won't find it such a task after all."

Etienne was dumbfounded. "I'll be damned! Who *is* she?"

Negu shrugged. "I'm not too sure. All I know is that he adopted her some time ago. Maybe some distant relative. Some child left orphaned. I don't really know."

"Where has she been living all this time?"

"In a convent. The good soeurs have been raising her, and she will know so little of the outside world. The poor little thing will be frightened. So far from a home she has always known. It will be good if you meet her and bring her out to the plantation. You seem to have an assuring way with girls of all ages."

"The poor *petit enfant*," Etienne said sympathetically. "I'm surprised at those nuns letting her travel all this distance without a nurse. I'll be happy to meet the child."

Negu put her hand to her mouth and turned away, making muffled sounds as she did so.

"What's the matter?" Etienne asked.

"I'm—I'm holding back a sneeze," she told him. Yet, her shoulders were shaking and he could not see her face. He suspected Mama Negu was laughing.

Chapter Nineteen

Asya stood in front of the small oval mirror in her cabin for a last inspection of her appearance before going ashore. She was not pleased with what she saw. In her heavy brown dress, which seemed to take its color from the old pine walls of the cabin, she felt as drab and unnoticed as a hare in a hayfield.

The only bright spot was her nose, and that, more than anything else, displeased her. It resembled a tomato. A very red tomato. It had been such a pleasure to get away from the long dark halls and airless rooms of the convent where the windows were kept tightly shut against colds and fever, that she had spent hours walking the deck, breathing in the fresh air. Captain Hampton had warned her about too much sun, but she was tired of being warned against the enjoyments of life, and, as a show of rebellion, she walked longer than she had intended. The nuns had always cautioned, "If you don't listen, you will pay for your disobedience." Well, now she was paying for it.

Asya stepped back from the mirror. Defiantly she put on the old brown bonnet. She hated it, but one could not go bareheaded to claim one's inheritance. Soon, she would get a lacy new one, a larger one, so she could wear her hair piled up instead of down like a schoolgirl.

I don't need anybody's help anymore, *ever,* she told herself. I'm rich and grown up now, and I can look after myself. Nobody will ever make me cry again. Nobody!

233

"Here you are," a voice boomed into the cabin, piercing her soliloquy.

Startled, Asya turned toward the doorway. It was Captain Hampton. I've been looking for you. Here is a gentleman who has come to take you ashore."

He stepped aside and Asya found herself looking up into the bemused eyes of a tall stranger. Her heart did something it had never done before. It flipped.

"This is M. Grenier, my dear. It is not every girl who gets so handsome a man to welcome her to Haiti," the captain chuckled. Asya stood staring, her cheeks warm with embarrassment.

Then, in a sudden feeling of self-defense, she drew herself upright and said haughtily, *"Bonjour, monsieur.* I am ready to leave the ship." She must remember her new role. She was a rich woman, and she needed help from no one. No, not even this handsome stranger.

But M. Grenier continued to stand in the doorway, his arms folded across his chest, a big straw hat dangling from one hand and those laughing eyes appraising her from the top of her old brown bonnet to the toes of her sabot-shaped school shoes. They were hazel-colored eyes and twinkled down at Asya as though their wearer were enjoying the situation. Could he be laughing at her? Asya did not like to be laughed at. She thrust out her chin in a combative gesture.

"Well, I'll be da—dumbfounded," were M. Grenier's first words. Asya tightened up at the sound of his voice, for the amusement in his eyes had crept into his tone. She glared at him, ready for battle.

"I thought I was to pick up a child, and instead, I find a full-grown female. How Negu must be chuckling!"

"I fail to see the joke," Asya said icily. "After all, when a girl has been on this earth sixteen years, she can reasonably expect to be full grown."

"Pardon. Pardon." He sounded contrite, but the mischievous twinkle in his eyes belied his repentance. With a wide sweep of his arm, he made a low bow.

234

"Welcome, my beautiful mademoiselle. Welcome to Haiti. Had I known that the heir was so lovely and so grown up—" she did not like the way he emphasized *grown up* "—I would have worn my state uniform. Pardon my casual attire."

"Your attire is of no concern to me," Asya said coldly. "Since the purpose of my trip was to come to St. Domingue, and since the boat has already arrived, may I go ashore now?"

Even to her own ears, her voice sounded horribly formidable, but somehow she felt more at ease behind this hard exterior.

The laughter in M. Grenier's eyes disappeared and a look of kindness took its place. He said gently, *"Ma cherie,* you may go wherever you wish. I am your friend who has come to help you."

Asya was ashamed of her snobbishness. She wanted to run up to him, place her hand in his and tell him how happy she was that he had come, but she did not know how. This was a man and she did not know how to be friends with one unless he was like old Butte. Instead, she spoke as to a slave. "Good. My baggage is there on the floor." She pointed disdainfully. "You may take it ashore. I will see you on the pier."

With a toss of her head, she walked past him and out the door. Captain Hampton followed. "Mademoiselle," he explained, "you must not refer to this land by its old French name of St. Domingue. The citizens here do not like it. It is now called Haiti."

"It is no concern of mine what they call it," she said flippantly, and ran down the gangplank to get away from the pesky old man. He was always telling her what she must and must not do. She shook her shoulders as if to flick off all authority but her own.

But when she stepped out on the deck, Asya was greeted with her second surprise of the day. The pier was crowded with Negroes. Asya had never seen a black man before. She had heard of the Moors in Europe, but none had come as far north into France as

Chalon-sur-Marne. She stood fascinated. She did not know what she had expected, but certainly not these varying shades of skin. Some were so shining black that they looked as if the Lord had recently covered them with stove polish and rubbed them to a high gloss. Others were a dull gray, like the fur of a convent mouse. Many had a golden skin which accented their black eyes. All were shoeless, and she was surprised to note that their heels and soles were pink, the same as her own feet. To her, so recently released from the colorless world of school uniforms and monastic habits, the gaily colored clothes of the inhabitants were as delightful as bright flowers in a window box.

Here and there, groups of children scurried happily about like brown leaves swished to and fro by a prankish wind in the autumn. The whole seemed to wave "Welcome! Welcome, Asya. Here you are free."

Asya smiled. She was going to like St. Domingue. No, Haiti. The natives were right. That name was more suitable for this colorful land.

"That's better," a voice spoke behind her. "You look less grim now."

At the sound of his voice, her lips automatically closed in a tight line. Why, she wondered, did Captain Grenier bring out her most ornery instincts? There was something about him. Something that frightened her. She thought of Kaspar, the only other man she had ever known, and she shuddered. No, he certainly was not like Kaspar. This man seemed gentle, even kind. Yet there was something about him that made her keep her distance.

"I brought a phaeton for you. I thought you might like it better than a closed carriage," he was saying. "This way." She felt his hand on her elbow as he guided her along the crowded pier. She stiffened and wanted to shake off his touch, but she remembered that she was now a lady and must accept these little gallantries. When they came to the phaeton, he tossed the one bundle with all her possessions onto the floor and then, just as easily, turned around and, taking her by the waist, swung her up onto the seat. Asya almost burst with humiliation.

"Are you trying to show off your strength," she snapped as he seated himself beside her, "by picking me up as though I were but a child? I am old enough to climb into a phaeton by myself, I can assure you."

He nodded, "It *was* a feat of great prowess, wasn't it?" She looked up at him as they started off, but she could not tell if he was laughing at her or not, for his eyes were shadowed by the large straw hat he now wore.

In exasperation, Asya turned away from him to study the town through which they were now driving. To her amazement, the stores along the street had no windows, only great arched doors with wide-open shutters on either side. As they passed by, she looked in and saw their wares. One had shelves of yard goods which reached to the high ceiling; another, rows of figurines and bowls carved out of black wood. In another commercial establishment, one woman had ridden her burro into the center of the store and was doing her shopping while still astride its back.

Everywhere were women walking about the dusty streets, balancing huge straw hampers of vegetables or fruit or clothes atop their heads. At one corner, two of them were resting in a squat position, chatting away, seemingly unaware of the great load each was carrying.

Soon, the open carriage was beyond the business section and approaching a residential area. Tinted in pastels of blue and pink and green, decorated with lacy iron balconies and trellises hung with purple flowers, the homes were reminiscent of the fancy pastries Asya had seen in a patisserie in Chalon-sur-Marne. This was a land of color and warmth, a far cry from the cold shadowy halls of the convent Asya knew as home. But that was forever behind her across the sea. Haiti was her home now. She would live in this colorful fairyland like the princess in the stories Butte had told her.

On either side of the road large red flowers waved like welcoming flags among the green leaves. The wind blew against her face, warm and caressing, at the same time carrying a strange fragrance to her nostrils. Asya sniffed the air and looked about trying to see from where this heavenly perfume came.

She must have been very obvious, like a dog sniffing a scent, for M. Grenier, who had been silent since they had left the pier, explained, "Those are orange blossoms you smell. I noticed them too the first time I came here."

Asya breathed in deeply. "It's wonderful. Better than the smell of incense."

"All the brides of Haiti carry bouquets of orange blossoms. It brings them luck." He added, "When you are a bride, you will do the same."

"I don't know anybody to marry." Her tone dismissed the subject.

He leaned over and his face was close to hers as he whispered, "You know me."

She jerked herself away. "I know nothing about you. Besides, I shall never marry anyone."

He shook his head and said mournfully, "What a shame. So young to be dedicated already to the single life."

She tried to change the subject. "All I've seen so far are natives. Are there other white people on the island besides yourself?"

"You saw the shops, didn't you?"

"Oui," she wondered why he asked.

"Wherever there are shops, there are English businessmen. They travel all over the world. Some have families. Some are looking for families."

She could feel his sidewise glance and shrugged. "I wish them luck," she said indifferently.

"Oh, they will look upon you as a bit of good luck when they see you. Young, beautiful, and an heiress.

Commendable attributes for the wife of a man of commerce."

"I couldn't be less interested."

"That's of little moment. You'll be deluged with offers of marriage."

"Thanks for the warning. I'll be on guard," she said coldly. "Are there any other whites here besides these enterprising shopkeepers? Any Creoles?"

"A few. Some came back to claim their lands after the revolution. You'll meet them. Every last one of them since they'll vie for your—" he hesitated "—shall we say, friendship?"

She was curious. "Why?"

Etienne chuckled. "Because, my dear, you are the richest Creole in Haiti!"

"Oh!" She was astounded. It was true after all. She no longer had to pretend she was rich. She *was* rich! The richest woman in all of Haiti! Out of the corner of her eye she noticed her companion smiling. Suddenly he reached across and wiped her mouth with his handkerchief. She slapped his hand away. "What was that for?"

"You were drooling, *ma cherie,* as you mentally counted your money bags, and it was showing." He laughed out loud.

Asya looked up at him defiantly. He was making fun of her. Well, so what. Let him laugh. It was of no concern to the richest woman in the land.

Then, as if he had read her thoughts, he said aloud, "Don't misunderstand, mademoiselle. I am laughing *with* you, not at you."

"I wasn't laughing," she said angrily.

"Young girls *should* laugh. Perhaps someday you will. I hope so. Before you grow old and formidable."

"I shall laugh when there is something humorous," she replied haughtily. "Until then I can't go about with a leer on my face."

Etienne turned his attention to the road ahead.

"That wouldn't be so bad. It might be a welcomed change," he said in a quiet voice. She was rebuked.

For a while they rode in silence. She felt small sitting beside this broad-shouldered stranger. Her eyes fell to his hands as they lightly held the reins. They looked strong and capable, accustomed to making things happen. The sun had darkened them to a rich bronze color, as it had his face. She wondered how long he had been on the island.

To break the awkward silence, she asked, "Did you know my papa?" Perhaps this would be a safe subject.

"André Drapeaux? Was he really your father?" he asked, his eyes considerably wider but still on the road ahead.

"No, I was told he was my adopted father, but," a note of longing crept into her voice and she could do nothing about it, "he was all I had. So I like to think of him as my papa."

Monsieur reached over and patted her hand which was resting on the seat between them. Asya stiffened, while at the same time her heart somersaulted crazily in her breast. She shut her eyes so she would not glance down and see her body quivering from the turmoil within.

M. Grenier removed his hand from hers. Had he sensed how his touch had affected her? Asya could feel the blood rushing into her cheeks at the thought of such a possibility.

"No, I did not know your papa personally," he spoke softly, "but I did hear that M. Drapeaux was a very well informed gentleman." The man beside her spoke slowly. He turned and smiled at her, and Asya noted that his eyes, when gentle, were a mixture of green and gold. For the first time, she smiled up at him.

Asya sighed. "I wish I had known him. Do you know how he died?"

"I believe it was his heart. He was planning to remarry and perhaps the excitement was too much. He died suddenly."

240

"Remarry?" The thought made Asya feel like a lonely orphan again. "Remarry?" her voice rose with disapproval.

"A perfectly natural step for M. Drapeaux to take after his wife had died. Didn't the good sisters at that convent school tell you that God said it is not good for man to live alone?"

"Oh," she frowned up at him in exasperation. "They also told me that people find excuses in the Bible for all their sins."

"That's right. A great book." He nodded approvingly. "We sinners need it as much as you saints."

"I'm no saint," she denied.

"Oh, a wicked sinner then?" He turned and looked down at her, the trace of a smile at the corner of his mouth.

She shut her lips firmly and did not answer.

"Don't look so grim, *ma cherie*," he cajoled, "or you'll never get a chance to become a sinner."

"Is that a coveted role in your estimation?" she asked snippily.

"No." He drew out the word as though he were mentally selecting what he might say next. "No. Nor is it a role to be condemned. There is many a saint who is only so because she has never been tempted."

She tossed her head. "I'm not interested in your discourse on theological trivia."

After a few moments of silence Asya shook her head. "My father, had he remarried, would never have sent for me. I only count now, after everybody is dead, and I'm all that's left around." She was bitter.

M. Grenier pulled on the reins and the horses came to a halt. Taking Asya's face in both his hands he tilted it up, bending down to her at the same time, so that when he spoke she could feel his breath upon her cheek. "What you have never had you cannot miss. Don't start feeling sorry for yourself by dwelling upon good fortune that did not come your way. Your papa was very happy his last few days. Do you begrudge him that? He loved you enough to make you his heiress in his will. Now he is dead and your life begins. Make the most of it."

While Etienne spoke, Asya's eyes were on his lips. What was it like to be kissed by this man? Shocked at the audacity of her thoughts, she jerked her head from his hands and moved to the edge of the seat. She felt awkward and prim, sitting so far away from him, but she was frightened of him too.

From the corner of her eye, she saw that he had picked up the reins again. Leaning back, half-reclining, and with his hat pulled down over his eyes, M. Grenier was once again seemingly oblivious to her presence. For a while they rode in silence. Then he began to whistle, whistle in time with the horse's trot. Ordinary, aimless whistling she did not mind, but this whistling in rhythm with the horse's movements was to her a game to ward off his boredom. She was uncomfortable, a nuisance to him.

Whether from the turmoil of her own feeling or from the warmth of the sun beating down upon her, Asya began to feel suffocated. Untying the strings, she removed her bonnet. A breeze fanned her hair and she raised her face that it too might be refreshed and cooled.

The whistling beside her stopped. "I wouldn't do that," M. Grenier spoke languidly from beneath his hat.

"Why not?" Asya snapped. "I'm hot."

"Better hot than burned," he answered slowly in a philosophical voice.

"I'm sick of all your axioms. You sound like a mother superior."

A chuckling sound came from beneath the hat. "I've been called a lot of things, but never that."

Defiantly Asya leaned back and let the breeze caress her head. However, the sun soon became a hot flame that licked her face and her pinched burned nose. She had regrets about having removed her bonnet, but death at the stake was better than letting M. Grenier know he was right.

When Asya thought she could bear the heat on her head no longer, the man beside her spoke, "By the time we arrive at your new home, the folks there will think the new heiress wears a poinsettia for a nose."

"What's a poinsettia?" She was glad to be talking again.

He pointed to the large red flowers at the side of the road. She followed his glance. "You exaggerate." Asya tossed her head, but her nose did hurt. She conjured a picture of her face with a huge red flower poking boldly out from the center, and what she saw weakened her determination.

Slowly, the man beside her unfolded himself from his slouched position and, leaning over, picked up the bonnet from her lap. "It looked bad enough when you got off the ship, but let's not cook your poor nose any further." Carefully, M. Grenier placed the bonnet on Asya's head and tied the strings into a bow.

"There, that's a good girl," he said, as he gave her an approving pat on the head. "You're coming along fine."

Asya could have kicked him in the shins for his patronizing tone of voice. He made her feel like a child taking her first steps.

For a while they rode along without speaking. The road was now close to the sea and Asya found herself listening to the sounds of this new land. The waves boomed offshore like the low-pitched tympany of a concerto, while the rustling of the wind in the trees sighed its pianissimo accompaniment.

Then, too soon, they had passed the shore and were driving along a plain which ended far ahead at the foot of a towering jungle-covered mountain. The sun beat down upon Asya's back and her brown woolen dress sucked its warmth through to her skin. Reluctantly, she admitted to herself that she was glad M. Grenier had insisted she wear her bonnet. But the damage had been done. Her poor sore nose. How the wind and the sun kept bumping against it.

Again, as if he had read her thoughts, Etienne interrupted the silence. "You know, *cherie,* even with that bright red nose you are really quite pretty."

Asya could feel the blood creeping up into her cheeks. Annoyed that she still blushed like a schoolgirl, she did not answer, but dropped her eyes to her hands in her lap.

Etienne put his hand under her chin and tilted her face upward. She tried to turn away, but he held it firmly cupped in his hand. "Now let's just take a look and see what we have here. Long black hair, entirely too straight by ladies' standards, since they seem to prefer a foliage of curls, but from the way you let it hang down your back, curls would be of no help. Negu will show you how to dress your hair. High and sleek."

Abruptly he turned her head to the side. "Oui. A good profile. A slightly turned up nose. That will add a touch of sauciness. In you it is probably more orneriness, however. Good ears too. Small and flat."

He jerked her head frontward and his eyes again examined her face. "Very dark olive skin, but it only serves to highlight the unexpected color of your eyes. Let's see." He raised her chin to get more light.

"Are they blue or gray? Blue today because the sky is blue. Gray on a rainy day. They are like a chameleon, taking their color from the world about them."

"A chameleon?" She was angry but curious.

"A chameleon is a lizard which changes color. It's a fascinating little creature."

"Oh, so now I'm being compared to a lizard. And all this time I thought I was a mongrel pup." She raised her eyebrows in annoyance.

He wrinkled his forehead as he weighed her words, but the smile on his lips belied his seriousness. "Now that you mention it, you do have houndlike tendencies. You bark too much." He laughed again. "Just wait until Mama Negu meets you! The two of you will be some match!"

"Just who *is* this Mama Negu?"

Etienne became serious. "She's very special. You'll like her."

"Special?" Asya's curiosity was again aroused. "How so?"

"Well, first of all, she is aware of everything that happens on the island, and yet she seldom leaves the plantation. She probably knows right now which people will come to call upon you even though as yet no one has heard your name. You should listen to her advice. She will dress you in the latest Paris fashions even before they've left Paris, and she will tell you what the other girls," he looked at her slyly and said, "your competition, you know, will be wearing to a ball long before the day arrives. Negu will be your best friend."

Asya was delighted. "It will be wonderful to have a best friend. Is Negu my age?"

M. Grenier laughed. "Your age? I don't think Negu was ever your age." He spread out his arm as if to embrace the atmosphere. "She's the wind, the church, taxes. She's always been with us."

"You make her sound like a spook," Asya scolded. "Tell me what she's really like."

"Let me think." He looked up and studied the sky. Then he turned toward her and said brightly, "She's like a good fairy in witch's clothing. Oui, that's what Negu is like."

"You're impossible. I want to know," she insisted, "just what will I see when I look at Negu."

"Oh," he shrugged, "just an elderly black woman with a bright kerchief about her head."

"Black!" Asya shouted. "Black! You expect me to be friends with a black woman? To take advice from a black woman? Let her boss me around?" she asked arrogantly.

His quiet answer made her own voice sound raucous. "Friends do not boss. Friends have a respect for each other no matter what the age or color."

"If you don't mind," she said icily, "I shall choose my own friends."

Etienne looked at her in disgust, but said nothing. She would have to learn for herself, and what an education it would be. He slouched back in the seat, pulled his hat down over his eyes, and resumed his whistling.

They turned off what must have been the main road and onto another dirt road, which was much narrower. Tall, thick trees lined the way like sides of a deep green gorge. Buried in the dense foliage she saw remnants of a charred chimney protruding above what seemed to be the vine-covered ruins of a dwelling. She wished she could ask him about it. But every time she opened her mouth to speak, she seemed to stir up a spirit of antagonism between them. She said nothing until M. Grenier reined the horses before a black iron gate.

"Why are we stopping?" she inquired.

The whistling died away. M. Grenier sat up, pushed his hat far back on his head, and lazily stepped from the phaeton. "We're here. Do you expect the horse to climb the gate?" he asked.

Asya's heart hammered out her excitement. She would see it all now. She could hardly contain herself as she watched M. Grenier swing back the gate. Why was he being so slow? Couldn't he sense her eagerness?

And then Asya saw it. A cold slimy feeling chilled her, and she shivered. On top of the gatepost. That horrible skeleton. She shut her eyes to blot out the diabolical image, but when she opened them it was still there. Like something from Hell, grinning down with its large teeth as if threatening to devour her. Even in her warm dress, Asya was cold. She folded her arms across her breasts and tried to snuggle her hands under her armpits to warm them.

As he climbed back on his seat, M. Grenier noticed

her distress. "What's the matter, Asya?" His voice showed concern.

She pointed to the top of the gatepost. "That head," she stammered. "That horrible-looking head."

He followed her glance and laughed. "Oh, that? Think nothing of it. It's part of the establishment. Like the kitchen or the shutters or the fireplaces. Call it the family coat of arms."

"That's not funny," she retorted.

"Of course not. It's an ugly thing," he agreed. "But it keeps away witches and bad luck and evil spirits. Things like that. It's a voodoo charm."

She was disgusted. "I don't believe in witchcraft. This is an enlightened age. Only superstitious ignorant natives believe in those things."

He had hopped back into the phaeton and as they moved slowly up a wide stone drive, he said in a low voice, "Don't ever underestimate the powers of voodooism." He turned to her, and she saw that his face bore a serious look. "You will regret it," he warned.

For a fleeting moment she was uneasy. His words carried a foreboding. Asya tossed her head as if by so doing, she could dispel her uneasiness. "Nonsense," she told herself. "He's been stuck out in this backward island too long." She was educated. She'd have nothing to do with that hocus-pocus.

The drive turned, bringing them out from the shadows of the trees, and there ahead, surrounded by the greenest grass Asya had ever seen, was her new home. It was pink, the loveliest, most delicate pink. Across the entire front, like a frothy lace trimming, was a white veranda of ornamental iron, its decorative pattern repeated in a balcony along the second floor. The roof of the upper balcony was a mass of purple flowers which spilled over the sides, entwined about the pillars, and spread down to the veranda below. To either side stood several great trees. They fanned the house with the enormous brown saber-shaped pea pods that dangled from their branches.

Asya drew in her breath and let it out again in a long ecstatic sigh.

"You like it?" she heard M. Grenier ask, but she could not answer him. For the moment nothing existed save her and her house.

"Home," she whispered to herself as in prayer. "I am home at last."

Mesmerized, she lay back against the seat and watched this glory come closer. She was floating on one of the clouds, floating right along to Paradise. Her Paradise.

"It should have a name," she sighed in her dreamy mood. "Every beautiful home should have a name, especially this one. It will be so dear, so precious, since it is my very first, and I have wanted it so long." She sat erect. "I have it." She turned to her companion. "I shall call it 'Cher Château.' Yes, that's it. Cher Château. Dear, dear home."

Suddenly all the happiness she felt gathered in her heart, filling it up until she thought it would burst. At the same time, the phaeton pulled up to the entrance, and Asya jumped to her feet.

"Wait, I'll help you down," M. Grenier offered, but who could wait for gallantry at the most exciting moment of her life?

Asya leaped to the ground, but as she did so, her skirt caught on the side of the phaeton and she tumbled forward. While she put out her hands to break the fall, she still went forward with such force that her head struck the stone drive.

M. Grenier was at her side immediately. "You poor dear," he said as he helped her to her feet. "Are you hurt?"

She did not know. All she felt was humiliation, but she could not tell that to M. Grenier. Where before there had been only happiness, irritation stirred within. "I'm all right," she snapped. As she reached up to

248

straighten her bonnet, she noticed for the first time a small group of people standing in the shadow of the doorway. They must have seen everything. She could feel her cheeks warm with embarrassment. What an awful first glimpse of the new mistress! And she had wanted to sail in upon the scene like a grand lady with her nose up and her skirts sweeping.

Shaken and unsure, Asya stood quietly while he re-tied her bonnet. "Now you look tipsy," he teased, "and if you walk a little sideways, no one will see the rip in your skirt."

"Rip! I didn't know it was torn." She frantically looked down and examined the folds of her skirt. There was a long rent through which her white flannel petticoat showed. For one fleeting minute, Asya wanted to run away. She heard Monsieur's voice. "Chin up. This is not Versailles, but if it were, would it matter if you were its queen? This is your home, and those people on the porch are waiting to welcome you. A bump on your head and a tear in your skirt will not make them love you less."

He removed his hat and with great exaggeration made a sweeping bow. Then he straightened and clicked his heels to attention.

"Lady Asya," he said in a mock-formal tone, "may I escort you into your castle?"

With great dignity, he offered her his arm. Asya looked up and saw that his eyes were smiling, inviting her to share in the fun. She resented his attitude, his attempt to make light of her predicament. There was nothing amusing about an heiress coming to claim her estate with a tattered skirt, a red beet for a nose, and a lump that felt like a potato growing out of her fore-head. She would show him. She would show all of them.

Ignoring Monsieur's proferred arm, Asya flung back her bruised head and haughtily walked toward the people waiting on the veranda.

Chapter Twenty

By the time Asya had been at Cher Château a whole year, life before her arrival in Haiti seemed never to have existed. Here, she was the duchess of the palace, the mother superior of the convent, the midwife of the maternity ward. All looked to her for their orders. That was, all but Negu.

From the moment Asya stepped onto the veranda of the house and her eyes had met those of Negu, she knew she could never dominate the Negress. Her first reaction had been of repulsion. Those deep black eyes had looked at her wildly, growing wider and fiercer until Asya shuddered lest the spirit of the woman behind them leap out and devour her. Negu's welcoming smile had been a snarl, like that of a cur baring its teeth for attack. Only later did Asya realize that a malformation of the lip created the antagonistic effect. Even so, she could not warm to the housekeeper.

Nevertheless, she realized the woman was indispensable. She knew everything about the house, the stables, the crops, the books on the library shelves, and even the age of the hams in the smokehouse. In a low, soft voice, which Asya could not associate with so ugly a woman, Negu almost reverently introduced her to Cher Château. It was as though she had been its creator and still wondered at what she had fashioned. A twinge of jealousy stirred in Asya's breast as she realized Negu also loved Cher Château. Asya resented the older woman, and she did not know why. Perhaps it was because Cher Château had two lovers.

In addition, Negu's constant presence made Asya uneasy. She was forever at her side, those fierce black eyes beating down upon her, like a wild animal ready to spring upon its prey. There were times she wished she *would* attack. Then they could have a good brawl like back at the convent school, and each would understand where the other stood. But now, she was a lady, an heiress, one who maintained a cool air of sophistication at all times. The mistress of the house was above anything so crude as brawling.

The other help posed no problem. Evadne, the cook, and her husband, Nassy, acted like the well-trained servants Asya remembered on Eleanore's mother's staff. Pleasant, but subservient. Evadne never brought any of the problems of the kitchen to the new mistress. She prepared bounteous delicacies, Nassy served them, and Asya, with her voracious appetite, ate them heartily. Evadne and Nassy were the kind of dutiful servants who befitted a rich woman such as herself.

Cilla was different. She was young, Asya's own age. When Asya first met her on the veranda the day of her arrival, the daughter of Evadne and Nassy welcomed her with a smile which said, "I'm glad you've come," and it diffused some of the combativeness which possessed Asya at that time. At first, Asya tightened at the thought of the friendship proferred by the young Negress, not because she was black, but because she did not know how to be friendly with a servant. The girls at school had always disdained such a relationship. Futhermore, she had never had a servant, and Cilla was to be Asya's very own personal maid. Upon introduction the shy black girl had beamed upon Asya as happily as the nuns in the hospital regarded each newborn infant.

Later, in the bedroom, Asya was glad to be alone with Cilla. She did not realize how tired her trip to this new land had made her. As Cilla unhooked the warm brown dress and pulled it over her head, Asya let out a long sigh. It was not so much the excitement which had sapped her energies as it was those fighting tendencies she had experienced since the ship had docked. Now, in her very own room, away from critical eyes, the tension went out of her, along with her exhaling breath.

"You must be tired, Miss Asya," Cilla spoke in such a soft hushed voice, that Asya was reminded of the nuns in the hospital nursery when they tried to croon a colicky baby to sleep. A pang of homesickness stirred within, and she longed for the warmth of loving arms, familiar arms like those of Mère Denise, about her. As though to be closer to the land of her birth, Asya walked to the tall open window and stepped out upon the balcony. Her eyes sought the horizon. Was it that way lay France and the Hospice of the Sacre-Coeur? Home.

There was a warm, caressing breeze. It fanned her face and flowed over her bare shoulders like the waters of a christening washing away the past and leaving one cleansed for a richer life. She thrust out her chin. She was an adventuress now. She must not look back. Yet, she held her chin firmly lest it quiver.

"Are you thinking of home?" Cilla's voice came from behind her. It went on to ask excitedly, "Or maybe a beau you left back in France. A boy you liked very much? *Oui?*"

Cilla's hopeful prying into a possible romantic interest was what Asya needed to dispatch her momentary gloom. She giggled. "Silly. I never had a boyfriend. You can't meet boys in a convent. The nuns scare them away."

However, it had been flattering to be suspected of having amorous entanglements, and Asya was happier as she re-entered the rose-colored bedroom.

"Nobody scares boys away in Haiti," Cilla announced as her eyes sparkled with the promise of happy events to come. "You wait and see. You're going to have lots of beaux." Her eyes fell upon Asya's nose and her voice became woebegone. "But first, we got to do something about that nose of yours. No self-respecting gentleman would give a second look to a white woman with a fiery red nose."

Asya put her hand to her face as though she could determine its color by touch. "Is it that bad?" she asked.

"Awful! Just awful! But don't you worry none. Cilla will help you make it better in no time." With that promise, she flew from the room, and was back in seconds holding an earthenware mug. Ever so gently, she rubbed some of its contents on Asya's sunburned nose.

"Oh, that feels so good," Asya exuded in relief.

"It'll snuff that fire smack out of your nose in a hurry," Cilla consoled. "Ain't nothing like linseed oil and limewater for putting the skin back on white folks who stay out in the sun too long."

"I'd never been around sun this hot." Asya had to give an explanation for her foolishness.

"You got too smart too late," was the maid's comment as she stepped back to study the result of her ministrations. Then her eyes fell upon Asya's many petticoats. She shook her head in disapproval, remarking, "Where you came from it's either mighty cold or people are awful respectable."

"Why, Cilla?" Already she was comfortable with this gentle girl. "How many petticoats do you wear in Haiti?"

"None," Cilla answered casually. "Why clutter up ourselves with so much material." Asya must have had a startled look upon her face, for the girl hurried to add, "Of course, I'm only speaking about myself. You will have to wear more clothes." She sighed. "Too bad, that's the trouble with being rich. You can't be comfortable like us poor folks."

Asya laughed. Cilla was fun. She was easy to be around. Not only was she happy and willing, but also spoke better French than many of the patients at the Sacre-Coeur. Her speech was nothing like the gibberish that know-it-all Captain Hampton said the natives would be speaking.

"Tell me, Cilla," she asked, "how did you learn to speak such beautiful French? Nassy and Evadne talk patois and I supposed you would use the same dialect as your parents. Negu too. She talks as well as the mother superior of my school."

Cilla smiled. "Negu taught me. She reads and writes. She knows everything in the books in M. Drapeaux's library and she's making me study them too. She and I are among the few black people who are educated. I forget once in a while and slip back to my own tongue, but Negu never forgets."

"How did she learn?" Asya was amazed.

"Oh, she's a high priestess. I guess Dambolla taught her. I don't know. Maybe she's like Jesus—born knowing. The real problem now," Cilla said, dismissing the subject of her education as inconsequential, "is what will you wear?"

In the weeks that followed, that problem was solved. Like magic, merchants from Cap François arrived at Cher Château with samples of materials from which Asya selected her wardrobe. Outstanding among these businessmen was M. Rowbottom. From the very first, Asya liked the English merchantman. He made her feel like a femme fatale, a woman of irresistible charm. When she had first walked into the little parlor where he was waiting with his wares, M. Rowbottom started toward her and then abruptly stopped as though overcome at the sight of her. With his weight on his heels and his head thrust back, he flung out his arms as if trying to take in this overwhelming loveliness.

"Ah, it is Mlle. Drapeaux," he spoke in a voice of rapture. "The beautiful Mlle. Drapeaux." Whereupon, he made a sweeping bow, and hung there like a worshipper in humble adoration. He remained bent over so long that Asya was uneasy as to what to do next. She said, *"Bonjour."*

Her voice sounded like a schoolgirl's rather than
that of an enchantress. She must learn some clever rep-
artee like Eleanore had always used.

At her words, M. Rowbottom straightened.
"Mademoiselle, you are lovelier than rumor has reported," he said admiringly, while Asya fleetingly wondered how rumor could have reported anything since
she had so recently arrived. She immediately dismissed
the thought as the merchant went on to say, "My poor
laces and linens will make a sad showing along such
beauty as your own." His shoulders drooped in dejection, and he shook his head while saying sadly, "My
poor wares. I have nothing worthy of such loveliness."

Asya walked close to him and touched his arm.
"You are very kind, monsieur, but let me decide about
your wares."

Immediately his whole attitude changed. He lifted
his head and a big smile instantly appeared, suffusing
his face with happiness. Everything about him was radiant. His blond hair seemed to reflect the sunlight,
and his strong white teeth shot out little sparks of light.
Even his cheekbones were polished with a high gleam
of pleasure.

"Ah," he clapped his hands as he spoke, "allow me
to show Mademoiselle to a chair, and I shall be delighted to display my merchandise."

It was fun shopping with M. Rowbottom. Before
uncovering each bolt of material, he first piqued her
curiosity with a lively description of what she was
about to see.

"This next linen, a singing linen," he said as he held
a finger to his ear and listened. Then he closed his
eyes. "Ah, when you wear it, you will make men's
hearts sing. It was made in Ireland, close to where St.
Patrick first landed. Irish lasses sing the whole time
they weave, and it is said that the flax is raised by the
leprechauns themselves."

He sounded so excited that Asya wanted to buy the
linen before she saw it. The same was true of his laces.

They were crocheted in the convent of St. Geneviève in southern France and before they were sold, the good soeurs placed their handiwork in the chapel and prayed a novena to St. Geneviève that its wearer would marry the man of her choice. Asya must have the lace, lots of lace. Not that she wanted a husband, not yet anyway, but it is well to look to the future.

"And the most magnificent of all," M. Rowbottom closed his eyes in ecstasy, "is a brocade from Florence. It is a blue, a heavenly blue woven in the same pattern that Lucretia Borgia once wore. Wait until you see it. You will be the most provocative lady at the dance. The gallants will not be able to take their eyes from you and the girls will be weak with envy. I have sold this to no one as yet. You will be the only one in all Haiti to have a gown of this material." The merchant paused. A sadness came over his face and he turned to her. "How foolish of me. Forgive me. I should not have brought the Borgia piece."

Asya was immediately alarmed. "Why not?" She must have that brocade.

He shook his head. "It is so expensive. So very expensive. I am embarrassed to have to ask the price."

Asya laughed in relief. "Don't worry about the price, M. Rowbottom. I'm a rich woman." She sat tall in the chair and said proudly, "I can pay whatever I wish for my clothes."

The happiness came back to M. Rowbottom's face, and without knowing why, Asya felt guilty for having been the cause of its brief disappearance.

"Good. Good." The merchant threw up his hands in excitement. "Wait until you see it. Shut your eyes. I shall drape it around you and you will see for yourself how irresistible you are. No, no. Don't open them yet."

Asya could hear him dragging something across the floor. "Now. Now, my dear."

She opened her eyes and saw herself in the gold mirror which he had moved from the other side of the room. The brocade shone as though it were made of

256

tinted silver, and yet it had the blue color of the sky on a cloudless day. She did not know her eyes could be so blue, and yet their very blueness gilded her skin and called attention to the jet blackness of her hair. She did look pretty at that. Maybe what she had needed all along was some fine clothing.

"You look like a painting in Windsor Castle." The man sighed. "Never have I had the pleasure of selling to so beautiful a lady." He bowed.

Unused to such flattery, Asya did not know what to say, so she asked, "Isn't brocade too hot for this country?"

M. Rowbottom laughed. "Of course, but beauty must not be practical. All the young ladies here wear brocade dresses to the balls. Of course, they buy a lighter weight brocade, which is not as beautiful, but cheaper. Perhaps Mademoiselle would prefer what the others wear." He reached to remove the silk from about her.

"No. No." Asya drew back. "I am used to warm clothes. The weight means nothing. I will take the brocade."

M. Rowbottom cocked his head and looked at her admiringly. "The silk was made for you. Mademoiselle has exquisite taste." He sighed. "A new queen has come to Haiti."

In a businesslike manner he briskly picked up the heavy mirror and returned it to its corner in the room. "I must not keep so great a lady waiting. I must show her what else I have brought."

As the selection of materials for her wardrobe continued, a thought came to Asya which she confided to M. Rowbottom. "Where shall I wear all these beautiful clothes? As yet, I don't know anyone to invite me to any parties. Perhaps I should choose only drab heavy cottons for riding over the plantation to see what's growing?"

M. Rowbottom stopped unrolling the bolt of embroidered cotton he held in his hands and turned to look at Asya. His eyes half closed while he regarded her speculatively. Suddenly they shot wide open as excitement flashed out. "I have it. I know just the right person to introduce you to Haiti. My daughter," he announced. "My daughter, Eloise. She knows everyone."

"Oh." Asya leaned back in her chair. Suddenly she remembered. She thought she had heard the name Rowbottom before. Of course! It was an Eloise Rowbottom whom M. Grenier had mentioned as her father's betrothed. She had planned on disliking Eloise. Asya tossed her head. How silly, she told herself. I might even like the girl. If she takes after her father, I'm sure I shall. Inwardly she found herself hoping M. Rowbottom's daughter might even become her friend.

A few days later, Eloise Rowbottom came to call. Asya thought her the most beautiful girl she had ever seen. Even prettier than Eleanore. She was dressed in pink linen from head to toe. Even her slippers were pink. The only contrasting touch was the lining of her bonnet, which was the same shade of blue as her eyes. She was dainty and feminine, like a Dresden figurine.

Asya liked Eloise at once. She loved listening to her tell about the exciting times the young people had on the island. Her father had been right. Eloise knew everyone of importance. She and M. Rowbottom were wrapped up in a social whirl, and Asya envied them. She so hoped she would soon be included in some of the gay parties.

"Father just loves being with people," Eloise drooled. "I think that's why he is engaged in commerce, so he can meet people. This selling of merchandise," Eloise's voice came down an octave and she spoke disdainfully, "is only an avocation. A whim he allows himself and, mind you," she now sounded surprised, "he loves it. But that's Father. Always having fun."

"You know," she confided, "we have a lovely home in England, but Father found it boring being a country gentleman, with nothing to do but collect the rents

258

from his lands. So we ventured to the New World, the land of opportunity, as he calls it. And here he is so happy."

Eloise looked about the sitting room at Cher Château, with its Aubusson-covered chairs, the Chinese pink hooked rug on the floor, and the purple bougainvillea waving in from the open doorway, and gave a deep sigh. "I miss our country place," Eloise said longingly. "We have to live in a town house in Cap François, and it's so much smaller than the plantation homes of our friends. But Father says," her voice sounded as if she were parroting a sermon, "we must live where our business is. Our friends will like us for ourselves and not for the house we live in."

"I think your father is a wonderful man," Asya said admiringly. "So full of verve. Not dull and staid like most men." Inwardly she reminded herself that she was expounding a lot for her limited knowledge of the male world. However, her remark did sound sophisticated.

"Oh, that darling father of mine," Eloise actually trilled in her evident pleasure over the possession of such a parent. "He's so young-looking. Not even a gray hair yet. Of course, the men in the Rowbottom family have always married young." Then she leaned companionably toward Asya and giggled, "But not the women. Drat it!"

Asya laughed. It was easy being friends with Eloise. "You probably have so many beaux you can't make up your mind," she said.

"I'll introduce you to them," Eloise offered, "and you can help me decide."

For a moment she sat in thought. Suddenly she burst out in excitement. "I'll have a party for you. A big party. I'll invite as many people as our house will hold, especially the eligible men."

"Oh." Asya almost collapsed in her chair and her heart sank at the thought of meeting strange men. "Oh."

Eloise looked at her in bewilderment. "What's the matter? Wouldn't you like a party?"

"Oui. Oui. It's only that," Asya hunted for some explanation of her apparent reluctance. "It's only that I have nothing to wear. As yet, I do not have any seamstress to make up the dresses from the materials I selected from M. Rowbottom. Negu is getting me a dressmaker, but she will not be free to start until next week. I am told she is the best in all of Haiti."

"Oh, those niggers! They don't know how to hurry. Negu's probably getting one of her relations to do the work. They all stick together. Let me get someone for you," she suggested. "I'll speak to Father. There are a few Englishwomen in town who do beautiful sewing and they won't take forever."

Asya was amazed. It was nice having a friend who was interested. She felt light-hearted. "Will you, Eloise?" she asked eagerly. "I'd be so grateful."

Patting her hand, Eloise assured her, "Don't you worry anymore. Father knows how young girls want new clothes in a hurry for a big social event. He'll send one, maybe two or three, seamstresses out tomorrow, and your dress will be ready in time." She stood up. "I'm going home and start making plans right now."

Later, when Asya told Negu about the English seamstress coming the next day, they had their first open disagreement.

"They're probably some of M. Rowbottom's poor relations trying to horn in on a good thing," she said caustically.

A feeling of loyalty to her new friend welled up inside Asya's breast. "Don't you talk like that about Mlle. Eloise," she ordered. "She's a kind, sweet girl, and if those are her poor relations, which I know they aren't, then it is generous of her to see that they have a livelihood."

"Englishwomen know nothing about fashion," Negu snapped. "They'll dress you to look like some washed-out, watery-eyed, sickly-looking wench."

"Don't you talk like that about Mlle. Eloise." Asya was enraged. "This is my first friend and I want her spoken of with respect."

Negu said icily, "I made no mention of Mlle. Row-bottom's name. If you think that unflattering description fits her, that was your conjecture, not mine." Negu walked from the room.

The next day, the seamstress arrived and Asya dismissed Negu's disapproval from her mind. Eloise came too, and it was exhilarating to be the center of so much attention. Cilla was invited to share in the exciting selection of patterns, but when her opinion did not coincide with that of Eloise, Asya no longer consulted her.

"Niggers have such wild tastes," Eloise confided to Asya when Cilla had gone to the kitchen for a pot of chocolate. "They know nothing about what a lady of breeding should wear."

Asya was flattered to be referred to as a lady of breeding. It was like being treated as royalty.

In the matter of dressing her hair, Asya again placed herself entirely under Eloise's tutelage. That proved to be a more frustrating problem. "You must wear curls hanging down over your cheeks, and the rest of your hair pulled in a tight little bun on top of your head," the English girl asserted. "That is the way the queen wears her hair, and she sets the style."

Eloise cut some of Asya's hair on either side of her face and after wetting it, rolled it in kids. Later, however, when she took it down and tried to brush it around her finger in an attempt to shape it into wiry-looking curls, Eloise despaired. No matter how much she brushed or how wet she made it, Asya's hair maintained its rigid straightness. "It's like curling straw," Eloise complained.

When Asya looked at herself in the mirror, she gasped in horror. The hairy arrangement on each cheek stuck out like the clump of hay on either side of a horse's mouth when he has greedily taken too big a bite.

"You will have to wear false curls," Eloise conceded defeat. "Father happens to have some in the store for just such emergencies."

The knot of hair on top of Asya's head was another problem. After working with it for a half-hour, Eloise shook her head despairingly. Surveying her handiwork, she said "It looks like—I hate to say it, but it looks as though you're wearing a big black cook pot on top of your head."

After Eloise had departed, Cilla comforted in her soft reassuring voice, "Don't you worry none, Mam'selle Asya. I'll fix you up. You don't have to look like the queen. You're French and have more hair than those wispy-headed English girls. When the Lord gives something beautiful, don't hide it. You got to show it off, or maybe He'll think you aren't grateful. It'd be awful if He took away your gift." She rolled her eyes in apprehension. "Beaux don't go for bald-headed girls."

Asya laughed. "You say the silliest things, Cilla, Who ever heard of a bald-headed girl?"

Cilla's face took on a solemn look. "I hear that all the nuns are bald-headed under those veils."

The humor of the remark poked Asya in the stomach and she bent over double with laughter. "Cilla, where did you ever get that idea?" she gasped. "They shave their heads."

"Maybe so." Cilla was dubious. "But when they keep cutting off what the Lord gave them," her voice took on a pedantic tone, "after a while He just takes it away. God's truth."

"Have you been going around checking convent heads?" Asya teased. "Well, since you know so much about heads, what will you do with mine?"

"I got plenty of ideas."

At Eloise's suggestion, Cilla and Asya arrived early for the party. "Since you're the guest of honor," her hostess said, "you don't want to look all sticky and weather-beaten from a long ride into town. You'll need a lot of time to dress so you will look cool and composed when the guests come."

Asya did not feel cool and composed. It was her first party and she was excited. Her heart had been somersaulting wildly all day. It was as though the party started with the thought and would last as long as her memories. Who wanted to be calm on the most exhilarating day of her life?

Eloise was busy and, after showing Cilla and her mistress to their rooms, excused herself to attend to some final details. "The curls are lying over there on the bureau." Eloise pointed to a box. "Cilla can pin them on you. I'll look in later to see how she does. We were so lucky that Father had your shade."

When the door had closed, Cilla ran to the bureau. "Let's see what kind of curls grow in M. Rowbottom's store?"

When she had lifted the lid of the box, the maid stepped back, turned her head away, and wrinkled her nose. *"Mon Dieu!"*

Asya laughed. "That bad?"

Cilla giggled and reached into the box. Holding the curls on either side of her head, she turned around for Asya to see. They looked like three long dull black screws hanging stiffly down Cilla's brown cheeks. Asya had her first moment of doubt about current fashions. "They surely look skimpy," she laughed. "Do you think they match my shade of hair?"

Cilla began to dance prankishly around the room. As she did, the curls flew out wildly and one dropped to the floor. Immediately Cilla stopped her cavorting and languidly pointing to the fallen adornment, said to an imaginary dancing partner in a high affected voice, "Sir, I've dropped my postiche. Would you be good enough to hand it to me? My laces are too tight for me to bend?"

Both girls laughed and, with the laughter, Asya's apprehensions were soon forgotten. It was going to be a wonderful party.

Cilla had a manner of instilling such faith and confidence in her ability to do a job, that when she half-playfully and half-seriously suggested it would be more fun if Asya did not look into the mirror until she was completely dressed and coiffured for the affair, her mistress agreed. It would be a beautiful surprise. Somehow, Asya knew that Cilla would not let her down.

When at last Cilla said, "Now you may look," and excitedly led her to the long mirror between the windows of the room, Asya was dumbfounded at the sight of her own reflection. The person looking back at her was a stranger. Someone new whom she had not known she had been living with. Someone grown up. Her hair fascinated her. It was all done up like a Greek goddess. Except for those side hairs which Eloise had cut, all of Asya's thick hair was pulled back from her face and piled on top of her head. Cilla had divided it into several strands and curled and entwined them about each other until they looked like a nest of shiny black eels. The short loose side hairs were greased and shaped into one flat curl sleeked against each cheek. Then Asya noticed her eyes. "They look blue," she said excitedly. "I didn't know I had blue eyes."

"It's your dress," Cilla said delightedly. "It's the blue of your dress which gives them that color."

Asya put her hands up to touch her cheeks and quickly drew them away. "These little curls. They seem to be pointing right up to my eyes to tell everyone to look at the new color I have in them."

Asya opened her mouth to tell Cilla how happy she was, but her exuberance left her without words. Cilla had done this just for her. Cilla, who would not be going to the party. She flung her arms around the Negress and kissed her. "I love you."

"Well! Indeed!" Eloise, unnoticed, had entered the room. Asya turned around to find her hostess standing in the doorway looking very much aghast as her eyes went reprovingly from maid to mistress.

"Look how beautifully Cilla dressed my hair." Asya was like a trumpet blaring forth good tidings. "I feel so elegant."

Eloise looked at Asya's head, and her eyes widened in disbelief. She suddenly snapped them shut so tightly that her nose wrinkled with the effort. She opened her eyes again and raised them slowly and warily to Asya's coiffure. Eloise shook her head. "I thought I was seeing things, but they're still there."

"What's the matter?" Asya was deflated. "Don't you like it?"

In her high-pitched voice, Eloise spat out in disgust, "How can anyone admire a bunch of wiggly-looking snakes writhing together on top of your head?"

Asya's chest contracted so much it sat on her breath; she could not say a word. Instead of a glamorous belle, she was once again the ridiculous little schoolgirl in a hot brown uniform.

"The guests will be here any minute," Eloise complained, "and we don't have any time to change your hair to something presentable. I'll get Father. I don't know what to do." Eloise was approaching hysteria.

As though summoned by some spiritual messenger, M. Rowbottom appeared in the hall outside the open door. "Are you girls ready to go downstairs and bowl the young gallants over with your charm?"

"Father, come here!" Eloise ordered frantically. "Come in here."

"So," M. Rowbottom drawled teasingly, "am I so old and harmless that it is safe to invite me right into the boudoir? Well, never mind, I'll not question it. I'll take advantage of it."

Asya watched him as he walked easily into the room, his round face shined up with happy pleasure, and she felt her confidence return. This man would make everything all right again. At the moment, he was happiness, sent to hand it out to those who needed it. She held up her head, the better to display the monstrosity she wore upon it.

M. Rowbottom stopped in shock. His eyes grew big and round. His mouth dropped open as though there was not enough room inside him to absorb his reaction to the sight before him. Then approval danced in his eyes and he threw out his arms. "Delightful! Delightful!" he reiterated. Coming close, he gently touched Asya's hair, after which he took her hand and beamed upon her. "This will be the greatest honor in my life. To present from my house the most beautiful woman in Haiti." He bent and kissed her hand.

Chapter Twenty-one

Long after the guests had gone, Eloise and Asya, who was spending the night at the Rowbottom house, stayed up to relive the party. Asya could not have slept anyway, for her head was still whirling with the events of the evening. She had never talked with so many boys at one time, and to her amazement she had felt as poised and as relaxed with them as if she had grown up surrounded by beaux. It was all due to that kind M. Rowbottom, who had built up her confidence through his lavish admiration of her appearance. Asya had never felt so happy.

"I think it was the nicest party I ever gave," Eloise said smugly. "I think it was because everyone was so anxious to meet you that they came. Not one regret, mind you. You're a very important person on this island, Asya, and people envy me because I am the first one to be your friend. From now on, you'll have lots of friends." Eloise paused while she mulled something over in her mind. The thought must have troubled her. She pouted, "I hope you won't forget about me."

Spontaneously Asya placed her hands on Eloise's shoulders and playfully shook her. "Don't talk like that. You will always be my very best friend, for you came when I had no one."

Eloise gave a sad little smile. "Many people don't like me because Father engages in commerce. They call him a—" she swallowed hard "—a shopkeeper, and the way they say it, one would think it was a dirty

267

word. Here in Cap François, one has to be a soldier or a landowner to be important."

Asya's heart went out to Eloise. She remembered her own hurt when she had first gone to school and been discriminated against because she was not royalty. "If I am as important as you say I am, then I will not go to any parties unless you are also invited. I promise." She held up her right hand as they used to do in school. "They take the two of us, or neither."

"Oooh," Eloise cooed. "We shall have great times together."

And they did.

Asya wondered what excuse people had used in Haiti to socialize before she arrived. Everyone wanted to honor her at some convivial gathering or other. And she went to all of them, in spite of Negu's warnings that she be careful of fortune-hunters.

"She doesn't know her place," Eloise complained one day, when the housekeeper disapproved of a drab gray fabric Eloise had chosen for Asya. "In all the other houses we go to, the black help only say, 'Yes, mam'selle. No, mam'selle,' but not your nigger. She acts like a mother hen, the way she orders you about. Really, Asya, you ought to talk to that bossy black woman of yours."

But Asya never did reprove Negu. She rather liked being noticed, even if everything she did was all wrong in the older woman's eyes. And Negu was right about the color. Asya was becoming aware that the Creole girls on the island wore flashier colors than those Eloise selected. Cilla had intimated she knew some Haitian seamstresses who could sew as well as any in Paris, although how Cilla knew about Paris, Asya was not able to figure out.

However, she hesitated about discarding Eloise's suggestions on dress, for she did not want her friend to think she was ungrateful. It was an ordinary dinner and musicale which caused the revolution. Eloise had driven out to Cher Château. There the two girls would dress and then depart for the plantation of their hosts. Asya wore a new dress for the occasion. When she had selected the material, M. Rowbottom had draped it over her shoulders and across her breast so as to get the effect of the color against her face. Throwing out his arms in his usual ecstatic manner, he had exclaimed, "Magnificent! Like the sun from the skies of Egypt which sent me this silk. Spun only for a princess. A golden princess."

Asya thought it looked more tan than golden, but Monsieur assured her she was seeing it in a poor light. "At night, by candlelight, you will be an apparition from the courts of the pharaohs. Ah!" He closed his eyes as if he were already envisioning the scene of her triumph at the musicale, although inwardly she did not think she had to be quite that ravishing for only a small dinner party. But he seemed to know best.

Now, in her bedroom, Asya knew the dress had been a mistake. When she looked at her reflection in the mirror, she was depressed, even though Cilla had carefully arranged three hibiscus in the coils of her upswept hairdo. They peeped out like red eyes on the curled snakes, as Eloise referred to her coiffure.

"Do you like this dress, Cilla?" Asya asked, studying herself in the looking glass.

Cilla obviously swallowed before she answered. "It's nice." She could have been reading the answer from a book for all the spontaneity in her voice.

"It would look better if you'd pull in your stomach," Eloise observed as she thumped Asya on her protruding part. "You've lost a lot of your adolescent weight since you've been here, but you'll have to flatten it out more." She ran her hand over her own flat stomach. "Look at mine. No pot at all."

Asya did look and sighed. "I guess I'll have to stop eating."

"You can eat. You don't have to starve yourself. Just don't eat so much that people get the impression you swallowed a ball."

269

Asya laughed and felt better. She stuck out her chin. She had gotten this dress for the party, and it was what she was wearing. So she had better make up her mind to have a good time, she told herself philosophically.

But, for all her resolve, the evening got worse instead of better. She had only shortly arrived when, while listening concentratedly to an Englishman whose accent was more difficult to follow than most, she suddenly had the feeling that someone was standing beside her. Someone tall. He was watching her, for she could feel his eyes upon her. Her heart skipped excitedly, and she talked longer than she ordinarily would for she was savoring the suspense of wondering who her admirer might be. When she was able to disengage herself politely from the loquacious Englishman, she turned. Her alluring look changed to one of shock. She was staring up into the amused green eyes of none other than Captain Etienne Grenier. Her mouth snapped shut. Otherwise, her heart might have leaped right out.

"So nice to see you again, *ma petite enfante*." His voice still held that teasing note. "Although I must say you are no longer an *enfante,* but a lovely young lady." His eyes wandered over her figure so brazenly that Asya knew she was blushing by the warmth in her cheeks.

His eyes traveled to the top of her head. "The coiffure is enticing. No Englishman designed that."

"I'm glad it meets with your approval," she said with a toss of her head, as if to shrug off the compliment.

"If one is a wild tiger lily on the roadside, then one should wave her blatant colors at those who pass by. Why try to hide them?"

"Indeed." Asya wanted to slap him. When he said something nice, why did he not stop instead of going on and muddling up a pretty speech? "You make the tiger lily sound very common. Ladies prefer to be compared with a shy, delicate flower like a rose," she reprimanded.

Etienne laughed. Plainly, he was enjoying her annoyance. "Perhaps I did make a wrong comparison. I was forgetting that roses show their beauty first, and then when you know them better, their sharp thorns. I agree. The rose is a better comparison for most females."

Asya stepped back and made a big pretense of looking M. Grenier up and down. "Your appearance is most becoming for the occasion," she observed, "but you forgot something."

"What is that?" He was enjoying their tilt.

"Your manners," she snapped.

The amused look vanished from his eyes, and he took her hand. "I go too far with my teasing. Forgive me," he said, and bending, he kissed her fingertips. Her heart sank, leaving a quivering, empty place where it had been. What would she do now?

As she was struggling to recover some measure of calm, a feminine figure suddenly sprang between Asya and M. Grenier. It was Eloise. Eloise in soft white voile, looking like one of those exquisite Viennese figurines.

"So this is the famous Capt. Grenier." Mlle. Rowbottom's voice gushed up and up like water in a fountain. "Ooh," it splashed down, "it's so good to meet you."

M. Grenier swept Eloise a low, graceful, but long-drawn-out bow. He had not bowed when he had first seen her, Asya observed, and now he was making quite a performance out of his greeting to Eloise. He also kissed her hand, not just her fingertips. Asya was exasperated.

"You are as beautiful as I was told, Mlle. Rowbottom," M. Grenier was saying.

"I didn't know you knew my dearest friend, Asya," Eloise said to him in a breathy voice. Turning to Asya, she asked half-teasingly, half-reprovingly, "Why didn't you tell me you knew M. Grenier?"

271

Asya's heart was now back in place, but it was heavy with gloom. "Such a small matter. I probably didn't think it important enough to mention." And with that, she walked away, tears stinging her eyes. Delicate rose, garish tiger lily, golden princess, who cared what they called her. She still felt as if she were back in school, dressed in her old brown uniform and playing grown up, with her hair piled on top of her head. After one bright flash of excitement, the evening loomed dull and long. Asya was in a black mood, and frankly, she did not know why.

The bubbling enthusiasm of Eloise, back at Cher Château, didn't help any. "M. Grenier is so exciting," she cooed, as she pulled back the covers to climb into bed. "He's really a roué, a wanton no-good," she went on. "No proper young lady would ever be caught flirting with him." She heaved a deep sigh. "But, then, when I'm with him, I never think of propriety."

"Why do you say that?" For some unaccountable reason, Asya wanted to defend M. Grenier.

"Haven't you heard? The whole island talks about it. He lives with a nigger mistress! Refers to her as his housekeeper. Not even a mulatto with a little white in her. This one is big, built magnificently, they say. I guess she makes a good bedful, and that's what he likes."

"Eloise!" Asya was shocked. "You talk like a—like a peasant discussing the breeding of his livestock."

"It's all the same. Bull and cow, sow and boar, man and woman. The only difference is that a woman makes a little more pretense at disguising her intent than does the cow or sow."

Eloise noticed Asya's revulsion. "You're young and probably have romantic notions about mating, such as marriage and fidelity, and rosy skies forever after. Man and wife are no different than the animals, who for monetary reasons are mated by their owners. I want a man who can provide me a comfortable barn and good fodder. If I'm to be no more than an animal, and that

is what women are, and give birth to a bunch of calves
for the good of the strain and the farm, I'd rather pick
an interesting bull to do my procreating with. Life can
grow dull standing around in the stalls, eating hay, or
pasturing in the meadows all day long. And as a cow, I
don't give a damn what shade of rival cows my old bull
chases out in the field, as long as I'm the one who gets
sheltered and fed and pampered."

Asya shook her head in amazement. It was the same
attitude Eleanore had professed. Was she, Asya, the
only naive one? Was romance only for legendary
characters in books? Had Mère Denise and the soeurs
been wrong when they spoke of love and the beauty of
having babies? She remembered how delightedly each
baby was welcomed at the Hospice of the Sacre-Coeur.
The nuns fluttered and beamed over each new arrival.
They folded their hands and, raising their eyes to the
ceiling of the nursery, prayed, "Thank God for this
precious little soul. May it be happy and good." Was
that all meaningless?

"I don't believe what you say," Asya protested. "At
the hospital where I was born, the nuns taught that animals were placed here to serve God's people. Why
should we rate ourselves on the same level as the animals?"

Eloise looked at her in disgust. "Do you believe all
that hogwash the nuns shoved down your throat? Why,
they've never been out in the world. Most of them
joined the convent because they couldn't get a man,
else why would they want to hide themselves in white
robes behind monastery walls."

Asya's gloom had turned to anger. It was the same
kind of rage she had felt years ago when Eleanore had
insulted her heritage. But what did Eloise know of the
nuns? They were her friends—for years, her only
friends. How dare she presume to mock them!

Something cold, like a wind on a rainy day, blew
over Asya's heart, putting out the glow which had been
enkindled there by the friendship of M. Rowbottom

and his daughter. In the morning she must ask Cilla about the Haitian seamstresses. She would be a tiger lily, perhaps. Vulgar. Common.

But at least, she told herself, she would have no thorns.

Chapter Twenty-two

The Rowbottoms were quick to sense Asya's disaffection. In return, they slowly, but steadily, pecked at her friendship as a woodpecker does a tree. The first time Asya appeared in a gown sewed by the Haitian seamstress Cilla recommended, Eloise gave it a casual glance and commented, "There's a thread hanging from the hem. Very careless of the dressmaker. If you give me a scissors," she went on in her high sweet voice, "I'll be glad to snip it for you." Not a word about the garland of bright red roses embroidered across the waist of the white dress at just the right height to call attention to the form of her breasts.

"It's the French touch," the seamstress had said. "At your age, the female body is so beautiful. All us dressmakers have to do is add a little bright sign on you to let the menfolk know where to look first."

Then there was the night the opera opened in Cap François. President Christophe was there. Everyone with any claim to importance would be there to show his interest in Haiti's first cultural endeavor. Asya was invited to a buffet before the performance. However, it was northeastern season and the rains had been coming off and on without warning that whole day.

"It will be very hot indoors tonight," Cilla said. "You must wear something cool, and yet a dress that won't wilt if you get rained on. Umbrellas don't help none when these northeasterns blow."

Asya went to the buffet feeling very elegant in a blue

linen gown. It was a rather dark blue, and yet bright enough to cast its reflection in her eyes and give them the color of a deep sea. At least, that was what Cilla insisted. The maid had contrived a new coiffure for the occasion. At the very back of her head, Cilla wound Asya's hair around and around until it resembled a neatly coiled rope. From here, two long round curls hung down her back. Asya had no idea how Cilla had managed to get something curly out of her straight hair, but with the aid of rags and a mysterious concoction, Cilla trained the strands to her liking. The coil was encircled with gardenias. Asya wore no jewelry. Cilla insisted she was too young for the elaborate pieces left by the late Mme. Drapeaux. As a substitute, Cilla sewed a strip of gardenias across her *décolletage*.

Asya inspected herself in the mirror and announced gaily, "I look like a major with my medals of honor splashed across my breast."

Cilla snickered. "Just don't let any gentleman get too close. Those posies won't take the pressing like medals will."

At the buffet, Eloise seemed to make a point of not seeing Asya, even though the girls and their escorts had planned to meet there and go to the opera together. When finally they met over the pastry table, the English girl made a big show of scrutinizing Asya's neckline. "Goodness," her high thin voice could be heard in the most of the room. "I think, Asya, you have dandruff on the back of your dress."

Asya wanted to crawl under the table and hide, until she heard Godefroy, her companion for the evening, say, "That's not dandruff. That's the sugar from my pastry. Asya looks so elegant and smells so good I like to stick close to her, even when I'm eating."

He moved closer to her and rubbed his nose in the flowers of her hair. "You're so sweet," he cooed, "I'd like to take a bite out of you."

Raising her eyebrows, Eloise said in a snide voice,

276

"While you're nosing flowers, Godefroy, don't ignore Asya's other floral arrangement." She let her eyes fall suggestively to the gardenias across Asya's breast.

It was the first time Asya had made a blond jealous. How exciting!

But, Asya soon forgot all about Eloise. The opening night of the opera held too many other highlights. First, there was the audience. People had come from all over Haiti to attend the event. It was not that they loved opera, but this was the new country's first step toward cultural achievement, and President Christophe had insisted that all who could afford must attend. His people were no longer slaves. Now they were civilized, and ready for polish and refinement.

Except for church, it was Asya's first racially mixed audience, and she was amazed at the apparent wealth of the Negro opera-goers. Judging from the number of satins and brocatelles and other silks in which the black members of the audience were costumed, M. Rowbottom had done a landslide business. The Englishman was not the only merchant to profit. The jewelers of the town must have emptied their vaults onto the ears, necks, and arms of the former slaves. Each woman looked as though she had hung all her jewels upon her person at one time. The men, wore wide satin ribbons across their chests, emblazoned with brilliant jewels. One man had surpassed the others. In his lapel he wore a jeweled sunflower, life-size.

Ten minutes before the curtain went up, trumpets blared as if preluding a coronation, and President and Mme. Christophe appeared in their royal box. Before the candles were blown out, Asya saw a tall figure quietly enter and take his seat behind Mme. Christophe. It was M. Grenier. Her own little trumpets sounded in Asya's ears, and her heart insisted on hopping to the music they made.

At the close of the first act, Godefroy and Asya walked to the lobby. Eloise and her escort followed. "I must give them credit," Eloise said sweetly. "These niggers are a very receptive audience."

Godefroy looked down at her and frowned. "Why are you always picking on the natives? You talk as though they were something to put on the dissecting table and study."

"That's so true. They are different. They are servants who are assuming the class of gentry. In England, no menial would think of stepping out of his class." She began to laugh. "They're so amusing as they try to imitate their betters."

"It *is* amusing, isn't it?" a voice said sarcastically from behind Asya. "Some of them display better manners than their so-called betters."

She did not have to turn to see who it was. That giveaway heart of hers was acting like a drum as it beat against her breast.

While Eloise stood with a perplexed look upon her face, trying to digest the intent of M. Grenier's remark, he nodded recognition to the men and took Asya's hand. "The trumpets should have sounded for you. You look so regal tonight." Etienne bent and kissed her hand and this time it was not only the fingertips.

Then he straightened up and turned to the others. "Will you excuse Mademoiselle for a moment? M. President has asked that I bring her to his box."

Asya happily noticed that Eloise's eyes and mouth were three little O's of surprise as M. Grenier led her away.

As they walked toward the royal box, Asya was thankful for the support of M. Grenier's arm. She had never met a president and her knees were quivering.

M. Christophe rose as Asya came toward him. She had to look up, for he was tall, tall as Etienne Grenier, but much thinner. Without waiting for an introduction, he spoke to her. "So, you're the young lady from the great Drapeaux plantation. Already you have been here a year, and it is time we met."

Asya bent those unsteady knees in an attempt at a curtsey. She had the notion she was being scolded for not having made an effort to meet him sooner. When she stood up and raised her head, she saw that there was a kindly look in his large brown eyes, a look such as a father might bestow upon a favorite daughter. She must have been mistaken about his disapproval, yet an uneasiness remained.

It disappeared abruptly as he turned and introduced the woman in the chair beside him. "This is Mme. Christophe. She too has been hoping to meet you."

At first glance Asya saw only a black face atop a big blur of white material which draped down over the chair like a pile of snow. Automatically, Asya dropped in a curtsey. As she rose, her glance took in the softness of the material in the gown the president's wife was wearing. It was very full, like a nun's habit, covering any semblance of a figure. Except for a large white pearl at her neck, Mme. Christophe wore no jewelry. Only then did Asya look into her face.

It was thin and drawn, the face of a nun at the close of the Lenten fast. The cheekbones were high, giving an ascetic appearance. Then Asya saw the eyes. To her surprise, they were slanted and green, green as the Caribbean on a cloudless day. Asya had never seen a Negress with green eyes, especially ones which slanted. Mme. Christophe wore her sleek black hair, which was heavily oiled, pulled up tight to the top of her head and bound into the shape of a little muffin. Asya could not help but wonder if the Oriental slant of the woman's eyes was caused by the tightness of her coiffure. When she let down her hair, did her eyes resume normal shape?

Without evidencing any expression, those green eyes stared straight up at Asya, giving the impression that their owner had already examined her and arrived at an opinion. Favorable or unfavorable, they did not divulge. Asya thought of a cat. A wild cat. Lissome, sinewy. Ready to spring for the kill, or curl up in a corner and purr.

Finally Mme. Christophe spoke. She had a warm throaty voice, which softly reached out and patted one lovingly on the head. "I hope Etienne soon brings you to the palace. My daughters want to know you." Turning to M. Grenier, she asked, "You will bring her, won't you? Amethiste and Athenaire would love it."

"*Ma chère femme*," he said, his voice lovingly hovering over the words, "for you, of course."

Something swelled up inside Asya's breast and little needles pricked at it painfully. He spoke so lovingly to the president's wife. Never had he spoken to *her* like that. Something told her he never would. She bit her lip. Asya did not like Mme. Christophe.

Her thoughts were interrupted by a laugh from the president. "Such sweet talk. Before my very eyes too. My wife and my most trusted confidant. *Amour, amour.*" He shook his head. "It is well that I am a broadminded man." He addressed Asya, and she saw the amusement in his eyes. "You can see that the problems of a president are not all concerned with matters of state." He chuckled and his shoulders shook with enjoyment of the situation. Asya smiled stiffly. She did not think it very funny. In fact she thought it all quite silly. Certainly no behavior for a president and his wife.

By now, her knees had regained their customary stability. How stupid she had been to get excited about a couple of fools aping aristocrats. Why, anyone could wear a crown and call himself a king.

"I think it time I rejoin my party," Asya said primly. Then, with mock civility, she made an exaggerated curtsey. She would show them. She, too, could put on an act if she wished to.

"I have heard so *much* about you," she oozed. "It was most," Asya paused, and went on sarcastically, "most enlightening meeting President and Madame Christophe."

In an instant Asya felt M. Grenier's firm hand on her elbow. "It is time I take you back to where you belong. Come, *enfante*."

Asya detected the anger in his voice. She tossed her head. This was fun. The way his fingers gripped her arm betrayed his annoyance with her.

To further bait Etienne Grenier, Asya asked as they walked along, "Isn't it amazing that someone who grew up as a slave, a servant girl, such as Mme. Christophe, can suddenly acquire the manners of a lady?"

"Not as amazing as someone who has been raised a lady and grows up with the manners of a servant girl," he snapped.

Asya giggled. "I do believe you are trying to lecture me."

His grip on her arm tightened. For a moment she thought he might shake her right there in the opera house. She wished he would. That would create some excitement among her friends. Instead, he swung her around to face him. He had a big, fixed smile, but his eyes were cold. "For your information, so that you will not be so ignorant in any future discussions you might be having with some of your social-minded friends, you should know that Mme. Christophe was never a slave. She was the daughter of a wealthy innkeeper who served only the finest ladies and gentlemen on the island. It is well that you were not in Haiti during those days, since you would not have qualified for inclusion in their clientele." He gave a short snappy facsimile of a bow and walked away.

That night, Asya received her first proposal of marriage. It came at the tail end of a long and dreamlike evening and Asya had to pinch herself to be sure she was hearing correctly. This was the highest compliment a girl could be paid and Asya felt all tingly and unsure of her judgment. But she had no intention of marrying Godefroy Laborde. While he was older than she, he seemed scarcely more than a gawky youth in the early stages of learning to manipulate a razor. A date for a gay evening was all Godefroy meant to Asya. Furthermore, she did not like the way his ears stuck out from the sides of his head. If she married him, she could visualize herself surrounded by a coterie of children whose ears protruded like their father's.

Asya cooed as she patted Godefroy's cheek, "You're a darling to ask me to be your wife, but I'm too young to know my own mind yet. Too silly, too," she added as an afterthought. He reached up for her hand on his face and slid it around to his mouth where he pressed a kiss into the palm. Gently, he folded her fingers and said, "There. When I kissed you, I placed my heart in your hand. It's yours to hurt, to cherish, or to throw away."

Asya was touched. At once she was ashamed of herself for dismissing his suit so lightly. Maybe his children would not inherit his protruding ears after all. He was rather sweet and easygoing.

But Asya remembered the firm grip on her elbow and the strength emanating from the man whose hand it was. Her heart took breathy little skips as she thought of Etienne's handsome face. Then she looked at Godefroy and sighed. "I don't think I shall ever marry, at least, not for a long, long time."

Chapter Twenty-three

The next morning Asya awoke late and found it hard to rouse herself from her bed. She wanted to lie there, watching the sun seep lazily in through the window, and remember every luscious detail of her first night at the opera. But a knock at her bedroom door forced her out of her reverie.

"Asya," Negu's voice urged through the door. She opened it a crack and saw that her mistress was awake. "Asya," her soft voice spoke excitedly. "You must dress quickly. We have an honored guest."

Asya wrinkled her brow in annoyance. She did not want to get out of bed. Not yet. And had her ear caught the word "we"? Why did the Negress always talk as though everything at Cher Château concerned the two of them?

"It is Abbé Brille," the housekeeper continued. "The chaplain to the president." She bent and whispered into Asya's ear, "This is not a religious call. He is here for a special reason. Of that I am certain."

Pooh, thought Asya, as she dressed in the clothes Cilla had laid out for her. Chaplain to the president! Hopefully he would have more manners than the president himself!

Abbé Brille was waiting for Asya in the library. As she opened the door to see him standing there, perusing the bookshelves, she almost shrunk back in shock. Never had she seen a man so big. For a moment she thought the Holy Ghost himself had come to call. The Abbé was so tall that the top of his head almost brushed the ceiling. As for his girth, he was as round as a carriage wheel, and, as he walked toward her, his voluminous white cassock swished from side to side across the floor like a billowing duster. His face was large, but handsome, for with all the bulk of his body, the priest carried but one chin. At first glance Asya thought him bald, but then she noted that his light brown hair, tanned to the same shade as his skin, started far back on his head. He smiled at her, and his teeth looked strong and white, giving the impression that the man could chew into anything, physical or spiritual.

Asya hurried across the room and knelt before the priest for his blessing. He mumbled the Latin words of the religious incantation so quickly that it might have been no more than a *bon soir* he said over her head. Then he put his big hands under Asya's arms and lifted her to her feet.

"So, you're the little angel," he said, beaming beatifically upon her, "who's come to roost in the Drapeaux house. Such a little mite to run so big an establishment." The Abbé Brille patted her on the head like a puppy. "But, you'll do. Little women are like little shotguns. Very potent."

"*Merci, Père,*" Asya laughed. "I'll try not to fire off too often. Have a chair." She indicated the largest in the library.

"Non. Non." He waved the suggestion aside and walked to the bookshelves. "I see my old friends are still here—Homer. Vicente. Dryden. Epictetus. You have made their acquaintance? Oui?"

"Well," Asya hesitated. "Frankly, *Père,* I read so much in school and in the hospital while I was growing up that now I find it a welcome change to get acquainted with people. But I'll come back to my earlier friends one day, for I love to read."

The Abbé Brille nodded his head in approval. "M.

Drapeaux would have been happy to hear that. A brilliant man. A student of history, especially the early history of Haiti. Knew the island almost as well as the early Carib Indians. Was forever delving into their old-time customs and hunting through the wild parts for buried artifacts from their civilization."

Abbé Brille spoke in a breathy tone, the tone of a runner who has just come in from the race. And no wonder, Asya thought, when his breath has to struggle up through all that mountain of flesh.

"You knew my father well?" Asya asked eagerly.

The abbé smiled, and his eyes had a faraway look. "We were good friends, *très bons amis*." He paused as if taking a look into the past and then went on in a musing voice, "Such talks we had. In this very library too. Ah, the bottles of Beaujolais we consumed, but never did we arrive at an agreement. Always, I had to come again another day to pick up the discussion— and—" With an obvious effort he extracted himself from his memories and added in a sly voice, "And another Beaujolais."

"You would like a Beaujolais now, Père?" Asya inquired. "As yet, I have no discussion to offer."

The laughter rolled easily from his lips. "Non. Non. Not yet. First we must get acquainted." With a flourish Abbé Brille gathered the folds of the huge cassock which encompassed him and seated himself. He placed his hands on his widely spread knees and, looking at Asya, said in a neighborly voice, "Now. Let's hear about you. What wonderful school was this which taught you the love of reading?" Before she could answer, he reached out a big hand and drew a chair before him. "Sit down. Make yourself comfortable. M. Drapeaux always did. Said he couldn't stand on his feet as long as it took me to run out of breath." The visitor laughed. Asya was fascinated by the way his stomach reared and shook with his merriment. However, when

285

he laid his hand against it, as if on signal, it obediently subsided.

"It was St. Clothilda of the Woods in Hesse," Asya hurried to say before the priest found her staring rude.

His mouth opened with surprise. "*Deutschland. Vie schoen*. I am part German. On my mother's side. That's where I get all this fat." Sadly, he shook his head. "When one is German, one can't help being *gut dick*. We are born with such great hungers and thirsts that we must eat and drink too much. You should see my mother. I take after her. When I left the Sorbonne, I was as large as I am now, and yet beside *meine Mutter*, I looked like her little boy."

Asya giggled at the mental picture the priest had conjured. She liked him. He was easy to talk to.

"You were at the Sorbonne?" she asked. "I thought priests only went to monasteries."

"Non. Non. We cannot learn all about the wicked world if we shut ourselves up in a monastery like a bunch of frightened nuns in a convent. Some of us have got to go out and get contaminated so we know what sinners have to put up with and can go back and tell the other seminarians. I think my superiors selected me as their representative for worldly education because I was so immense that evil couldn't throw me." Again that laugh and the accompanying upheaval of his middle.

Abbé Brille continued, "However, I'm glad I didn't take after my skinny French father. Of what good is it to be a priest if your flock can't find you?" He raised his shoulders, at the same time turning up the palms of his hands to indicate such purposelessness. "I'm big around." He flung out his arms to accent his size. "When I walk down the street, my people can see me. The wind whips at my cassock and it flaps in the breezes like a big flag at the head of a parade, only I'm the parade too. They know their priest wouldn't come sneaking around to catch them in their sins. They know I've come to help them before they sin, and if I'm too late—well," he drawled, "I'm on hand for the shriving."

"*Quel dommage*," Asya said, then could not help but ask: "Why did you come here to Haiti? You studied at a great university and now you are only doing missionary work among Negroes who can't read or write. If you had stayed in France or Germany, you could be a bishop by now. You have too much talent to waste it here."

Abbé Brille did not answer at once. His hands slowly dropped to the sides of the chair while his eyes studied Asya. Had she said something wrong, she wondered.

At last he spoke. "When the people are smart, they don't need a teacher. It's the little ignorant ones who need the learning. And what would I do as a bishop, shut up all day in my study as I pondered over the affairs of my diocese? Only seeing my people when I place my hands over them once in their lifetime for the blessed sacrament of Confirmation. To them I would but be a beautifully dressed shepherd with a silk mitre and a golden crosier. Like a prime-minister shepherd who sends out edicts by courier to the working shepherds on how to fatten the flock. No, no, my little angel." He shook his head reprovingly. "I like to gambol in the pastures along with my sheep. How else can I know if the grass they are eating makes them sick or the stones are too sharp for their little feet? My sheep are not old rams, toughened and wise in the ways of the church and of life. They are but little ewes, still in need of guidance and much, much training."

Asya laughed at the thought of the Abbé Brille trying to skip through the fields along with a bunch of silly lambs. "You make it sound like fun, but what does the president say concerning his chaplain taking time to roam through the pastures? I understand M.

President is a fiend about his people keeping profitably busy."

"True. True. But M. Christophe is a smart man. He has great respect for my learning and position. So he takes advantage of it. Since I have been to the university, and he has no knowledge of book learning, I——" the priest paused to raise his great chest before he announced proudly, "I am in full charge of establishing a school system. I am responsible for importing the good soeurs who will staff the schools. I am the author of the course of studies. In fact——" He sat back as though a thought had struck. "In fact, you might say I am the minister of education."

Asya bowed her head in mock homage to the man in front of her. "Congratulations, Minister. I am sure the Bishop of Paris is jealous of your high position here."

The prelate raised his eyebrows. "Of a certainty, he well could be. With his office, he inherited the mistakes of his predecessors from the past hundreds of years. How he must flounder as he tries to correct them. But as for me," the priest crossed his arms over his chest and sat very straight as he said proudly, "as for me, I have no one's mistakes to clutter up my work. Nor do I have anyone's brilliant record to surpass. I am like the *Bon Dieu* in the beginning of time. I am creating a new world to the best of my ability and in my own way."

Asya listened carefully. A question was forming in her mind as he spoke. A question which had lain dormant in her subconscious for a long time. When he had finished, it burst from her lips. "Père, is it worth it? What good will it do to educate these black people? While they are no longer bought and sold, they can never rise to the high social level of the white people they are trying to imitate. They will never be more than domestics or field hands. They are tamed savages created to be subordinates of the white man."

"Oh." Abbé Brille's eyes opened wide. "I didn't

know that. Glad you told me about it. In all my years of study of the Bible, the Lord gave no hint about the superiority of the white race. It only said He created *man*. So Adam and Eve were *white*, were they?" He fixed his eyes upon Asya. They wore an innocent, inquiring look.

She squirmed in her chair. "Well, I think so. I always regard Adam and Eve as being white."

Her reply caused the priest to sparkle with pleasure. "Glad to hear it," he said. "That's very encouraging in my work. There were those two dumb white folks owning nothing in the world. No parents to train them and smack them when they pulled a dumb one. No book knowledge. Not even a stitch of clothing to cover their bare behinds. And from them came this wonderful social level you talk about. Well, if they can do it—" He stood up and stepped close to Asya.

"If they can do it, my little black flock can do it better. Already they wear clothes because they know about modesty. They have papas and mamas who can paddle them good if they so much as talk a word with old Lucifer. They are used to working because they didn't get born in Paradise with everything handed to them. They know about education, and they want it. I'm going to see they get smart through books and not by picking an apple from the wrong tree. Already my people have a head start on Adam and Eve. It will be easy to make kind, God-fearing ladies and gentlemen from my children."

As the impact of the priest's message beat down upon her, Asya thought of the advantage of being a terrapin with a shell into which to pull her head. Maybe sometime she would learn to keep her mouth shut.

"However," the Abbé Brille reached down and taking her by the hand pulled her to her feet, "it is time we talk of other things." His voice was now that of a friend engaged in amiable chatter. "Let us walk to the chapel before lunch. It is far too long since I have been there. I mustn't grow so worldly," he said in a self-reproving tone, "that I think of food before prayer."

As she left the house and walked by the priest's side along the stone walk to the chapel, Asya hoped she would not be embarrassed. She had completely forgotten about the chapel. Only once had she entered it, and that was when she first arrived and Negu had taken her on a tour of the plantation. She had no idea if it was locked and if so where the key was kept. All the chapel had been to her was one more possession, a part of the property she had acquired along with Cher Château. She tossed her head. Too late to worry now.

The chapel had been built in the shadow of eucalyptus trees which stood clustered together at the end of the flower gardens. The abbé paused in his walk to remark, "How beautiful! How beautiful!" He stood silent for a moment and then shook his head in obvious amazement, seemingly overcome by the scene about him.

"These flowers," he spread his arms out in an expansive gesture, "are among the most wonderful gifts of God to mankind. Not even the great artists could copy the colors of these little flowers. And their fragrance." He inhaled deeply. "Like a foretaste of Heaven to come."

"Everything grows easily here, Père," Asya commented.

The abbé was thoughtful. Slowly, he rubbed his chin with his big hand. "Sometimes I wonder why God did not stop His creation after He made the flowers. He could have saved Himself so much trouble. But no. He went on to create man. That was His greatest work. All He had made before were but gifts for His beloved man. Like a dowry is for the bride.

"But man is so stupid," the priest went on in a tired voice. "All about us is God's will, God's lesson, but man thinks he knows better and refuses to learn."

Asya was perplexed. "How do you mean?"

"Look at these flowers. The pink cosmos, blue stephanotis, red poppies, white lilies. How they all grow together in one patch. They wave their little heads in the breeze and seem to call a friendly '*Bon soir*, Abbé,' as I come by. The lily does not spread itself and take all the sunshine as its due because the Lord mentioned it in the Bible. The poppy does not assume the rain is for its thirst alone, since its ancestors long ago came from faraway China. They share together, they nod together, and together they make a splendid bouquet. A thing of beauty for the world and a tribute to God's work."

He sighed heavily. "Why can't man learn the lesson of the flowers. With all races living together side by side, each sharing God's graces, growing toward Heaven. Ah—" His voice died away as though its owner were suddenly weary. He said simply, "Life is so easy if only man did not go out of his way to complicate it."

Asya strolled ahead of the abbé. When she reached the entrance of the Chapel of St. Geneviève, Asya waited in the shade of the eucalyptus for the priest to catch up to her. He came, panting and winded. "That's the trouble with being fat," he said in his breathy voice. "Every little effort saps my energy. Blessed are the skinny, for they are stout of heart."

They entered the chapel together. The red vigil light was flickering in front of the main altar, seemingly pointing toward the tabernacle to let one know the Lord sat waiting for a visitor.

"It's been a long time since there was a service in this little church." The abbé's whispery voice filled the edifice. "That was a sad occasion. M. Drapeaux's funeral. It was my privilege and my sadness to read the Requiem Mass for him. God rest his soul. Let us kneel and say a prayer that he may be at peace."

Asya went into a pew across the aisle from the

prelate. She knelt up straight since she knew she ought to look reverential in the presence of the clergyman, but her joints hurt on the hard kneeler. That was the trouble with being a Catholic. Catholic girls had rough knees. Eloise would have tender, soft ones. She was a Protestant.

Asya looked up at the crucifix above the altar. It was made of black, heavily carved wood. Mahogany, she supposed. The figure of Christ was of white ivory. She had never cared for ivory. She liked glittery things better. Like jewels and shiny gold. She remembered the cross in the hospital chapel. It reminded her of Soeur Denise.

Soeur Denise liked to tell the story about the first time she took Asya to Mass in the chapel, and Asya talked during Consecration.

"Shh," Soeur Denise had whispered. "You must not talk in church. God's up there on the cross and He'll see you."

"That man can't see," Asya had countered. "He's dead."

Asya felt a twinge of nostalgia. She must write Mère Denise soon.

The abbé rose from his pew and walked up the aisle, his white cassock swishing from side to side. He opened the gates at the Communion rail and walked briskly into the sanctuary. He stopped at the foot of the main altar and, to Asya's amazement, studied the stone flagons on the floor. He nodded his head in a set rhythm as though he might be counting their number. Then, like one pacing off arithmetical measurements, he took so many steps toward the Blessed Mother's altar on the left. His computations brought him around to the far side of that altar, where he stopped. For a moment, he stood in thought, his lips pursed, his eyes half closed. Then his head gave an abrupt nod of confirmation, and he turned toward Asya. His face wore a smug look as he curled a fat finger, gesturing her to come to him.

Asya hurried up to Abbé Brille, expecting to hear some legend about the wood of the cross or of some statue of a saint.

With his folded hands resting at the top of his mountainous stomach, the priest beamed upon the woman before him. "I have a surprise for you. You will now receive your greatest inheritance of all." If possible, the abbé looked larger than ever, so puffed up was he with the pleasure of what he was about to do.

Asya smiled indulgently. Probably some spiritual gift, like a famous blessing for the Drapeaux family or holy water from the River Jordan. To please him, she asked, "What can it be? I'm excited."

Quickly, for one so large, the Abbé Brille dropped to his knees. His fingers felt along the stone roses carved into the steps about the Virgin's altar until they came to rest on one particular rose. Slowly he turned the flower, unscrewing it loose from the steps. In the same way, he removed the rose beside it. Then taking a firm hold on the metal stakes which protruded from the spots where the flowers had been, he lifted out a section of the steps, revealing a large opening.

"Now for the surprise," the priest panted as he looked up at Asya who was hovering over him in astonishment.

Reaching in, Abbé Brille slowly slid out a silver box. "All solid silver," he commented in his breathy voice. "M. Drapeaux wanted nothing but the best container for his prize possession. The box alone is of great value."

With a few short blasts of breath, the priest blew the dust from the lid of the box. Picking up the skirt of his cassock, he began to shine the silver with the underside. "A little dirt on the inside of my garment will never show," he chuckled.

"But what's in the box?" Asya was really curious now. Laboriously, the prelate sat his great bulk down on the altar step and nodded at Asya to sit beside him. With the box on his lap, he motioned her to open it. Asya's hands trembled as she lifted the lid.

When she saw what was inside, Asya let out a disbelieving gasp. Her eyes opened wide as if better to encompass the sight of what lay displayed in the box before her. "Oh—oh," her breath went out slowly and quietly in her wonderment.

"You like it?" Abbé Brille asked in a hushed whisper.

For a moment, Asya could not find enough voice to answer. At last she managed to say, "Never have I seen anything so beautiful. It is something from out of the stories of old dynasties."

Asya could not take her eyes from the object that lay inside the box. It was a chalice reposing on a bed of black velvet. It was not the chalice itself which fascinated Asya. That was of a heavy dark gold. It was the ornamentation that surrounded it which dazzled her. The chalice was completely encrusted with gems arranged to suggest that the actual cup rested in the center of a bower of red roses. Each petal was made from one ruby so perfectly contrived that the effect was of blooming, velvety flowers. So natural did they look that Asya caressed a rose, certain it would bend on its stem at her touch. The leaves were of a green stone. Emeralds? She looked closer, for what gem had so many varying shades of one color? She saw that they were made of many stones, so tightly fashioned that they resembled the natural leaf, veined and shiny. Scattered throughout the bouquet, on a petal here or a leaf there, sparkled dewdrops of diamonds.

Carefully, almost reverently, Asya picked up the chalice. She set it on the palm of her hand and held it out from her, the better to admire it. This was hers. This beautiful, jeweled chalice was hers.

In a vibrant voice she asked, "Where did you get it?"

"It is the chalice of the Abbé Casals, given to him three hundred years ago by the Queen of Spain, Isabella herself."

"But," said Asya impatiently, "how did it get here? Please, Abbé Brille, tell me the story of the chalice. There must be a story."

"Yes, yes, my dear. I shall tell you. But first let me put it back to rest. This is a long story, and it will be too heavy for you to hold." Taking the jeweled object from Asya's reluctant hands, the abbé placed it carefully in the silver box beside her. Then, puffing himself up as though he needed more wind to speak, he began his tale.

"When Columbus and the Spaniards first came to Haiti, there were about a million Carib Indians living on this island. But you know how those Spanish are. They take a place in the name of God and the King and then proceed to act like neither God nor the King would think of behaving. They made slaves out of those poor little Indians. Well, the Indian cannot live and multiply in slavery. By 1514, mind you, 1514, there were only around fourteen thousand left. The Spanish were savage, cruel masters.

"Queen Isabella who had been very proud of her red-skinned subjects, sent over the Padre Casals to check on the stories of the atrocities her representatives were perpetrating on her beloved Indians. When she got his reports, she was outraged. She announced that the Caribs could no longer be used as slaves. The Spanish must find someone else to do their work. She meant business too. Abbé Casals stayed around to see that the natives were protected and, naturally, to convert them.

"The Queen, to show her great love for her new subjects, sent over this chalice as a gift to them."

"A gift? A jeweled chalice as a gift for Indians?" Asya was puzzled.

"*Oui. Oui,*" the prelate said as though no further explanation were needed. "It was a wonderful idea. The heathens were converted and they could all share in the gift when they received Holy Communion. It is said that Isabella herself designed the chalice as the red rose was her favorite flower. She wanted something very beautiful, very special, so the Caribs would understand how great was their queen's love for her adopted people."

"But how did it get *here*?" Asya asked impetuously. "Here in my chapel?"

"M. Drapeaux placed it here so the Blessed Mother and St. Geneviève could watch over it."

"But how did M. Drapeaux acquire Abbé Casals' chalice? Did he inherit it? Did he steal it?"

The priest was shocked. "M. Drapeaux was not a thief. He gave, he did not take." Then dropping his voice to a casual tone, he added, "He found it."

"How could a priest be so careless," Asya asked disbelievingly, "as to lose his chalice?"

"He did not lose it. He hid it. Abbé Casals knew that after his death someone might steal and sell it for the precious stones that ornament it. At that time, they were worth a kingdom. The Caribs did not know its monetary value. They probably liked its looks and knew that it belonged to them, but what could a bunch of simple Indians do against some grasping Spaniard's dagger? M. Drapeaux thought Abbé Casals probably confided its place of concealment to one of the leaders in the tribe, but," the priest shrugged, "but who knows. The leader might have died or been slaughtered or the tribe moved away since the history of this island is nothing but blood."

"And, now?" Asya asked anxiously. "Are you—and I—the only ones who know of the chalice?"

"We are the only ones alive who know its whereabouts," replied the abbé, and then, as if in warning, added, "but there are others who know of its existence and its value."

Asya's blood began to run madly through her body. "Sounds like plotting and intrigue could revolve about this chalice," she said almost hopefully.

"No, no," the abbé answered in a reassuring voice. "There will be no world upheaval for the possession of this treasure, since those who want it are willing to pay its price."

"How much?" Asya asked eagerly.

"You are not expecting to sell it?" Abbé Brille looked amazed.

Asya laughed arrogantly. "Of course not. I merely want to know how much I am offered for something I alone possess and someone else desires, but can never buy from me."

The priest cocked his head and looked over at her with a raised eyebrow. "One buyer offered half a million pounds. Lord Essex, a collector. However, I understand that the Emperor Alexander of Russia will double that amount to possess it."

Asya threw back her head in delight. How wonderful! She, an orphan, owned something an emperor desired. It made her feel heady with power. Never would anyone part her from her jeweled toy. Never.

"All this must be kept in the greatest secrecy," Abbé Brille said seriously. "I did not want to know of the hiding place of the chalice, but M. Drapeaux deemed it wise that always two people know. In the event of a sudden death, as did occur in his case, there is always one left to divulge the place of concealment to a trusted second person. The fact that for so long I was the only living person who knew the whereabouts of the chalice has bothered me. Now I have placed the worry in your hands." He gave a deep sigh of relief.

"Possessing something of beauty is not a worry," Asya said lightly. "It is a pleasure."

"Good," the priest agreed emphatically. "However," he went on to say, "if the time should ever come that you wish to dispose of the chalice—"

"Never!" the girl interrupted, reaching out to clutch the silver box beside her.

Abbé Brille raised a hand to silence her. "We can never tell what sacrifices we are called upon to make in a lifetime." Moving her hand, he reached into the silver box, lifted a fold of the velvet lining, and extracted an envelope.

"Just so you know this is here," he said, showing it to her and then replacing it. "In this envelope is the address of the agent who will handle the sale of the chalice. It is a British firm with offices in Jamaica and London. Even though years should pass, this company will always be in existence."

"How can any company know that?" Asya asked dubiously.

"It's British, isn't it? There'll always be a Britain." Abbé Brille laughed in appreciation of his joke and his stomach shook in sympathetic collaboration.

When he had enjoyed his mirth, the priest stood up. "You have worshipped at the heathen altar of the golden calf long enough," he cautioned. "Return it to its hiding place and forget about it."

Asya reluctantly closed the lid on the silver box and returned it to its place of concealment in the floor.

The prelate went on with his talking. "You must forget about the chalice, Asya, or it will possess you. Constantly you will tell yourself that you own what no one else owns. You will be tempted to show someone merely for the pleasure of flaunting your wealth. Wipe it out of your mind, or it will be a canker, growing, festering, blighting your outlook on life, making you an arrogant, possessive old woman before your years.

"In its place, bend your energies to your plantation. Grow new crops. Work for your wealth, and by working show that you deserved what was handed to you by the

298

generous M. Drapeaux. Many in Haiti turn envious eyes on your land, because you were not born here. Show that you have a right to contribute to the well-being of your adopted country. Make yourself useful."

Abbé Brille terminated the lecture when he dropped his voice and asked coyly, "And now, can I have that bottle of Beaujolais?"

Chapter Twenty-four

Etienne Grenier was mad as hell this morning. He viciously dug his spurs into his horse, for only by riding at this maddening pace could he control the explosive feeling inside. He wanted to contain it all in its entirety until he arrived at Cher Château.

It was the letter from Tante Sophia, which had come in the morning post, that so violently disturbed him. The nuns of the Hospice of the Sacre-Coeur at Chalon-sur-Marne had asked her to write for them as they did not know how to go about making an inquiry. One of their orphans, Asya Drapeaux, had come to Haiti. Already it was two years since she had left them, and as yet, they had received no word from her. Their solicitor assured them that she had arrived safely, but was she happy? Had she married? The soeurs felt they were Asya's family since they had raised her, and they wanted some assurance as to her well-being. If he could learn anything about the girl, Etienne's aunt wrote, the nuns would be most relieved.

The selfish ingrate! All those little sisters wanted was to hear a little family chitchat about one of their members. Woman's news, but she wasn't woman enough to put a little gossip down on paper to cheer up the drab lives of those dedicated saints. He'd tell her. He'd bellow loud enough for the idea to penetrate that numb-skulled head. No use appealing to her heart. She didn't have one. The self-centered bitch.

Etienne approached the iron gate at the entrance to

300

Cher Château and saw that it stood open. The old nag's skull leered down from the top of the post in fiendish delight as though it might have been expecting him and had itself pushed back the gate for him to enter.

"You old devil," Grenier saluted as he dashed by, "I don't doubt but that you might have done it, too. Thanks for the cooperation. I'll give her hell."

In an ornery mood, Etienne headed his horse across the lawn and toward the front entrance. "Dig those hoofs in but good, boy" he urged the animal. "Knock out big clods of her precious grass. This is war!"

Reckless with anger, and propelled by an urge to lash out at anything that belonged to the object of his ire, Etienne rode the horse onto the veranda, through the open front door, and into the marble hallway.

"Asya! Asya!" he roared. "Wherever you are, come here damn quick." Impatiently, he headed the horse to the entrance of each room which opened onto the front hall, and looked in. "By God, if I have to I'll ride this animal right into your bedroom. Where are you?" His voice rose until it must rock the chimneys as it blasted up through the house.

"If you quit roaring like the silly Don Quixote you resemble," said a quiet voice, made more quiet by contrast with his own vocal barrage, "you'll find me standing right behind you."

Turning, he saw her leaning against the door jamb of the front entrance. "I was watching your berserk performance up my front lawn," she said coolly. "If you hadn't been in such a hurry to get here as to forget to leave your horse outside the door, you might have seen me." She gazed up at him with a supercilious, indifferent look upon her face. Plainly, she was bored with his antics. He wanted to spank her.

Leaping from his horse, he strode toward Asya, at the same time roaring, "Negu! Come out. I know

301

you're peeping around somewhere. You wouldn't miss this. Negu!" he raised his voice again, "come here."

He was right. Like magic, the housekeeper appeared from one of the doorways and stood by his side, her big eyes regarding him solemnly. "Oui, monsieur?"

"Get someone to take my horse to the stable. I have business with this filly, and it will take a while. She needs a little breaking in."

Asya's chin shot up. "Don't you give orders around my house to my servants." Turning to Negu, she said in a cutting voice, "Don't touch his horse. Both M. Grenier and his beast can get out immediately. It will be my pleasure if they go as quickly as they came."

Placing his face close to hers, Etienne hissed, "We did not come here to give you pleasure. We came to ask a question. Why haven't you written to the soeurs back in Chalon-sur-Marne? They're upset that they haven't heard from you." Then he added, "They ought to thank God they are rid of you."

Disdainfully she turned her face away. "Have you nothing better to do than to check on young ladies' correspondence?" Emitting a forced laugh, she said in a suggestive tone, "Or perhaps it is of interest to a small mind like yours?"

He grabbed her chin and jerked her head around so she could look at him. "I'm asking you, why didn't you write? Can't you hear or shall I shout?" Taking a deep breath, he roared, "*Why*, Asya?"

With her fist, she knocked his hand from her chin. "None of your business," she said slowly, emphasizing each word as she spoke. "I think you're the one who should go to the stable. You're the beast. The horse acts more like a man. At least, he's quiet."

"Beast or man. There's no difference. But you didn't know that, did you?" Swooping her up in his arms, he carried her down the hall toward the stairs which led to the upper floor.

Her coolness vanished. "Don't you *dare*!" she screamed. "Don't you dare, you animal!"

Her fists pummeled his head and face. For the first time since the letter had come this morning, the irritation which had been exploding inside him evaporated. He laughed as he carried her past the stairs and into the library where he set her down. "So, you thought I was going to carry you upstairs to your bed, did you?" Crossing his arms over his chest, he looked down at her in amusement. "Just a little wishful thinking on your part, oui? Next time, don't be so premature with your happy anticipations."

"I'll kill you." Her face was red with her fury.

"They'd hang you."

"They would not. I'm a woman."

"You've got a neck, haven't you? That's all that's needed for hanging." He was beginning to enjoy himself.

"If you've finished your little comedy, will you tell me why you brought me into this room?" She pressed her lips together in a firm line as if forcibly to hold back the vituperation her thoughts were conjuring.

"To write a letter," he announced in a flat voice.

"Oh, no," she spoke with a note of finality. "When I write, it will be when and to whom I please, not at the order of a vulgar yokel."

"Your flattery won't soften me any." This was fun, he thought. Much more pleasurable being aide-de-camp to the little nuns than to M. Christophe. Looking around the library, his eye caught the settee and with an exaggerated show of indolence, he pulled it across to bar the doorway. Lazily, he sprawled himself down upon it with his head resting on one of the arms and his feet dangling over the other.

"You've got your nerve," Asya shouted indignantly.

Etienne shook his head. "Not nerve. Merely concern for my comfort. At heart, I'm really a sybarite." Waving a hand toward the chair at the desk across the room, he casually suggested, "Please do sit down. You can't write your letter standing up."

"No!" she snapped. "I won't sit in the same room with you, and—" she sucked in her breath before spitting out, "and I'm not writing any dumb old letter."

"*Non, non.*" He shook his finger at her as he might to a naughty child. "Not a dumb letter. A brilliant, newsy one befitting your personality and education. You wouldn't want the nuns to think your mind has slipped, would you, from such high living? Granted, it probably has, but we do want to fool them and keep them happy, don't we?"

She clenched her fists and said nothing, only stood there glaring at him from the middle of the room. Slowly, he propped himself up on an elbow, and twisting his head around to see into the hall, he called out, "Nassy. Nassy! I need a little service. Where are you?"

"He's in the kitchen where he belongs," Asya said testily, "helping to get lunch. He can't hear you."

Etienne chuckled. "That's what you think. He wouldn't miss this for all the lunches in the world. He's close by somewhere taking in every sweet word you're whispering to me."

"Yas, suh. You call me?" The butler was all at once standing beside the settee, his sleeves rolled up and a polishing cloth and silver teapot in his hand.

"Nassy!" Asya's voice was sharp. "You know you're not to appear in the front of the house without your coat."

"Oh," the Negro's eyes were large with apprehension. "M. Grenier call. I come fast. He's in a bad, bad humor."

"Nassy, you were out there in the hall listening. Don't you know better than to eavesdrop on your betters?"

"Sure he does," Etienne interjected. "Only in this case there are no betters around."

"You shut up!" Asya's eyes blazed.

304

"Naughty. Naughty," he chided. "Your dignity is slipping."

Nassy broke in with a stutter, "Well, I jist think I better be on hand case anybody needs mah help."

"Good thinking," Etienne approved. "I need some help."

"You?" The butler spoke disbelievingly. "You look lak you got de situashun well in hand."

"That's right, Nassy," Etienne agreed, "but I'm bored. I need a bottle of wine to while away a dull day. Select a very dry one. When you come back, I may just need you to fetch me an article of a more personal nature. That, of course, is up to Mademoiselle." He chuckled to himself, as Nassy left the library.

When he looked back at Asya he almost laughed out loud. Her chin was stuck out, her eyes squinted shut, and the lower lip overlapped the upper as though her features had arranged themselves in battle formation. "Relax, honey," he said soothingly. "In your present mood, you are reminiscent of an English bull terrier."

Asya gave him a look of venom and did not answer.

Etienne dropped his feet to the floor and sat up. He put his elbows on his knees, leaned toward her, and spoke quietly: "Let's have a little talk." His change of voice made her wary. She gave him a sidewise glance, plainly showing she was expecting some wily surprise from the enemy camp.

"I'm serious. Listen closely," he went on in a low, but firm voice. "I mean business. You have to write that letter. I'm staying here until you do. The only reason you are stubborn is because you know you are wrong."

She raised her eyebrows, indicating the whole situation was boring. Not worth the bother of an answer.

Etienne said in an unruffled voice, "The silent treatment will avail you nothing. You had better look at the facts. I have indicated that I shall stay here in this room with you until you write that letter. One day, two days, all week. It does not matter. You will have nothing to eat. A little water to drink. If you should die from starvation, then, of course, I shall take the liberty of writing the good soeurs at Chalon-sur-Marne to impart to them the good news of your demise."

"You're wasting my time. I refuse to stay in this room with you any longer." Angrily, she walked toward Etienne. "Get out of my way. I'm tired of looking at your hateful face."

From his place on the settee, Etienne stretched his arms, yawning as he did so. "Don't try to change the subject by talking about my handsome visage, however, despicable it may be."

To his surprise, Asya kicked him in the shin. "Get out of here! Get out of my house!"

Quickly, he reached out and grabbed her arms, pinioning them against her sides, and set her down on his lap. "You pesky little mosquito," he grinned down at her, "I admire your spunk, but I think I'm going to have to swat you."

Her forearms flailed out and she tried to hit him with her fists, but he kept a tight grip on her elbows, and she could not reach him. "Don't you touch me! Let me go!" Asya threw back her head and screamed, "Nassy! Nassy! Throw this wild man out."

"What are you trying to do? Have that big bruiser intimidate me?" he asked in mock fright.

Laughing, he set her on her feet and released his hold. "Now behave yourself and get back to the little spot you're wearing out on the carpet," he said chidingly, "while we finish our discussion."

Asya shot across the room, rubbing her arms at the same time. "Look what you've done," she accused. "Look at the red marks you made on me."

"Better there than on some other part of your anatomy where one of these days I'm going to spank you. At least, you can show people these bruises. The others you will only talk about."

He grew businesslike. "Nassy will be back any minute with my wine. Have you reached a decision?"

Asya turned her back to him.

"Very well, I shall ask Nassy to bring me a nightshirt and more wine. If I am to have a holiday here in your writing room, I may as well be comfortable."

"It's only noon," Asya spun around and flung the words at him. "You'll be drunk before night."

"You underestimate my tippling ability, *ma cherie.*" Etienne heard Nassy's steps behind him and, without turning his head, ordered, "Put up a table in the hall, Nassy, and leave the bottle there. I don't want it within easy reach of anyone who might let it fly against my head."

"Yas, suh," the butler said in a hushed voice. "Is dat all?"

"One more thing. A nightshirt. I'll be staying a while."

"But, but," Nassy stammered, "we ain't got no menfolk in res'dence here. Where I gonna git me a shirt?"

"One of yours," M. Grenier answered casually, "will be fine."

The butler shook his head. "I dunno 'bout dat. Mine ain't so fine. Better I ask Evadne."

"Hers or yours. It makes no difference. My hostess won't mind, will you, *Cherie?*" He leaned in her direction, but Asya only wrinkled her nose in answer.

Nassy came back soon with a brilliant orange garment over his arm. "It's a li'l short for yuh, but plenty wide 'cross."

"Just the thing." Etienne took the shirt and, getting up from the settee, he shook it out, saying to Asya at the same time, "Beautiful color, isn't it? You won't mind my sleeping in the same room where you plan to spend the night standing, will you?"

He took off his shirt.

"Don't you dare. Don't you dare!" Asya yelled at

him. "I won't have you lying here drunk, sprawled out in that ridiculous orange monstrosity on my settee."

Etienne studied the nightshirt. "It *is* rather bright, isn't it?" He turned to Nassy. "Do you have another color. Mlle. Asya doesn't like orange."

With a show of indignation, Asya put her hands on her hips and glared at Etienne. "I hate you!" she shouted. With that, she turned and walked to her desk.

Etienne remained at Cher Château for lunch. Not that Asya had invited him. When she finished the letter, she threw it at him and, without a word, disdainfully left the room. He had other matters to take up with her, but they could wait.

He wandered into the kitchen, and there found Evadne elbow-deep in dough.

"How's my favorite cook?" he greeted.

The Negress gave him a big grin. "Yuh comin' to make trouble in mah kitchen too? I'se too busy for foolin' 'round." She dipped her hand in the flour in the barrel by the table and generously spread it over the dough she was kneading, at the same time enveloping herself in a white cloud.

"Trying to camouflage yourself in that flour?" Etienne teased. "You can't fool me. I know you're there." Taking the end of her apron, he wiped the splatters of flour from her face, saying as he did so, "A white face can have black freckles. That's all right, but, Evadne, a black face just can't wear white freckles." He put his arms around her and gave the cook an affectionate hug.

Evadne giggled. Spontaneous giggles which shot out in spurts of merriment, shaking her whole body. Even her hand rose and fell in the dough like busy moles working away under little white hills.

"Yuh stayin' for lunch, hain't yuh?" Evadne asked hopefully.

"Seeing as how you've asked, I'll postpone my de-

parture until I have a belly full of your good victuals."
Etienne gave her an affectionate pat on the head and
walked over to sit in her rocker by the window.

The cook shook her head. "I allow as how yuh's not
goin' to find Mam'selle Asya a likely table partner.
Lord, she sure's in a bad spirit."

Etienne picked up a persimmon from a hamper
nearby. "I have an idea she's going to be in worse spirits if her lunch is late. Those goings-on in the library
surely did slow up the work schedule in this house. Behind which door were *you* watching?"

Evadne did not answer. She lowered her head and
tittered to herself as she fashioned fat little loaves of
bread from the white dough.

When Asya entered the dining room and found M.
Grenier holding a chair out for her, she marched up to
the table and curtly asked, "Who invited you for
lunch?"

In amazement he spread out his hands. "You mean
you don't want me?" he asked.

"That's right. I mean I don't want you," she
snapped, eyes glaring hatred.

His hands dropped to his sides. "I can't believe it. I
can't believe your lack of hospitality. What has happened to the famed Drapeaux hospitality that a hungry
guest is turned out at mealtime? How the bones of
those bygone mistresses must be rattling in their sar-
cophagi over the bad manners of this younger generation."

Her lips curled in disdain. "Your poor clowning only
bores me."

"As a final gesture of goodwill, at least allow me to
seat you at the table before I leave. See," he pointed at
the chair, "I already have it pulled out for you."

Ignoring him, she walked to the other end of the
table where Nassy was also waiting to seat her. "You
may begin serving, Nassy."

"Me too? What a magnanimous hostess!" Etienne

beamed. "She has allowed me to stay after all." With a show of delight, he sat in the chair which was to have been hers.

Looking prim and aloof, she said from her end of the table, "You may do as you please. Whether you stay or not interests me not at all. I'm not letting a little inconvenience like you interfere with my lunch. I'm hungry."

He chuckled to himself, for he had counted on her young girl's appetite to win him this round.

Through the whole luncheon, not a word was spoken. Negu came into the room several times, ostensibly as a conscientious housekeeper on routine checkups, but Etienne preferred to attribute her presence to curiosity. While they waited for dessert to be served, Etienne broke the silence.

In the voice of one who has just happened to remember something which had slipped his mind, he said, "Oh, by the way, I have a message for you from the president, M. Christophe himself. It is another reason why I had to come today."

One shoulder shrugged in indifference and with a show of boredom Asya languidly turned her head to gaze out the window on the opposite side of the room.

"Oh, no, no," Etienne said amiably, "don't look out there for him. The president is not coming here."

Asya gave an affected little sigh of relief. "*Bon. Bon.* On some days, one has to be grateful for the smallest things in life."

"Don't be troubled, my dear. You have never invited him. He won't come here."

"I wasn't sure. One can never count on how an untutored oaf will act." She gave Etienne a supercilious smile. "Thank you for reassuring me."

Leaning his head against the back of his chair with his eyes half closed, Etienne appraised the girl opposite him. He found her most provocative.

"That untutored oaf, as you refer to M. Christophe,

is still the law of the land," Etienne explained in clipped, precise tones. "Absolute law," he emphasized. "What he wants, goes."

Tossing her head, as though with a mere gesture she were done with the whole distasteful business, Asya said, "Perhaps in his little black world, he's God to all those illiterate niggers, but I'm not impressed. Whatever message you brought from him for me, take it right back undelivered. I'm not interested."

Anger flared up in him, and had she been closer, he would have picked her up by that pile of black hair on top of her head and shaken her like a rag doll. Instead, attempting to control his voice, he said, "Will you get it through that numb skull of yours, that this is a black man's land, and you are merely permitted to live here so long as it suits him to have you in his midst."

She opened her mouth to speak, but he held up a hand to silence her, and went on, conscious of the fact that Negu was standing outside the open door. "Perhaps you feel strong in the knowledge that by law, a law which is only evidenced by a slip of paper in the solicitor's office, you are the legal heiress to this plantation. Today in Haiti, there is no law but that which Henri Christophe permits. He could send a platoon of soldiers out here to burn your land—if he wished to."

"He's a savage. They're all savages here!" Asya shouted, pushing her chair back from the table and starting to rise.

"Sit down," he ordered in a harsh voice, "and keep your mouth shut so you can learn something."

Glaring across at her, he continued, "Of course the president is a savage. Everyone who is black here is a savage. They didn't go to a convent school and learn how to drink chocolate and wear silk nightshirts. Many were born in the jungles of Africa and ran naked in the tribe like a pack of hyenas. When they were hungry they learned to feast on such delicacies as the raw liver of a pig and for strength they drank the warm blood as it gurgled from the cut throat of a lion they had speared. A man who did not wear the same feathered headdress as your own tribe was an enemy and you killed him before he killed you. No trial. No questions asked, and you celebrated the conquest of your enemy by inviting your friends to a feast and sharing the dead man's flesh with them, and when you finished you hung his bones around your neck as a badge of honor.

"The floors of their huts were mud, not marble. They had no windows with latticed shutters or ornamental iron balconies. They had no windows at all lest the predatory varmints of the jungle creep in at night and devour their children as they lay sleeping. For a beauty treatment, the women bathed their faces in their own urine and set their hair with the dung of goats. They accepted the flies on their rotting stinking meat as natural to their food, the way leaves are to a tree. Always it was so. No one questioned the order of things for life was all too brief in the jungle. They did as their ancestors had done, even as you in your growing up follow the pattern of those who have come before you."

He noticed her skin now had a greenish pallor and she kept swallowing as though her mouth were always full. Etienne went on but the harshness left his voice. "Asya, those savages, as you call them simply because they know a different way of life from yours, are suddenly, forcibly, transported into slavery in another land. They are bewildered, angered, disconsolate by our enforced morality, our language, our harshness, our dress, our laws—all of it so strange to them. Suppose you had suddenly been snatched from your familiar sheltered convent and thrust into the jungle to survive as best you could according to its way of life. How stupid, how awkward a figure you would cut in the eyes of the natives. But you would try, wouldn't

you? You would do your stumbling best to reshape
your life with the tools at hand.

"That's all the black men of Haiti are doing. They
put on the Creole's clothes, live in his houses, eat his
food in imitation of their former masters. Sure, they're
fumbling, but they keep trying, so put out a hand to
help them. You laugh at their manners, because they
are unsure as they use a knife and fork, instead of their
fingers, as they were accustomed. How graceful would
you look to a Chinaman as you tried to manipulate
chopsticks for the first time? You and your friend
Eloise made fun of them at the opera because they followed their inate love of decorating themselves and
wore too much jewelry. Had you been in a jungle fes-
tival, I'm sure the other girls would have laughed at
the inept arrangement of your head feathers."

A trace of a smile appeared on her lips. She must
have been seeing herself in jungle garb and found it
amusing.

Lifting his chair, he carried it to the other end of the
table and sat down beside her. Her hands were resting
in her lap. He reached for one and held it in his. She
tried to jerk it away, but when he did not let go, she
relaxed and let him hold it.

In a low voice she asked, "What am I supposed to
do?"

"Show a little warmth of friendship."

She looked shocked. "To M. Christophe?"

He threw back his head and laughed. "Get that little
mind of yours out of the gutter. This is purely on a
platonic level." His remark embarrassed her, for her
cheeks became flushed.

Hurriedly he continued: "M. Christophe's feast day
is next week. In the past, it has been customary for all
his friends, both political and genuine, to come to the
palace to pay their respects to him. This morning, he
expressed the hope that you would deign to remember

him too. You know you have never shown him or Mme. Christophe the courtesy of a call."

Asya answered flippantly, "If that's all he wants, I guess I could go and extend a few words of felicitation."

Etienne patted her hand approvingly. "That's a smart girl." Tilting back in his chair, Etienne said casually, "Since this is your first visit to court, may I suggest you do it with a flourish. Make it something eventful."

Asya's eye narrowed. "I think there's a catch to this whole scheme," she said warily.

"Don't be so suspicious," her luncheon guest chided in a light tone. "I think it would be appreciated if you took Cilla with you and stayed a few days to get acquainted with the Christophes' daughters. Amethiste and Athenaire would love having you."

Indignantly, she drew herself up. "Are you mad? I'm not amusing a couple of black nursery brats."

He wagged a finger at her. "Temper. Temper. Are you forgetting my little sermon already? These girls are not infants. They are little girls. They want to meet other gracious young ladies. These are the first ladies of Haiti. They in turn must be an example to others, but to be that, they first must get their own polish. Asya, so far you have taken everything in Haiti for yourself. Now it is time to share."

She gave him a look of disgust. "What will my friends say? Showing off for the blacks."

"You will be surprised," he answered seriously, "to find many of your friends at the palace licking a few boots for their own good."

"Here," Etienne continued. "I brought you a note from the president and his wife asking you to be their guest." He held a letter out to her. "They thought perhaps you might be shy and needed a written invitation."

Asya made no move to take the message. Instead

314

she sat staring speculatively at him through narrowed eyes. "You once said that neither of them could read or write. M. Grenier, I suspect you're tricking me."

"Naturally, they don't write. They never learned. But they can talk, can't they? They're very well spoken, I might add. I wrote the message just as they dictated it to me in their own words. I'll read it to you." He reached for the letter which he had laid on the table, but she placed her hand on it. "Don't bother," she said indolently. "I accept the invitation."

"There's one other thing," Etienne said. "A gift is in order since it is M. Christophe's feast day. I thought we might discuss what you would like to give."

"I would like to give nothing," she answered tartly, "but since a gift is in order, I think the most appropriate offering would be a first-year reader. I'm sure there must be one stuck away in some corner of my library."

Giving her an admiring glance, he said, "Smart girl. How did you know that was going to be my suggestion too?"

She gave him the startled look of one who, having thrown down the gauntlet for battle, has found his antagonist on his side.

"You're teasing me," she accused.

"Not at all. I am in perfect accord with your suggestion," Etienne said truthfully. "You have named the perfect gift. Books are what are needed in Haiti. Do you realize that I am the only member of the president's staff who can read and write? That is, except for Abbé Brille."

Asya looked surprised. "But," Etienne continued, "do you think *one* book is quite enough for the richest planter in Haiti?"

"What do you mean?" Asya replied indignantly. "What does my wealth have to do with this discussion?"

"Just this, my dear. The children need many books.

Thousands of books. And you can afford to supply them."

Her eyes and mouth opened in amazement at his effrontery, but he went on speaking as if he had not noticed. "The perfect gift. Just the other day, Abbé Brille—he's the minister of education, you know—the good father presented his requisition for the books for the schoolchildren of Haiti. M. Christophe was dejected. He did not know where he was to get all the money. The people themselves are building the schools and Abbé Brille has lured some French nuns from Canada to staff them, but no gourds to pay for the books," Etienne finished sadly.

"You relate such wonderful tales, M. Grenier," Asya commented, reaching up to wipe a pretended tear from her eye. "They wring my heart with sorrow. Do tell me another, only this time make it a happier one."

Watching her closely, he said in a slow voice, emphasizing each word as he spoke, "I am not fabricating myths. I am seriously suggesting that you donate all the schoolbooks for the children of Haiti and call it your gift to M. Christophe."

Asya jumped to her feet, hurling her chair to the floor. "You're crazy! I'll do no such thing. Get out—!"

Before Asya could finish, Etienne sprang toward her. In one quick movement, he righted the chair and brutally flung her back upon it.

"You'll listen to me," he bellowed, "if I have to force you to listen."

Asya looked up at him in shocked bewilderment. "You—you pushed me." Her voice stuttered in disbelief. "You laid a hand on me."

"There will be more than my hand upon you if you don't listen to some advice. For God's sake, Asya, how do you think your black neighbors, former slaves, got their plantations? They took them. That's how they got them. They took them because their former white or mulatto owners were too scared to come back to claim their own property. Now you come, a stranger. Not a Creole. Born in France, a land they hate and for good reason. You dare to come here, take the best plantation of all, and turn your nose up at anyone who isn't white."

"I've done nothing to them," she snapped defensively.

"Nor for them, either," he added. "You accuse them of being savages. You're right. They are when it comes to survival. They are not enough years removed from the jungle. Do you know how the unclaimed houses and fields were parceled out?"

For an answer, she gave him a black look.

"M. President simply told those followers who had been of service to him to take whichever they wanted as their reward. Now some of his ministers are working hard for Haiti, and they want better pay. More land. A better house. M. Christophe doesn't care where they get an increase in income so long as they do their job for him. That's where Cher Château comes in. Some of the top brass want this plantation. You do nothing for M. President. Why in hell should he shelter you? That's why it is so important that you make a big show. Give this generous gift to the schools and everyone will look upon you as the good angel of Haiti. The president will then need you. No one would dare kill the philanthropist of his country." Etienne gave a mirthless laugh. "A generous woman who loves all the little children so very much."

Asya let out a low moan. "That would cost hundreds and hundreds of gourds."

"No," he corrected in a cold voice, "thousands and thousands of gourds. Not only for one year but for every year."

"That's bribery," she exploded. "That's what it is. Bribery!"

"Of course it is. It's done all over the world. Isn't

the protection of your home worth a little—" he became sarcastic "—insurance on your part?"

Negu came into the room, presumably to arrange some dishes on the buffet, but Etienne knew it was to be closer to the conversation. He called to her, "Isn't that so, Negu? Wouldn't some of the pompous biggies, one in particular, like to get their hands on Cher Château?"

With her eyes looking wide and solemn, Negu slowly approached the table. Her voice held an ominous note as she answered: "*Oui*. Everyone wants Cher Château. It would not be here today if it was not for Dambolla. That is why we are always careful to keep the torch burning at the gate so thieves and murderers can see the Nagshead. The sign of protection."

"If the old voodoo gods are taking care of me," Asya taunted, "why then should I pay out protection money?"

Etienne was exasperated. "You have heard of fallen-away Catholics, haven't you? There are fallen-away voodooists too, when it suits their purposes."

"You talk nonsense," she said angrily. "All this talk about spooks and skeletons. You'd think some kind of black magic runs this island."

Etienne did not answer. He was watching Negu's face. Her cheeks were slowly sinking as if she were sucking them in and her eyes narrowed to mere slits like curtains drawn upon her thoughts. She spoke in a low menacing voice. "There are many evil gods, Asya. Sometimes they grow strong." She paused. Then slowly opening her eyes, she fastened them upon the girl.

Visibly stirred, Asya squirmed and looked away. "I do not remember asking for your advice. Our dessert has not yet been served. M. Grenier and I are ready for it."

Turning to Etienne, Asya ordered, "Sit down and finish your lunch. I'll think about the books."

Etienne said nothing and took his place at the other

end of the table. He knew she was upset by the way her brows were drawn together like two black storm clouds, and her upper lip was hidden by the lower one in a pout. It had been a spirited day and Etienne enjoyed the meringue glacé Nassy placed before him. However, he noted that Asya was aimlessly poking her fork into the food and ate nothing. Her mind was far away, probably figuring out how many crops of sugar cane she must give away.

At last, she inquired in a dubious voice, "Are you sure I must give such a big gift?"

Etienne pushed himself away from the table. His voice was cold and flat. "Suit yourself." He stood up. "I don't give a damn what you do." He started to walk from the room.

"Wait, wait," she called to him.

He stopped but did not look toward her. Quietly she came up to him. "I—I have decided to take your advice," she said with great effort. "Will you ask Abbé Brille to send me his invoice for the books?"

With an unexplained feeling of relief, Etienne placed his hands on her shoulders and affectionately shook them. "That's using your head, Asya. Don't you feel better?"

"No." She seemed downcast. "I always loved meringue glacé and today I lost my appetite for it." She looked up and Etienne saw that her eyes were twinkling.

Chapter Twenty-five

As she had promised Etienne, Asya took Cilla and departed for the presidential palace. She was in an irritable mood and not quite sure why. It was not the munificence of her gift that annoyed Asya, for having once made up her mind to provide the books for the Haitian school system, she accepted it as one of the unpleasant, but necessary, exigencies of being a landowner. Like repairs or wages or too much rain.

It was the exhausting preparation for the trip that had really disturbed Asya. Negu had been particularly aggravating, with all her fussing over what clothes Asya should wear while a guest of the Christophe family. Between them, the housekeeper and Cilla selected Asya's entire wardrobe.

"Isn't anyone going to ask *my* opinion on what I might like to wear?" Asya knew she was being snippy. But the two women went on with their chattering over the selection of her apparel, ignoring her presence. She might have been a child with no eye for fashion as yet.

"For this very, very great occasion," Asya asked sarcastically, "would it be too much to ask for some of that ultra-dazzling jewelry I am supposed to have inherited and which Negu never seems to remember the hiding place of. After all, why should the country's great philanthropist go unadorned like a pauper?"

At Asya's words, Negu paused to look at her. Through half-closed eyes she studied her mistress as though mentally decorating her, jewel by jewel.

"Yes, I know. I know. Don't tell me." Asya was exasperated. "Unmarried girls don't appear with expensive earrings and bracelets and pins splashed all over them. It's vulgar ostentation." Her voice was parroting someone, and Asya hoped Negu recognized whom.

Cilla giggled. "Why don't you get married? That would solve your problem." She added slyly, "M. Godefroy would like that solution."

"Why don't *you* get married?" Asya retorted. "Then I'd only have Negu to contend with."

"No hurry. I have no jewels to complicate my life." Cilla's eyes twinkled. Plainly, the maid was enjoying what to Asya were chaotic preparations for nothing. A comic-opera court with a bunch of serfs playing the lead roles! How Eleanore would have snickered.

Eleanore. It was a long time since she had thought of her former school friend. Or had she been foe? Eleanore with her golden curls and rustling taffetas. Walking in silk sandals over the white marble floors of her family castle. Jewels radiating from her like the crystal chandeliers sparkling in her parents' ballroom. Dancing in the arms of a graceful partner. And all around them, musicians, hundreds of musicians, wearing powdered wigs and lace ruffles. Bowing, curtseying. That was a *real* court reception. What barbed remarks Eleanore would make about the Christophes' affair! Asya could see that turned-up nose, turned up higher than ever as she showed her disdain by holding her nostrils with her fingers. She smiled at the picture in her mind.

But Eleanore did not live in Haiti, and Asya did. If she must visit the president and his family, Asya wanted to go and get it over with. Waste no time on unpleasant preparations. She felt restrained. Bound. She wanted to leap out the front door, drive to Cap François, and be done with the whole distasteful excursion.

The voice of Negu broke into her thoughts. "I have

something for you." The housekeeper held out a large, flat box covered in red satin. "I happened to find it only this morning. Perhaps you might like to take it along."

The way Negu dropped her eyes as Asya reached for the box, the mistress of Cher Château knew its discovery had been no mere accident. A feeling of excitement pushed aside her grumblings and stirred her heart, just a little. Asya opened the box.

She gasped. An emerald lay blazing on a bed of red velvet. Its edges were encrusted with rows of small diamonds which sparkled like all the stars in the firmament had gathered to display the beauty of the green gem, and then meandered off, one by one, into a stream of light to form a diamond chain for the wearer's neck.

Asya spoke in a hushed voice. "It's beautiful. Just beautiful."

Her hand shook as she reached for the necklace, but she drew it back. "You put it on me, Negu. It must be a dream. I don't want to touch it and find the dream gone."

Negu lifted the necklace from the box and fastened it about Asya's neck. It was no dream, for it lay cold against her skin and its weight tugged at her neck. Asya ran to look at herself in the mirror. She gave a smug smile. Even Eleanore's jewels looked tawdry beside this necklace. Asya caressed it with her fingers. This was hers.

That had been in the morning.

Now, as they approached the presidential home, even the possession of the lovely emerald could not ease her apprehension. I'm not afraid, Asya assured herself, but I'll be happy when I'm back to Cher Château again.

She was angry with herself. What's the matter? Are you a coward? taunted a voice inside her. She straightened her backbone, raised her head, and gritted her teeth as a denial of this unheard of temerity.

She, who could run the biggest plantation in Haiti, supply schoolbooks for the country's illiterate brats, give parties whose food and drink were the talk of Cap François, need have no qualms about meeting some of its important citizens.

Perhaps it was her naïveté in political matters that worried her, but why? Surely she need have no qualms about *her* lack of knowledge. The Christophes could not even write their own names. It was a disgrace that an educated woman like herself had to stoop to mingle with a bunch of ignorant natives in order to assure the safety of her own home.

As they drove along the Plain du Nord, Asya was more than ever aware of the thatched hovels that lined the main highway into town. They were not solidly built like those of the peasants of France, but feebly put together as though the builders were too weak to properly bind the branches. She could see through the crevices in the walls right into the inside of the houses. They were cluttered like old attics with scattered dishes, broken-down furniture, and rags thrown about on the floor. There were strings of vegetables hanging everywhere to dry, pigs and chickens wandering inside the houses and out among the numerous children playing in the mud. Asya wondered how a few years' schooling could benefit the offspring of such a home. Suppose they could read and write. Then what? In a few years each of those children would be grown, half-heartedly build his own hut, get married, and clutter it just as had his parents before him. Nothing would change. Even his livestock would be but the offspring of those on which he had fed as a youngster. Asya hated to think of her nice new schoolbooks lying among the litter in those shacks. How foolish the president was to waste money on education. These people looked happy enough as they were. If the Haitian did not know any better, how could he miss anything better?

Asya was not sure what she expected to find in the Christophe household. In her mind it had never been quite clear how the more affluent Negroes lived. Perhaps it was because she had dismissed them as not worth her concern. But now, Asya was squeamish about meeting the black man on an equal social basis. Could it be that he might be aware of her uncomplimentary regard for him and feel constrained toward her? Asya smiled at the silly thought. How could they know. The whole trouble lay in her being pushed into something against her will.

Well, she would try to make the best of it. But what does one talk about with former slaves? Mère Denise always maintained everyone had something to teach us if only we exert ourselves sufficiently to find out what. Nonsense. What did a nun know about society?

Asya straightened her shoulders as she and Cilla drew up before the Christophe home. The presidential palace, as Asya mockingly referred to the house, was not unknown to her from the outside. She had passed it many times and thought it a fitting abode for a one-time slave of a black innkeeper. The structure was square and tall like a barracks or a crude church without glass in its windows. Somewhere Asya had heard that the Christophes had once owned the prettiest house in Cap François, but Christophe had burned it along with the town when the French invaded the island years ago. What a waste!

A black butler in white wig and silk breeches opened the door for Asya. She stepped in upon a white marble floor and sat upon a chair carved from black mahogany while the servant quietly went for Mme. Christophe. The room opened upon a large courtyard in the center of which was a pink marble fountain. It struck her as a happy fountain which gurgled and laughed as it tossed its waters up. Birds, hidden in tall trees, sang out gay little tunes, and flowers from the blooming bushes danced in time to a soft breeze. Why, this was really rather lovely, thought Asya.

Before she had time to adjust to this unexpected environment, Mme. Christophe came hurrying into the room.

"So nice of you to come to our home," she said in her warm voice. "You are most welcome." The president's wife placed her hands upon Asya's shoulders and drew her close, placing a kiss upon each cheek. Asya stiffened. It was the first time she had been so greeted by a Negro.

Asya found her voice, feeble as it was, and managed to answer, "I am flattered that you asked me."

"You must be tired after your long trip into town," that warm voice was saying solicitously, "and I'm sure you might find some pastries refreshing. Come into the salon where we can eat and visit at the same time."

The salon also opened onto the happy courtyard, as Asya already thought of it. To her amazement, it too was furnished exquisitely in a style reminiscent of a queen's sitting room. On the floor lay a thick hand-woven rug of a glowing red color with a pattern of beautifully designed green leaves entwined throughout. The furniture was gilt, upholstered in varying shades of green brocatelle. White silk covered the walls whose only hanging was a gold-framed picture of a horse. It was obviously a wild horse, for it seemed poised and ready to dash off into the woods, but as yet undecided as to which direction to take. The background of the painting was dark, almost black, but the last light of the setting sun shone on the horse's flanks, making them look so real that Asya wanted to reach up and pat the animal.

Mme. Christophe noticed Asya's interest in the picture. "I see you like my painting. It is my favorite of all. It was done by a Dutch painter, Van Rijn. I forget what its original name was, but I call it 'The Wild One.'"

"Why?" Asya was curious.

Her hostess's slanting green eyes took on a dreamy look. "Because it is a spirited, beautiful animal, but it does not know which way to turn. Lives only by instinct. It is the same with my people."

Asya squirmed. To bring the conversation to a more practical turn, she asked, "How ever did the work of such a famous painter come to—?"

"A Negro?" Mme. Christophe finished quickly.

Asya's body tensed in indignation. That was not what she had meant. Was her hostess deliberately trying to embarrass her? "No," she said testily, "I merely wondered how it came to be in Haiti?"

Mme. Christophe's shoulders moved in the faintest of shrugs. "The French left many beautiful things when they pulled out of Haiti. Perhaps General Leclerc's wife had brought it to decorate her home. I understand her brother, Napoleon, took what art he wanted from the museums of Europe. Who knows? Perhaps he gave it to Mme. Leclerc so she might have a touch of culture in this savage land." The corner of her mouth moved in a little smile. Was she being sarcastic?

Asya was annoyed. Clearly, she was in enemy territory. Was this the charming, kind lady whose praises Etienne had sung? At that moment a servant appeared with a tray of meringues and Asya was relieved at the interruption. While Mme. Christophe poured coffee from a tiny silver pot, decorated with carved bees, Asya could not help but admire the poise with which her hostess conducted herself. For an innkeeper's daughter, she somehow had acquired the movements of a queen. Asya's eyes went to the picture on the wall. She thought of the wild horse as it might be. Trained and poised. Tail arched. Head high. Dancing in time to the music of a marching band.

Asya was glad when her hostess showed her to her

room. "I am sorry," Mme. Christophe apologized, "but we are somewhat crowded and have only one room for you. When our new home is completed at Milot, you must come again. There you will have an entire wing."

"Your home is lovely," Asya answered. She meant the compliment, for as Mme. Christophe took her through the halls and various rooms, she was amazed at the furnishings. Oriental rugs, crystal chandeliers befitting a castle, oil paintings in wide golden frames large enough almost to cover a wall. Golden furniture. Golden wall tapestries. Gold. Gold. Gold. Yet, it was in excellent taste. The amazing part was the unexpectedness of it all. It was like entering a hut and finding a fairy castle inside.

"M. Christophe loves beautiful things," his wife offered in a voice which surprisingly held about as much animation as if she was referring to the weather. "He is supervising the entire building of our new home, It will be called Sans Souci. I have not gone out to see it. I hear it is—" Mme. Christophe hesitated. She sounded weary as she added, "a palace equal to Versailles."

Asya was amazed. "Has M. President been to Versailles?"

The wife of the president gave her a sidewise look before answering in that sweet, low voice, "Of course not." Asya received the impression she had asked a foolish question.

Mme. Christophe continued: "Etienne has told him about the palace and even managed to obtain sketches of it. My husband has always been interested in building. In his younger years he was a bricklayer. You see," Mme. Christophe turned and looked directly at Asya, "we had to work hard for all we have acquired. Nothing was handed to us." Asya noticed a little smile playing again about the corner of her hostess's mouth before she turned away.

Asya wanted to clobber Mme. President right on that tight little muffin on top of her head. Instead, she sucked in her breath and closed her mouth firmly, as she reminded herself she had come as a lady and would leave as one.

However, when Mme. Christophe stopped before one of the golden doors, Asya's indignation slipped away as her eyes fell upon the figure of a little straw man dangling from a hook on the outside. It was dressed in tattered clothes and carried an empty sack in one straw hand. From its mouth, a tiny pipe protruded.

"That is Mait-bitasyen, the god of the house," her hostess explained. "Very effectual in keeping out evil spirits and—" she paused "—and intruders."

"What does he do?" Asya laughed, ignoring Mme. Christophe's pointed implication, "slam them over the head with the empty sack?"

The president's wife did not deem the remark very humorous, for she coolly turned away, saying only, "This is our family quarters," as she opened the door.

Never had Asya walked into such a room. It was a large room, and its furnishings under ordinary circumstances could have been similar to those of the rest of the house, but it looked as though the rugs, chairs, pictures, tables, everything, had been dumped in from some mammoth box and were allowed to lie wherever they fell. It was golden confusion. Mme. Christophe stood motionless, an angry look on her face. She called out in a voice like a whip: "Amethiste! Athenaire! Where are you?"

Asya saw something black rise up from behind one of the overturned chairs. She recognized it as a head whose kinky hair stood straight up. Then followed two big black eyes. The face of a little girl appeared. It broke into a smile which gradually quivered away and left only a guilty look.

There was a noise behind a table which lay on its side, and another little girl, somewhat smaller, stepped out. The look of apprehension was already on her face.

"Who did this?" Mme. Christophe demanded in a quiet, but firm voice.

"*She* did," said the girl behind the chair, pointing at her sister.

"She *made* me do it," insisted the one by the table.

Slowly, but purposefully, Mme. Christophe walked across to a cabinet which stood askew in one of the corners of the room. While Asya watched, she opened a door and withdrew what turned out to be a breadboard with a handle. Both little girls began to whimper.

Unmindful of Asya, Mme. Christophe casually took each girl over her knee and gave her a thumping paddling. Asya was amazed at the vigor of so slight a person.

"Go to your rooms," the president's wife said quietly. She could have been offering a second cup of chocolate, so amiably did she speak.

Mme. Christophe explained to Asya, "Their governess resigned a fortnight ago and returned to Philadelphia. Amethiste and Athenaire have declared their independence."

With that, she gracefully picked her way amidst the rubble on the floor. "Come, I'll show you to your room. I am sorry we do not have space for your maid, but she won't mind sleeping on the floor. Probably more used to that than a bed," she added airily.

That remark Asya could not let pass. "Cilla has never slept on a floor." Now it was she who affected the sweet smile. "But don't let it concern you. We shall manage very well."

Later, when she and Cilla were alone, Asya denounced her hostess. "The nerve of her! Thinking you could sleep on the floor. Does she take you for a stable hand? Does she think we live like savage tribes at Cher Château? You'll sleep in bed with me."

"I don't mind the floor," Cilla protested. "It's all right. It's all right. You have a good time and don't worry about me."

329

"Of course I'll worry about you. I brought you, didn't I?"

"Yes, but," Cilla hesitated, "Negu might not like it if I sleep with you. After all, I—I am your black maid," she finished feebly.

"No, you're not. You—you are—I don't know what you are. You belong to me. You're my friend." Her voice rose as she declared, "And I'll always look out for you."

Protectively putting her arms about the slim girl, Asya looked peeved. How much simpler things had been back in the hospice de Sacre-Coeur, she thought. How complicated it was sometimes to be an heiress.

M. Grenier had been right about those of her friends who came to the court of M. President. When Asya entered the salon for the first of the celebrations, she was surprised to find none other than Eloise Rowbottom. The blond girl was equally shocked.

"Well!" Eloise raised her eyebrows, approaching Asya's chair. "And what favor are *you* after that you bother to visit this bunch of niggers?"

Asya found the girl's comment distasteful. She suspected that Eloise made equally unflattering remarks about her when she was not around to refute them.

"No favor," said Asya coldly. "It is the president's big day, and I came only to bring him my best wishes."

"And a gift too? I hope you didn't forget that. It's the important thing if you want any favors."

"I told you. I'm not asking for anything."

"Well, everybody else here is. That's why I'm here. Father said we must come and be friendly, since now he has so many customers among the court gentry. Gentry. Humph!" she said disdainfully.

"I think everyone looks very nice tonight," Asya defended. "They look as magnificent as the people I saw at a palace ball in Europe." Asya was sincere in her comparison. She had to admit that the president's

circle of friends had come a long way since she last
saw them at the opera. They seemed to have acquired
manners and poise along with their wealth, and no
longer wore all their jewels at one time. Etienne was
right. They were trying.

"When were you ever at a palace ball?" Eloise
laughed, a nasty laugh.

"I didn't attend as a guest," Asya explained. "I was
only a schoolgirl at the time and visiting my friend over
the holidays. We peeped from the balcony and watched
the dancers."

"With the rest of the scullery maids?" Eloise asked.

"Yes. We were all jolly girls together," Asya
snapped.

Eloise tittered. "I was only teasing. Don't be angry.
You and I have got to stick together here in this stupid
country. Ladies amidst all these pretenders."

"I don't know why you say pretenders." Annoyance
crept into Asya's voice. "You can't blame people for
trying to work themselves into high society."

"Now you sound like a vicar at Sunday-school
class," Eloise teased.

At that moment, the stentorian voice of the an-
nouncer of the guests came through the room, "Count
Lemonade, Secretary of State, Minister of Foreign Affairs, Member of the Royal Chamber of Public Instruc-
tion of Haiti, Honorary Member of the English and
Foreign School Society of London."

"See what I mean." Eloise spread out her hands.
"Clowns aping their betters. It's like a farce." She
giggled. "Do you know there is also a Count of
Limeade and a Duke of Hencoop? They were announced before you came in. Limeade is wearing a
lime-green satin suit, special order from Father, and
Hencoop has short legs and a big chest. His hair stands
up on edge as though it were made of feathers and he
struts about like a bantam rooster in a barnyard.
Dresses like one too. Shiny black satin pants and red

coat with gold buttons the size of turkey eggs. The buttons are made of solid gold too. I know, since the firm of M. Rowbottom imports them especially for His Highness of Hencoop."

Eloise changed the subject. "Father is giving M. Christophe a gift of a bolt of red velvet and just kilometers of white fur trim. Real ermine too. I suggested he make it hare, since it's so very much cheaper, and our unschooled president would not know the difference. But," and she sighed in exasperation, "that Papa of mine insists we must be lavish, especially to up-and-coming customers who can do so much for the business."

"How very wise," someone beside her chuckled. Asya knew it was a man, not from his voice, but by the speed with which Eloise turned in his direction.

"Godefroy!" she squealed. "How wonderful to see you. A white friend amidst the Black Sea." M. Rowbottom's daughter placed two fingers against her mouth and tittered, "I didn't know I could be so descriptive. Maybe I have buried literary talent and am letting it go to waste."

Godefroy took Eloise's chin in one of his big hands and shook it teasingly. "Don't bother to excavate it," he said.

She slapped his hand away. "How very discouraging to a future author!" she said in mock indignation. "And after all the encouragement I've been giving you about your sheep too."

Asya looked at Godefroy. "What's this about sheep?" The young Englishman shook his head. "Nothing. Nothing much. Just a silly idea, which—" he waved a big hand in dismissal "—which will never get born."

"Of course it will. Don't you talk like that," Eloise reprimanded in her high-pitched voice. "There's lots of money in sheep raising, and you can't dismiss a money-making scheme." Turning to Asya, she explained, "Godefroy has been talking about importing sheep into Haiti. That is why he's here tonight. Nobody may start a new industry here unless he gets permission of the benevolent black god who has only our interests—and his percentage—at heart." Eloise's prattling bothered Asya's ears and she turned to Godefroy to comment, "What a wonderful idea to raise sheep on your land. I think you are very enterprising."

In his easy manner, Godefroy answered, "It's all up to the sheep."

"And guess what he's giving M. Christophe for a gift," Eloise interrupted. "It's most original. A pair of lambs."

"Nothing like some furry things to soften a tyrant's heart," Godefroy answered, his large brown eyes twinkling with humor. At that point, Godefroy's attention was attracted across the room. "There's Mama waving frantically at me," he said resignedly. "Excuse me while I see what the emergency is this time." In his slow fashion, he loped over to her.

"That Mme. Laborde treats her son like a baby," Eloise sneered, "and what's worse is that he lets her."

"Godefroy doesn't want to hurt her feelings," Asya asserted.

"That doesn't mean he has to let her dominate him. She owns the land and runs things to suit herself even though she doesn't give a damn about the plantation. Why, she won't even let Godefroy try a different crop to see if maybe they can make more money out of the land. She hopes to sell someday and go back to England. But," Eloise shrugged her shoulders, "who would want to buy her run-down property?"

"Mme. Laborde must have had a change of heart," Asya said, "if she is letting Godefroy try his hand at sheep raising."

"Those sheep will never graze on *her* plantation," Eloise corrected. "She wouldn't have them where she could see them. She owns a small piece of land somewhere in the mountains near Gonâve and she's letting him use that for his sheep."

"But how can they afford to buy the sheep if they are so poor?" Asya wanted to know. "Godefroy doesn't seem at all concerned about where the money is coming from."

"Why should he be?" Eloise asked airily. "He already has the money. Mme. Laborde borrowed it on her plantation. Father advised her how to go about making a loan. With all those debts of hers, she only got it because the lender was a friend of Father's. But I'll tell you this." Eloise came close to Asya and whispered into her ear: "She's had one of her convenient headaches ever since, worrying over whether she did right or not."

Eloise shook her head in disgust. "Some businesswoman. They don't even have their sheep yet, and she's crying that all is lost. I can't stomach someone like that."

It was then that Asya saw Godefroy coming back toward them, his big arm thrust up over the crowd of people, waving as he approached.

Before he reached them, however, someone stepped between her and Eloise and his voice greeted, "How are my two girls? Wonderful to see you both. Best-looking women here."

Etienne Grenier put an arm lightly about Asya's shoulders, but her pleasure was short-lived when she saw him put the other one about Eloise's.

Godefroy came up then and with a lopsided grin on his face announced happily, "I no sooner turn my back than a rival appears."

Looking adoringly up at Grenier, Eloise whined, "I'm so thirsty, Etienne. Let us get a drink."

"Of course. And you will come too?" Etienne, looking more debonair than ever in his white dress coat and golden epaulets, inquired of Asya.

"Oh, no." Asya was definite in her refusal. "I don't

care for anything right now." Turning to Godefroy, she gave him her best smile and said in a voice of sugar, "I want to hear all about your sheep. As yet, you have not told me one word. It sounds so adventuresome."

Eloise's nasty laugh came floating back as she and Etienne walked away. "I never did like tales of adventure," she was remarking to Etienne.

Asya looked at Godefroy. His face was serious, and if he had heard Eloise's parting remark he gave no indication.

He asked in a slow, almost disbelieving voice, "You *really* want to hear about my plans with sheep?"

"Of course, I do," Asya encouraged. "I see two chairs over there against the wall, and if we hurry we can get there before anyone else takes them." She reached for Godefroy's hand and lightly ran across the room, pulling him along behind.

"There." She dropped down into a chair, at the same time playfully shoving him into the vacant one beside her. "We made it. We can have a nice visit together. Someone is starting to read a long list of gifts M. President has received for his feast day, and everyone will be too busy measuring his offering against that of his neighbor to miss us. Now, let's hear about your sheep."

Godefroy leaned toward her, but said nothing. His dark brown eyes regarded her seriously. In a coquettish mood, Asya reached up and lightly kissed him on the cheek.

"Wake up," she laughed. "If some witch doctor has put a magic spell upon you, I have broken it. You are able to talk again. Speak to me, Godefroy," she ordered.

Godefroy took her hand and held it between his two big ones. He said simply, "I want to marry you. I love you."

Involuntarily, Asya drew back. She had not expected this serious turn and she wanted to be free of encum-

brance. She opened her mouth to make some light retort, but Godefroy shook his head. "Don't answer. I
know, you're thinking this is my usual routine proposal, but this time it is different. I have a future to
offer you. Before, I had nothing but a run-down
plantation over which I had no control. Now, I am
starting off on my own. This will be mine, not my
mother's. I am going into the sheep business, and I
know I can succeed. My plans and contacts were all
made in Jamaica, and what I need to get started is only
the nod from M. Christophe. As soon as I get that, I
shall leave immediately. In the meantime, Asya, will
you remember what I have asked? When I am in a
position to support a wife, I'll come for your answer."

Asya said nothing. Her hand in his felt warm and
protected. A moment of lassitude came over her, and
she thought how nice it might be to be looked after.
Asya glanced up into Godefroy's deep brown eyes, and
realized he was no longer a boy. He seemed to have
become a man, a strong man.

He turned her hand over so that the palm faced up
and kissed it. "I once told you that here lies my heart.
It is yours for always. To hurt, to cherish, or to throw
away."

Asya bit her lip. She did not know what to say.
Somehow she had the feeling she had been singled out
for a great honor and was not worthy of it. Nor did she
desire it.

At that moment, Asya became conscious of a
stillness in the great room. She looked up and found all
the guests—there must have been hundreds of them—
staring back at her and Godefroy.

In bewilderment Asya whispered, "Godefroy, why's
everyone looking at us? What have we done?"

Without taking his eyes from her face, he answered
with a touch of not quite repressed exuberance in his
voice, "We've fallen in love."

"Godefroy!" The old suitor would have blushed, the

redness in his cheeks visible to the ends of the room. But this new one had assurance. Rather appealing, his debonair attitude infected her, and Asya smiled amicably at the sea of eyes. However, the eyes came closer, converging upon her and Godefroy. Exclamations of "How wonderful!, How marvelous! What generosity!" erupted from the crowd, which by now stifled her with its enthusiasm. Whatever was the matter with everyone?

Then the crowd parted and the voices died down as Henri Christophe walked up to Asya. Looking upon her from his great height, the president said in a deep voice which shook with emotion, "In our need God must have sent you to us." He held out his hands, and Asya, rising from her chair, placed both hers into his. She started to curtsey, but he restrained her.

"It is we, the people of Haiti, who should pay homage to you, Mlle. Asya Drapeaux, for your wonderful gift of books to our country." With that the president bowed low and long, and his court, taking the cue from him, followed suit.

Looking over the bowed heads, Asya was bewildered by the swift turn of events. To be thrust from sitting unnoticed in a corner with an ardent suitor to being the cynosure of all eyes was exhilarating. Frightening. Wonderful. It was being as famous as Eleanore. No, Josephine. The Empress Josephine! Asya opened her mouth and drew in a deep breath. If the girls back at school could see her now, she thought smugly. Queen Asya. She thrust out her chin. Wealth *was* everything, after all. She would never be without it, ever.

M. Christophe must have had tears in his eyes, for as he spoke to her, he gave a quick flick at one of them with his fingertip. "You have insured the future of our poor little country. Like in the Bible, all generations will call you blessed."

Why had she ever been uneasy about this darling old man with the red-streaked eyes? He was really a black Moses in modern dress. A leader of his people. It was an honor to win his approbation. Because she wanted to, Asya curtseyed to M. Christophe.

While floating to ethereal heights with all this honor and limelight, Asya remembered Godefroy. To her surprise, she found him standing by her side, practically at military attention. The lopsided carelessness of the gangling boy was gone, and, straightened up, Godefroy looked almost as tall as the president.

She gave M. Christophe a sweet smile and said, "May I present my dear friend, M. Godefroy Laborde. He, too, is happy to be here in honor of your feast day, M. President."

A look of amusement flickered in Henri Christophe's eyes. "Ah, yes. The giver of the lambs. A most original gift. In fact, I might say, the most active on the list."

Asya's mouth dropped open in amazement. "How did you remember, M. President, with all the gifts you have received today?"

M. Christophe chuckled. "Easy. My memory was trained long ago when I was a waiter in a tavern and had to remember which guest ordered what drinks. I can't write," he explained easily, "so I have to stick everything in my head."

Addressing Godefroy, the president asked, "Have you ever thought of raising sheep on the island, M. Laborde? You impress me as a young man with a patient, even temperament who enjoys handling animals. A growing nation can use new industries. Any endeavor in animal husbandry would win my approval and encouragement."

Godefroy looked as surprised as Asya at the turn of the conversation, and he did not answer at once. Was the president a mind reader, or truly a Moses inspired by God? Asya gave a timid little smile, but before she could speak, Godefroy found his voice. "Thank you, sir. That was exactly what I had in mind." He was having trouble clearing his throat. His voice became stronger. "I shall leave for Jamaica tomorrow to initiate plans for such a venture."

"No hurry, no hurry," M. Christophe said in his soft voice. "I didn't mean to mention business in the middle of pleasure."

Godefroy gave the president a broad grin. "You don't understand, sir, but there *is* need for hurry." He looked significantly at Asya. "The sooner I take care of business, the sooner I have time for pleasure."

M. Christophe gave an indulgent laugh. "My blessings on *all* your intentions, M. Laborde, but right now, may I borrow your intention?"

Turning to Asya, the president offered his arm. "Will you sit by me at dinner, my dear? The honor will be entirely mine."

For Asya, this was triumph. Complete triumph.

After that first night of acclaim, Asya longed to return to Cher Château. True to his word, Godefroy sailed for Jamaica the next morning, and there was no one at the palace to squire her around. Other young gentlemen, both English and Creole, were present, but they were so obviously at court to nourish their own political interests that they had no time to dance and be gay. All the old ladies of both colors were most gracious about offering their congratulations to Asya upon her gracious gift to the nation, but Asya had not come to please old ladies. She wanted to laugh and be flirted with by handsome young men. Of what purpose was it to wear a spectacular emerald necklace about her neck if she was but something to exclaim over like the gold-framed pictures on the wall.

After two wearings even that jeweled boost to her morale had to be hidden away in her bedroom. It was General Prophète who had made her uneasy about wearing it. From the first meeting with him, Asya disliked the red-coated Dahomey. He was so sure of himself, arrogantly sure, like a goateed Satan who is proud of being evil and smiles derisively at good, for in evil lies all the fun the good are missing. During any conversation, M. Prophète's eyes never moved from her neck. At first, she thought it was her natural charms on which he was concentrating, but she realized it was the emerald necklace when he said, "Your choice in jewelry is excellent, Mlle. Drapeaux."

Whereupon, in his superior manner, he reached out his hand and lifted the pendant, juggling its weight in his palm, all the time a calculating look in his narrowed eyes. "Just as I thought," he said more to himself than to her. "Easily a thousand karats."

Cilla, too, had abandoned her. She had met a young man at court. Watusi Motti. It was he who had read out the list of Christophe's gifts that first day of the festivities. He was a mulatto, born in New Orleans where he had kept books for a cotton exporter. Cilla was vague about how he had come to Cap François except that she knew M. Grenier had secured him through his own shipping contacts. Watusi's job here was to keep books for the government treasury.

According to Cilla, Watusi was fascinating. When pressed for further details, she could only sigh, "Like I said, fascinating." Feeling like a duenna, Asya insisted upon meeting Watusi. To her suprise, unlike his name, he was a little man, shorter than Cilla. He had a long-beaked nose, which should not have added to the attractiveness of so small a person, and yet he wore it well. It gave him an appearance of strength. His brown eyes were sharp and unwavering when he spoke, conveying the impression that he stood behind what he said. A little scrapper, Asya concluded. Yet when he smiled, it spread so far across his face that his long nose jutted down like a brown peninsula across a white sea of teeth.

Asya liked Watusi. When he talked with her and Cilla he did so in a soft, gentle way, flattering them with a respectful gallantry. No wonder Cilla found him fascinating.

Asya knew she should curtail the number of hours Cilla spent with Watusi, for the roosters were already crowing each morning when the girl came to bed, and yet she was loath to interfere in the romance. However, when Mme. Christophe made mention of the scandalous time of morning Cilla said goodnight to her gentleman friend, "a very bad example to the other maids of the court," Asya was positive she would say nothing at all to the happy lovers. Cilla could do as she pleased.

And what right had Mme. Christophe to complain about someone else's bad behavior? Asya had seen the president's wife hovering about Etienne Grenier, their heads bent together in serious conversation. Once she saw them leave the dancing early in the evening, not to appear again. "Bad example" indeed, thought Asya.

But, to be honest with herself, part of her anger was rooted in jealousy. She had expected to have M. Grenier, Etienne as she privately thought of him, dancing attendance upon her like a lovesick swain. Instead, he was treating her like a visiting elderly cousin with whom one speaks the amenities simply because a relative must be tolerated. As in a ritual that must be performed, he danced with her once each night, and then sought a new partner to favor with his charm. She hated him.

It was Eloise, however, who gave her the final jolt she needed to make up her mind to cut her court visit short and return home. "Poor Godefroy," she said to Asya, as she came up to her one evening when everyone was sitting about waiting for a harpsichord concert to begin. "He's missing all the fun by going off to Jamaica on business."

Her high voice carried through that section of the room, and the other guests stopped in their conversation to listen.

341

"I think Godefroy has fun wherever he goes," Asya answered in a flat voice.

"Who would be knowing better than you?" Eloise tittered, at the same time bending over to give Asya a knowing look.

Asya was perplexed. "What are you talking about?"

Eloise raised innocent blue eyes to the ceiling and smugly announced, "I know you're engaged to Godefroy. Don't hold out on your best friend."

Asya was dumbfounded. Her mouth opened, but no sound came. Had Eloise been drinking too much wine? And that high voice of hers must have carried all over the room, from the way the women about her were nodding and smiling happily in her direction.

"Tut-tut. Don't deny being in love with that marvelous boy. Or," she asked archly, "are you trying to keep the wonderful news from his mama?"

Nearby, somebody snickered. Eloise always did love playing to an audience.

After the first shock of this astounding accusation, Asya managed to control her vagrant voice. "I am not engaged to Godefroy Laborde," she announced sharply. "We are friends. Nothing more."

"You're acting too flustered to be telling the truth," Eloise drawled in a smug, know-it-all way. "I saw the way he looked at you before he left for Jamaica. Love in his eyes, and you looked interested, too, that is, interested for you."

"You are making up stories." Asya turned her head away in disgust. The best way to handle this little chit was to ignore her.

Eloise, however, was not one to be so easily dismissed. "Then there is an understanding between the two of you," she persisted, "and I'm not the only one of that opinion."

By now, all the guests were smiling at Asya like a bunch of Cupids whose arrows had hit the target.

"Etienne agrees with me," Eloise babbled on. "I

called his attention to the cozy little rendezvous you and Godefroy were having in the corner the other day, and he says it was undoubtedly a proposal and you looked most receptive to the honor offered. Why not?" Eloise raised her eyebrows and went on in a snide tone, "It isn't every girl who gets the chance to marry a nice young man whose mama is letting him try his little hand at sheep raising." The crowd snickered.

Asya jumped to her feet. In a clear voice so that all these gossip-lovers could hear every word, she announced succinctly and firmly, "I am not engaged to M. Laborde now and never shall be. At no time in the future do I plan to marry him. He is still eligible so that any girl who is interested may pursue her suit." She looked meaningfully at Eloise. "Better hurry before some nice girl grabs him."

Slowly and casually, so that no one might think her upset by the conversation, Asya left the room.

But Asya *was* upset. She was seething. It was all Eloise's fault that Etienne had dropped the camaraderie they had always entertained between them. Not that it was a friendly relationship, but it had been an exciting one. And Godefroy. *Mon Dieu!* Waste her talents, her life on that simple soul. It was all a plot on Eloise's part to get M. Grenier for herself. The fool! Right now he had eyes only for Mme. Christophe. He would always have eyes for somebody else and each few days a different somebody else. He was fickle! Fickle! Fickle! An adulterer. A *roué!* A devil. He was horrible, and so was Eloise. She was as bad as he. She hated them both. And what was making her angriest of all was that deep down inside, she was aware that Etienne, even without Eloise's help, had never regarded her as a candidate for lovemaking. She was still a little girl to fight with. She hated him. She was going home. Even without Cilla, she could pack. She would be ready when Cilla came in from her evening with Watusi. Being a servant had advantages, she told herself irritably. Nobody cares whom you spent the evening with.

When Asya entered the Christophes' family quarters, she was relieved to find the place deserted. *Merci, mon Dieu*. She would not have to answer any questions as to why she had left the festivities. She had at least expected to encounter Amethiste and Athenaire and battle her way to her own room. However, all was quiet.

And then she opened the door to her own bedroom.

At first Asya thought she had come to the wrong place. A band of drunken pranksters must have topsy-turvyed the room. The furniture—the highboy, the bed, the chairs—could not be distinguished one from the other. Everything was covered with clothes, tossed carelessly into misshapen piles. Even the pictures were draped with skirts or shawls hanging at crazy angles. The carpet—she thought there had been a red carpet—was completely hidden by bedclothes twisted up with some green silk which somehow resembled the shade of dress she had worn the night before. The only piece of furniture which was able to maintain its identity was the full-length mirror which feebly peeked out from behind strands of varicolored sashes. Even in this state of disarray, the clothes looked familiar. Asya had a sinking feeling they were hers.

From somewhere in the room there came a happy little chirp. At least it sounded like a chirp to Asya, but when it came again, her ears recovered from shock and once more took up their job of hearing.

"*Bonne nuit*," the chirp said.

Amidst the dishevelment, Asya's eyes could not immediately pick out a human form.

"I'm up here. Up on the highboy." The chirp was now a voice. "I'm the highest of all."

Asya looked in the direction of the voice. *Mon Dieu*. It was Amethiste. Amethiste standing up there with her head against the ceiling dressed, or wrapped up, in the new orange gown Asya intended to wear the next day for the grand ball. Her gorgeous dress. Ruined! That brat had chopped off the bottom.

A great many vituperative epithets seethed inside Asya but before she could select the most vitriolic for her opening volley, she heard a giggle on the other side of the room.

"But I'm the prettiest of all."

Asya spun around, certain the situation could not be worse. But it was. Athenaire stood poised on top of a pile of hats, her naked body encircled by Asya's boa of white feathers. Hanging from its diamond chain, her emerald sparkled against the skinny black chest.

"You damn nigger brat!" Asya spat out and made a lunge for the girl. Athenaire, like a wild animal, leaped away, but her foot caught in the boa and ripped it in two, at the same time pitching its wearer to the floor.

Asya pounced upon her, pulling her to her feet by her kinky hair. The child began screaming in fright, but the sound of her voice only further churned the anger boiling in Asya's breast. With both hands firmly gripping Athenaire's hair, Asya wildly shook the girl, unable to stop, for the storm inside poured out through her arms in a senseless, uncontrolled fury.

From somewhere in the room, another hysterical voice joined in with the frightened wailing of Athenaire. "Amethiste! You're next, you black brat," Asya shouted. "I'll teach you to put your filthy nigger hands on my beautiful clothes. I'll shake the hide off the two of you until no one knows what color you were born. You damn, damn, damn niggers!"

"You'll do no such thing," a cold voice whipped out behind her, while at the same time two strong hands grabbed her wrists.

"I will. I will. I will. Let me go!" Asya tried to struggle free, the unspent fury inside driving her on with unaccustomed strength. "They ruined my clothes. I'll kill them for this."

But the hands on her wrists tightened their grip until

she had no feeling and let go in momentary exhaustion. Athenaire scooted away.

The interloper spun her around. It was Etienne. "Have you lost your mind?" he demanded angrily.

"No. Only my clothes." Asya spoke through clenched teeth.

"Too bad. The other would have been of less value." His eyes looked her up and down in scorn. Then slowly he turned away and walked over to the highboy where Amethiste was crouching, her arms reaching out to him, big sobs shaking her small body. Without one word of admonishment, he lifted the child down and carried her toward the door, where Mme. Christophe was standing.

Etienne set the child down beside its mother, turned her toward the door, and gave her a propelling smack on the behind. "Get off to your room and wait for your mama."

His words brought renewed vigor to Amethiste's lungs, and she went howling away like a departing banshee.

In amazement, Asya put her hands on her hips. "You act as though you're the father around here," she flung at M. Grenier. "You ought to do a better job of training *les enfantes*."

Etienne regarded her in contempt.

"Don't look at me that way. I'm the innocent victim. My clothes are ruined. What are you going to do about it, *Père* Disciple?"

Mme. Christophe spoke from the doorway. "Your pardon, Mlle. Asya, for my daughters. I deeply regret their conduct toward a guest in my home. Your clothes will be replaced. Here is the necklace I removed from Athenaire on her way out of this room." She walked over to the dresser, pushed aside some clothes and laid the emerald down.

She started to leave the room, but Etienne placed a

346

restraining hand on her arm. "Wait. I believe Mlle. Drapeaux has a word for you."

"I've said everything I'm going to say except adieu." Asya snapped her mouth shut into a firm line.

Etienne looked at her through half-closed eyes. His nostrils were quivering, and she thought she had never seen him so angry. "Your language was most unbecoming before the children and your hostess."

Asya shrugged. "If you had knocked before entering, you wouldn't have heard so much."

"Don't be facetious. You owe your hostess an apology."

Asya's head shot up. "Well!" she exploded. "Well!" Her chin jutted out in indignation.

Looking very fragile. Mme. Christophe interrupted in a soft voice. "*S'il vous plaît*, I shall go. This is all most unfortunate, and we need not prolong it."

"Wait." Etienne spoke quietly, too quietly.

It happened so quickly that Asya had no chance to protest. Etienne's strong arms grabbed her waist, and throwing her over his knees, he spanked her, spanked her soundly.

"Stop it!" Asya found her voice. "Stop it, you savage! Stop!"

As quickly as he had seized her Etienne dropped Asya to the terrazzo floor, where she landed on the chastened part of her anatomy. Eyes blazing, she screamed up at him. "How dare you humilate me like this!"

"It was easy," he said scornfully. "And now your apology. Mme. Christophe is waiting."

Asya was furious. She could feel tears of anger and humiliation welling up in her eyes. But she knew she had no choice. She rose and turned toward the door where her hostess had been standing, but Mme. Christophe was gone.

"Your dear friend obviously grew bored and left,"

Asya snapped. "Couldn't stand your comedy." She fought back the tears.

Etienne gave a quick glance about the room. Then, without a word, he strode out, slamming the door behind him.

"Damn!" Asya shook her fist at the closed door. "Damn you, Etienne!"

Chapter Twenty-six

For days after her return from the presidential palace, Asya knew only anger. She would show them. She would show Etienne and his noble lady. She would marry Godefroy. That was what she would do. As soon as he came back from Jamaica. No one would ever spank her again. No one would raise a hand against M. Laborde's wife. They would have to treat her with respect. Asya and Godefroy would be the richest people in Haiti. Between his prosperous sheep business and her plantation, they would be loaded with gourds. They would have parties which would be talked about as far away as—as—Eleanore's palace in Europe. And they would never invite Mme. Christophe or M. Grenier. Never.

Except for Cilla, Asya confided her nuptial plans to no one. Cilla was her confidante in the matter of the stormy encounter with M. Grenier and was truly sympathetic. The maid had been aghast that anyone had dared strike her mistress. She shivered during Asya's account of the altercation and shook her head in wonder.

"A big man like that hits hard. You must have a big hate. There's so much of him to hate."

"I hate him. I hate him. I hate him," Asya chanted. "I hate him. I hate him. I hate him." She walked about the bedroom in time with her voice. "I hate him."

"That's good," Cilla encouraged. "You just keep on hating that man. And he'll be sorry too when you are

349

Mme. Laborde, but it'll be too late, and it'll serve him right."

Momentarily Asya was taken aback. "What do you mean?"

"When a man hits a girl that hard, he likes her."

"Cilla, you don't know anything about men. You've always been sheltered by your parents and Negu. Where did you get such stupid ideas?"

Cilla rolled her large eyes up toward the ceiling. "Us black girls are *born* knowing about men."

"This time you're mistaken. M. Grenier likes Mme. Christophe; he likes Mlle. Eloise; he likes his big old housekeeper. In fact, he likes everybody but me."

"*Non.*" Cilla was most emphatic. "When a man likes a girl, he wants to change her to his way of thinking. If he has no feeling for her, then he does not care what she does." She wagged a finger at her mistress. "Wait and see. He'll cry at your wedding."

"Rubbish," Asya said brusquely, hoping to snuff an annoying little flutter which stirred in her breast. "He won't be invited to my wedding. I shall never look at him again. I shall never speak to him again. I hate him. I hate him."

"That's good. You keep on telling yourself how much you hate him," Cilla encouraged, "so that you stick by you intention to marry M. Laborde. Don't go weakening like all the girls do when M. Grenier comes sidling up to them with sweet talk."

Asya raised an eyebrow. She was certain this was not the customary counsel given a future bride, but she guessed it did apply to her case. "No one will stop me from marrying Godefroy Laborde. No one," she answered.

But someone did.

Godefroy was still in Jamaica, when Eloise Rowbottom arrived at Cher Château one afternoon.

"Oh, Asya, you're not still cross with me, are you?" Her voice was syrupy and her eyes looked soulful.

Instinctively, Asya was on guard. The English girl had not made the trip out to Cher Château simply to check on its mistress's degree of friendliness. "*Oui*. I am. You had no business making a public announcement about my personal affairs, which are no concern of yours or anyone's."

Eloise bowed her head and pouted. "You don't understand." Her voice was tearful. "It's my romantic nature. Sometimes it runs away with me."

"Why didn't you ask me about it?" Asya snapped.

"Oh, Asya, don't talk to me like that, or I'll cry." She sniffed as an indication she was already prepared to burst into tears.

"Eloise, stop that!" Asya ordered. "Save your act for some susceptible male. On me, you're wasting your talents."

"You don't like me, do you, Asya?" Eloise accused in a wounded tone. "You don't like me because I'm not as rich as you. I'm your poor friend. I was good enough at first when you knew no one, but now you don't need me anymore. You don't care about me, do you?"

Asya stood fascinated by Eloise's histrionic display. The girl was ridiculous. Momentarily at a loss for a suitable reply, Asya said nothing.

Eloise brightened. "See, you can't answer. You do like me, don't you?" She ran to Asya and affectionately flung her arms about her neck. "I'm so glad I'm still your best friend. I knew you would forgive me."

Asya gently, but definitely, pushed her caller toward a chair. "Sit down. Relax. We won't talk about that unpleasant episode anymore. I'll order some chocolate and you can tell me why you really came to call this afternoon." She walked over and pulled the bell.

"Oh, Asya, you are a real friend. You put up with my silly idiosyncrasies and like me in spite of them. But that's the way a friend should be. Understanding of one's weaknesses." The English girl became serious. "If I had freckles or my ears stuck out or I had a club

351

foot, you would not deny your friendship with me because I had these physical deformities about which I could do nothing. Just so," she concluded breezily, "a true friend accepts one's character shortcomings and likes her in spite of them. Just as you like me even if I am too romantic and talk too much and can't correct it." She paused. A mischievous look came into her blue eyes. "Do you suppose I could have a brandy instead of chocolate? Papa needn't know."

When the brandy arrived, Eloise rolled it over her tongue and smacked her lips in genuine delight. "Umm, this is so good. It's just what I needed. Sometimes I hear Papa talk about a bracer. I guess now I know what he means. I surely needed this, for the most awful thing has happened."

From the obvious pleasure the imbibing afforded her visitor, Asya was thinking that nothing very momentous could have upset her. However, with Eloise's next words, it was the young mistress of Cher Château who became upset.

"It's well that you are not marrying Godefroy, because by the time he returns from Jamaica he and his mama will be as poor as swamp niggers. No girl will marry him then."

Asya looked at Eloise in disbelief, at the same time annoyed that her guest would manufacture such a tale. "Whatever are you saying?" she rebuked.

"Just that." Eloise was very matter-of-fact. "They are going to lose their house, their lands, and," she giggled, "even those silly sheep."

"Eloise, wherever did you pick up such horrible gossip? The Labordes have been here for years and nothing is going to make them paupers overnight." Asya was irritated. Eloise's tale-bearing always rankled and Asya had become skilled in refuting it. Yet, she had an uneasy premonition that something was wrong. Her caller wore too knowing a look.

"You'll see." Eloise shook her finger at Asya.

"You'll see." Casually she reached for the decanter which had been left on the table and poured herself another brandy. "This is good. You don't mind if I have one more, do you?"

"Not if your father does not mind."

Eloise placed her finger against her lips. "Shh. We won't tell him, will we? He's so old-fashioned. He thinks girls should only drink wine until they are married. As old as I'm getting and still not married, I'd never know how brandy tastes if I listened to him." She took a sip. Her blue eyes rolled in ecstasy while her tongue licked her lips. "The second glass is even better than the first," Eloise announced. Then she looked at Asya and said brightly, "You know what I'm going to do? I'm going to tell you what I heard about the Labordes, because you are so good to me."

"I'd be lying if I said I wasn't curious," Asya admitted, "but I hope nothing awful has happened to them." Since she had made up her mind to marry Godefroy, Asya had already come to regard him and his mother as family.

"Awful? Of course it's awful. There isn't anything more awful than losing everything you own, and that's what's happened to the Labordes." To emphasize the point she was making, Eloise swept the palm of her hand across the table by which she sat. "Just like that. Dusted off clean."

"How?" Asya asked, still not believing.

Leaning toward her hostess, Eloise confided in a malicious tone, "If you remember, I told you when we were all at the palace that Mme. Laborde had borrowed money from a friend of my father's to give Godefroy for his try at the sheep business. Well, now my father's friend says he made a mistake. His superiors insist he should not have lent her all that money since she did not have enough something or other on which to borrow. I think it's called collateral." She shrugged. "I don't know all the technicalities of the mess, but—"

her voice became emphatic "—she has to pay it back. Right now!"

"But if Mme. Laborde has no money, what will she do?" Asya shook her head in dismay.

Eloise shrugged a shoulder. "Too bad. That's her problem."

"She won't lose everything, will she?" Asya persisted.

"Everything." Eloise punctuated the word with the definite click of the brandy glass as she set it on the table. "Everything. She owes so much money to everyone that her creditors will all pounce upon her at the same time as soon as they hear about this huge sum of money she can't pay back. Like buzzards on a corpse. She'll be picked clean in no time." Slowly Eloise raised both arms in an arch above her head and then let them flutter out in a wide circle as though she were beginning a ballet right there in the chair. At the same time, she began to sing, "Good-bye, Mama Laborde. Farewell, Mama Laborde. Adieu, Mama Laborde."

"Eloise, you're drunk!" Asya accused.

"Nope." Eloise shook her head. "I'm blithe. I'm celebrating. Cheers. Cheers." Her voice trailed away as she blinked her eyes in an obvious effort to grasp some elusive thought. With a perplexed look she turned to Asya and asked, "Aren't three cheers the customary number in time of rejoicing?"

Before her hostess could answer, Eloise nodded her head. "Yes," she told herself. "Always it's three cheers and I've only had two. What a laggard I am." She laughed. "Imagine that. Forgetting my third drink." Eloise reached for the decanter and began to refill her glass.

Quickly, Asya took the bottle from her visitor. "You've had enough," she rebuked. "Besides, if what you say is true, the Labordes' misfortune is no reason to celebrate."

"Oh, pet, you don't understand." She gave a

crooked smile. "Father and I want to get back to England. And, anyhow, it was all fair and square."

Scattered thoughts ran through Asya's head. "Eloise," she finally found her voice. "What are you saying?"

With a smirk on her face, Eloise haughtily stood up. "Why, nothing. Only that the transaction was entirely legal. My father would never refer a friend to a quack. Mme. Laborde herself signed the agreement, and it definitely stated that she would repay the money—and the interest—in twenty days. The twenty days will be up tomorrow."

"Twenty days!" Asya was dumbfounded. "What do they expect from sheep in twenty days? And I don't recall Godefroy mentioning anything about a time limit."

"You know how flighty his mama is. Maybe she forgot to tell him."

"Maybe Mama didn't know?" Asya accused.

Eloise tossed her head. "That's her fault if she didn't read the fine print before signing. Now she can do nothing about it but pay back the money tomorrow, and that is something the fine lady does not have."

"What will happen?"

"Oh," Eloise rolled her eyes as though happy visions danced inside her head, "they'll have to take her house and her lands and her carriage and her one skinny horse and her smoked hams and her silver teapot and her imitation jade earrings that she's been trying to fool everyone with all these years and—"

"Shut up," Asya ordered. "You're actually gloating over Mme. Laborde's misfortune."

"—and the house should bring a good price," the English girl continued, the same pleasured look on her face. "There are so few of those fine old ones left around here, I just know those nigger potentates down at the palace will knife each other in outbidding for it."

"Shut up!"

For a brief moment, Eloise was quiet. A slow smile

355

crept over her face. "I can see Godefroy now as he steps off the boat. He'll look as dumb and bewildered as the bleating sheep trailing behind him when the deputy steps up and announces his wooly cargo belongs to somebody else. I might just go down to meet Godefroy when he lands. I'd hate to miss the fun."

"Get out," Asya shouted. "Get out! You and your father are nothing but a couple of thieves!"

"Come, come," Eloise cajoled in her high sweet voice. "Your terminology is all wrong. It's not thieves we are, but businessmen, very sharp businessmen." Trying to maintain an air of dignity, Eloise weaved from the room.

At her guest's departure, Asya stood by the table in dismay. Her eyes fell upon the brandy glass Eloise had drunk from. She snatched it up and flung it furiously against the wall, the sound of its breaking somewhat mollifying the anger she felt. "Thieves! Swindlers!" Asya announced loudly to the room.

The sound of her own voice stimulated Asya into action. Those plotting peddlers would never get away with it. She had an idea. Excitedly she ran to the bell cord, calling out at the same time, "Nassy! Nassy! Send for the carriage. I want the fastest horse. Nassy! The carriage."

The butler came running from the dining room, flapping like a black bird in a dirt bath as he struggled to put on his coat. "I'se comin'. Soon's I git prop'ly dressed," he sputtered breathlessly.

"Don't bother with a coat now," Asya ordered. "Get the carriage. I'm going to town."

She pulled up her skirts and flew up the stairs two at a time. It had been a long time since she had been so exhilarated. It was a wonderful feeling.

"Is you sick?" the concerned voice of the butler called up the steps after her.

"No." Asya turned and grinned down at him. "I'm going to war." Then she ran down the hall to her room, shouting as she went, "Cilla. Cilla. Help me change my dress. I'm in a hurry."

Asya was madly pulling out clothes from her closet in an effort to find something suitable for her call, when Negu came into the room. "Is someone dying?" The breathiness of her voice betrayed the speed with which she must have climbed the stairs.

"Worse." Asya kicked off her house slippers. "The Rowbottoms think they are going to get rich off the Labordes by stealing their plantation. Well, they won't. I'll see to that."

"I don't know what you're planning to do," Negu said in a deliberate tone, "but whatever it is, I am in favor of it." After a pause, she snapped, "Never liked those two." Pushing aside the younger maid, who had just rushed into the room, Negu took command. "I'll tie the petticoats. You get the dress, Cilla. Wherever Asya is going, it looks like she had better hurry."

While her housekeeper and maid literally flew about the room in their efforts to dress her, Asya told them of Eloise's visit. She was so wound up with enthusiasm that for the first time Asya felt no restraint in speaking freely before Negu. Asya wanted to shout a war cry as she eagerly welcomed battle, and Negu was but another trusted aide-de-camp, as she readied for action.

"But what are you going to do?" Cilla asked. "How are you going to stop them?"

"I'm coming to that. Wait until you hear. But—" she paused suddenly to give both servants a severe look "—don't breathe a word to anyone. No one. Understand? Not even your parents," she admonished Cilla.

"No. No." Cilla shook her head quickly. "I know when to keep my mouth shut. But I'll die if you don't quick tell us what good wicked plan you got in your head for outfoxing those English Rowbottoms. They don't belong here anyway with us Haitian folk."

Asya stretched to her fullest height so as to give the

357

exhilaration bursting inside room to swell. Taking a big breath, she proudly shouted, "I am going to buy all the Laborde properties right out from under the noses of those conniving Rowbottoms and their sneaky friend. Everything—their household furnishings, the sheep which haven't come yet, even the no-account land in the mountains where Godefroy is planning to graze them. There won't be a thing left of any value that those thieves can steal. I'll show *them* who's the sharp businessman in this land. They can go back to England penniless for all I care!"

"And good riddance," Cilla joined in. Suddenly a frown wrinkled the brow of the young Negress. "Are you sure Mme. Laborde will want to sell? She's—" Cilla hesitated before going on: "It's only hearsay, of course, but I heard she's not very smart and—and if she likes M. Rowbottom, she might not want to sell without getting his advice."

"No. Don't worry about her," Asya answered, sure of herself in that direction. "If I know Mme. Laborde, she's floundering in despair with one of her headaches as her only comfort. She'll grab at anything."

"I never thought headaches very comfortable," Cilla said dubiously.

"If you're used to them and can call one up at a moment's notice, I guess they can be a help. Like sulking in a dark room when you're upset. Not very comfortable, but it's what you enjoy doing at the time." She pointed to the top shelf of the clothes press. "I'll wear my little straw bonnet. I'll look more like a businesswoman in that than in a big floppy one. Hurry. Hurry."

"I am running as fast as my black feet will carry me." Cilla set the hat on the head of her young mistress and sighed. "Oh, how I wish I could go with you."

The thought struck Asya. Why not? "You can," she announced jubilantly. "Then we can laugh and talk about all we're going to do the whole way into town and back. We'll be in this together, Cilla. More fun that way. Quick. Get into your going-to-town clothes. Never can tell when you might meet Watusi," she called after Cilla who had already scampered out of the room. "Got to look alluring."

Asya was wound up with happiness. It was good to have money. With money one could change the world. Right now the world was hers.

Too excited to sit, Asya walked to the window while she waited for Cilla to return. Negu, picking up the clothing that lay scattered about the floor, asked in a quiet voice, "How do you know how much to offer Mme. Laborde for her properties?"

Perplexed, Asya bit her lip. "Really, I don't know. I'm not sure of all the details. I just know I must buy out the Labordes."

"Why not go to see M. Rosseau at the bank in Cap François? He would know the market value of the Laborde house and land. He has been here a long time and could advise you as to a fair price."

"Good," Asya agreed, surprised at herself. It was the first time she had accepted advice from Negu without argument. Today, nothing could upset her. "Excellent suggestion. Then, when he tells me a fair price, I shall raise the price in my offer to Mme. Laborde."

"What!" It was the loudest Negu had ever spoken.

"You heard me. A big raise." Happy spurts of laughter danced in Asya's breast over the amazement in her housekeeper's face. What fun!

"Mama Negu, you look shocked." Cilla, dressed for town, had returned.

"I told her I'm going to pay Mme. Laborde too much for her property," Asya explained, "and it seems to surprise her."

"Me too." Now Cilla wore a quizzical look.

"Why?" Asya asked in unconcern. "Did you forget that I'm going to marry Godefroy?" As soon as she said it, Asya's hand went over her mouth. "Me and my flapping mouth."

She turned to Negu. "Cilla was the only one who knows I am marrying Godefroy when he comes back from Jamaica. Now you know too. But," she shook a finger at Negu, "don't you dare tell a soul. Promise?" She walked up close to the Negress. "Promise? Raise your hand and swear."

Still looking startled, Negu raised a hand. "I swear. But I never would have picked M. Laborde to be the man of this house. Whoever marries M. Laborde marries his mama too." Negu sounded like an oracle foretelling doom.

Asya laughed. "Not when I'm the one M. Godefroy Laborde marries. That's why I'm such a generous purchaser. In this case, money will cut that maternal tie that binds. Mama Laborde will have enough money, after wiping out all her debts, to return to the beloved England she's been crying for. Then Godefroy and I can live happily ever after." She giggled. "He and I and the sheep."

Asya ran out the door and started down the stairs. "Hurry, Cilla," she sang out merrily. "It's Creation Day for us. We're remaking the world and we have much to do."

Three weeks later Asya was growing impatient. Godefroy, whom she was expecting to overwhelm with both the news of her coming engagement to him and with the cleared titles to what would soon be their land together, had not yet returned from Jamaica. Nor had she heard anything from the Rowbottoms, though what she expected of them she really was not sure. That they were miffed with her, she was well aware, since at the various social functions at which Asya saw Eloise, the English girl stared straight through her without a sign of recognition. At first, cocky over her victory in the battle with the Rowbottoms, Asya said, "*Bonjour.*"

She enjoyed the malicious pleasure it afforded her to see Eloise turn haughtily away and then immediately beam her saccharine smile up at some other guest. Male, of course.

However, her former friend's feline performance soon lost its power to amuse, and Asya decided she had better turn her attention to the matter of collecting a trousseau. With Godefroy still away, this was the time to make her selection of materials and discuss the patterns with the seamstresses. A diabolical thought raised its two-horned head. What if she were to buy her wedding silks and linens from M. Rowbottom? With a chuckle, she smothered the thought. But it would have been a master stroke of irony!

To allay any suspicions the sewing women might have in regard to all the clothes she ordered, Asya explained she was planning a trip. Really, she was. A honeymoon. Only Cilla and Negu knew the truth, and she pledged them to secrecy each day before the sewers arrived. Cilla and Asya made all the selections between them. For the first time, Negu showed no interest in Asya's clothes.

"It won't make any difference," she explained listlessly when asked for an opinion about some aspect of fashion. "A man like M. Laborde will like you in anything, or," after a significant pause, "out of it."

Cilla tittered, but Asya was taken aback. She had never thought about being without clothes in front of Godefroy. A shiver of uneasiness ran up her back and involuntarily she shuddered.

"Scared?" Cilla teased. "Hadn't thought about what happens after the parties are over and the wedding guests have gone home." She spread her hands over her face, and by the way her shoulders shook, Asya knew the girl was enjoying a quiet laugh.

"If I hadn't thought about it, why are you?" Asya snapped.

"Don't be angry," Cilla reprimanded in her happy

way. "All brides are scared about a man seeing them for the first time without their clothes on. You'll get over it."

"*Non*. All are not scared," Negu announced in a pedantic voice. "Only those foolish ones who marry the wrong man."

Asya flashed the housekeeper an angry look. She knew what was going through her mind, what had been going through it since she first made the announcement. If Negu had had her way, it would have been Etienne Grenier with whom she marched down the aisle. Pooh, thought Asya. That rascal. More than once Asya had imagined herself the bride of the handsome captain, but that was in her younger days. Then she, too, had been taken in by his charm. No, she told herself, she was not marrying the wrong man. Godefroy would make a loving and devoted husband. And, anyway, Etienne would never marry her. Probably, he would never marry anyone.

"Mama Negu," Cilla teased. "How would *you* know?" Cilla laughingly danced away to avoid the black hand that shot out in her direction.

"You fresh thing." Negu fixed the young servant with a stern eye. "I may never have been a bride, but I know a few things about selecting a proper groom."

"Who wants a proper groom?" Laughter sparkled from Cilla's eyes.

"Will you stop your battling," Asya ordered, feeling like a matron beset with two squabbling imps.

When Godefroy returned to Haiti, Asya did not know. Later, as she thought back over that awful day, she wondered why Negu had not been aware of it either. Negu, above all, was usually informed on news almost the moment it occurred. But the Negress had said nothing. Perhaps she really had not known.

But on that memorable day, Asya, hot and perspiring after standing through many fittings, had come down from the upstairs sewing room to walk out on the veranda for some air. As she came through the doorway, Asya saw a man helping a girl from a carriage in front of the house. She did not recognize him because his back was turned. His companion was looking down to watch her step so that her broad-brimmed bonnet hid her face.

The man turned toward the house. It was Godefroy! In surprised delight, Asya started to run toward him, calling, "Welcome. Welcome." But the girl with him raised her head and Asya stopped. It was Eloise. Eloise looking lovelier than ever, her big affected smile in full bloom across her face. "Godefroy insisted we drive right out here," Eloise gushed. "So here we are."

Asya knew something was wrong. It was not with Eloise, though. She always looked that way when with a man. It was Godefroy. He was sneering at her. Godefroy, who was always happy, smiling. His eyes twinkling. Now, they were half closed in bitterness.

"Godefroy, Godefroy. What happened? What happened in Jamaica? Didn't you get your sheep?" Asya cried. Something had gone wrong.

"Yes. I got my sheep." He spoke each word slowly as though by so doing he could inject more venom into his voice. "You'll find them all there. It should please you to know that not one died en route."

Asya's mouth opened to speak, but she was too bewildered to know what to say. Whatever was he talking about? Feebly she asked him, "Won't you come in."

"We'd love to," Eloise sang out in her usual high key and started to sashay across the veranda and toward the door into the house.

"Eloise!" Godefroy barked. He had never barked before. "Stay here. We'll say what we came to say. Then leave."

Asya looked from one to the other. "Whatever is it that I should know?"

Eloise rolled her eyes coquettishly at Godefroy,

looked at Asya, and simpered, "We eloped. Just this morning."

"Eloped!" Asya was stunned.

"Of course. Don't look so surprised," Eloise chided, cocking her head to one side, a smirk on her face. "People do, you know." She gave a deep, lovesick sigh. "He simply swept me off my feet, Godefroy did. I couldn't resist him."

Asya stared, disbelieving, at the lanky figure that was now leaning against the white iron column of the veranda. He looked beat, whipped, as though without support he would surely slide to the floor. The only life in him was the violent contempt for her in his eyes. Asya took a step toward Godefroy, but stopped when she smelled his breath. "Godefroy, you've been drinking." This must be the excuse for his odd conduct. "You're drunk," she repeated, more to assure herself. "This is all a joke."

"What do you mean? A joke?" Eloise actually shrieked out. Then she paused to gather up her usual dulcet voice before going on. "One never makes jokes about matrimony. It's very serious. This ring is not a joke, is it, Godefroy?"

He did not answer. He moved his mouth, but it was only to curl his lip in derision.

"He was celebrating. He said he had to drink to the bride. Oh, it's so wonderful. It's so remarkable. After being neighbors all these years, a man's eyes are opened to the girls about him, and he picks one for his wife." Eloise snickered. "Just goes to show what sort of little jokes Fate plays on us unsuspecting girls. Isn't that so, Asya?"

Eloise picked up her husband's hand and placed it against her cheek. "Isn't it amazing, pet, here we are so happy over the big step we took this morning, that we never thought to tell my future mama she has a daughter now." Then she looked at Asya. "It's all so romantic and complicated too. Papa and Mme. Laborde!"

Eloise giggled. "I'll have to say Mama now. They are planning to marry too. These last few weeks they've had eyes for no one but each other. You should see them." As she talked, Eloise let go of her husband's hand and it dropped limply to his side. "Every time they open their mouths," Eloise rattled on, "it's 'honey' or 'darling.' Whatever have you been doing, Asya, these last few weeks that you were not aware of the big love affair between the old folks." She shrugged. "But then, I suppose you've been busy getting ready for when your sheep got here. But you can have your sheep." She reached up and patted Godefroy on the cheek. "I have my own little lamb right here."

"Godefroy," Asya broke in, "those aren't my sheep. They're yours." She shook her head in dismay. "I don't want any sheep. I don't know what to do with sheep."

"You'll learn." His voice was cold.

"But they're yours," Asya insisted.

"Not anymore. I saw the receipt. You paid for them. You paid for everything." He was standing on his own now and his voice was like a whip. "You bought my home while my back was turned. I'm thankful M. Rowbottom advised Mama to hold out for a good price, otherwise your grasping little hands would have snatched it for the cost of the mortgage. You always knew she wanted to return to England. That's why you waited until I was gone before tempting her with your money bags. If it hadn't been for Eloise's meeting me at the pier I never would have known of your sneaking thievery. Thanks to Eloise, I woke up to you. She had the courage to come to me and tell the truth about you. Acting as though you're my friend, encouraging me in this new venture, when all the time you could scarcely wait for me to get out of town to snatch my future away."

He paused, and a wistfulness crept into his eyes. "I've always wanted to stay in Haiti." He spoke quietly now. "I had ambitions of founding a new Laborde dynasty.

365

But that's all over," he said with an effort, as he again rested a shoulder against the iron column. "You took care of that." The fight was gone from him.

"Godefroy. Godefroy," Asya cried. "You misunderstood. It wasn't like that at all."

"Yes?" he asked indifferently. She had already been judged and condemned.

"I didn't—" Asya stopped. How does one go about telling a man that his bride is a liar? Angrily, she turned to Eloise, but the English girl was wearing one of her innocent smiles.

"Of course you couldn't know how upset Godefroy would be." Eloise was very sweet. "However, don't worry about us. We shall all be so happy in England." She let out a coquettish giggle. "Godefroy and I with Mama and Papa."

Eloise put both hands on Godefroy's arm and said suggestively, "Come, pet. This is our wedding day, you know." She kissed his sleeve. "Let's not waste precious time on another woman, or your little wife will be jealous." Eloise threw Asya a quick look of appraisal and turned up her nose as indication she found no competition there. She shrugged a dainty shoulder. "Our boat sails this afternoon. The old folks are going at the same time. The captain will marry them at sea. Isn't it remarkable! Through the years, we four can celebrate our anniversaries together!"

"You, you are leaving so soon?" Asya addressed the question to Godefroy. She did not want him to go without knowing the truth.

"Soon?" He let out a mirthless laugh. "That's funny." He looked down at Eloise. "Soon, she asks. What's there to get ready? What's there to pack? It won't take long. She left me nothing."

"Come, pet." Eloise tried to pull at her husband's arm, but he lay against the pillar like a dead weight. "We've made our happy announcement. It's time to get back."

Godefroy did not move. His cold eyes were on Asya, looking hard at her as if he were trying to make up his mind exactly how much he damned her.

"Godefroy," Eloise insisted, "let's say good-bye and go."

Brusquely, he shook her hands from his arm. "Get into the carriage and be quiet," he snarled, never taking his eyes from Asya's face.

"Oh!" Eloise's mouth flew open in disbelief and slammed shut almost as quickly. It was a stern-lipped bride that flounced down the steps and without assistance hopped into the carriage.

"Godefroy, you must hear my side," Asya said immediately, feeling freer to speak with Eloise gone.

"No. I don't want to hear anything from you but good-bye." Hate, blazing from his eyes, communicated the unspoken vituperation of his thoughts. He left the support of the pillar and walked close to her. He seemed so weak and devoid of life that he staggered, and she wondered how he could stand up. Taking her hand he turned it over, and stared at her palm, saying nothing.

Slowly, his eyes traveled to Asya's face, and she saw that the hate was gone. Only his misery looked out at her.

"Twice, I placed my heart in your hand." He spoke slowly, like a tired old man. "It was yours forever, to hurt, to cherish, or to throw away." He paused. With great effort, Godefroy continued: "You threw it away, but I don't want to leave you empty-handed, Asya. You must have some memento of me."

He cleared his throat and, at the same time, his face suddenly contorted with the passion of his contempt. He spit in her hand. "My parting gift. Carry it forever."

Godefroy turned around and, sustained by the strength of his emotion, walked without staggering to the carriage.

Asya watched him drive off as she shook the spittle from her hand. She should have been angry, but unexplainably she was relieved. Now she would never have to take her clothes off before Godefroy.

Chapter Twenty-seven

In the days which followed, Asya seldom thought of Godefroy Laborde and his hastily acquired family even though he was the source of her present difficulties. What to do with all her new acquisitions? She had been around Cher Château long enough to know that owning land was not enough. It must produce. Asya had taken Peter, her own field supervisor, over to the Laborde plantation to get his opinion on its state of productivity, but he discouragingly shook his head at everything he saw. The only definite suggestion he offered was to abandon it. About the sheep, he knew nothing. However, he would inquire among his relatives. Perhaps a cousin could be found who had some knowledge of them. If he was lucky enough to find one, Mlle. Asya would have to offer big pay. Sheep handlers, smart ones, that is, would come high.

The big brown eyes of the supervisor peered cautiously at Asya to see if she was receptive to this offer. The mistress of Cher Château was well aware of the Haitian tendency to look after the welfare of myriad relatives. Somewhere in the clan there was always an expert for the job.

Recalling that sheep had grazed on the grounds of the hospital of the Sacre-Coeur to crop the grass which also served as fodder to fatten them for the slaughterhouse, Asya did not really think an expert was necessary.

"Don't bother," Asya told Peter. "I'll have the sheep

hauled out to the Laborde lands, and they ca
scrounge around for food. They'll be all right until
decide what to do with them."

"Oh, I dunno." The husky Negro spoke with appre
hension. "Dat's no good. Dey gotta have a shepherd
Like in de Bible. Even in dem days, folks stole. If de
stole in de Good Book, dey steal better now after a
dese years of practicin'. *Oui*. Yuh better git a shep
herd."

"Stealing? You think the people around here woul
steal my sheep?"

"I shore do. Dem good mutton chops soon make u
Haitians de fattest folk in de Caribbean . . ."

"Us?" Asya asked reprovingly. "Would you stea
them too?"

"*Non. Non.* I got too big a position to go 'roun
thievin' like a no-'count nigger. But," his white eye
balls loomed large in their innocence, "whin I git a bi
fat mutton chop given me, I don' ask no one where i
come from. I jus' eats."

Asya tried to keep a straight face while, inside
mirth tinkled like a little bell. "I guess you had bette
look around and find one of those relatives of yours."

"Dat's good, but," he frowned in thought, "but
don' guess one shepherd is 'nough. All dem sheep i
gonna need plenty of eyes lookin' after dem."

Asya laughed, remembering the gregariousness o
these people. "All right. If you can find three of you
relatives who know anything about sheep, hire them
With three shepherds, the job shouldn't be so lonely
and I know the sheep will feel happier about it too."

In the matter of the Laborde house, M. Rousseau o
the bank was of no help. "Although it is run-down, i
could bring a good price if properly refurbished. How
ever, I advise you to sell it as it is, and quickly." H
lowered his voice. "We are all aware that M. Presiden
condones the stealing of untenanted homes by his so
called statesmen, and there are too many *nouveau.*

riches amongst them who, in the interest of status, want one of these fine Creole residences. One day you will ride out to the Laborde house to find it occupied by some officious Chairman of Bilge Water or one of those stupid titles by which his black pirates call themselves. He'll have hired a couple of cutthroats as guards who'd think nothing of cutting off your head with a swing of a machete. Get rid of it. Get rid of it, Mlle. Asya."

"I don't want to." Asya was irked. "I won't be pushed around or have my own property stolen from me. M. President is a just man and a kind man. He would see that I got it back."

M. Rousseau shook his head disapprovingly. "You are young."

"Because I am young does not mean I am wrong. Why should I grovel and pay homage to the government thieves. I am not afraid. I shall call upon M. Christophe and ask for his protection."

Spreading his hands in a helpless gesture, the banker said, "As you please. But on the other hand, what makes you think M. Christophe would favor you over his tax collector if his tax collector stole the Laborde house. Or his architect who supervises the new palace going up at Milot? Or Gaffie, the executioner, who removes the heads of uncooperative associates? Sure, everyone knows that you paid for the schoolbooks, but that was over two months ago. A gift once received diminishes in importance and recedes to the back of the mind as fresh favors come pouring in. Furthermore, you already have a château. Those fellows up in the palace might be inclined to think one was enough for any woman."

Asya frowned and said nothing.

"You may know how to run a plantation," M. Rousseau continued, "but stay away from politics, especially in a new nation. You never know when you're the one to be cut down so the ambitious one behind you can stand on your dead body to take a step higher."

"I don't believe all those cruel stories people whisper about the president," Asya retorted. "If thievery and backbiting go on, it's because those he trusts are betraying him. I'm sure M. Christophe would not sanction his assistants acting like murdering savages."

The banker's face reddened with indignation. "Assistants, you say. The almighty one himself is a savage. The other day he was walking through a field, saw a laborer sleeping, and shot him. Without warning. His excuse was that he was sleeping on the job. To me, that's savagery, pure and simple."

Asya turned away in disgust. "That's only gossip. M. Christophe is too busy to have time to walk through a field. If a man was shot, this distorted version of the slaying which you have just repeated sounds to me like an alibi the real murderer would invent. The whole story should be reported to the gendarmes."

The banker looked at her disbelievingly and shook his head. "How can you be so naive? It is fine for the young to be idealistic, but not to such an extreme. You must learn to face up to evil, because by God, it exists!"

"Don't get so ruffled, M. Rousseau. I only asked for your advice, not a dissertation on the blindness of youth. After all, it is my problem," Asya reminded him.

"Thank God for that. Sometimes I think you young people create your own trouble as if you were looking for it."

For some unaccountable reason, Asya laughed. The banker seemed like a fat, waistcoated toad, plumped there on the chair, rooted to the easy, legal escapes from the wonderful challenges of life. She left the office chuckling to herself. What awful things M. Rousseau would have to say about this younger generation when he and his cronies next gathered at the café.

Now Asya was more determined than ever to keep the Laborde house. The banker had not frightened her with his warnings. Instead, he had enlightened her on how the enemy played its hand. One peep into the opponent's cards, and Asya had the idea of the game.

That same afternoon she went to her overseer, Peter, and made a deal with him. He, with the assistance of his countless kinsmen, would protect the Laborde house against vandalism and thievery, by whatever tactics he deemed necessary, during its refurbishing; and the day she sold it, the overseer was to select for himself one-fourth of the sheep which still survived on the grounds.

Peter had pursed his big lips and scratched his bald head. "I dunno," he said. "Dat sure take plenty protectin'." For a while he was thoughtfully quiet, studying the ceiling as though mentally chalking off the number of available heads among his relations. "I dunno," he repeated, giving Asya a shrewd look. "Might. Jist might, but Ah not sure."

"Of course," Asya casually commented, "all those sheep should have a ram."

"I might jist look 'round farther and inquire. Dat need my wife's folks too. Mighty big job. Mighty big job."

"On second thought," Asya announced, "with all the sheep you will acquire, I'm sure one ram will not be enough. You had better select two from the flock when the job is done." She stood up as an indication the deal was closed.

Peter gave her a sly glance and nodded. He understood that she would offer no more. "Dat's right. One ram might git hisself too worn out. It's better if dey share de work. Now I'd better git. Much to do," he mumbled to himself as he hurried away.

That evening at dinner, Asya was so excited she could hardly eat. She had done well. Now, not only would she be rid of a goodly number of those bothersome sheep, but she could safely take her time in turning a seedy old house into a desirable mansion which she would then sell at a marked-up price. In the back of her mind, she was also aware that she needed expert advice on what to raise on the land which would not be sold along with the house. There was also the mountain property on which it had originally been intended for the sheep to graze. Someone with sharp business acumen ought to be able to sell that land for her along with the remaining sheep. "You need a husband," Negu suggested. "Someone to look after your properties."

"When I get a husband, he'll look after me, not my properties," Asya corrected the housekeeper.

Negu gave her a skeptical look. "That's too difficult. Not many men around here qualify for that job. I only know one ornery enough to handle you and he's not about to give up his freedom ever. Not that I blame him."

"Your job is to run this house," Asya haughtily reminded the older woman, "and I'll look after everything else. When I need a business manager, I'll hire him, not marry him."

Negu shrugged. "I still think it easier to get him through matrimony."

Asya did get her business manager through matrimony. But someone else's not her own. It was Cilla who got the husband and Asya the business manager in the same happy stroke. Engrossed as she was in the demands of her new acquisitions, Asya had forgotten about the romance between her personal maid and Watusi, until one morning Cilla shyly announced she would be leaving Cher Château to be married. A sudden pang over the prospect of being separated from her friend became a weight in Asya's heart, and yet when she saw the stars in the young Negress's warm brown eyes, a happy giddiness filled her, and she spontaneously threw her arms about Cilla.

"Happy, happy, happy, I am for you!" she cried. "It's wonderful. Wonderful! Marvelous! I can think of no one I'd like better for you than Watusi." She thought for a minute and then asked warily, "It *is* Watusi, isn't it?"

"Of course," Cilla giggled. "He's the only one I've ever had. I'm no femme fatale," she giggled again, "with so many suitors that it's a surprise which one I pick." Now she threw her arms about Asya, and the two girls laughed and hugged and whirled about.

"I shall give you the wedding," Asya announced breathlessly. Her heart somersaulted with joy, tossing off the weight of impending separation. "We'll have the wedding here, at Cher Château."

"Oh." Cilla looked appalled, the eyes in her thin face large with uncertainty. "I don't know. Black folks' weddings are big."

"And so is Cher Château," Asya announced emphatically. "Invite your friends. All your friends. We'll have dancing and music and food like for a royal wedding. The wine will flow," her voice exuded enthusiasm, "and the waiters will wear their most formal uniforms and a thousand candles will light up the ballroom. Your bridal gown will be the most beautiful ever worn in Haiti, *ever*." She grabbed Cilla about the neck and whirled her about singing, "Oh, what fun, what fun, what fun!"

"But, but," Cilla finally managed to gasp, "all that costs so much money."

"So what, I have money," she answered lightly. Taking Cilla's face in in her hands, Asya spoke seriously. "I have never had a sister, and you have been one to me. You are my sister. Is it not right for one sister to give the other her wedding?"

Cilla began to cry.

"That's no way for a bride to act," Asya teased. "Your eyes will get all red like—like M. President's, and when Watusi looks soulfully into them he will think of his boss instead of you."

Cilla laughed as she cried. "Getting married is very

upsetting," she blubbered. "Not at all like I thought. It's the same as having a hurricane inside, blowing you sometimes one way, then all at once another."

While the plans went swiftly ahead for Cilla and Watusi's wedding, Asya could not overlook the growing heaviness in her heart over the prospect of Cilla's leaving her. Naturally, the young couple would have to live in Cap François close to the palace where Watusi worked, but Asya found it difficult to reconcile herself to a life without Cilla. It was going to be worse saying adieu to her personal maid than it had been leaving all the nuns at the Hospice of the Sacre-Coeur. Cilla had been closer to her than even Mère Denise, for Cilla was her own age. They had shared everything, disappointments and delights. And now she would be gone.

Asya sighed. There was nothing to be done about it. She sighed again. A deeper, more labored one. She was thinking of all the bookkeeping she had neglected for the more pleasant flurry of wedding preparations. What a mundane thing to have to do while romance and excitement surrounded one! Then there were the sheep who required her attention. The dumb animals. What a time to pick to have to be shorn. Peter promised to see to that, but she would have to find a market for the wool. How does one go about finding a market? Go down to the pier and hail a ship going to England and ask if it has room to haul the wool to the mills there? Dumb Godefroy. He probably never thought ahead about what one does with sheep after they had carried out their part of the investment. Whom could she ask? M. Rousseau might know, but she could not bear the unctuous toad and his eternal I-told-you-so's. In the back of her mind, she was well aware who probably knew all the answers, but no, that was out of the question. She would scatter the wool along the road before she asked M. Grenier's help.

Negu was right, but she would never let her know it.

Asya needed a man to run her business. One who could dicker for contracts, jot figures down in books, oversee construction of sheds. Do miniscule things like pay bills and find new markets, leaving all the fun part of running a plantation to her. She loved to ride the fields and check on her crops. Whenever she came close to one of her stables, the wonderful fragrance of the hay and the animals called her in. She had not realized how much she had learned about growing things by helping, more likely pestering, the farm hands on the grounds at Sacre-Coeur. Asya thrilled to the tangible things of her wealth. The sight of it meant more than the long columns of figures in the profit column in a book.

Suddenly, the thought struck. She knew just the person to be her business manager. Why had she not thought of it earlier? Watusi! He knew everything about record-keeping, and what he didn't know he would learn. Selfishly, she realized, he could not very well refuse her offer, in the face of her present generosity; but on the other hand, she would make it worth his while. Being rich had its recommendations.

Having made up her mind, Asya lost no time in going into action. That night she hired Watusi. Now not only did she have a business manager, but by the same transaction she retained her personal maid.

The wedding was everything Asya had hoped it would be. At her suggestion the smokehouse was stripped, the wine cellar raided, and the ovens sent out succulent aromas for days. Abbé Brille performed the marriage ceremony in the chapel of Cher Château. The mother of the bride, enfolded in a red empire-style gown, pinched in beneath her ample bosom, rustled and shook like a palm tree in the wind during the ceremony. At first, Asya did not recognize Evadne. Never had she seen her cook in other than a plain white uniform fronted with a blue apron. The red kerchief about her head had been supplanted by a huge yellow bonnet which stuck out from the sweating black face like the petals of a sunflower. Nassy, whose experience in buttering had given him more experience in public appearances, conducted himself with aplomb. In his yellow satin waistcoat garnished at the neck and cuffs with lace ruffles, the father of the bride bowed and beamed at the guests as though it were a customary occurrence for him to marry off a daughter in sumptuous style.

Cher Château swarmed with well-wishers for the happy couple. Not only did Cilla seem to have as many relatives as Peter had laid claim to, but Watusi, despite his recent arrival in Haiti, was likewise honored by a host of government friends from the palace. M. Christophe himself arrived, not in time for the ceremony, but later in the afternoon, when the guests had drunk sufficient wine to feel at ease in his presence. When she saw him come through the doorway, Asya surreptitiously looked beyond him, fearful lest Mme. Christophe had accompanied her husband. She sighed with relief. Thank God. The woman had enough sense to stay at home. But how nice of M. President. So big a man to take time to greet a little bookkeeper on his wedding day. Asya hurried over to welcome the great guest.

"*Bonjour*." Asya extended her hand. "Our house is honored, as are Cilla and Watusi."

The tall man took her hand in his. He did not kiss it, but bowed low over it. Then straightening to his great height, he smiled benignly down on Asya and spoke in his warm voice, "*Chère femme*. This is a wonderful thing you are doing for your friend, and in your kind action, you exhibit the spirit of democracy. Citizens like you give me hope that our revolution was a success." He bowed again.

Asya hoped her face did not betray her bewilderment, since she had had no such altruistic motives in planning this affair. All she had intended was to give her friend a happy wedding. But if Mr. Christophe thought she had done what he said, then she was pleased.

"Merci," she smiled, "but it is your presence which makes it a real democracy."

At that moment, Nassy, by now well primed in his role as father of the bride, fell upon M. Christophe and, in a flourish of expansive hospitality, carted him off to drink a toast to the bride. Asya was certain the butler could hear trumpets blaring as he triumphantly escorted this prize guest among the merrymakers.

There were many others from the palace. The Duke of Hencoop had come too. She had forgotten his name, but when her eyes saw the pinfeather hairs standing upright on the top of his head, Asya remembered. Eloise had been cruel to make fun of him. He had a round happy face which beamed with pleasure at being included in the celebration. There was something about him which made one chuckle when he spoke. She was glad Eloise was not here. Somehow, she would have spoiled the fun of the day.

Prophète came too. Asya still did not like him. She was uneasy in his presence. However, she greeted him as she had done the others, for it was an honor for Cilla to have the commanding general of the palace army at her wedding. Asya gave him her hand, hoping he would not know how reluctantly it was offered. Prophète made a great production about bowing, and when he kissed her hand, his goatee, rubbing against her skin, made Asya think of a rat brushing her fingertips. Inwardly she shivered. His piercing eyes laughed at her as though he knew her thoughts and was glad he had caused them. Haughtily, he looked about like Satan leering over the prospect of his next ravishment. However, he did not immediately move on as Asya had hoped, but stood holding her hand. "I have been here a while," he almost purred, "but I did not come in immediately. I was outside admiring your home." His tongue slowly crept out and outlined the Cupid's bow beneath his well-clipped moustache, conveying the impression that he was digesting a mental delicacy. "It is beautiful," the low purring voice continued. "And inside more so." Languidly he let his head roll back while his greedy eyes examined the ceiling. "This ballroom must have more chandeliers than any other room in Haiti." He leered.

"And sufficient candles to show them off." It was Asya's attempt at levity, but the general only gave her a blank look. Then, with an expression of disdain, he dropped her hand as though he had suddenly discovered he was holding something tainted. Giving her a pitying smile, Prophète strolled out of the ballroom. Later, Asya saw him wandering about the rooms, like a prospective buyer assessing everything in sight. She felt uneasy and wished he would go.

When a familiar voice spoke into her ear, Asya immediately forgot Prophète for a more rigorous denunciation. "Pardon, mademoiselle, but your dislike is showing."

Glaring, she whirled about, ready for battle. However, before she could open her mouth for action, M. Grenier shook his head in warning. "Don't let the general see your disapproval. It will only flatter him, for he enjoys being hated."

"How *dare* you come into my house! Get out!" Such sudden anger exploded within her that Asya could scarcely restrain her voice from screaming out.

"Tut-tut," he cautioned. "Mustn't be shrewish. Most unbecoming to a beautiful lady."

"I *like* being shrewish. Get out! Get out!" In her fury, Asya took M. Grenier by the arm and tried to push him toward the door.

But he stood his ground and laughed at her efforts.

"Get out! Can't you hear? Get out! No one wants you here."

Etienne took her hands, which were thrust against his chest, and held them firmly in his own. "You're too

380

frail for a sergeant-at-arms," he teased, "so try to act like a lady."

Unable to free her hands, Asya drew herself up in indignation and glared.

"That's better," he soothed. "Now the guests who are watching behind your back will think you are struck speechless with joy over my presence and have forgotten to withdraw your hands from my warm, welcoming clasp."

Asya snapped her hands free. "You are not welcome at Cher Château."

His face assumed a perplexed look, which Asya knew was feigned. "How strange. Watusi himself asked me to come. In fact," he insisted, "I am here at his invitation, not yours."

"I happen to own Cher Château," she reminded him. "Will you please leave?"

"No." He grinned at her. "I did not come to see the owner. I come as a guest of the bridal couple. Why do you try to stop me?" As an afterthought he inquired, "Are you a relative of the bride or of the groom that you take it upon yourself to screen the wedding guests?"

Asya opened her mouth in disbelief. Quickly she shut it. Better to not answer so ludicrous a question.

He chuckled. "Of course, I should have known. You are the *maître d'hôtel* of the affair. As yet a little pompous. Inexperienced help is apt to be."

With surprising quickness, M. Grenier placed his hands on her waist and raising her up from the floor as one might a child, he carried Asya into the ballroom."

"Put me down," she hissed. "You fool. Let me go."

He set her down, but kept his hands firm on her waist. "If you will dance with me." For a fleeting moment, his eyes were serious. "The music is starting for the merengue."

"Guests don't dance with the *maître d'hôtel*."

"If she's a beautiful woman, they do."

Asya pressed her lips together in annoyance.

"Don't squeeze your mouth like that," Etienne grinned at her. "It makes you look like you forgot to put in your teeth when you got up this morning."

"Good. You'd never be seen dancing with a woman without teeth. That excuses me."

"Oh, I never minded dancing with a woman whose teeth don't show because she has them sunk in me."

"As I recall," Asya said coolly, "the last time we spoke we were not on friendly terms. Why this sudden crass interest?"

This time, Etienne did not answer immediately. He was gazing down upon her, all signs of laughter gone. His eyes were clear and steady with a hint of tenderness in their depths. "I want to," he said in a quiet voice. "I want to very much. Would you do me the honor of dancing with me, Asya?"

Taken aback by this sudden reversal of tactics, Asya was momentarily at a loss for a reply. One sweet sentence was not going to make her catapult into his arms, although—although she had trouble telling her cavorting heart to quiet down. "I don't think I should," she managed to say hesitantly. "If I dance this once will you leave then?"

"If you wish me to." The same low voice. The same steady look.

And so, they danced the merengue. And, in his arms, her mood softened. How could a man who made her so angry also make her feel so heady with happiness! She would worry about that later. Now the music embraced her and lifted her up with its beat while her madcap heart danced double-time in her breast. It was a wonderful wedding.

At the end of the merengue, Etienne gave her his arm and they strolled away from the dancers. Asya wished she had not been so insistent on one dance, for the music was playing a minuet. It was more intimate than the merengue. Perhaps he would continue to be nice to her if they danced again. But she was supposed to be cross with him, she justifiably reminded herself.

"You still dance well," he smiled as they left the floor. A nice friendly smile like he might bestow upon a maiden aunt. She much preferred a fighting smile.

"Still? What did you expect? Have I aged so much since we last danced?" She tried to keep the irritation from her voice.

"I was thinking about our little altercation at the palace. How's your little derrière? Still sore?"

M. Grenier withdrew his arm on which her hand had been resting and swung it behind Asya. For an instant she thought he was going to swat her on the buttocks. Right there in front of everyone. She flipped her hips sideward, away from him. He chuckled. "So, it *is* still tender?"

"Where you hit me is not a subject for social discussion," she told him primly. "If you had any gallantry about you, you would apologize for your brutal behavior." Asya started to walk away. "You've had your dance. Go now."

She felt his firm hand on her elbow. "I am, but you are going with me. Outside where we can talk." He steered her toward the front door. Common sense told her to break away and run, but her feet ignored the misgivings of her mind and Asya trotted stiffly along.

Etienne took her across the veranda and along the stone path which led through the flower gardens. At the first eucalyptus tree, they stopped. He turned her around so that she faced him. His hand dropped from her elbow and half-smiling, half-serious, he looked at her.

Under his stare, Asya was ill at ease. "I thought you were going to take me to the chapel to say a rosary," she spoke flippantly.

He leaned against the tree and laughed. "Have you

383

been a bad girl, Asya? Is your conscience bothering you?"

"Of course not."

"Naturally not. I forgot. You have no conscience."

"I'm not referring to my conscience. I've not been bad. And if I had been," she demanded, "what's it to you?"

"I like to keep an eye on you. Since I saw you first, I look upon you as my protégée. Got to help mold you as you're growing up."

"I am grown up. I am nineteen. I am fully grown," Asya announced.

Etienne's head shot up and his eyes brightened. "So you are." His voice affected surprise. "Hadn't noticed before." Carefully folding his arms, his eyes moved in slow appraisal over Aysa's body.

Having completed the inventory, he commented drily, "Shaping up nicely."

Asya flared up. "How dare you look at me that way."

"How?" he asked, feigning innocence.

"How?" she repeated. "I'll tell you how." Asya took a deep breath. "You look at me as though you'll ravish me. And then—" she hesitated before determinedly going on "—and then as if you've found me wanting and lost interest."

Etienne threw back his head and laughed heartily.

"What's so funny?" Asya asked testily.

"You are. You're not bothered by the way I look at you. Only by the fact that I may have found you wanting."

Asya slapped him across the mouth.

Etienne's eyes blazed, and for an instant, she was afraid. "Don't ever do that again!" his voice whipped.

Asya stuck out her chin, the fear inside her gone as quickly as it had come. "I will if I want to."

Swiftly he reached out for her, and, too late, Asya turned to run. Etienne pulled her roughly to himself,

and his lips came down on hers. Asya struggled to free
herself, but his arms were strong about her, and she
soon relaxed against him. His body was warm and
firm. Asya's arms crept up about Etienne's neck, and
with every ounce of passion that burned within her, she
kissed him back.

Chapter Twenty-eight

In the months that followed, Asya wondered if she had dreamed the episode with Etienne under the eucalyptus tree. She had hoped he would ride out to Cher Château to see her, or at least send a message. The more she thought about him, the more she wished she had slapped his face when he kissed her, instead of allowing her passion to have its way.

It was Watusi who told her that M. Grenier was in England on business. Asya felt better knowing that he had not purposely neglected her, but at the same time, she was annoyed that he had not sent her a farewell note. Silly, she told herself. He'd never have gotten away had he taken the time to say adieu to everyone. Yet in her heart she pouted.

Among Asya's coterie of friends, Etienne was not missed. They were too busy indignantly discussing the coronation. Henri Christophe had declared himself emperor. He was to be crowned in June in the cathedral in Cap François. The thought of an emperor who could neither read nor write, the former slave of a black man, was distasteful to the Creole landholders of Haiti. The English residents were more taciturn in their remarks since most of them engaged in commerce, and with the preparations for the momentous ceremony, business was booming. The cathedral, damaged during the various uprisings of the past, had not been restored in all these years. Now, in two months' time, it was made ready for the coronation. When the invitations were sent—Watusi said they had been engraved in

Kingston—the tenor of the criticism changed. Those who had been mollified by being invited to the festivities looked upon the occasion as a gala social event. The uninvited were less kind. They made snide remarks about a black savage engaging in a barbaric ceremony in a Catholic church. The fact that all Haitians were Catholic did not seem to enter their minds. A travesty such as this should be held in the woods, they maintained. It was a sacrilege for the Abbé Brille to crown the usurper emperor in the same manner as Charlemagne or Napoleon. The Pope should be told about it.

The abbé was quoted as saying that the Holy Father had enough problems with one emperor marching all over Europe. Now was no time to ask his blessing on another one.

Asya was invited. About the self-elevation of an imperial family in Haiti, she had no concern. If that nice man wanted to wear a crown instead of a straw hat on top of his kinky head and not have to concern himself with laws and constitutions, that was his prerogative. Right now, the coronation was the social event of the season, and she was invited, and that was all that mattered. As long as Cher Château was not involved, she did not care whether Haiti was ruled from a throne or an unpainted milk stool.

Her main concern was what gown to wear to the coronation. From her own seamstresses, Asya learned that most of the women were planning on heavy brocades. To be different, she selected an Egyptian silk. White, frothy, cloudlike. She had visions of herself, cool and lovely, floating gracefully among the heavily garbed competition. The outstanding touch on this simple dress was a design made from colorful macaw feathers, embossed around the neckline. Her earrings would be large crescents of amethyst, surrounded by rows of pearls. The brilliant reds, greens, and blues against her dark skin would make Asya feel like an exotic princess from the travels of Marco Polo. She sighed. Surely Etienne would return for the coronation.

M. Grenier did return. He was there in the cathedral, close to the emperor. He wore a white suit with golden buttons. No ribbons, no medals of honor, and yet, to Asya, he stood out in that sea of rustling silks and glittering gems and golden candlesticks like the moon in a starlit sky.

Through the long ceremony, Asya never took her eyes from Etienne's face. She became impatient to be done with what was now, to her, dragged-out folderol.

During the recessional, Asya lost sight of Etienne, but as she was standing amid the crowds in front of the cathedral, waiting for her carriage to take her to the palace—royal palace now, she must remember—there he was before her.

"M. Grenier! What a surprise!" Asya spoke as though she had at that moment only laid eyes upon him.

He took her hand in his as he looked upon her with admiration. "You are beautiful." He leaned close and said in a low voice, "But why so formal? The last time we were together you kissed me. That leaves us well enough acquainted to use first names, *oui?*"

"I did not kiss you," Asya denied emphatically. Her voice must have carried, for a buxom woman in front of her turned around and beamed.

"If you didn't, yuh sure better, 'fore some other purty girl does. Ah jist might as well do it myself." True to her word, she reached up and took Etienne's face between her two fat hands, pulled it toward her, and kissed him right on the lips. "There. Don't be so pokey," she cautioned Asya. "If a girl wants a man, she better git 'im while she has a notion to. There's always someone like me 'round waitin' to snatch 'em from you."

"Countess Marmalade-Lemonade." Pressed in by the crowd, Etienne bowed as well as he could. "You old flirt. One of these days your husband's going to lose you to one of us younger men who appreciates you more."

"Dat's fine, s'long as I don't lose him." Her big shoulders shook with merriment as she moved on to her waiting carriage.

"Seems to me," Asya said coolly, as she withdrew her hand from Etienne's grasp, "that you have very familiar friends. Are they all that forward?"

"Everyone," he agreed.

At that moment her carriage drew up and Etienne helped her in. To her surprise, he followed. "Mind if I ride with you? It's easier than walking."

"How did you get here?" Asya discouraged.

"Oh, you do mind? Driver, stop the carriage," he called to the man in the front seat. "This lady prefers to ride alone."

The horses stopped so suddenly that Asya was thrown forward. Etienne grabbed her and solicitiously set her back in the seat.

"What are people going to think?" Asya asked reprovingly.

"That we're having a lover's spat. They're all watching. Look for yourself." He already had one foot out of the carriage.

He was right. Women were giggling and pointing up to her and Etienne, and the men were waving their hats in fraternal understanding.

"Get back here," she ordered. "Of course you can ride with me."

He gave her a skeptical look. "Are you sure?"

"*Oui*. I'm sure. I want you to ride. I didn't say you couldn't. I merely asked how you had come." She grabbed his arm and pulled him back onto the seat.

He gave a big sigh of relief. "So nice to know I'm wanted."

"You're exasperating," she announced.

"Now, now. Let's not quibble anymore," he reminded her. "Let's just try to make friendly conversation."

389

"Nice crowd out today." She put her hand over her mouth, pretending to stifle a yawn.

"That's *mon petit chou*. Bored when not doing battle with me. I might as well be talking to a comrade-in-arms, for all the sweetness I get from you."

"You surprise me." Asya gave him a sly look. "I thought you viewed every woman as a comrade-in-arms."

He chortled. "Your wit grows, Asya."

"So does my temper when I'm around you." Riled, she turned her head away from him and looked at the crowd along the Place d'Arms.

"Quit glaring at the people. They're nice people. Smile at them like the gracious lady you're not." He was obviously enjoying himself.

"If not for the presence of those so-called nice people it would be my pleasure to smack you into remembering your manners. Luckily for you, I'm being restrained by their presence."

"Is that all that's holding you back?" Etienne asked in the voice of one upon whom the light has dawned. "We'll remedy that."

He spoke quietly into the ear of Asya's coachman, who immediately nodded his head like an accomplice, fully aware of the details of a plot. Feigning indifference, Asya pretended to be engrossed in the spectators who had come out for the coronation parade.

Suddenly she was aware that her carriage was not following those in front. It was turning off onto the Rue Martin, a narrow street which led away from the palace. *"Bougez-vous!"* her driver waved his whip over the heads of the parade-watchers. He guided the horses through the crowd. "Out of the way!"

For a moment, Asya panicked. "Where are we going?"

"To my house." Etienne stretched out his long legs in unconcern.

"What?" Her voice was rising in protest.

"You said you wanted to be alone with me."

"I did not," she denied.

"Asya, why don't you make up your mind?" He sounded exasperated. "You wanted us to be alone so you could smack me. Remember?" He spread out his hands in a helpless gesture. "I'm only trying to please you, but you are being most difficult."

Asya gave him a long look of disgust. Then she spat out at him, "I happen to be fortunate enough not only to be alive when history is made and an emperor is crowned, but also to be invited to participate. But you, *l'espèce d'idiot,* have to drag me off to some deserted hideaway to give you a lesson in manners. Well, I'll be—"

"Careful of your choice of words, Asya." Etienne teased as he held up an admonishing finger.

"—damned," Asya finished defiantly.

Etienne threw back his head and laughed. "Your true colors are showing at last, Asya. Our highly touted philanthropist, society leader, cream of the gentler sex, has a common streak in her, which she displays for my enjoyment alone."

"I don't have a common streak," Asya denied emphatically, "and if I seem to, it's only your vulgarity brushing off on me." She gave the man beside her a hateful look. "You annoy me."

"You don't want everyone to see you looking so cross." Etienne reached for her parasol, which lay on the floor of the carriage, and, opening it, offered it to her. "Take this and hold it low over your head. Then you can sulk all you want and no one will be able to see your sour looks."

Asya yanked the parasol from his hand and fiercely hurled it out into the street, where it landed at the feet of a little Negro boy who was ambling along in the dust. He jerked to a stop and blinked disbelievingly up at the occupants of the carriage before swooping down to pick up the parasol and go running off with it bouncing crazily over his head. He shouted excitedly to a woman some distance ahead, "Mama! Mama!"

"That was a sweet thing you did," Etienne praised. "Think how happy his mama will be to have a new silk parasol!"

Asya turned her head. She would not give him the satisfaction of an answer. They rode in silence until the carriage stopped in front of a house with a high pink stucco wall. Etienne alighted, opened the gate, and the carriage rolled through. Then, he closed the gate and climbed back up into the seat beside Asya. The carriage continued on, passing through a long avenue of eucalyptus trees. Asya could see the house ahead. Pink like the wall, but so covered with vines of blooming flowers that she could tell nothing of its design. Tall, wispy-trunked trees leaned lazily against the house, giving the impression they had grown too high and lacked the strength for their own support.

"This is your home?" Asya asked, making an effort to sound civil.

"It is. Welcome to—" He paused. "It has no name. Perhaps you could suggest one?"

'My first impression is of a house in the woods. I should call it 'Maison dans le Bois.' "

"Good," he agreed amiably. "That it shall be."

"You have lovely eucalyptus trees." Asya spoke in the same polite tone in an attempt to maintain an air of peace between them, but in her own ears her voice sounded flat.

"Just as Cher Château. Shall we get out and stand under one again? As I remember, the last time we did, our relationship was most pleasant. Most pleasant indeed," he added with evident relish.

Asya gave him a quick warning glance. "My visit here is purely platonic."

"I was afraid of that." He was laughing at her again.

Asya turned and gave Etienne a direct look. "The trouble with you," she announced, "is that you're always baiting me, and then you have the audacity to accuse me of going around with my feathers ruffled.

392

What is a red-blooded girl to do? Blow kisses and murmur, 'How charming?' "

He became serious. "You're right, Asya." Resting on her, his eyes were clear now, the bantering look which always separated them, gone. Suddenly she was at ease.

They pulled up to the front of the house and Etienne lightly jumped from the carriage and reached up for her. Asya's irresponsible heart soared in song as he put his hands about her waist and swung her to the ground.

Taking her arm gently, Etienne led her toward the house. As he did so, he could feel her stiffen slightly. "My real reason in bringing you here," he reassured her, "is to give you a gift I brought back for you from Europe."

At his words, she raised her eyebrows in surprise. "You're trying to bribe me," Asya accused. "You hope I'll forget about my threat to smack you for your earlier impudence this morning."

Eitenne laughed heartily. "Your temper doesn't frighten me, my dear. Quite the contrary. I find it most attractive." He gave her àn approving glance, "Now, shall we?"

He opened the front door and bowed her in. No sooner had she entered than her eyes went to the bright center of the house, where the sun seemed to be captured and walled in for the private benefit of the dwellers.

"How delightful," Asya exclaimed, running ahead. "Your house is built around a garden. I love it." She walked into the sunlight. The same tall, thin palms which abounded on the outside of the house leaned against the pink walls of the courtyard like bored street loafers waiting for something to happen. "And a fountain! And lacy iron benches on which to sit!" Asya babbled enthusiastically. "And so many flowers climbing right up to the bedroom windows."

Taking her by the hand, Etienne walked with her to

the fountain and sat down on its stone brim. Grinning up at her, he said, "Well, Mademoiselle, if you still wish to strike me, I am ready."

Asya looked at his upturned face. Even in jest she could not slap him.

"What are you waiting for? This suspense is torture."

Asya laughed. "That's half the punishment. Not knowing when the blow will fall." Etienne pulled her onto his lap, and she made no attempt to resist.

"Sit and be comfortable while you make up your mind."

"What makes you think I'm comfortable here?"

"Aren't you?"

Asya gave him a coquettish look. "You're hunting for a compliment."

"Is that bad?"

"For you, yes. You're spoiled enough as it is. I refuse to be a sheep that follows you around with her tongue drooling, baaing out your charms for all to hear."

Etienne chortled. "Spoken like a true female. But," he turned his face to her, "when do I get my punishment? Let's be done with that, and then I can give you the gift I promised." While he teased, his eyes regarded her fondly.

Asya's heart hummed. "You know I can't smack you with one hand while I reach out for your gift with the other."

"Good. Then we'll call it even. No punishment—and no gift."

"No." Asya frowned. "That's not fair. I'll die of curiosity knowing you brought something for me, and I have no idea what it is."

He started to speak, but she playfully put her hand over his mouth. "You are impertinent. I've never had a gift from you. Never once. And you know I won't smack you."

Taking her hand from his mouth, he gazed at it with

amusement. "You're so right. This dainty little mitt was made for more tender purposes." Slowly and lovingly Etienne kissed the palm of her hand, and Asya's heart gave a wild leap. No one had ever kissed her as tenderly as this. Perplexed by the sudden fervor of his lips, and wary lest she make a fool of herself by letting him see how he had stirred her, Asya felt the need to take cover behind words. "Well, well—" She had to say something. "Did you forget why you brought me here, or are you only procrastinating?"

Etienne's head jerked up, and Asya saw disappointment in his eyes. "Of course," he said in a flat voice. "The gift." Brusquely, he set her firmly on her feet and walked out of the courtyard. Asya was annoyed with herself. She was acting like a schoolgirl who had never spoken to a man before.

Etienne was not gone long. He returned with a small blue velvet box which he placed on the wrought-iron table in the courtyard. "This is actually a gift from an old friend of yours." He spoke with formal cordiality.

Asya stared at the box, saying nothing. The excitement of the gift was gone. What did she care about old friends? She had presumed the gift was from him. Her heart curled up in a corner of her breast, sniffling away.

"I have no old friends who would send gifts," Asya said forlornly. "All my friends were nuns and all they could send would be prayers."

"You forget about one." His voice was warm again. "A very wealthy friend, Asya. The Queen of Prussia."

"Queen Sophia! I did forget about her." Asya brightened. "She was always very good to me. As she was to all orphans," she added. "But, I thought you had gone to England."

"I had, but I finished my business there and took a quick trip to the Continent to catch up on the news."

"But if they had caught you, they would have shot you," Asya warned. "The French military are all over Europe."

Etienne grinned. "I didn't know you cared so much about my safety. However, I had no worry. Napoleon is having too much trouble in Russia to be concerned with one fugitive officer. It was good to see old friends again."

Asya shook her head. "Imagine your knowing the queen."

"She married my Uncle Frederick Wilhelm. That made her my aunt."

Asya gave him a surprised look. "Why did you never tell me Queen Sophia was your aunt?"

"You didn't ask me. But, then, why should you? You haven't even thought enough of your old friend to write her a letter after your arrival in Haiti."

Asya caught the rebuke. "She has so many charities," she said airily, "that she would not be interested in a letter from me. I mean nothing to her."

"You must mean something," he reminded, "else she would not have sent you so precious a gift."

Clasping her hands with delight, Asya enthused, "It must be jewelry. Maybe something from the olden days, way back in history. Worn by one of her famous ancestors."

"You're close,' Etienne encouraged, smiling knowingly. "It *is* from the olden days."

"A gift from the Old World to the New! How wonderful! I can't wait." Excitedly, she reached for the jewel box on the table, but Etienne placed his hand over it.

"Shut your eyes while I open your present. It should bring back happy memories for you. At least, that's what the queen hoped."

Asya squeezed her eyes shut and her heart danced with crazy excitement as she waited. She heard the clasp snap open, and after an almost interminable silence, the voice of M. Grenier said, "You can open your eyes now."

And she did.

When she saw what Etienne was so proudly holding

up, Asya's heart turned to ice. She shivered like one who has taken the chills.

"What's the matter, Asya?" Etienne was bewildered. "Don't you like it?"

But she could not answer. It was the other black necklace made by Butte.

"Don't you remember? Aunt Sophia said you would. It was made by her coachman and given to her when she was a little girl. I understand he had made you one too. Since you and Butte had been such good friends, *Tante* Sophia wanted you to have both of them. She knew of no one who would appreciate the necklace more."

Asya did not put out a hand to take the necklace. All she could see before her was the hateful pimpled face of Kaspar leering above her own beloved necklace, as he dangled it tauntingly at her behind his mother's back. The queen's gift had brought back the whole horrible scene and she felt defiled again as she had so long ago in Eleanore's home. She placed her hands over her face in remembrance of her shame.

"Take it away," she ordered. "Take it away. I don't want—the ugly old thing."

Etienne was looking at her in disbelief. "What's the matter? While the necklace has no jewels, it's not ugly."

"To me, it is," Asya snapped. "If you don't put it away I'll—I'll throw it in the fountain. I hate the sight of it."

"Asya, why are you so vehement? It's only a necklace. A small remembrance from an old friend."

How could she tell him it was a reminder of a horrible humiliation. Looking at it, she could feel Kaspar's hot breath on her neck and the pressure of his hands on her breasts. No, she could not take the gift, and Etienne must never know the reason why. She would have to contrive some excuse.

Looking up at him, she tossed her head and arrogantly announced, "You are right. It has no jewels.

397

What would I do with such a poor gift. One would think a queen could afford better."

"What did you expect," Etienne asked in disgust, "the crown of Charlemagne?"

"Not quite. That would be too heavy," she retorted. "But some fetching little tiara would have been most welcome. However," Asya was being deliberately patronizing, "the gift need not go to waste. You might give it to your housekeeper with my blessing. I'm sure she would be thrilled to have a gift from a queen."

His eyes clouded. They were now cold and contemptuous, shutting her off from him. "Desaix is as you," his voice whipped out. "She accepts only jewels."

Slowly, like one who is making an effort to control his anger, Etienne placed the black necklace in its case and snapped it shut.

Asya shrugged. "Save your compliments. Sorry you had the bother of carrying it halfway around the world. You should have tossed it into the Atlantic."

Etienne ignored her comments. In the voice of an indifferent stranger, he suggested, "It is time to get to the palace for the coronation festivities. I would hate to deny you the pleasure of making the other girls envious of that new feathered dress of yours. I must caution you, however, not to show your claws. They're very sharp."

Taking her firmly by the arm, Etienne led her outside to her carriage. She felt like a reluctant cat being put out for the night. He helped her in, and stepped back. "Adieu," he said.

"Aren't you coming with me?"

"*Non,* mademoiselle." He offered no explanation, but turned on his heel and marched stiffly back to the house. When he reached the doorway, he spun around and said in an icy voice, "Adieu, Asya."

The carriage moved away, and as it rolled along the avenue of eucalyptus trees, Asya shook uncontrollably. She reached for the feathered shawl that lay folded in the corner of the seat and wrapped it about her shoulders. Where before she had been too warm for its use, she now found herself chilled despite the increased heat of the day. The cold was coming from inside where her heart used to be, and the wind was blowing through the void left by its departure. For Asya, the pleasure of the coronation festivities was gone.

Chapter Twenty-nine

Henri had been crowned emperor June 2, 1811, and now it was September of the following year. In all that time, Asya had not seen Etienne. Rumor was that he was on the diplomatic mission of persuading various countries of the Western Hemisphere to recognize the government of Henri Christophe, Emperor of Haiti. By popular demand the name of the capital city had been changed from Cap Haitien to Cap Henri as a testimonial to the man who rebuilt it, or so the emperor announced.

"One thing we must admit about Henri," Negu intoned in the flat voice of one discussing an idiosyncratic kinsman, "he's not modest."

"No one might have thought of the idea if he didn't tell them," Cilla giggled. "You got to let people know about any big thoughts you get."

"Well," the housekeeper snapped in disgust, "in my lifetime, that town has had three separate names. It makes a lady feel old, like she's been living through history. And speaking of history—" Negu turned a sharp eye on Asya who was sitting at her toilette table while Cilla dressed her hair "—someone I know around here is going to become an old relic if she doesn't snap onto some eligible young man sometime soon."

"Haven't the slightest idea of whom you are speaking," Asya denied. She whistled a saucy little tune. That always annoyed Negu.

"Ladies don't whistle," the older woman scolded.

"Spinsters do," Asya interrupted her song long

enough to answer airily. "Spinsters can do anything they wish. They are free." She resumed her whistling and began swinging her shoulders in time to the beat.

"Free to do what? Sit home alone and count their money while other young ladies go to balls."

Asya stopped whistling. Drawing herself up in annoyance, she slowly turned to face the housekeeper. Carefully enunciating each word, she declared, "I am not going to the ball tonight. I want to stay home. It is my own stupid idea to stay home. I shall be very happy here, all by myself, counting my gourds like an old miser."

"Then *look* happy," Negu retorted in a short voice.

"I think she's already got her heart set on one man," Cilla teased, "but he ain't around right now. Wait till he comes back, then the fur will fly." She giggled knowingly to herself.

"You stay out of this," Negu snapped at the maid. "You got yourself a man, and after two years you haven't even gotten a baby yet. In my day, a wife always got a baby right away."

"Even if it didn't take nine months," Asya flung the words at her housekeeper. She gave a nasty laugh. "Tell me, Negu, were the girls more impetuous in your day?"

"I can tell you this. They were more polite." Negu stomped from the room.

Like two conspirators, Asya and Cilla laughed together. "What's eating her," Asya explained, "is that you don't have a baby so she can boss you around and tell you how to raise it."

"Right," Cilla agreed. "That's the bossiest woman. She got to manage everything. That's why I'm not telling her that Watusi and I want a baby bad. We're so upset 'cause we have no children yet. She thinks we're one of those fashionable couples that don't want babies. Honest," Cilla shook her head, "honest, I wouldn't know what to do to keep from getting a baby. I'm dumb that way. I say my Rosary every night for a baby. But if I tell Negu about our disappointment, she'll mix up something voodoo."

"Don't worry," Asya patted her maid's arm. "You'll have your baby Cilla. Just be patient."

"I don't know. I say my Rosary every single night before I go to bed, praying that this is the night."

"Every night?" Asya gave Cilla a quizzical look. "Why don't you try skipping it once in a while?"

"The Rosary?" Cilla asked in amazement.

"Not the Rosary. I was referring to," Asya said slyly, "to what happens *after* the Rosary."

Cilla blinked her eyes. She was obviously trying to follow her mistress's meaning. Suddenly her face lit up with comprehension. She laughed a shy, sheepish laugh, while she covered an embarrassed face with her hands.

At that moment, the door opened and Negu strutted in. "Well, you were speaking of the devil," she said in a clipped voice. "So now he is here."

"Who?" Cilla asked. Asya said nothing. She knew by the tone of Negu's loving announcement that it could only be Etienne. Her heart fluttered.

"M. Grenier of course. Isn't that the secret love in this household?"

"Of course not," Asya denied. "I have no loves, neither secret nor public. And I'm sure if I did you'd be the first one to find out." She gave the housekeeper a snippy look.

"That's right," Negu agreed. "And I found out. Now get on down there. He's waiting for you. And the captain don't like to be kept waiting."

Asya flounced from the room in disgust. At the top of the stairs she hesitated, her bravado gone. "I don't want to see him," she told herself.

Yes, you do, her heart shouted back, and began to pummel her chest as though by its action it would push her down the steps and into his arms.

"He probably has some outlandish reason for coming here. Perhaps he's still angry with me over the necklace."

Go find out, her heart urged, or you will never know.

Slowly, Asya started down the marble stairs.

Etienne must have heard her footsteps, for when she was almost at the bottom, he was there, his arms spread out in welcome. "Heard you coming and couldn't wait to see you," he shouted, at the same time putting his hands about her waist and lifting her down the rest of the way. He held her from him, while his eyes appraised her.

"You're more beautiful than ever, *mon petit chou.* Just looking at you assures me I'm home again."

Etienne looked tired. He had lost much of his tan, and his face was thinner. She wanted to put her arms about him and cradle his head at her breast. Instead, she said, "You make me feel like ye olde cook pot bubbling with your favorite stew which you haven't tasted since you left home."

He gave her a slow grin. "Same old warring sweetheart. Time doesn't soften you."

"What do you expect me to do? Fall down on my face and look up at you adoringly."

"From that angle you would only get a worm's eye view," he chortled.

She had to laugh in spite of his unflattering comment. Then she sobered. "You never wrote me. Not a word."

Etienne put an arm about her waist and led her toward the library. "You are the worst correspondent I know. If I had written to you, and you did not answer, I might worry the whole time that my *billet-doux* had gotten into the hands of the wrong girl. I might not have ever come back, for fear that some scandal was here, waiting to confront me."

"*Au contraire,*" Asya chided. "If you thought there was some scandal waiting for you, you'd have come back faster. Not waited fifteen whole months."

"Ah," Etienne sounded diabolical. "So you were counting the months of my absence. You did miss me."

Asya tossed her head. "Of course not. Why should I care how long you were away?" She seated herself in a chair and looking up at Etienne, coolly reminded him, "As I recall, at our last meeting you did not seem to be concerned about whether you ever saw me again or not."

His answer was simple. "That's right. I wasn't."

Taken aback by the man's directness, Asya was quiet. She could feel his eyes upon her, but she would not look up at him lest he see the hurt in her own.

"Asya," he said after a pause. "I want to talk with you."

"Oui, Père Confesseur. How kind of you to interest yourself in this sinful person!" She was being facetious, and enjoying it.

"Someone should," he snapped. "In a new country like this it's dog-eat-dog, and those with the fastest teeth survive."

"Oh," she crescendoed in a high falsetto key, "how interesting."

Ignoring her interruption, he continued: "As you know, the emperor has recently completed the new palace. It's called Sans Souci, and it is a lifetime ambition fulfilled. It has the elegance of Versailles, and yet—" He paused.

Asya stared up at the man who stood before her. His eyes had a faraway look. Had he known Versailles and loved someone there? Was it his homeland calling to him? A twinge of jealousy pricked at her heart.

"—and yet it is not a home." Etienne took a deep breath and looked hard at Asya. She had the feeling he wanted her to listen carefully to what he would say next.

"It is a monument to M. Christophe's success," he said. "It's a beautiful monument, one he can be proud of. But with its completion have come new problems. His co-workers, former slaves like himself, have also worked hard for Haiti. They, too, might deserve a little Versailles, but a new country can afford but one extravagance. I only returned last night, but already I see evidence of jealousy, resentment. Each minister, each public servant, thinks he too should be handsomely rewarded. He, too, should have a palace to live in. The wives of these men are putting pressure on their husbands to set them up in more elaborate dwellings."

Asya leaped from her chair. "No. No. The answer is no!" she shouted at Etienne.

He gave her an odd look. "Have you lost your mind?"

"If I keep listening to your logic, I will. Every time you come to see me, you want something. Well this time the answer is no. NO. I've given schoolbooks to the children, but I refuse to build homes for their bickering parents." She folded her arms across her breast and glared. "That's final."

For a moment, Etienne looked at Asya in amazement. Then he turned his back on her, his shoulders convulsed, and he doubled over with laughter. Watching him from her militant position, Asya began to regret she had ever listened to her heart.

At last, he turned toward her, and between chuckles managed to say, "Asya, you sometimes think up the most refreshing ideas. I'm glad I came out here today. You're what I needed."

Her voice frigid, she snapped, "Well, I'm glad I'm good for laughs anyway." Then with vehemence she added, "The answer is still NO."

Putting his hands on her shoulders, Etienne cajoled, "Sit down, *ma cherie*. Let's talk."

Asya did not budge, so he pushed her gently down into a chair. Drawing another to her side, Etienne casually seated himself and crossed a leg over his knee like a guest preparing for a long visit.

Leaning back, with his hands behind his head, Etienne drawled. "When I was in Mexico, I came upon a pair of beautiful thoroughbreds. Fastest of all breeds.

405

Bought them cheap from a banker. They're having a revolution over there, and he was anxious to sell them before they got butchered some night."

"What has that to do with me?" Asya asked impatiently.

"I bought the horses for you, Asya." She looked up at him quizzically. "Well not exactly for yourself," he went on, "but for you to give away." He spoke slowly so that his words could sink in. "I thought you might give them to the emperor and empress as a sort of palace-warming gift."

"I knew it. I *knew* it," Asya spat out between clenched teeth. "I knew you had some subversive purpose in coming here."

"That's right." Etienne was unruffled. "I like to look after your welfare."

"You're only trying to make me spend money. I'm not buying those horses from you."

"I'm not selling them. I'm merely offering them to you to give as a gift to the imperial family."

Asya had not expected this answer. Her aplomb was shaken, and to cover up the break in her defense, she sneered, "Ha. Ha. Imperial family of a country that's but a speck on the globe."

"Your sarcastic change of the subject does not answer the matter we were discussing." Etienne spoke with patience.

With recovered assurance, Asya stated, "I'm not interested. I see no reason to give a gift to the imperial family, as you refer to them. If I wished to give a gift, it would be of my own selection and paid for from my own purse."

Etienne applauded. "Spoken like a real idiot."

Asya turned her head in disdain. "Sweet talk will get you nowhere."

"Good. Then I can give you facts. In the past two weeks, fourteen of the better homes around Cap Henri have been seized and occupied by some of the higher dignitaries of the court while the owners were away."

"They can't do that," Asya denied, unmoved. "That's robbery. The emperor would not stand for any such wanton disrespect for the law."

In a patient voice, Etienne explained, "The emperor is too busy with affairs of state to be concerned with the domestic squabbling of his associates. If the practice became a nuisance, he might hand the matter over to Prophète who would march some of his platoons around the city as a show of imperial concern over the issue. However, Prophète is casting his eye about for a better home too. One more fitting his high station. So he is not likely to advocate the elimination of the sport."

Asya lost some of her rigidness. She was remembering the drooling look on the general's face when he had come to Cher Château for the wedding of Cilla and Watusi. "You—you're just saying that to frighten me," Asya scolded. "I haven't heard about any of this crime you're talking about."

"Of course not. Where would you? Most of those who were robbed are Haitians with whom you disdain to mix, since they used to be slaves. But, a house that was seized only yesterday belonged to an Englishman. A wealthy lumberman. No attempt as yet has been made to seize a Creole home. Perhaps that is because for years the Creole was god on this island. However, there is always someone who will not be cowed. Therefore, you must, even if it is only for selfish reasons, make friends with these neophyte citizens. If you are not their friend, then you are most definitely their enemy."

"What do you want me to do?" she asked hesitantly.

"May I give the thoroughbreds to Henri and his wife in your name as a sign of your friendship?"

"No." Asya pulled her hand from his. "No. They have already been paid enough for my protection. I'm no coward. Anyway, even if all you are saying is true, which I don't believe it is, I'm not going to pretend I

407

want to be their friend. I like my life as it is. I wish to choose my own friends and do as I please."

She stood up and said in a tone of finality, "The answer is no. If you wish to unload a pair of cheap Mexican horses on me under the guise of loyalty to the realm, you've got the wrong person. Give them to the emperor yourself."

With a sly grin, Etienne looked up at her. "He already has them. I sent them this morning with your compliments."

Asya clenched her fists in anger. She could have poked him in the middle of his smug face. "You didn't," she stormed. "You didn't have the effrontery to offer a bribe in my name."

"Not a bribe. Merely a friendly gift from a loyal subject to His Majesty. So, tonight at the ball, when he thanks you for your munificent gift, bow that stiff little neck of yours and accept his gratitude with humility."

"I'm not going to the ball," she stated flatly. "I've already sent my regrets."

"So the empress mentioned to me. However," he lazily unfolded his long legs and stood up, "I told Her Majesty that you had changed your mind since my return. Before my departure last year you had asked that I look about for a pair of horses as a gift worthy of Their Majesties. Your heart was set on having them here in time for the completion of Sans Souci, and when you had not heard from me, your disappointment was so great that you could not come empty-handed to their new home. But now," and his voice took on a gay lilt, "but now that I have returned in time, with mission completed, you beg to be included among their guests tonight."

His eyes were laughing at her, so that she could not tell of what he might be thinking. She hated him. "Quite an ingenious tale and you're stuck with it. I'm not going."

"Not immediately. We'll wait until you change your

dress, since I am sure you will not want to wear that one to the ball tonight."

"What do you mean?"

"I'm taking you with me."

"Didn't you understand? I'm not going." Her voice rose. "I'm staying here. Right here at Cher Château."

"Don't be so adamant about it," Etienne warned. "You could be wrong." He started toward her, but she backed out of the room, shouting defiantly at him, "No. No."

He lunged, but she was too fast for him. Whirling about, Asya was up the stairs in a flash, Etienne after her. She reached her room just ahead of him. The door banged and the key turned. She had locked herself in.

Etienne tried the knob, but there was no give. "Asya, he ordered, "open the door.

She did not answer.

"I'm coming in."

He placed the flat of his hand against a panel to test its strength. "I'm coming in if I have to break down the door," he shouted.

"Ha, ha," her taunt floated into the hall. "Big tough fellow."

Stepping back, Etienne threw his shoulder against the door, giving one of the panels the full force of his weight. It splintered. In one more try, it gave way and Etienne stepped through the opening, at the same time calling out behind, "Come out of that shadow in the hall where you've been listening, Negu, and get in here. Asya's going to the ball after all."

"I am not." Asya's eyes flashed in defiance. "You— you animal! Look what you've done to my beautiful door."

Ignoring her, Etienne strode toward a tall white and gold press which stood near a window. To Negu, who, with an amazed look on her face, had just stepped through the broken door, he called back, "Is this where she keeps her party dresses?"

"No you don't," Asya screamed defiantly as she

leaped between him and the press. "Don't you dare go through my clothes with your big dirty paws."

Etienne pushed her brusquely aside and pulled open the door. "Well, Negu," he asked as if Asya had not uttered a sound, "what shall we select for Mademoiselle tonight?"

"Nothing!" Asya yelled.

"Oh." He slowly turned, giving her a suggestive look. *"Mal elevée,"* he chided. "What would the other girls say?"

Etienne returned his attention to the well-filled rack of dresses. "Now let's see," he asked Negu, "how does she look in this white one?"

"You can't make me go. I'll refuse," Asya shouted from the middle of the room. "I won't budge from here."

"White is for sweet young things," Etienne confided to the black woman at his side. "Let's put this one on her. Maybe in this color she will fool some of the guests into thinking she's a lady."

"I don't want to be a lady," came the protest. "Besides, I can't wear that anyway. I wore it only last week."

"Mon Dieu!" Etienne dropped the garment as though it was contaminated. "Why keep this old rag to clutter up the press? Mademoiselle has already worn it."

"Let my clothes alone." Asya pummeled Etienne's back with her fists. "Get out of my bedroom."

Etienne made little scolding sounds with his tongue. "You are the first woman to tell me to get out of her bedroom." Then he grinned at Negu, who was trying to keep a straight face. "A new and challenging experience for this old *roué.*"

"If you don't go, I'll call for help," Asya threatened.

As though she was not there, Etienne leisurely examined each dress, stopping now and then to confer with the housekeeper as to its suitability.

"Help! Nassy!" Asya's lungs gave their all to her cry for assistance.

"Don't wear yourself out, my little shrew," Etienne cautioned. "Save your energies for the dance. Nassy can't come. He's too fat to get through the hole in the door."

Asya ran to the door, but Etienne was there before her, barring her way. "Such haste to get to the ball," he teased. "You almost forgot to put on your party dress. But don't you worry your little head. Negu and I will work fast. You'll be ready in no time."

Quickly he took off his coat and, hanging it on the doorknob, started toward Asya. Seething, the mistress of the now second most stately home in Haiti turned and gave a flying leap into the middle of the bed. "No you don't. Don't you touch me," she screamed.

Etienne walked to the bed. "Are you going to get up and dress? Or do I come get you?"

"No." She clamped her mouth shut, stiff and unyielding, like a suture across the lower part of her face.

"But, Asya," he teasingly admonished, "it's so early in the day to play jump-into-bed-after-me games, although I must admit you do look fetching. Come now. Get dressed."

Except for her eyes, which bombarded him with wrath, Asya remained immobile.

Slowly and methodically, he unlinked the cuffs of his shirt and rolled up his sleeves. "I see I have a job cut out for me here," he said slowly, while his eyes looked her over with anticipated pleasure. "A most spirited opponent in a very enjoyable jousting bout. Too bad you haven't a chance for victory."

In one motion, Etienne grabbed Asya by the ankles, pulled her to the edge of the bed, flicked off her slippers, and rolled her over on her stomach. Before she could reach back to claw at his face, Etienne had her dress unhooked and pulled halfway over her head, where it constricted her flailing arms and muffled her protests. "Negu," she heard him ask, "do I take off the petticoats too?"

"Oui," the Negress answered. "Everything. For a ball, a lady must wear her very best lingerie."

Asya felt his fingers undo the string which held up her petticoat, and she tried to kick backward with her bare feet. For the effort, she got his knee in her back.

"Let me up!" she yelled. "Let me go. I'll dress myself." She was suddenly frenzied.

"I can do it faster," was his calm answer, "and really I don't mind. No bother at all." Down came her petticoat.

"Please let her go," said a quiet voice. It was Cilla's. "I'll help her dress."

Etienne's knee came off her back, and Asya shot upright, at the same time pulling her dress from about her head.

"A lady cannot go to a ball all flushed from fighting, monsieur," Cilla stated with simple dignity. "If you will wait downstairs, Mlle. Asya will be ready to accompany you to the ball very shortly."

Etienne studied his antagonist. "I'm not so sure. I thought I was doing a pretty good job all by myself. Maybe if I help," he looked slyly at Cilla, "we'll get done sooner."

"Your specialty is undressing. What do you know about dressing?" Asya accused from behind the shield of her rumpled dress. "Now get out, you—you monster."

Etienne chuckled as he strode toward the bashed-in door and stepped through the hole he had made. Before disappearing down the hall, he looked back and waved at Asya, who was still seated in the center of the bed.

A half-hour later, Asya was ready. When she walked into the parlor and Etienne stood up to greet her, she knew by the surprised admiration on his face that Cilla had done her job well. The dress was of apricot *mousseline de soie* with stars embroidered in silver thread about the hemline. Her hair was tightly pulled back to the top of her head and then wound into little rolls which entwined each other like a nest of black snakes. Except for a wide silver band about her waist, her only other jewelry was a pair of large diamond clips in the shape of a dagger which Cilla had fastened into her hair just at the temples. The sharp tips pointed upward, standing out like glittering horns against her black hair.

"I look like a satyr," Asya exclaimed when she first saw her reflection in the long mirror.

"That's good," was Cilla's comment. "If a satyr is anything like a Satan, your dress captures your mood."

Etienne must have had a similar thought, for, after taking in every detail of her attire, he remarked, "You look like the devil." However, before Asya could make a sharp retort, he hurried to add, "A she-devil."

Asya was pleased. She even felt wicked. Perhaps it would be an exciting evening after all.

Just then, Negu appeared with a decanter of wine and two glasses. "A little wine," she commented as she placed the tray of refreshments on the table. "It helps relax a body from the cares of life and mellows her for a gala evening."

"I think she's talking about me," Asya informed Etienne, ignoring the housekeeper as if she were not present. "Negu thinks I should shower you with affability and adoration." Asya emitted a mirthless laugh.

A smile flickered at the corner of Etienne's mouth. "And why not? All the other girls do. Don't you like me?"

"I hate you." It was a flat statement.

"Good. Let's drink to that dénouement."

Etienne poured the wine, and as Asya watched, she had a thought. A diabolical, delightful thought. But as she reached for her glass, his voice warned, "I wouldn't carry out that intention which is so plainly written on your face, Asya. This is the suit I'm wearing to the ball, and if you toss your wine on me, I am still wear-

413

ing it. People will wonder about the sloppy beau who escorts you tonight, and I shall tell them. This is what I'm wearing, wine-splattered or not."

"You—you wouldn't wear that plain old coat to Sans Souci." Asya's eyes wandered disapprovingly over his attire. "It looks like a—a work coat."

"That's right," Etienne airily agreed. "When one dates you, that's work."

Without another word, Asya drained her glass in one swallow.

Chapter Thirty

Asya was glad Etienne had insisted she go to Sans Souci. She had a wonderful time. The wine which Negu had offered before their departure had done its job, for by the time she and Etienne reached the palace, Asya had not an irritation in the world. When her eyes first fell upon Sans Souci, she had to admire genuinely the magnificent structure. It was set partway up a great mountain and built over a waterfall that dropped down into red stone-lined channels which wound away into the woods. Constructed of yellow stucco, four stories high, the palace blazoned like a golden temple in the late-afternoon sun. Its red-tiled roof matched in color the gardens of red flowers which already grew in profusion. The tree-covered mountain in the background framed Sans Souci like a giant green fan. To reach the entrance, Etienne and Asya walked up marble steps that arched gracefully up either side of the waterfall.

"The waterfall is so lovely," Asya remarked as she stood over it and watched it gush from the keystone of the arch below. "It makes everything nice and cool around it. It's like a breeze-maker." She raised her head to let the cool air bathe her face.

"That's the idea," Etienne said. "It cools the palace. Henri designed this waterfall."

Asya laughed. "I know you think the emperor is all-powerful, but after all, he can't move mountains and create waterfalls."

"Maybe he didn't move a mountain, but he surely

moved a mountain stream." Etienne looked smug with some secret knowledge.

"Don't tell me how," Asya said quickly. "Let me guess. Did he make a bargain with the Devil?"

"His Majesty makes bargains with no one, not even the Devil."

"Excusez-moi." Asya bowed her head in mock contrition. "I should have remembered that." Then she brightened. "I know. He made a novena to St. Christopher. *'S'il vous plaît,* move me a mountain stream,' he begged."

"Wrong again. He never begs."

"Oh dear," she sighed. "I guess he did it the same as God in the Bible. He stood on the mountains and ordered, 'Move me a stream. Let it flow down in a little waterfall, so that when Asya comes it can blow its cold breath upon her.' "

Etienne was amused. "Asya, I think that wine Negu served was a little strong."

She giggled. "Perhaps if we went inside, we might find a weaker one."

"In your present mood, any wine's too strong," he cautioned.

"Your worry," she said flippantly. "It was your idea to bring me. Now that I'm here, I plan to have a gay time." It was Asya, with an impish glint in her eye, who took Etienne by the elbow and pushed him toward the entrance.

Inside the palace, the air was pleasantly cool.

"Really, Etienne," Asya asked as they waited to be announced, "how did Henri do it?"

"He rerouted a mountain stream so that it runs under the first floor and cools the whole palace. You saw where the water comes out through the keystone in the arch before the entrance. Pretty smart old man, wouldn't you say?"

She thought for a moment before answering. "Real smart," Asya laughed. "Anytime he runs out of food, the cook can look under the kitchen floor and catch a fish."

Etienne gave her a speculative look and then smiled indulgently. "I have an idea I had better keep a sharp eye on you tonight. You are in a capriciously unpredictable mood."

They were announced and as Asya curtseyed before the emperor, she completely forgot about her supposed gift to him until Henri said, "Mlle. Asya, it is I who should bow before you. Her Highness and I are deeply grateful for your most generous and unusual gift of the horses."

His big smile enveloped her like a protecting ray. How could anyone fear this man?

However, Asya soon forgot about the emperor and the foreboding gossip about his grasping friends. Let the others worry about diplomatic maneuvers. A handsome stranger had come to the party. A redhead with hair as flaming as the carrots the scullery nun used to cook in the kettle in the Sacre-Coeur kitchen.

"Who is he?" Asya excitedly asked Etienne.

"The new consul from London, Sir Roger Tuthill. Very eligible bachelor, but you wouldn't be interested." His voice dismissed the man. "After all, he's English and I know how you feel about the English."

Asya gave Etienne a scathing look and turned her attention back to the new arrival from London. "Ah," she sighed, "such gorgeous red hair!"

"Asya, you're acting like a hound dog that has spotted the fox. I can hear your panting."

Ignoring his comments, Asya whispered, "His emerald-green coat and the golden epaulets are a perfect frame for the burnished hair."

"You're drunk."

"You're jealous."

Etienne handed Asya a glass of wine. "Drink this. Maybe it will dull your senses since you're not using them anyway."

Keeping her eyes glued to the red-headed stranger,

Asya sipped the wine. "This is good," she said. "My senses aren't getting dull. I can feel them sharpening already. Sir Tuthill is looking my way."

"Your hot little glances are seering that cold English head and causing him to turn to see what voodoo witch is casting a spell upon him."

"He's still looking my way," Asya said breathlessly.

"More than that. He's coming over."

"Of course. I invited him."

"How? You never said a word."

Asya gave a pleased laugh. "Didn't need to. Just winked."

It was hours before Asya saw Etienne again. After his presentation of the Englishman to her, she and Sir Tuthill wandered about the marble-floored palace, having a different wine in each room opened for the inspection of the guests. Sir Tuthill knew everything about the polished woods which paneled the walls, the origins of the tapestries and the renown of the paintings. When Asya stopped to admire a magnificent silver troika displayed on a refectory table of carved ebony, Sir Tuthill was informed about that too.

"It's a gift from the Czar Alexander of Russia," he announced proudly.

"How did it get over here?" Asya asked.

"By English ship." He looked smug. "We're the only nation he would trust to deliver it, the only one who does not run from the French fleet. To bring it to Haiti is but a thumbing of the nose at Napoleon, one might say."

Asya frowned as she tried to digest this information. "And all the time," she said, "I thought it was a nice friendly gift from the Russian emperor to our own nice little emperor on the occasion of the opening of Sans Souci."

"Nice little emperor!" Sir Tuthill laughed as one might at a child who has given a comic answer. "Mlle. Asya, you are a sweet naive darling." The sound of music was heard in one of the other rooms. He held out his arms. "Shall we dance?" They did. Right there around the emperor's troika.

Asya never knew when the sun set and the candles were lit in their crystal containers. She danced and she drank and she dined and she laughed. When she thought at all of Etienne, it was only when she felt that his eyes were watching from somewhere, and her immediate reaction was to step up her flirtatious conduct with Sir Tuthill. Only once did she actually see him. It was late in the evening and Sir Tuthill had momentarily left her side to bring her another pâtisserie. She sat waiting for him on the edge of a marble fish pond, amusing herself by trying to catch a large goldfish which swam through the water like a fiery dancer in flowing veils.

Suddenly he was beside her. She did not look up. She knew it was Etienne. "Still hungry?" he asked.

Asya gave him a sideways look. "I won't eat him. Just trying to catch him."

"How do you know it's a him?"

"Trying to get away from me, isn't he?"

"Naturally," came his sardonic reply. "It's the protective instinct of the male in any species. Self-preservation."

Asya giggled to herself and went on playing with the fish.

After a brief moment of silence, Etienne asked coldly, "Why are you bothering those poor devils. You've already hooked your fish for today. Isn't Sir Tuthill big enough to please you?"

Asya gave him a sly look. "What's the matter?" she taunted. "Is no one putting any bait out for you?"

"I'm no adolescent," he answered brusquely. "And speaking of adolescents, don't you think it's time you stopped hanging into the water like an *enfante* seeing her first fish? Dry your hand and act like a big girl."

"All right," she airily agreed. "Anything you say."

Whereupon, Asya reached up and dried her wet hand on a tail of his waistcoat.

The man did not move. Only watched her in disgust. "Is that your idea of a joke? If so, it's a poor one."

She shrugged off his disapproval. "I didn't think you would mind. After all, it is only your work coat. Surely you would be disappointed had you worn it in vain." Then she looked at her hands. "There. All dried. Now you have served your purpose, M. Grenier, so why don't you go off and give the girls a treat by dancing with them."

Before he could answer, Asya reached down into the water, and, scooping up a big fat goldfish, dropped it into Etienne's coat pocket. Then she ran to join Sir Tuthill who was coming toward her with a plate of sweets.

Asya did not see Etienne again until very late in the evening. Everyone was dancing the minuet when, suddenly, loud guffaws and high feminine squeals of laughter broke out. The dancers slowed, looked about, and gravitated toward the center of the merriment. Count Marmalade was doing a solo dance. With his chest thrust out and his mouth open in the shape of a square, he resembled a gorilla. His legs were bent like the hind ones of a cat as he wobbled in rhythm from one awkwardly pointed toe to the other. The guests encouraged his ludicrous antics with applause and shouts.

Asya thought him the funniest entertainer she had ever seen. "Didn't know Count Marmalade had it in him," she laughed.

"It looks just like *him*," a woman beside her shouted to no one in particular. "Exactly the way *he* used to do it. It's him all right."

"Who?" Asya asked her.

"Good old Emperor Dessalines," she managed to wheeze out between convulsive outbursts of laughter. "He danced like a rhinoceros in silk pants. You should have—" But she went off into peels of laughter and could say no more.

Suddenly the fun and the noise were gone. It was as

if a giant machete had cut them from the room. The emperor strode into the midst of the guests and like a wild man he confronted Count Marmalade. His eyes flashed in fiery rage and when he opened his mouth to speak, Asya expected red flames to come roaring out. His voice was quiet, but it whipped through the room.

"You are engaging in a vulgar display unbecoming in an imperial residence. You will leave immediately, I repeat, immediately, for the garrison at St. Marc, where you will be in command. From this moment on, you are Captain Marmalade. There is no longer a Count Marmalade."

With his fists clenched and his back stiff with the effort of self-control, Emperor Christophe walked pompously from the room. The ensuing silence was like a vacuum in which even the air could not stir. Timidly, a violin squeaked out a note and encouraged the other strings to join in the music of a minuet. The shuffle of a few hesitant feet across the floor signaled the slow awakening of the bewildered dancers from the impact of their host's exit.

"By Jove, he gives it to them right sharp!" Sir Tuthill commented to Asya under his breath. "Feel sorry for the poor chap, Marmalade. He was only having a bit of fun." He turned to his partner. "Shall we dance?"

"Oui," Asya answered, somewhat shaken by the emperor's outburst. "Let's dance right up to the nearest wineglass. That mean old emperor spoiled my fun. I thought he invited us for a party, not a state funeral."

In the foyer just outside the ballroom, Sir Roger Tuthill and Asya found a silver tray of untouched glasses filled with a sparkling amber wine.

"Like magic." Asya went up on her toes, arched her arms above her head, and pirouetted around the table. "This palace is a house of magic. The owner says, 'I am hot. Bring me a waterfall,' and it comes. I say, 'I want wine,' and it appears. Wonderful, wonderful house," she sang out.

"A charming way to look at it," the Englishman said, "but I'd wager it was set here by a servant who went off to gossip about the recent happening we just witnessed in the ballroom, and forgot about serving the guests."

"Oh. You make it sound so mundane," Asya pouted. "I like my version better." She brightened. "Let's drink to this magical house. May it last forever."

"Right." Sir Tuthill raised his glass. "And to the beautiful woman I met here this night."

"May she last forever too," Asya tittered. "I'll drink to that." Without a pause, she finished her wine and set the glass firmly upon the silver tray. Looking at the rest of the filled wineglasses, Asya nodded her head at each one as she counted. "One and—ad infinitum," she finished with a wide sweep of her arm. "That's six for you, Roger, and twenty-six for me."

"Right," Roger agreed. "That comes out even. A toast to your brilliant mathematical mind."

"Well." Asya blinked her eyes in amazement. "I didn't know I had one. Since we just discovered it, I should drink to it too." She touched a wineglass to her forehead. "To my brilliant mind. Welcome home." This toast she finished ahead of Sir Tuthill, and shook her head at him in disapproval.

"You need more practice in toasting." Asya pushed two glasses of the bubbling wine toward him and picked up one for herself. "Now you drink two to my one," she told him, "and try to finish at the same time I do."

Sir Tuthill thought this over for a minute and then nodded. "Right."

"Put your hand on your glass and I'll put one on mine. We must start together. Those are the rules. We must be fair."

"Of course." Sir Tuthill drew himself up and remarked with great dignity, "We English are a sporting race you know."

"Well!" Asya placed her hands on her hips and

asked indignantly, "If you're so sporting, how come you have two glasses, and I only have one?"

Her companion looked bewilderedly from her glass to his. "So it is. Where's your other glass? Do you suppose you left it under the table?"

"I don't know. I don't remember being there," she answered blankly. "Maybe I'd better look."

Slowly, Asya bent over and looked under the table, but all she saw was Sir Tuthill's face also peering under from the other side.

"Hello," she called gaily. "Didn't know you were under here. I lost a glass of wine. Did you see it?"

"No. Can't say I have."

"You're upside down. Did you know that?"

"So are you," Roger answered.

Asya thought a moment. "Maybe that's because we're in a magical house. How do you suppose we get changed to right side up again?"

Sir Tuthill chuckled. "I suppose we have to stay this way."

Asya giggled. "We'll look funny going around upside down. Let's see how the other people look. Maybe they're upside down too."

They both straightened and stared in surprise when they saw each other across the top of the table. "You're right side up again," Asya spoke first.

"So are you."

Asya bit her lip then wondered aloud: "How did I do it?" Her eyes fell upon the remaining glasses of wine. "Let's have a drink," she suggested, "while we discuss our topsy-turvy powers."

As she raised her glass to her lips, Asya caught sight of Etienne coming toward her from the ballroom. "Wait a moment," she told Roger. "We're having company. It's not polite to drink up all the wine before a guest arrives. Let's wait and ask him to join us."

But Asya never got that last drink. Etienne took the bowl of the glass in his hand and deftly unwound her fingers from about the stem. "You've had enough," he announced as he returned the full glass to the tray. Grasping her firmly by the elbow, he said brusquely, "It is time to go home." Ignoring Sir Tuthill, Etienne ushered her through the foyer and outside to his waiting carriage.

"Not so fast," Asya pleaded. "I don't want to leave." But she had no strength to protest. No sooner had he swung her up into the carriage and set the horses in motion than Asya leaned snugly against his shoulder and fell happily to sleep.

"Sleep, my angel," Etienne whispered softly. "Sleep well."

Etienne drove slowly, his mind obviously not on the road. The moon was high in the sky, and in its light, his face looked grim. When one of the horses stumbled and the carriage jerked slightly, Asya awoke with a start.

"Oh," she moaned. "My head. My poor head." Then, suddenly remembering where she was and who was beside her, she sat stiffly upright. "Where are we going?"

He gave no answer.

"Ah, what difference does it make," Asya sighed. "It was a wonderful party."

Etienne turned to glare at her. "Wonderful. Except for a few people who made asses of themselves."

"Oui," she agreed. "The emperor *was* revolting, wasn't he? The old party-spoiler."

Etienne said nothing. He gave her a look of disgust and turned his eyes back to the road ahead.

Asya tried again. "Do you think Count Marmalade is upset over his new appointment?"

"Wouldn't Lord Nelson be upset," Etienne asked, his voice cold, "if he suddenly found himself in charge of a river barge?"

"Well," Asya pondered a moment, "if you put it that way, the count *didn't* exactly get a promotion."

Etienne's answer was a sneer.

"What makes you so cross?" Asya wanted to know. "It's no concern of yours."

'Count Marmalade is my friend. He fought well against the French and worked hard for this new country. He deserves better."

"Then tell your good pal Henri he made a mistake," Asya answered blithely.

Etienne looked steadily at the road ahead and said quietly, "I did."

Realizing for the first time how upset he was, Asya attempted to buoy his spirits. "You did your best for your friend. Now stop worrying."

"What you don't understand," he replied, "is that tonight you witnessed not only one man's humiliation, but the fanning of an unrest which is already deep-seated in Haiti. The emperor made a powerful enemy out of a valuable ally and is sending him off to St. Marc, which is already a hotbed of potential traitors."

"I should think it smart of him," Asya announced unconcernedly, "to put all his enemies in one spot. Then at least he knows where they are."

"The logic of a female!" Etienne snorted derisively

Asya moved up close beside Etienne. "Aren't you glad I'm a female?" she cooed.

"No," he barked. "If I never saw an ass drink before, I saw one tonight."

Asya giggled. "Wasn't it terrible? Roger simply can't drink. And Englishmen are usually so perfect in all their endeavors."

Etienne glowered. "It wouldn't have hurt *you* to be less adept."

Asya turned on him. "You're no fun to be with. Just sitting there, primly driving along the road on this gorgeous moonlit night. Here." She reached for the reins. "Let me drive. Even the horse is falling asleep."

Before he could protest, Asya snatched the reins from Etienne's hands and called out loudly, *"Va! Va! We'll show this dullard how to drive."* At the sound of Asya's voice, the horse made a quick leap forward, the carriage lurched, and the surprised Etienne was almost hurled from his seat.

Asya laughed as they rolled on with gathering speed. "Watch how a real driver handles a horse."

"Asya," Etienne shouted, trying to take the reins from her, "the road is full of holes. Slow down." But she flung his hand from her arm, and at the same time stood up to step away from him.

That was when it happened. There was a crashing sound, and the carriage leaped like a frightened animal, tossing Asya into the air. The stars and the moon flew by and then there was darkness. When Asya opened her eyes, she supposed it was the same night. The stars and the moon were still whirling overhead, but now the face of Etienne was leaning over her, whirling too.

"Asya, are you hurt?" Even in her hazy state, her heart heard the anxiety in his voice and purred.

"*Non.* Just dead." She sighed happily. "I wasn't such a bad girl after all. I made heaven."

"*Oui. Oui,*" he agreed, "but can you move? Can you stand?"

"Why? Why should I?" she asked dreamily. "I'm flying now. I'm flying right up to Heaven, and you're going too." Her voice trailed off and she was content. His hands were behind her head, raising it, and now her breath came more easily. The sky stopped spinning, and she was being helped to her feet. "Are we there already?" she asked. "Time to get off?"

"*Oui, mon petit chou.*" Etienne put his arms about Asya and held her against his breast. "My willful little cabbage head. Someday, you're going to lose it."

"I have," she whispered quietly to his cravat. "To you."

Etiennne set her away from him and, looking down into her face, he scolded, "You could have killed yourself. It's only luck that you're still alive."

"Oh, you mean I have to make the trip to Heaven all over again?" She put her arms about his neck and laid her head against his breast. "And I thought I was already there." Asya gave a big sigh. "As long as I'm not going anywhere, I like it where I am."

His hand touched her hair, then wandered to her cheek in a gentle caress. Asya raised her face and looked at him.

"Dear little *chou*," he said tenderly.

"Can't you call me anything else but cabbage head?" Asya demanded.

Etienne answered softly, "Yes, but you wouldn't like it." Then his lips were on hers, and Asya blissfully drowned in his enveloping warmth.

After they kissed, Etienne placed his hands on her shoulders and held her from him as he lovingly gazed at her. Asya shivered and snuggled back into his arms. "It's cold out here," she murmured, as she rubbed her nose against his shoulder.

"That's because we're standing in a mud puddle," Etienne said dreamily.

"What!" Asya jumped from his arms and looked down at her feet. The edge of the moon and a few stars sparkled up from the liquid blackness in which she stood.

"You're wrong. I'm not in a mud puddle," she denied. "I'm on top of the world. See for yourself." She pointed with the toe of her slipper. "There's the moon." But as her feet moved the water, the heavenly bodies disappeared, leaving only ripples of light in a black sea.

Etienne and Asya had to walk back to Cher Château. A wheel of the carriage was broken, causing it to lean at a crazy angle in one of the holes in the road. Etienne unharnessed the horse. It bounded away and quickly disappeared in the fog which was coming down from the mountain.

"Look how it runs," Asya pointed in the direction the animal had gone. "I know how it feels to be unbridled. I felt the same way when I got out of my brown school uniform."

For a while, they walked along, saying nothing, the

427

silence broken only by the squishing sound of the mud in Asya's slippers. She said, "I like the feel of the mud on my feet. It's probably because I was never allowed to play in the mud while I was growing up at the hospital. The children of the Sacre-Coeur stable man were allowed to play in it. How I envied them. They made beautiful statues out of mud."

"Of the saints, I suppose," Etienne said.

"Naturally. What else?"

"Who was the most popular?"

"St. George," Asya answered immediately. "They liked shaping his dragon."

"Didn't anyone ever sculpt a nun?"

"Never. They were dull. All looked the same."

Etienne shook with quiet laughter and wrapped his arm more tightly about her waist. As they walked along, Asya snuggled close, for the fog was making the night cold and damp.

By the time they approached Cher Château the sun was red over the horizon, and the wind was sweeping the mist back up the mountain. Asya's heart hummed its contentment. She gave a little laugh of happiness, and at its sound, Etienne glanced down at her.

"You look rather cute with your mud-spattered face," he said. "The sun has put a red glow on your cheeks, and it's most becoming."

"And a red glow on my nose too," Asya added.

"No," he emphatically denied. "The red of your nose is not from the sun. It's from all the wine you drank at Sans Souci."

"I'm glad." Asya gave him a provocative look. "I'm also glad I wrecked the carriage."

"We should always walk home from a party," Etienne said. His hand tightened on hers. His voice became serious. "It will be a long time before we can be together again, Asya."

At his words, the bright morning became black night, and she shivered as though the fog had returned.

428

"You are going away again?" she asked, dreading the answer.

"Yes. Back to the States."

Asya gave a heavy sigh. "Will you be gone long?"

He shook his head slowly. "I do not know. They are at war with England. It might be the right time to persuade them to recognize the government of Haiti. The Unites States might see certain advantages in having their ships welcomed at a neutral port. But——" Etienne paused and he sounded tired when he continued: "—— but the senators from the Southern states are difficult. On my last visit to Washington, they left the room when I tried to speak. They will tolerate no negotiations with the black ruler of a 'nigger' nation, as they term this country. However," his voice took on a brighter note, "I shall try again. I am hopeful that one day the United States will recognize Haiti as an independent nation."

"Can't someone else go?" Asya complained.

"Who?"

Asya thought a moment, then shook her head. "I ——I don't know."

They walked along, holding hands, saying nothing, but Asya's heart was heavy. She felt an uneasiness, which increased when they reached the gate of Cher Château, for, across the way, roosting high in the barren branches of a long-dead tree, sat two huge buzzards, their bald heads shining in the sun.

Asya shivered. "I hate those birds." She picked up a stone and threw it in their direction, but they only flapped their wings and resumed their former waiting position on the limb. "I wish they'd go away." She waved her arms at the buzzards. "Shoo! Shoo! Go somewhere else."

The birds seemed to contemplate her antics and they made sounds as if they were discussing the situation between them. One moved to another branch, but the conference went on. Asya pointed to it. "I do believe

it's talking about us. What do you think it's saying?"
she asked Etienne.

"It's looking straight at you," he answered. "It's saying, 'She's mine.'"

"Then what's the other one screaming back to it?"

"'I saw her first.'"

Asya gave a quick laugh, and then suddenly
frowned. "I don't like buzzards outside my home,
watching it with their evil-looking eyes."

"Asya," Etienne reasoned, "they have to roost somewhere. They're only birds."

"To me, they're death, and I don't want them hanging around Cher Château."

Etienne picked up a large stone and hurled it at the
birds. It struck the branches on which one roosted, and
both buzzards flew off, noisily flapping their indignation
as they went.

"Let's forget about the birds." Suddenly Etienne
took Asya by the shoulders and turned her toward
him. He had a fierce look in his eyes, and she felt the
hardness of his hands as he pulled her close. "Asya, I
love you." His voice was low, husky, almost a whisper.
"I must have always loved you."

Chapter Thirty-one

Desaix was bitter. She had not been invited to Sans Souci. Prophète could have taken her as his guest, but at the suggestion, he laughed derisively. "Me, the captain of the palace guard, arrive at the opening ball with a housekeeper on my arm?" His eyes rolled over her body and his lips curled in contempt. "A fat one at that, whose legs are too heavy to dance." He had given a nasty laugh. "*Non.* Never does Prophète make himself a clown."

"But," Desaix whined, "kin I help if I'm gittin so fat?"

"Sure. You stuff yourself too much." Prophète pulled up her dress. "I seen fence posts what am weak 'longside the tree stumps what carry you 'round." In disgust, he kicked Desaix in the shin, watched with approval as a white mark appeared across it, and then disdainfully dropped her skirt. He brushed off his hands as if to rid them of all trace of vermin.

"My clothes ain't that dirty." Desaix gave the man a mean look.

Prophète raised his eyebrows. "Ain't they?" His tone indicated disagreement with her remark. He stepped back and his eyes slowly took in the woman before him. He shook his head. "You aint' much no more, Desaix. You'd jist better stick to cookin' victuals. No damn man's goin' to want you no other way." He turned and walked out of the house, but his sneering laugh, as he left her, rang tauntingly in Desaix's ears long after he had gone.

She hated him. Hated him. Desaix clenched her fists and shook them at the door through which he had disappeared. She wished she had his handsome face right in her hands. She would pull out the hair on his chin root by root with one hand and separate his head from his neck with the other. Just like a chicken readied for the pot. She knew him. She knew Prophète. He was a wild animal. A wild animal from the jungle. An animal that wore a uniform instead of fur, that snatched and chewed and killed to get what he wanted, then walked away on hind legs like a human instead of on all fours like the beast that he was. Big fellow! Guardian to the emperor! Did he forget that she—she, Desaix—had once slept in the bed of an emperor? The ass! Who did he think he was to turn away from her who had once been Emperor Dessalines' woman? Desaix's thoughts fanned the flame of her hatred, causing her blood to run madly through her body. Suddenly, she felt ill. Her head began to thump. Whatever was inside was growing bigger and bigger, pounding to get out. She held her hands against her temples lest they pop. Then a sharp pain struck her left arm and spread up into her chest where it became so intense that she was certain a dagger was plunged into her heart. Too weak to walk to her bed in the next room, Desaix dropped to the stone floor.

How long she lay there, she did not know, but in her agony it was an eternity. She called out to the blackness which teased in the distance, to come close, to envelope her and bring relief. "If you is Death, come git me. Git me. Give me sleep. I hurt," she blubbered. "I hurt. Somebody help me." But with her efforts, the pain grew worse, and Desaix subsided into quiet sobbing, stiffening herself as she did, so that no movement of her body might increase the pain. Tears of self-pity rolled down her cheeks. "Poor Desaix," she told herself, "nobody cares for yuh. Nobody gives two hoops in hell whether you is livin' or dead."

Well, then, she would have to care for herself.

Hadn't she always done so? The stone floor was cold. With her right hand she slowly pulled up her skirt, wiped the tears from her face, and carefully blew her runny nose.

Rolling her eyes about the room, Desaix called out as if someone were lurking there, "I's layin' here long 'nough. If you ain't comin' for me, Death, I ain't waitin' no longer. I's gittin' goin'."

With great effort, Desaix rolled onto her stomach and, with the help of her good arm, slowly pulled herself to the cupboard where M. Grenier kept his liquor. Still in a prone position, she rested her forehead on the bottom shelf, while her hand groped inside for the special bottle M. Grenier had brought back on his last trip from Jamaica. Finding it, Desaix agonizingly rolled onto her back and easily uncorked the bottle, glad that she had once sampled it, else she would not have had the strength to pull a virgin cork. She propped her head against the cupboard and took a gulp of the liquor. Like a hot snake, it slithered down her throat and coiled up in her stomach, from which spot its heat rose to bake her heart. Desaix slid her whiskey-soaked tongue over her lips, causing them to burn with its touch. It was a pleasant sensation.

"If this is dyin' and goin' to Hell, I wonder why I's bin fightin' it all these years. 'Taint bad. 'Taint bad." She contemplated the bottle. "The good ones is always tellin' us bad ones that we makes our own hell. I better git along with my buildin' by havin' another drink." So saying, Desaix tilted the bottle and let more of its warming contents gurgle down her throat.

Then she set the bottle on the floor and cradled it in her arm, a beatific look on her face. "M. Irish sure makes damn good whiskey. M. Grenier always says it's the best." She nodded her head. "I agrees. Damn good whiskey."

Desaix's eyes grew heavy and she closed them.

There was a warmth of contentment in her body as she floated through the darkness.

When next she opened her eyes, the moon was spinning past the window. She blinked. Everything was spinning. "I's goin' fast. With all sails flyin', but I still ain't arrived yit. Hell sure am far away."

Suddenly, her arm touched the bottle of whiskey, and she sat up, grabbed it with one hand, and shook it. "My God," she said aloud, "I ain't drunk it all yit. I hear it in there, callin' to me." The Negress put the bottle to her mouth and, without pausing for breath, finished its contents. Fires leaped within her, and their heat consumed the pain, leaving her exhilarated and light-headed. Desaix tossed the empty bottle into the air, and its crash on the stone floor was the last thing she heard before lapsing into oblivion.

An urgency of nature brought Desaix back to reality. She had to urinate. Even in her half-dazed state, the knowledge that her body was again reacting normally excited her. She must not be as sick as she had thought. With an effort, Desaix managed to get to her feet and wobble over to the slop pail by the chopping block. Straddling the refuse bucket, she stood there and let go. At the conclusion of the act, M. Grenier's housekeeper maintained her position while she nodded her head in smug satisfaction. "You're wrong, Prophète. I's still good. I ain't gonna swell up no more. What the old carcass was needin' all the time was M. Irish's bottled fixings." Desaix heaved a deep sigh of relief. Except for a soreness in her chest and a lightness in her head, she was her old self again.

However, a few days later, her spirit of cockiness ebbed when the Negress discovered she was again unable to pass her water. With M. Grenier's limited supply of Irish whiskey already dissipated, Desaix decided to cure herself with a voodoo concoction. Leaving the house, she padded barefoot down the road which ran in front of it, keeping a sharp eye on either side as she

434

went along. In no time at all, she found what she was looking for. A small clustered flower called a monkshood because of its resemblance to a friar's attire. Picking those which were in fullest bloom, Desaix hurried back to the house. There, she placed the flowers in a small pot, covered them with rum, and hung it from the hook on the hearth. Then she sat back in her rocker and waited for her panacea to brew. But as she waited and rocked, she suddenly remembered, and her remembrance was disturbing. The flower was poisonous. Very poisonous, and Negu, who had taught her the recipe years ago, when Desaix was learning to be a hounci, had cautioned that she use the right measures of the ingredients or the dosage could be fatal.

The longer Desaix rocked, the more certain she was that she had added too much rum. Or was it too little? Her recollection of the proper proportions was very muddled. Desaix stopped her rocking. Better not take any chances. She would go out to the Drapeaux plantation and consult with Negu concerning the mixture. Safer that way.

Setting the brew aside, the housekeeper banked the fire and headed for her bedroom off the kitchen. For her visit to the great house, Desaix must go in style. She would parade out in her very best dress, the yellow taffeta which Prophète had given her, and the white lace bonnet with the matching parasol. In honor of the occasion, although it was a painful part of full-dress regalia, Desaix would wear shoes—or at least she would slip them on when she arrived.

Desaix was excited as she dressed. Negu and her fine friends would see that she too had prospered. They would expect her to come calling from the back of a burro, but instead she would hitch up the barouche, the carriage M. Grenier always used when he wore his shirt with the lace jabot and ruffled cuffs for some big social function. It was time she flaunted her prosperity.

Buoyed up by her finery and the knowledge that she rode in a splendid carriage while other women were doing their drab morning chores, Desaix, as she drove through the streets of Cap Henri, gave the passersby a haughty smile and a patronizing nod. It was good to belong to the aristocracy.

Right through the front gates of Cher Château, Desaix rode, sticking out her tongue as she went by the Nagshead on the post. On this great adventure, the skull was but an unpleasant blot on the passing scene. Up to the veranda Desaix drove the horse and there alighted after first slipping on her bright green shoes with the silver buckles. With a great flourish of skirts, the visitor sashayed across the stone porch. After slowly closing her parasol, she threw back her shoulders and assumed a defiant stance. Satisfied that she was prepared for whatever might develop, Desaix gave the bell a rigorous pull, causing it to sound through the house like a ringing mandate.

She waited. After what seemed an interminable length of time, Desaix gave the cord another fierce yank. Was no one home? For a second her aplomb wavered in the face of an unexpected disappointment.

Then she heard footsteps, heavy and hurrying. It would not be Negu. The priestess was too sneaky to sound her approach. A man opened the door. A man with scared, wide-open eyes and dressed in the green uniform of a butler. It was Nassy.

Desaix saw that the butler recognized her, for disapproval, a look she had so often seen in the face of respectable hymn-singing folks, immediately supplanted his fright, and he asked in a voice of cold disdain, *"Oui?"* Evidently she was not worth wasting words on.

"I've come to see Negu," she said coldly and definitely, as one who expects to have her request granted.

"She's not here," the man announced curtly and started to close the door. However, before he could do so, a plump woman, whom Desaix recognized as

436

Evadne, thrust herself between him and the door.
"What's goin' on here? What's all goin' on here?" she
asked, breathless with excitement. "What's you shuttin'
from me so fast that I shunt know 'bout?"

Her eyes fell upon Desaix. *"You?"* she asked,
drawing herself up in shocked repugnance, her nostrils
quivering as though a stench had suddenly reached
them. "You darin' to come tartin' around 'spectable
folks." Evadne put her hands on her hips and spread
herself across the doorway. "Nassy," she called back
over her shoulder, while never taking her eyes from her
caller, "git to the kitchen. I smell the biscuits burnin'.
This ain't fittin' company for a gen'l'man to be seen
talkin' to. I'll handle it."

"Well, I'll be damned," Desaix announced in amazement. "I'll be damned. What the hell would I want
with that old man of yours. After beddin' with a
blown-up bolster like you all these years, he wunt
know what to do with a real woman."

Fire leaped in Evadne's eyes. "Iz zat so?"

"Yah. Zat's so," Desaix snapped back.

"Well, don't you come 'round here tryin' to show my
man none of your devil tricks." Evadne's chin slowly,
but firmly moved toward her adversary.

Desaix glowered. "Who you think you is anyhow?
You's nothin' but a kitchen biddy what ain't gone
nowhere but your kitchen and church. You ain't the
mistress here. Why you stickin' your nose out the front
door of this house whin you ain't got no manners for
nothin' but stickin' it in the stew kettle?"

"I knows 'nough 'bout manners to know that when
trash comes callin' it comes knockin' to the back door.
Front doors is for decent folks."

Desaix gave Evadne a venomous look. "And what
makes you think you is decent folk? What right you
got to say you is decent and I ain't? You's good 'cause
you ain't never had no chance to be bad. Sin ain't
never been interested in you and you's jealous. Tha's

what you is. Jealous." Desaix spat the word out. " 'Cause sin passed you by an' you's missing out on all the fun. *Oui.*" Desaix nodded her head vigorously. "That's the trouble with you."

"I ain't never had trouble till just now when trash with no manners comes ringin' my bell and gives a lady no mind." Evadne's eyebrows went up, pulling her head up along with them. "Now take your dirty black feet off our prop'ty and git goin'."

"You ain't the boss and you ain't tellin' me to git goin' till I see Negu."

"She ain't here."

Desaix shrugged her shoulders. "That don't bother me none. I'll wait." Languidly, she leaned against the door frame and sighed with martyrlike patience.

"She won't be back no more today," Evadne snapped.

Desaix stifled a mock yawn and drawled, "Where'd she go?"

"None of your business. She ain't here. She won't be back no more today."

"I'll wait," came Desaix's imperturbable reply.

The cook's voice rose in exasperation. "Tomorrow she might not be back neither. I don't know where she's gone. I don' go nebbin' into other folks' business."

"Non?" Desaix asked in a voice of surprise, which obviously was intended to taunt her adversary.

Evadne rose to the bait. "I mind my own business," she shrieked, "and don't you go sayin' I don'. Git off. Negu don' want to see you no time."

"That's for Negu to say." Desaix was getting irritated. "I's standin' right in this spot till Negu gits back."

"No you don't," the other woman shouted. "We don't want no gutter trash wrapped 'round our door all night." With both hands she gave Desaix a vigorous

438

shove which sent her sprawling backward across the stone floor of the veranda. Evadne slammed the door.

For a second, Desaix, taken by surprise, lay bewildered, Suddenly hot fury exploded inside her breast, and she jumped to her feet.

"You lousy bitch," she screamed, at the same time beating the door with her parasol. "Open up so I can kick you in the ass. You can't do this to me. I's gonna kill you! I'll kill you! I'll kill you!"

Desaix pounded on the door until the first wave of her anger had washed over her and reason began to assert itself, causing her to realize that beating on a heavy door was getting her nowhere. Stepping back, she raised a knee and broke the white lace parasol in two. Then she hurled the pieces against the closed door. "You stinkin' fat slob hidin' 'hind a door. I's gonna git you. All your high an' mighty airs is gittin' smeared in the dirt. You and that son'bitch you call a man ain't never goin' to throw Desaix out no more."

Jumping into the barouche, Desaix gave the horse a fierce lash and was off in a mad dash, shouting as she rode away, "I'll be back! I'll be back. I'll be back, you bitch! I'll be back!"

Desaix knew at once where she was going. In her fury and humiliation, she was no longer afraid. Wildness was rushing madly through her, spurring her along like a runaway horse.

She drove out the gate of Cher Château, careening onto the road at a crazy angle. One thought in her mind. To get to Sans Souci. They would let her in. She was afraid of no one. The guards could not stop her. She would demand to see Prophète, and if they did not take her to him immediately, she would lash out with her whip until they were no more than a bloody smear in the dirt. He would be glad she had come when he heard what she had to tell him.

Desaix let out a diabolical laugh which trailed the

carriage like the dust behind it. Tonight, she would take down the Nagshead at Cher Château.

Asya was glad that Cilla had come into the library this night to show her the clothes she was making for the baby. Cilla was glowing over the birth, two months' away, of the child she and Watusi had wanted so long, and her maid's infectious happiness somewhat dispelled Asya's uneasiness. During the day, when she had been busy with affairs of the plantation, Asya had been able to ignore the gnawing in her breast, but now that darkness was here, her problem was becoming a pest by its insistence that she recognize it. It had even injected itself between her and the books to which she had turned for relaxation after supper.

Asya was not accustomed to having misgivings about any of her actions, and it irritated her that such an inconsequential matter as firing Negu was tugging at her conscience.

It had all happened so quickly. This morning, she and Watusi had gone to the stables for their horses. He had wanted her to ride over the plantation to look at the crops. She was waiting outside the stable for her horse to be saddled, when suddenly there was a wild neighing from inside, mixed with the frightened shouts of the stable boy. Before she could go to see what was the matter, her mare came dashing out, reared on its hind legs, then loped off across the barnyard, leaped the fence, and disappeared in the woods beyond. In alarm, Asya ran into the stable. She found Gomer, the young Negro who had been saddling the horse, lying on the floor, his hands clasping his head, and moaning in pain.

"What happened? Whatever happened?" Asya demanded, her voice almost harsh with concern.

The boy, with his hands still on his head, looked up. "It's dat snake," he said looking toward the wooden box in the corner. "It cause all de trouble."

440

"Did—did it bite you?" Asya's heart sunk.

"Naw. Dambolla don' bite none. He jist havin' his fun."

"Let me look at your head." Asya pulled Gomer's hands away. Already his forehead had swelled out like a blowfish. "That's not my idea of fun," she commented drily. "What happened?"

The boy shook his head. "I dunno, but Dambolla sure has it in for dat horse. Every time he sees 'im, he rattles his tail and lets out a long hiss. I guess dis time de hiss was special long and scairt dat horse. He run like he got spirits inside 'im." Gomer's eyes grew big. "Maybe Dambolla did put spirits in 'is innards. I wunt put it past dat Dambolla none."

Anger welled up inside Asya. The whole episode was senseless. The boy could have been killed. Also, who was going to catch her favorite mare and calm her down?

"Gomer," Asya said, "go to the kitchen and have Evadne look at your head. At the same time tell her I want Negu down here at once." Her voice rose. "Do you understand? At once!"

The boy tore off toward the house, looking almost as frightened as the horse. "I git her, I git her," he called as he ran.

Asya was surprised at how quickly the old housekeeper came running down to the stables. "Did someone hurt my snake?" Negu called as she came up to Asya.

"What!" Asya almost popped with anger over the woman's audacity. "How stupid can you be?" she blazed. "A valuable horse is off breaking its neck somewhere in the woods, one of my servants gets clobbered on the head, and all you can think about is your ridiculous snake."

Without bothering to answer, Negu hurried over to the box and lifted the lid. Immediately, the head of the snake rose up. Asya shivered. Negu stroked its head, at

441

the same time talking in a voice too low for Asya to hear, but from the tone she was sure they were words of endearment. Seemingly satisfied that all was well with her pet, Negu shut and fastened the lid of the box and then turned an insolent face to Asya.

"You have your horse. I have my snake," Negu stated, her scarred lip looking more than ever like a snarl. "Each to his own choice."

"Yours is a crazy choice," Asya stormed. "A snake is a wild, dangerous creature."

"So was the horse before man tamed it," Negu countered calmly.

"At least, a horse doesn't go around frightening people."

"I don't know about that. I thought Gomer looked very frightened when he came into the kitchen."

Exasperated, Asya drew a deep breath. "We are not going to waste time. I refuse to argue with a servant. The snake must go."

"Why?" Negu's voice rose in anger.

"Because I say so," Asya snapped back. "I happen to be the mistress here. I own Cher Château. You are nothing more than a housekeeper paid for your services."

Negu's eyes closed until they were mere slits in her face, giving her a mean look. For an instant Asya thought the woman would strike her, but Negu's clenched fists remained rigid at her side. She seemed turned to stone.

Finally Negu spoke in a lifeless voice: "Very well. As you wish. Dambolla and I will both leave. Sorry we bothered you for so long." Without another word, she walked briskly from the stable.

No sooner had Negu departed than something came unplugged at the bottom of Asya's stomach, and her wrath drained away. She was uncertain. Perhaps she had been too vehement, but there was no reason to be

442

concerned about it now, she told herself. The horses were ready and Watusi was waiting. His only comment as they rode out of the stable yard was a quiet, "I shall miss her. Somehow, she belonged here."

That evening in the library, Asya argued with her conscience. I do not care. She should have gone long ago. She was nothing but a meddlesome old woman. Acted as if the place was hers, and I was but an irresponsible child. I did the right thing.

But Asya was still troubled when Cilla tiptoed to the doorway and timidly inquired, "May I come in?"

"Of course," Asya answered, welcoming a respite from the wrestling going on within her breast. "Anytime."

"Well," Cilla answered, "I wasn't sure whether you were in a sociable mood yet. I understand you got angry and dismissed Negu today."

"It was about time. She was becoming entirely too overbearing." Asya was annoyed to find herself on the defensive. She did not have to explain her actions to anyone.

Cilla shook her head. "Shouldn't have done it," she said ominously. "The voodoo gods won't like it. You know that Negu was a priestess. A real high-up one. Next to Joswee."

Asya laughed, but even to herself it did not sound very mirthful. "Rubbish. You're a Catholic, Cilla. You know better. There are no such things as voodoo gods."

"Negu was a Catholic too. We're all Catholic. We go to church. We pray the Rosary. We listen to Abbé Brille. But there are so many of us," the girl said matter-of-factly, "that the laos help out. They're the black folks' gods. Jesus and His mother and the saints have been used to white Catholics for hundreds of years. We're sort of late in making God's acquaintance, so the

443

laos, who knew us from when we were pagans in Africa, help God out."

Asya gave the Negress a look of disgust. "Cilla, you know better. You're educated."

"Because I'm educated," the girl answered, somewhat indignantly, "doesn't mean I have to slight old friends who have always been good to me. God understands that. The laos are His helpers."

"Bien. Bien," Asya answered with a sarcastic edge in her voice. "That's why Negu kept Dambolla as a pet in its box in the stable. Nice to have a lao handy."

Cilla shook her head in disapproval. "That snake was more than just an ordinary lao. That was Dambolla. He's the holiest of all. He's the top god."

"Don't be stupid. How can a cold, slithery snake be God?"

"That's easy to understand. They taught us in catechism class that God came down to earth in the form of man. God made man, and He made snakes too. So he can come down in any form he wants to."

"What makes you think He wants to be a snake? Why not a kitten, or something likable?"

Cilla looked disgusted. "You're arguing too much about religion. It isn't a geography lesson or a problem in raising tobacco. It's a feeling. Like love. You simply accept it because it is."

"But why an ugly snake?" Asya persisted. "What gives you the idea that's your great god?"

Cilla's eyes grew large and her voice dropped into a hushed whisper. "Have you ever looked at a snake's eyes?" she asked. "They're round and can see in all directions at the same time. Those are god eyes. God can see everything. So can a snake." Cilla gave a sharp nod to emphasize the fact. "That's the proof."

"That's enough dumb talk." Asya was weary of the subject. "What's that you have in your arms?"

Immediately, Cilla's face lightened. "Baby clothes," she answered, her voice rising in excitement. "I want to show you some of the things I've made." She placed the bundle on the table, from which she extracted a tiny white garment. "Do you think this saque is too little."

"Oh, Cilla, it's precious," Asya enthused, her problem with Negu immediately forgotten. "Of course it's not too little. Babies are tiny." Lovingly, she took the saque in her hands and placed it against her cheek. "It's soft and cuddly," she cooed. "Baby will love it."

"And here are some more," Cilla said eagerly as she spread various articles of clothing out on the table. "How do you like them?"

"They're beautiful," Asya admired as she gently caressed each little garment. "They're works of art. I especially love the nighties. You've scalloped the edges of the sleeves to match the color of the bow at the neck. I like that." She gave a happy laugh and said to the beaming mother-to-be, "I can just see our baby's fat little chin resting right in the middle of this blue bow."

"And look at the blanket," Cilla said, her eyes radiant. "It has the lily design all through it."

"Wasn't that hard to knit?"

"No," Cilla answered dreamily, "because the whole time I worked on it, I could almost feel my baby's warm body wrapped inside." She smiled with the serenity of a Madonna.

Asya put her arms about the girl's neck. "I'm so happy for you and Watusi. And me too," she added. "At last I'm going to be an aunt, and that's a big occasion. It means I'm not an orphan anymore. I'm starting to have family, like other people." For a brief moment she thought of Etienne. If she ever had a child of her own, she wanted it to be his. No, she flicked the

445

thought from her mind. He was miles away. No point in thinking about him now.

"Cilla," her eyes brightened with anticipation, "tomorrow, let's drive to the cabinetmaker's shop and see how he's coming along with the baby furniture. I'm anxious to have the nursery finished."

"Watusi and I are grateful to you, Asya, for giving us the nursery furniture. It is something we'll always have. Like our nice thoughts of you."

"Sisters always do things for each other. And you're the only sister I have," Asya reminded Cilla. "Besides, I'm tired of seeing only great beds and big chairs and big candelabra, and big everything else. It's time we had a cradle in the house and little chairs for little people, and tiny little doll clothes and—" Asya sighed with contentment. "It's all going to be so wonderful, our having this baby, Cilla. We'll feel like two little girls playing with a doll. Did you know," Asya paused a moment as remembered loneliness tugged at her breast, "did you know that I never had a doll? Never."

"I had lots of dolls," Cilla answered.

"That's because you had a mama and papa."

"No, they didn't make me the dolls. It was Negu."

"Negu!" Asya was astounded. "I didn't think Negu knew what dolls or little girls looked like."

"Oh, yes," Cilla went on enthusiastically. "She's always been wonderful. She used to make me beautiful dresses and when I outgrew them, she cut them up and made them into dolls. Once she even made a doll large enough to fit the dress. For years, I called that one *ma petite soeur.*"

"I'm surprised." Asya's conscience was rebuking her again. "Why would Negu do a thing like that?"

"I don't know except when I thanked her she poohpoohed her generosity and said she enjoyed making things for me, because I reminded her of another little girl about my age who was very dear to her. She lived far away, and Negu might never see her." Cilla gave a sad little smile. "I shall miss Negu. She was like having a grandmother around."

Asya said nothing, and it was during this pause that she became conscious of the sounds in the night. At first they reminded her of the buzzings of a distant swarm of bees on the move, but then she remembered with apprehension that bees did not migrate at night. Asya froze, her ears straining to recognize the noise. It drew nearer. She ran into the hall, to the top of the stairs, for now she knew what it was. It was the voice of a mob approaching Cher Château. She looked down to the floor below and saw that Watusi was already in the hall, standing by the front door, his hands gripping the bolt, listening, terror on his face. Fear clutched Asya's heart, causing it to pound hysterically against her chest. She could hear it all now. The cacophony of curses and jeers and arrogant threats screaming in the night.

Fear made her mouth too dry to call out. Cilla came to her side and together they stood there, clutching hands so tightly that their nails dug into each other's skin.

"Run!" Watusi shouted. "Run! Run to the attic and hide."

But they could not. Their feet were heavy and their legs had lost all power to move.

A pounding started on the front door. So strong was it that it shook the floor beneath Asya's feet. The door must hold. But the door gave, and in the flames of burning torches Asya saw a stream of wildly cavorting devils come spewing in from damnation.

She sprang to life. With her hand still clutching Cilla's, Asya dragged the girl along the hall. But the marauders were close behind. No time left to reach the attic. Asya pulled Cilla into her bedroom and slammed and locked the door just ahead of their screeching pursuers.

"What shall we do? They'll break down the door," Cilla sobbed.

Asya's eyes went to the large French windows. "Quick. Blow out the candles and we'll try to escape out the balcony."

But they were too late. Even as Asya spoke, two men stepped from the darkness of the balcony into her room. Asya stared in horror. They were two Negroes. One was tall and potbellied, and his bald head in the candlelight resembled a bloated black egg. He had a leer on his face as he eyed Cilla. "This one's mine," he announced and walked purposefully toward the cringing girl. Cilla came to life and ran to the highboy where she pressed against its side as though she would push herself through the wood.

Anger welled up in Asya, and she was no longer afraid. "Let her alone," she shouted, running toward Cilla. "Can't you see she's going to have a baby?"

"Good," the man snickered. "The bigger the belly, the better I kin bounce."

She tried to run to Cilla, but before she could reach her, a heavy hand grabbed Asya by the back of her dress, ripping it down to the waist.

"You're my honey," came the lecherous voice of the other man. His fingers were at once at her neck and he tore the front of her dress from her body. His big hands squeezed her breasts and he pulled her to him, his thighs already pressed tightly against hers.

It happened so fast that Asya had not seen the man's face. All she knew was that he was filthy. She smelled his unwashed body with its stench of old sweat, and his thick bushy beard scratched her face as he kissed her with wet lips, all the time his big slobbering tongue pushing against her teeth in its effort to enter her mouth. She clawed at his beard, but that amused him, for without taking his lips from her, he laughed. This caused him to slobber and he took a

448

fiendish delight in sliding his mouth around and over hers in the wetness of his spittle.

Strengthened by her revulsion, Asya managed to get her hands in his thickly matted hair and pull back his head. She got a look at her assailant. He was more furry animal than human. He was not young, for gray streaked the black of his hair, and his beard stuck out from his chin and cheeks like a wasp's nest from a bough. His brows looked like two black caterpillars resting above his eyes, and his large nose was flattened across his face, losing itself in the hair of the temples.

"I fucks better than I looks, gal. You'll see. I's a sight bigger man than it 'pears on the outside." He snickered, and as he did, a yellow pussy discharge bubbled out of one nostril.

"Let me go," Asya screamed. "I'll kill you. Don't you touch me."

"I's already touchin' you, and you feels good," came his answer in a sensuous tone. Asya pulled back his head as hard as she could, but not hard enough to break his firm hold on one breast while the other hand slid down across her naked stomach. With a superhuman effort, Asya brought up a knee and caught her attacker between his legs. He slumped to the floor with a sharp cry of pain.

Immediately, Asya whirled around to locate Cilla. She could not see her, but she knew at once where she was. The fat-bellied Negro was on the bed, his pants down, his big rear end stuck up like the ass of a black pig. From beneath him came the sound of whimpering.

Asya grabbed a heavy silver candlestick, burning candles and all. She ran to the bed and, holding the weapon high in both hands, crashed it down on the black, egglike skull.

At the same time, the sky above must have lost its supports and with an ear-splitting roar cracked down upon Asya's head. Pain and darkness engulfed her, and she remembered nothing more.

Chapter Thirty-two

Asya was swinging from a crescent moon. Her hands
were caught on the tip and she could not get down. It
was cold up here in the sky. She could feel the wind,
and the sky was so heavy. Perhaps that was why her
hands were tied to the moon. So she could not move
out from under the sky. Her head hurt. Why must she
hold up the sky with her head? The sky was too heavy.

She could kick her legs. She could kick all about,
but there was no place to rest her feet. She was tired of
dangling, and her wrists ached from the fiery thongs
that bound them. Her outstretched arms hurt with the
weight of her body. She could not be alone, for the
noise of screaming and shouting and singing was blowing up her head until she thought it would burst from
the pressure. Why did someone not help her? Asya
opened her mouth to call out, but if her voice came,
she did not hear it. The noise grew louder, banging like
hammers against her temples. What was going on?
This was crazy singing and what sounded like dancing. She could hear bare feet against the wood.
Wood? Why was there wood in the sky? Drums began
to beat. A thousand drums. Or was it a thousand hands
beating out time upon her head? Suddenly, hysterical
screams cut into the conglomeration of sounds like
lightning zigzagging across a black sky. They were
cries of terror, and Asya's eyes shot open. Only then
did she realize that they had been closed. But all she
saw was fire in the distance, waves of fire, and her eyes

involuntarily shut against its brightness. This must be Judgment Day, she thought, and I'm caught up here on the moon. They'll forget about me, and I'll be here forever.

With some foolish idea of attracting attention, Asya kicked out, but rough hands caught her legs and tied them together with coarse rope. She opened her eyes and saw the bare back of a black man, glowing in the firelight. Having secured her legs, he slithered away like a snake. Painfully, Asya raised her head. She had to force it to get it to move against the noise of all creation sounding off at the same time. Just ahead was the fire. It was made by burning torches held high in the hands of a mob of crazy dervishes. From their mouths came the maddening noise she was hearing. Slowly, Asya lifted her heavy lids and looked about. She was in a forest. It must be. There were trees, green trees, everywhere.

Asya felt a breeze on her body, and despite the fire of the torches, she was cold. Suddenly, she realized she was naked. She felt exposed, as if all the world were staring at her, and she tried to pull up her legs to hide her bareness. Asya looked toward the spasm of humanity whirling just ahead, but no one seemed to notice her.

Except for the drummers who stood about the edges, the rest of the wild mob was crazily gyrating on a wooden platform. Like that problem of the Dark Ages, they had all laughed about back in school. How many angels can dance on the head of a pin at the same time? Silly thing to think about. In the firelight, these looked like devils. Did devils take up more room than angels? From the way they jumped about, Asya thought so.

The formation of the dancers changed. The drums stopped and everyone leaped off the floor. Now Asya could see that the dance floor was nothing more than a large barn door. What a long way to carry a door just to dance on it. What was the matter with using the ground? But something strange was going on before her. The dancers were suddenly very still, and their silence blotted away the ear-splitting noises which had filled the forest. Everyone was watching the floor and in the firelight they stood as immovable as the trees about them. It was a ghoulish scene. Slowly, almost imperceptibly from where she was, Asya saw the floor move. Or did she? Now it was still. She must have imagined it, but even so, she knew it had moved. There it was again. Slowly, it was tilting to one side. Asya watched in fascination. Was it—the thought chilled her—voodoo? She wanted to make the Sign of the Cross as the nuns had always claimed it shooed away devils. Something moved out from under the wooden door, something dark, and as Asya watched it moved again and the light from the torches fell upon it. It was a human hand.

Asya's cry of shocked disbelief was swallowed up by the sudden screams of the dancers as they leaped back upon the barn door, shouting, swirling, stomping as though they would pummel the floor beneath them down into the bowels of the earth. Asya went limp. Her body detached itself from the bindings about her wrists, leaving them with their pain somewhere above as she slid down into darkness.

But even in darkness, Asya could not shut out the noise. From far off it came, but it was still there, pounding at her eardrums, stabbing at her temples. It was an evil thing, which would not let her free.

At last the noise stopped and Asya drifted away on her blanket of blackness.

An intense heat hit her body and brought Asya back to consciousness. It struck so suddenly that when she opened her eyes and saw great flames brushing the treetops, fear cleared Asya's mind. Now she remembered. The flat-nosed Negro. The horny hand sliding across her stomach. The sound of the candlestick smashing down upon the skull of the ugly egglike head. But why was she here? Asya tried to swing her body away from the fire, but that was useless, since the movement sent excruciating pain through her wrists, like knives cutting through. Some distance from the first fire, a new fire shot into the sky, spluttering and leaping as it strained to devour the boughs over head. In the glare, Asya saw people scurrying about; however, with the quick shadows and flickering lights, she could not make out who they were.

After their first outburst, the flames died down, content to lick at the stacks of logs piled on either side of the barn door. So it was not a nightmare after all.

The hushed business of the scurrying figures gave the night an ominous air. Like people preparing for the visit of Death. Then a new sound burst through the forest. It seemed almost ludicrous in the funereal atmosphere. It was the squeal of a pig. By the light of the fire, Asya saw it being dragged across the earth in the direction of the tree where she was hanging. Asya stiffened in fear as though by tightening her body she could shrink from the sight of these unknown persons. However, they passed her by, dragging the protesting pig along. They stopped at the tree beside her. With an uncanny feeling of horror yet to come, Asya watched, fascinated, as a rope was flung across a branch and the pig was swung up, its feet tied together the same as hers. Then the crowd quietly flowed away, Asya and the pig seemingly forgotten. A feeling of anger rankled in Asya's breast. She resented the ignominy of being in the same predicament as a pig, and she wanted to shout out her indignation, but common sense urged her to be still.

There was something macabre about the whole scene. All the moving figures were now standing motionless about the barn door, their hands raised straight above their heads. By the light from the two huge fires on either side, Asya could see they were naked, their bodies shining like polished statues dappled with shadows from the dancing flames. Then quietly, almost imperceptibly, came the sound of a drum far off in the darkness amongst the trees. Silence. It beat again, slightly louder, like a spirit calling that it was coming. A third time it came. It was closer. And no one moved. Suddenly the drum crashed through the night in a rash of beats, an arrogant voice shouting out its edicts. At the same time, a large woman leaped to the center of the barn door and stood motionless, her hands above her head. Her large fat breasts reached down over a bloated stomach, and her bulging navel reminded Asya of the eye of a Cyclops. The voice of the drum called out again and the woman began to dance. Slowly at first, with a languid, swaying motion to her hips. The drum beat faster, and was joined by the rhythmic voices of countless boulatiers beating out their encouragement. The big woman, with her hands still immobile above her head, swung her hips faster and faster until she looked like a great madly tolling bell. Someone jumped out upon the dance floor and placed a machete in the woman's hands. Immediately, the air split with the crashing beats of stronger drums while at the same time the dancer became a dervish, whirling and leaping in such a frenzy that the sound of her big breasts flapping against the skin of her belly could be heard through the night. When the drums, having reached a new peak of frenzy, relented, and the woman on the barn door could slow down, foam was falling from her mouth and sliding in a river of white down between her breasts and over her heaving stomach. The crowd took up a chanting shout, an accolade to the hounci for a performance well done.

Swiftly, for a woman who had already engaged in such rigorous activity, the dancer ran from the floor toward Asya, brandishing the machete as she came. The scream in Asya's throat died in relief when the hounci passed her by and ran to where the pig was strung up. There she paused, and a man sprang up and handed her a large bowl. Holding it below the animal's stomach, the dancer raised the machete and cut off one of the pig's teats. Quickly she severed one on the other side. Stunned, Asya watched as the rest of the pig's nipples were amputated and its blood oozed down its body into the large bowl. At the completion of this operation, the mood of the crowd changed. The jubilant chant became the wailing of a dirge, and the drums died down to overtones of sadness. Then with slow, mournful steps, two men shouldering a long spike between them approached the wildly squealing pig. The hounci handed them the large bowl, and, placing the edge of the machete against the animal's throat, slit it from ear to ear. As the blood gushed from the pig's maw, the men caught it in the basin. The excess splashed down over their arms and chests, leaving bright red splotches on their black skin. When the basin overflowed, the men held it toward the large priestess who pressed her white-foam-covered belly against the edge. Reverently she held her hands over the blood and blessed it as a priest might have done. Then she placed the palms of both hands over her face and slowly slid them down over her mouth and chin, against her throat and between her breasts, until the foam collected in a white ball upon her stomach. With a quick movement of her hands, she flicked it onto the sea of blood, where it lay like a fluffy mound of white meringue. The woman reached out, and, taking the bowl of pig's blood, raised it above her head without spilling a drop. Looking up to the heavens, she mumbled a low incantation.

Suddenly, the priestess opened her mouth and emitted a long loud, banshee call that screamed through the night like the voice of a macabre spirit warning all nature of its presence. With her head still thrown back, the hounci poured the contents of the basin into her open mouth, from where it spurted down over her chin and throat and flowed over her naked body. When no more blood came from the basin above her head, and only the cloud of white foam remained, one of the men reached up and, reverently taking the bowl into both his hands, knelt beside the priestess. Slowly, one by one, the men stepped from the crowd and, after rubbing their stomachs three times against the bloodied one of the priestess, folded their hands in an attitude of prayer, bowed from the hips, and touched their noses into the cloudlike foam lying in the bowl. As each man raised his head, revealing a white-tipped nose, the women, bunched together back by the first fire, called out to him in a cacophony of bloodcurdling screeches. The man then selected one of the women and together they ran onto the barn door where, after he had rubbed some of the blood from his belly onto hers, they began to rub their bellies against each other in a slow, sensuous dance.

When there was no more foam left in the basin, the man who held it let out a mournful wail, and those who had as yet not gone through the ceremony joined their voices to his. Angry shouts came from the women who still waited for men by the fire. The hounci, holding her head back so as not to spill the blood which remained in her mouth, put her arms straight out and slowly walked toward the pig where it hung from the tree. When her fingertips touched the animal, she spat out the rest of the blood, splattering it over the sow's body. A shout went up from the waiting men, and someone flashed a machete and cut down the pig. A spike was stuck between its tied legs and with its head hanging at a crazy angle, it was carried to the fire where the women were gathered. There, the animal was placed on top of the burning firewood, a corpse on a pyre, and its blood caused the flames to leap upward in great sizzling tongues, brushing the sky and seemingly setting it afire. The stench from the burning flesh of the pig made Asya gag and she became conscious of a pall of smoke crawling across the tops of the trees like a lid over hell.

Letting out a great shout, the women without partners ran toward the second fire, where they danced and frolicked in an obvious effort to attract the attention of the men who still clustered about the hounci. The men moaned and dropped upon their knees in a pleading attitude before the priestess. Slowly, she turned toward Asya, her large black eyes caverns of flames in the firelight, and Asya knew she was next. Her blood turned cold, drained away, and in its place her hysterical heart pumped tremors of fear through her veins. Asya pulled up her knees to kick back the approaching murderers and she tried to scream, but fear froze her throat, and no sound came. Viselike hands clamped upon her legs and thighs and arms, encasing her like a coffin, and she could not move. A weakness came over Asya, absorbing her resistance. She felt nothing. Life had gone, leaving only a body behind to watch itself die.

The bowl was pushed against the top of her stomach. If it was cold or hard, Asya did not know. All she knew was that it was there. Off somewhere, the crowd was still shouting and the drums were noisy, but that was far away, and her ears rejected the sounds. The large naked woman standing before her raised the machete high in the air. But before she could use it, a tall figure sprang out from nowhere and tore it from her hand. The naked woman turned upon him in outraged fury, but when her eyes fell upon her adversary, her bravado vanished.

"Joswee." Her voice quivered in disbelief and fear. "I—I—" she stammered, but the big turbaned man knocked her to the ground.

"You fool," he shouted.

The drums wavered in their beat and died off in confusion. The voices of those chanters about Asya grew silent, and the silence became a wave, spreading

457

out through the enclosure, blotting out all human sound. Only the snap of the fire and its occasional hiss of protest as it licked the wet blood of the pig broke the stillness. With the machete still clutched in his hand, the intruder stood fierce and angry as his eyes swept over the bewildered people about him. "You fools!"

Now a slow, measured chant was heard, and all eyes turned in the direction from which it came. Wide, staring eyeballs in black faces polka-dotted the night. Asya was confused. The tall man in the turban was familiar. Not that it mattered, but he had interrupted the ceremony. Why was everyone waiting? Asya sighed. She was tired. She was heavy with weariness. She sighed again. Suddenly she realized she was no longer restricted by the walls of her coffin. She could move. She could breathe. She could swing her legs. Forward. Backward. She was not dead. She was hanging from a tree. Like a— Like a what? A silhouette image of another figure suspended from a limb came into her mind. What had that been? She remembered. Like a pig.

The voice of the chanter drew nearer. Low, menacing. Evil. It was a woman. She came out from among the trees and in a slow, but unalterable step walked toward the fallen hounci who now scrambled to her knees. The chanter wore a bright yellow kerchief about her head, and a huge serpent encircled her body, its head thrust forward like the figurehead of a ship. The woman moved on. Her lip was drawn far back in a snarl, giving the effect of a wild animal baring its teeth to its prey. It was Negu!

A gasp rustled through the crowd of watchers. A gasp of fear and apprehension, and some started to back away.

"Stay where you are!" Negu ordered. "Stay so you may see how Dambolla punishes those who sin against him."

With a look of hate, she stared down upon the large woman who knelt before her. "So, Desaix," she accused in a voice hard with impending doom, "it is you who took down the wanga. You removed the Nagshead."

"No, no," Desaix shouted in denial. "It was Prophète. It's him what did it."

"You lie!" Her accuser spat upon her. "Even to death you lie. Prophète is a coward, but he is strong enough to obey Dambolla."

"But he wanted it. Me, I don' want it." Desaix spread out her hands. "I got a house. He's the one what stealed it. It was his men what taked it."

"But you took down the Nagshead," Negu hammered out her accusation, at the same time placing her hand on the head of the serpent and slowly moving it closer to Desaix's face. "Tell me the truth."

"*Oui. Oui.*" The cringing hounci nodded vigorously, her eyes bulging with fear. "*Oui.* But it was for him. For Prophète. Dambolla, he know that. I don' want it. It's all Prophète's fault. You talk to him. I don't steal nothin' from nobody."

Negu's eyes narrowed with hate. "All through the revolution Dambolla watched over the Drapeaux plantation for my granddaughter, and now you have taken it from her. You will die."

"Your granddaughter?" Desaix jumped to her feet. "What you sayin'?"

"Asya is my granddaughter. She is the child of my child, Celeste, and the daughter of M. Drapeaux. Cher Château is rightfully hers."

Negu released the head of the snake. In one swift movement it darted for Desaix's face and struck her in the temple. She screamed, but even as she did, the cry died in her throat. Her eyes puffed out and her face twitched with spasms. She reached out, aimlessly clawed the air and then slumped to the ground. Desaix lay still, her face turned upwards toward the red sky, the whites

459

of her large eyes glistening in the light from the fires like two glass eggs in a dark nest. Desaix was dead.

The giant with the red turban came to Asya. Gently, he put his arm about her and held her so she would not fall while he cut the rope that tied her to the tree. His arm was strong and warm, and Asya felt herself slipping into pleasant oblivion.

The sun was just coming up over the horizon as Joswee made his way through a sea of solemn black faces. There was silence in the forest as he marched slowly past, his arms draped with the limp form of Negu's granddaughter.

Chapter Thirty-three

Asya knew she was not lying in her own bed. This one was hard and its covers were rough about her body. There was so much darkness about her that even when her body tried to awake, her mind rebelled. Asya wanted to sleep on. To awaken was to be born again, and some inner core was rejecting this new life.

Asya heard a stir and her eyes opened. She was in a small enclosure with rough wooden walls. At one end was a table with a single candle. Slowly her eyes found a solitary figure sitting in a chair in a shadowed corner. It was Negu. Negu in whose image she would walk in this new life once she let herself be born into it. Asya closed her eyes. She did not want to come to life. If she lay still, perhaps they would think her dead and bury her.

But no. Asya felt a strong arm slide under her and she let herself be lifted to a sitting position. A hand gripped her chin and something hard, like a bowl, was placed against her lips. "Drink *ma cherie*," a soft voice urged. It was Negu. Asya closed her mouth and held her lips shut with her teeth. She wanted to be left along.

"Come, come, you are much better now. It is time for you to be up and moving," Negu encouraged.

Without answering, Asya shook her head.

"Do you want to stay in bed for always like a crippled old woman?" It was the coaxing tone one might use with a child.

461

Asya nodded. Her disagreeableness was making her feel stronger, and she tried to shake off the arm supporting her, but to no avail.

"Drink the soup. It will make you better."

Asya stiffened her body and tightened her lips. She did not want to be better. She did not want to be a part of this new existence.

Something clamped her nostrils shut and she could not breathe. Asya had to open her mouth before her stomach exploded, and when she did, the bowl slid between her teeth and a liquid, hot with spice, flowed down her throat. It burned and she swallowed it quickly to get it out of her mouth, but Negu just kept pouring more in. Asya wanted to push her away, but someone else was holding her arms against her sides and she could not move. She was angry and tried to protest, but her mouth only filled up with more of the strong liquid. She choked. Negu freed her nose and took the bowl from her lips. Asya commenced to cough and struggled for breath until she thought her stomach had come up past her torn throat and hurled its contents out through her mouth and nose. Negu took a rag and wiped her face, and the strong arms that were holding her released Asya. She gasped, "I can clean it—myself."

Asya wiped her face which was damp with perspiration and blew her nose. She sat hunched over, trying to take in deep breaths, her shoulders heaving with the effort, while Negu watched with concern on her thin face.

As Asya continued to cough, Negu walked away and returned with a chunk of bread in her hand. "Here," she said, holding it out. "Eat this. It will clear your throat."

Asya slapped it from her hand. "Go away," she panted. "Leave me alone." Gradually her breath became steady and Asya was conscious of a strange warmth in her body. Her heart beat fast and her blood raced through her limbs. A restlessness permeated her and it was impossible to be still. Flinging back the cover, Asya jumped from the bed. The room spun and she would have fallen had Negu not caught her and set her down on the side of the bed.

"Not so fast. You have been ill a long time and must take it slow."

Asya leaned against the black woman, but when the room steadied she pushed Negu aside and got to her feet. Asya stood and looked around. Except for a stream of sunlight coming in the open doorway, the room was without light. Asya realized she was in a dirty shack. Feeling contaminated, she walked toward the doors.

Immediately, Negu came after her, holding the cover from the bed. "You are naked, Asya," she called. "Wrap this around yourself till I find you something to wear."

Asya looked down and was startled, not because she was unclothed, but because her skin looked black in the dimly lighted room.

"It doesn't matter," she said bitterly. "I'm getting used to going without clothes." Again she started for the door.

Before Asya could reach it, however, a tall figure sprang from the shadows near the bed and barred her way. He wore a turban around his head. She remembered now. It was Joswee. It must have been he who held her while Negu fed her the soup.

"Listen to your *grand-mère*," he said brusquely.

"Don't you tell me what to do too." Asya was angry and tried to shove the man backward out the door, but he stood firm, his arms folded across his chest.

"Get out of my way," the girl ordered.

His eyes looked beyond her as if he were unaware of her presence. He said to Negu, "Have you found her a dress? She cannot go outside this way."

"Why all the sudden concern for my modesty?"

463

Asya flung out at them. "First you undress me, and now you insist I put something on. Why don't you make up your minds?"

Wearily, Negu walked over to where some clothes hung in a bunch from a peg on the wall. She selected a brown calico dress and held it out to Asya. "This will have to do for now." She spoke slowly. She looked very tired.

Asya drew back in revulsion. "I won't wear a black woman's rag. I'll go naked first. Where are my own clothes?"

Negu gave Asya a look of pity, and her lips quivered as though she were uncertain of what to say. Joswee answered for her. "It's all there is now," he said with authority in his voice. "Put it on."

"Non," Asya snapped back. "I want my own clothes. What have you done with them? Stolen them? Just because I happen to be the granddaughter of a nigger servant, doesn't mean I should suddenly wear nigger clothes."

Asya thought Joswee was going to slap her. He raised a hand, but Negu quickly said something in patois, which Asya did not catch, and he slowly lowered it with a great effort. His voice cracked like a whip. "Put it on. If you say just one more word of sass to your *grand-mère,* I'll spank your bottom."

Asya glared in defiance at the man who barred her way, but she knew he meant what he said. Rudely she snatched the proffered dress from Negu. "Don't think you two can keep me here in the bosom of the family," she shouted at them as she angrily pulled the dress over her head. "I'm not setting up housekeeping in a field hand's filthy shack. I'm going back to Cher Château, and don't you, neither one of you, ever set foot there again." Asya stepped up to Negu and put her face close to the scarred one. "From now on, I don't know you, and I'm not grateful for anything

464

you've done for me. I didn't ask you to save my life. I'd rather be dead than be a nigger."

With that, she pushed Joswee aside and tore through the doorway into the sunshine. The pebbles on the hard ground hurt her bare feet, but she did not care. She was running away from the blackness. Black walls, black shacks, the smell of black skin. Even the shadows the trees cast on the road made her flinch, for they reminded her of the race to which she now belonged, and she ran faster so as to be done with them. Asya wanted sunshine. Her side hurt, and she was forced to slow her pace. Suddenly, the earth rose up and she put out her hands to hold it back, but it smacked her in the face. Asya remembered nothing more.

When consciousness returned, Asya found herself back in the hard bed. There was something cold on her head, and she reached up to find that it was a wet rag. She threw it on the floor. Negu must be ministering again. She wanted nothing from that woman.

Asya closed her eyes. Maybe sleep would come again and blot away her changed world. As she lay, trying to court sleep, her hand rubbed idly over the mattress. She stiffened. She who had lain between embroidered linen sheets and under silken feather ticks was now resting on coarse sacking, filled with straw. Sleep was out of the question. Asya felt the need to move. Her body was finished with rest and would not be lulled. Her flesh won out over spirit and she sat up. There was no sunshine coming through the door. Asya saw that it was night. The light now came from a small fireplace. A black iron pot hung there, blowing steam out from around its lid. Asya sniffed. She knew the aroma. It was chicken boiled with shallots. Looking around, Asya saw that she was alone. She swung her feet to the floor and stood up. This time she would take it easy. She must not faint again.

Carefully, for she felt light-headed, Asya walked to

465

the fire and lifted the lid of the cook pot. Dumplings! Suddenly, she realized she was starved. She saw a gourd hanging by the side of the fireplace and dipped it into the soup. Then she sat down on a stool by the table and tried to drink, but the broth was too hot. The churning of her empty stomach made her impatient and she blew into the gourd in an attempt to cool its contents. Already I have the manners of a field hand, she thought, and feeling a slight twinge of conscience she fleetingly looked around for a spoon. But she was hungry and there was none. So she blew harder. Asya drank the burning broth, and the pieces of chicken wings she ate with her fingers. She threw the cleaned bones into the fire and, when she finished, she wiped the grease from her hands on the skirt of the brown calico and cleaned her mouth against its sleeves.

Asya sat by the fire. It was warm and bright and when her eyes wandered to the dark corners of the room, the flames drew them back. She did not think. Just sat there. She did not want to think, although she knew she would eventually have to plan some action. But for now, she was content to have her body toasted in this warmth, her mind lulled, her stomach full. Her eyelids became heavy and would not stay open and she nodded. With effort, Asya dragged herself up from the stool, using the table for support. Through half-closed eyes, she saw the bed, and putting her arms out for balance, she felt herself floating toward it. Sleep. Sleep. Some other time she would think.

It was day when Asya awakened. She saw it through the open doorway. It had laid a triangle of golden sunshine across the earthen floor. For a while Asya lay and looked at it from the bed. The light beckoned her to get up and meet the day. In the sunlight, everything would be fine. It was only the darkness which made one despair. But first, she must go home. At Cher Château, she could think. There she was protected.

There she was supreme. There she could shut out the blackness in her blood.

Quickly, Asya jumped from the bed. The earth was cold to her bare feet, and its chill made her tingle with life. Her body felt strong and rested. Asya threw back her head in arrogance. Today she could fight. Today she could do anything. In that mood, she stepped through the doorway and out into the sunshine. But the coaxing sunbeams had lied to her. She saw only the droppings of primitive man. Pieces of broken gourds, dried skins of oranges and the spears of a wilted pineapple top, sharp bits of coconut shells and rotten banana peels littered the ground. The carcasses of fowl, long since picked clean, caught the sun on their bleached bones, and dirty feathers lay scattered among the debris like clouds of gray dust. Scraggly chickens pecked in the dirt and noisly complained over the paucity of their findings. Stones, broken twigs, and mud holes filled with stagnant water added to the look of untidiness. A little black boy, wearing only a short white undershirt with a tear across the front, came running across the yard. He slowed down by one of the hens that was engrossed in its digging. Taking careful aim, he began to urinate, hitting the busy little fowl smack on its tail feathers with his stream of water. When it flapped its wings and strutted off in noisy indignation, the boy laughed and ran after it, still on target.

A movement caught her eye, and Asya turned to see a goat tethered to a rotten post by a clump of dusty bushes. A woman sat on a stool, milking the animal. It was Negu. Now Asya recognized the odor of which she had been half aware since she had emerged from the shack. Holding her nose, she approached the Negress. "There's an awful stink here," she said in disgust.

The woman did not answer. The only sound was that of the milk hissing from the udder of the goat into the wooden bucket.

Asya removed her hand from her nose. "Where am I?" she demanded.

Negu answered in a flat voice. "This is Peter's home. He moved out so that you might have a place in which to recover."

"Where did he go?"

Negu shrugged. "He didn't say. He has many relatives. Perhaps he is with one of them."

Asya had never been to this part of her plantation, since where her workmen lived was of no interest to her, but she had to admit that she was revulsed by the lowliness of her supervisor's home. He was a poor reflection on Cher Château and she certainly would speak to him once she got the reins back in her hands again. She looked around, but was unsure of exactly where she was. To cover her uncertainty, she asked in a haughty voice, "Which direction do I take to get to Cher Château?"

For answer, Negu pointed to a path which ran beside a woods.

"Is it very far?"

"What is far? Peter walked it. Maybe you can."

"Maybe I can't," Asya snapped. "Perhaps you had better send for a carriage. After all, somebody stole my shoes."

Negu raised her dark eyes and gave Asya a penetrating look. Then she dropped them back to the task of milking. "Did you forget," she said quietly, "that you fired me? You will have to order your own carriage."

"Merci for nothing. I'll walk."

Seething, Asya started toward the woods. She hoped never to see the former housekeeper again. The impudent old woman! And yet, even as Asya denounced Negu, she was aware of a little twinge of conscience shaking a reproving finger. She had not conducted herself as a granddaughter should. The thought angered her. If the only family she was ever to have was a nig-

ger *grand-mère,* then she preferred to be an orphan.
She had gotten along fine as an orphan.

The stones along the path hurt her feet. Even the
dust was coarse and abrasive. Asya wished she had
some shoes. She was no peasant. She was a wealthy
landowner, a gentlewoman, and she did not want big
flat feet from walking barefooted. A gentlewoman?
Would her former friends accept her back into their
world if they knew she had colored blood? Her friends
were white. Not even mulattoes were admitted to the
social circle of Asya's white friends. Perhaps sometimes
for business, but never for friendship. Asya pouted.
Gossipy servants! By now, everyone in Haiti would
have heard that Negu was her grandmother. She could
see her friends hiding their mouths behind jeweled fans
as they whispered the awful truth about her birth.

So intent had Asya been on her thoughts, at first she
did not notice the terrain through which she was passing. But now, she became conscious that everything
about her was charred. The path had widened into a
road which was littered with tree limbs from which
brown leaves, dead and crisp, still hung. The few trees
that still stood leaned their blackened trunks crazily
against each other like mourners weeping on each
other's shoulders. Shocked, her eyes went to the fields
beyond. She saw only a carpet of scorched matting,
broken here and there by a few blackened canestalks
hunched over in grief. Now she knew where she was,
and yet how could it be so changed? She was in that
part of her plantation where the sugar cane grew. She
shook her head in disbelief. Had the darkness from
which she had been running caught up with her and
blackened her whole world? Was she to be stripped of
everything she possessed? Now that her blood was
black was she ordained to live forever in a black man's
shack and wear a black woman's dress? *Non. Non.*
Never!

She still had Cher Château. That could not be

changed. She would run home and bolt the door. Lock
out the black world which was ungulfing her!

As Asya ran, her heart pounded more from apprehension than physical exertion. Cher Château would be
all right. Nothing could destroy it. Its beauty made it
inviolable. It was her home. Nothing could happen to a
home. For a fleeting instant she thought of the blackened wall she had passed on her way to Cher Château
that first day. Later, she had learned it was all that remained of a Creole mansion. *Non. Non.* Nothing as big
as her own dear home could be reduced to one burnt
wall. Asya ran faster. The path was sharp with stones,
and her feet hurt, but their pain did not register. She
must hurry to Cher Château and fight off all that endangered it.

Asya came out by the barnyard, or rather, where she
expected the barnyard to be. What had once been the
pigsty was but a rubble of stones. She had expected to
hear the crowing of the roosters and the honking of the
geese, and to feel the wind from the flapping of the
hens' wings about her feet as she walked, but the place
was still, as when Death passes through. Disbelieving,
Asya stood and listened until her ears ached from
reaching out for sound which never came. She walked
toward the stable, quietly, so as not to disturb the eerie
hush of the place. But she never entered, for the stench
of rotting flesh reached her nostrils and she stopped far
back from the entrance. Only the walls still stood, the
interior a mound of tangled, burnt timber.

Who could have done such a thing? She was angry,
and as Asya turned away, she saw the burnt rubble of
the hutches. Her poor little hares! She remembered
their big brown eyes, gentle and trusting, confident that
the hand which reached toward them held only a tur-
nip top or a piece of fresh grass for their pleasure. And
she had not been here to save them!

Again Asya's thoughts flew to Cher Château, and in
her fear she could feel the blood drain from her head

and down through her heart until her body was cold and she shivered. The same senseless destruction could not have happened to Cher Château.

Asya threw her head back and called out to heaven, *"Bon Dieu! Bon Dieu!* Save Cher Château. Save my home! You Who gave it to me, do not take it from me." She was hysterical and began to race toward the house, screaming as she flew, "You took enough. Leave me my home! I tell You, save Cher Château. Do You hear me? Save it!"

And then she stopped suddenly. What she saw ahead of her made Asya's racing heart stand still.

Chapter Thirty-four

As though carved from ice, Asya stared, uncomprehending, at the spot where Cher Château had once been. Except for one wall, all was gone. The lacy white iron railings, now blackened and tangled, lay like huge ugly serpents guarding the wreckage. The great marble stairway had toppled over and was pinioned in the rubble by heavy beams which jutted out at crazy angles. Collapsed and broken, the roof, the same red-tile roof that used to crown the house, was scattered throughout the debris. Doors, walls, furniture—all were stirred together into one burnt mound of rubbish. This was the funeral pyre of her hopes.

Asya walked slowly toward the ruins. The ice inside her began to melt. She stepped over the tangled serpents of iron, and as she did so, Asya heard a rip. Without looking, she knew her dress was torn. She was back exactly as she had been the day of her arrival at Cher Château a lifetime ago. Ahead, a glimmer of light flashed out from somewhere in the ashes, and she slowly made her way to where it was. Reaching down, she picked up a crystal drop from one of the ballroom chandeliers. She wiped it on the skirt of her dress, and it lay in her hand as shining and bright as when it had last glowed in the candlelight during a ball. She could almost hear the music of a dance, but it was poignant, like a final farewell. In her mind's eye, she saw herself in one of her beautiful ball gowns spinning around and around in rustling brilliance. She saw Eloise, and

472

Eleanore pointing at her and laughing cruelly. She looked down, and her splendid gown had turned into a torn brown calico dress, and ashamed, she tried to cover herself with her hands.

Suddenly everything inside Asya became unhinged and she was limp. Her lips trembled, her eyes no longer fought the tears. Asya wept.

Her body shook with uncontrollable sobs. Her heart ached as it tried to beat away the heavy grief which gripped it. Too weak to stand, Asya leaned against the one remaining wall for support, but the effort was too much and she slid down into the dead embers of Cher Château. Asya cried as she had never cried before. It was as though the hurts and despairs of all her life had lain dormant in her breast and now were trampling across her heart. She had sworn never to cry again, but her determination had only served as a dam against what nature knew all along must someday burst out. Now the dam had broken, and she let it have its way. Never did she want to fight again, think again, move again. It was a relief to lie here and let her body shake out its sorrow in tears and sobs. Always she had been one against the world. No one had ever really cared for her, loved her. Even Etienne preferred affairs of state to her. Mère Denise had gone off to Rome without saying adieu. All she was, was a name on a piece of legal paper. A chess piece who had been moved from one side of the Atlantic to the other because a solicitor must execute his duty as the law saw it. And Negu. She did not love her. If she did, why had she frightened her when she first arrived instead of putting her arms around her and loving her? No one loved her. Asya sobbed harder and shook her head in despair.

At first, Asya did not feel the hand on her shoulder, but it must have been there for a while before she was conscious of its sympathetic stroking. Wondering, she looked up and saw the face of Joswee.

"Cry, *enfante,* cry away everything that is hurting.

Scrape the bottom of your heart till it is all empty. Then we shall look around for new happiness to put in."

At his words, Asya's eyes swam in a fresh outburst of tears. "I shall never be happy again," she wept. "For me, there is no new happiness."

"You can still eat, can't you?" the black man asked in a voice filled with sympathy.

"Of course," Asya snapped. "What a silly question. Who cares about food at a time like this?" She was outraged. "Go away." Her sobbing was now from anger.

The houngan shrugged. "At least it's a beginning in a search for something to be happy about. Negu will cook you a duckling à l'Espagnol. You always liked that. Something good in the belly helps the mind look about for something happy in the heart."

"I'm no baby," Asya shouted in her weeping. "I'm no baby that has fallen and hurt her knee and must get her mind off her bruise by—by sucking a sugar stick. Now go away!"

"I am only trying to tell you that I'm sorry," the soft voice explained.

"I don't need your sympathy. I don't want anybody's sympathy. I want to be left alone." Asya covered her face with her hands and put her head back into the ashes of Cher Château, while her broken heart sent its flood of tears out through her eyes.

Later, as she lay on the soft earth weeping quietly, the same soft voice came again. "Night is coming. Let me take you home."

"This is my home." Asya felt weak with hopelessness. Her body would never move again. "I will stay here forever."

"You can't. The night is damp and you will catch cold."

"Good. I'll die quicker that way."

"You are too young to sit and wait for death. That is for an old crone."

"I feel like one." Fresh tears flowed. "I feel dried up and wrinkled and blackened by life. I'm just like Cher Château. I've been destroyed."

"Non. Non. You are alive. You will heal. Think ahead a year from now. All will be well."

The tone of consolation in the black man's soothing voice only served to make Asya cry the more. "That's what you say." She was blubbering now. "Everything's—all washed away inside me." She lifted a face streaked with tears and black ashes.

"All that's getting washed is your face." A cajoling note came into his voice as he added, "And I might say it could use it."

"Don't talk to me as though I'm a child." His obvious effort to amuse her irritated Asya. "Go away."

Joswee put his hands under her arms and lifted Asya to her feet. "Enough talk," he said. "Soon it will be dark and difficult to find the way back."

Asya tried to break away, but his grip was firm. "Will you walk?" he asked.

"No," she shouted. "Get your dirty hands off me. Don't you try to tell me what to do. I'm staying here."

"No, you're not," he announced in a patient voice as he flung her up over a shoulder.

"Let me down, you ape." Asya kicked his chest with her feet while her fists pummeled his back.

With one big hand, Joswee gripped Asya's wrists and ankles together. Powerless to fight, she bit him in the shoulder and his reaction was a sound smack on her behind.

"I wouldn't bother if I was you," the houngan warned in his quiet voice. "It's a long walk, and my big shoulder can hold up better than your little ass."

"I hope you get lost in the dark." Asya let her head fall down and wept in frustration. Everyone had pushed her around all through life, and now they

475

would not even allow her to die. Tears of self-pity soaked the shirt of the black man who carried her through the quickly gathering shadows of night.

Asya refused to eat upon her return to Peter's shack, and went straight to her bunk of a bed. There she collapsed in depression and weariness. The aroma of Negu's freshly baked bread should have whet her appetite, but her stomach was indifferent to its appeal. Truly, she was dead. As Asya closed her eyes, she hoped that the oblivion into which she was slipping would be eternal.

The buzzing of a fly circling her head awakened Asya the next day. It seemed frantically insistent that she get up, for no aimless swatting of her hands deterred it from its prescribed itinerary about her head. Around and around it flew. Noisily. Nervously. A pest. How could one spend a day in bed with this buzzing halo disturbing her. Asya got up.

The room was stifling and the sun coming in through the open doorway emitted waves of heat which reached Asya as she stood near the bed. The thought of fresh air and wind taunted her and she ran from the shack. Outdoors the sun beat down from high in the sky, making the whole world feel it lay before an open oven door on baking day. The hens had foregone their digging and roosted in blinking contemplation on the low boughs of the nearby trees. The smell of the goat hung heavy in the air, but it too must have taken to the cool shadows, for it was nowhere in sight. The only activity was that of the large black flies that buzzed in contention over the scraps of garbage which littered the yard. Her hopelessness returned and Asya began to weep. Was this what she should live for?

"Asya," a friendly voice called. "Asya, come over here. It is cooler under the trees."

Asya stood hesitantly. She knew that voice. It was Negu and she did not want to see her. The ugly face only served to remind her further of her wretched plight. Every time she looked at it, Asya saw herself

476

slowly crumbling into the image of her grandmother. But the sun was hot. And she was hungry. And she could not stand in this stinking spot forever. So Asya slowly walked in the direction of the voice.

"Here I am, *ma cherie*. Here in the shade."

Asya stiffened at the familiarity in the voice. She did not want anyone to speak kindly to her. She hated Negu and Negu surely must hate her in turn. However, Asya did not think it worth the effort to speak to her about it.

Negu was in a little clearing surrounded by trees. There was a small, roughly made table and a stump of a tree for a chair. A short distance away, Joswee knelt by a pile of burning logs, stirring something in a black kettle which was set down into the flames. It was bubbling out a delicious aroma.

"Come," Negu said as she indicated the tree stump, "sit down and eat. I have made you a leek potage. It was always one of your favorites."

"I don't want anything," Asya said in a dull voice.

"It is very good," Negu cajoled. "Joswee brought the meat this morning especially for you."

"He probably butchered that old goat you were milking yesterday. It stinks all over the yard." Asya was in a sullen mood. She wished they would quit fluttering over her. She did not want to be beholden to anyone.

"*Non. Non*," Joswee called out amiably from his place by the fire. "It is the meat of the hen the boy peed on yesterday. You must try some. It is delicious."

Asya glowered at him and said nothing.

"It is ready now. I will serve you some," the man offered as he dipped a gourd into the pot and brought it steaming and dripping to the table. "There," he announced as he set it down. "Try it. You will find that the boy's water did the flavor no harm."

He was making sport of her. That was what he was doing. Trying to spoil her appetite. She would show him. She would eat it to spite him.

Determinedly keeping her mind off Joswee's allusion to the source of the meat, Asya blew to cool the soup and when she was able to taste it, she found it was delicious. Asya drank it in big gulps, for her stomach was empty and partaking of something warm and tasty was comforting. In the midst of her enjoyment, she remembered the little brown hen in yesterday's scene, and her stomach convulsed. Quickly she put her hand over her mouth and swallowed several times to keep from retching. Beside her, Asya heard Joswee laugh and she looked at him with hate. He walked away, chuckling to himself as he went.

As Asya sat there on the stump waiting for her insides to stop their quivering, Negu placed some crêpes on the rough boards of the table. Asya looked at them, thinking to herself that now she was more like an animal than ever. Even the pigs had a trough for their food. She had nothing. Eating off the bare boards was no more than being a dog rooting in the slop that had been tossed out the kitchen door. She started to cry. The tears ran down her face, and she made no effort to wipe them away. It was a relief to let them fall.

By the time she had finished her cry, Asya forgot her squeamish stomach. The crêpes looked good. They were stuffed with kumquat jam, for she could see it oozing out the ends of the sugar-rolled pastry. She ran her tongue over her lips. She reached out and picked one up. It tasted better than she had remembered. Asya ate the rest of the crêpes and when she was finished wiped the sugar from her hands on the sleeves of her dress, thinking bitterly, as she did so, how easily destroyed were the lessons in manners which the nuns had drummed into her for years. She would never need them again. She was black.

Having eaten, Asya was stronger. She rose from the tree-stump chair.

"You feel better now?" Negu inquired as she wiped the sugar from the table with a handful of leaves.

Asya studied the thin face, with its wrinkles around

478

the eyes and the lip caught up by the pink thread of the scar. She looked at the wrinkled neck and the flat chest of an old woman, and she thought how one day she too would look like that. "What does it matter to you?" Asya answered in a surly voice.

"I would say she's better," Joswee commented from under a tree where he sat cutting a stock of sugar cane into little pieces. "Sounds like her old bad-tempered self."

Asya said nothing. Best to ignore the ugly old man who seemed to find pleasure in annoying her. She headed for the open barnyard.

"Where are you going?" The concern in Negu's voice pleased Asya.

"To Cher Château, and I'm not coming back again. So don't send that big lackey of yours," said Asya, nodding her head toward Joswee, "after me."

"You will be back before dark?" her grandmother asked. "You'll be hungry by then. I caught a fish this morning, and I'll poach it for you. Fish is good for building strength."

"I don't want any strength and I don't want any more grandmotherly solicitations from you. Why act as though we're bosom relatives, when I only want to get out of your sight."

"But the fish is very fresh," Negu stated in the tone of a long-suffering fishmonger trying to sell to a difficult customer.

Asya was aggravated at the woman's persistence. "I don't want any fish, I told you," she stormed.

"What shall I do with the fish?"

"Drown it."

"If you are going to Cher Château," the old woman said in a quiet, hesitant voice which betrayed her disappointment, "put on these sandals." Her bony hand held out a pair of leather thongs. "They will protect your feet until we find some slippers for you to wear."

Asya regarded Negu with scorn. "I told you to stop grandmothering me. I want nothing from you." Knocking the sandals from the old woman's hand into the dust of the barnyard, Asya walked out into the road which ran toward Cher Château.

As she went along and saw her land, scorched and useless, stripped, even as she, of everything alive and beautiful, Asya wept. She and the land were both dead. But the land was more fortunate than she. It had no heart that kept beating out in agony. It was all dead. It did not cry. It had no tears to shed. It was finished.

Asya wished that Negu and Joswee had let the voodooists burn her too. Then all would have been over. For what had they saved her? The old meddlers! And they seemed to think she should be grateful. Who wanted this ugly life? Colorless. Drab. A brown dress. Brown skin. Brown shack. Everything brown. Brown and dirty. Even the hens—the tears welled up again in her eyes—were an ugly brown. Not a brightly colored one among them. When her tears had had their way, Asya wiped her face on her sleeve. No sooner had she done so, than she cried afresh. What would she do when her sleeves got all used up? She had but one dress. A rainbow of dazzling colors flashed across her mind as she recalled how beautiful her wardrobe used to look when the door was open and she could see all the lovely dresses hanging there. Asya dried her face on her skirt. She must be careful not to get her sleeves too soiled.

When she reached Cher Château, Asya's heart was so heavy with misery as she stood in contemplation of her former home that she could scarcely draw breath. "*Mon Dieu. Mon Dieu,*" she prayed aloud, "let me die. The sight of what is gone suffocates me. Let me die."

But whether she willed it or not, her body went on with its struggle for air and her involuntary gasping for breath upset her. She wept. It was easy to cry, for she had neither the strength nor desire to hold back the tears. She looked at the rubble that had once been Cher Château and the wetness of her eyes made it a grotesque blur. Having lost her home was not the hardest part. Going on living without it was what she could not endure.

Asya picked her way through the debris to where the mangled staircase lay. It reminded her of something which had once been alive and beautiful, and the wooden beams which protruded from it seemed to be mammoth arrows which had made the wounds that killed it. Her knees folded and Asya collapsed in tears amid the marble ruins.

How long she lay there, Asya neither knew nor cared. She and her home were alone in a world of death, except that death had freakishly passed her by. If she waited in the graveyard, perhaps it would come back for her.

A voice broke into Asya's wake. "Your *grand-mère* is waiting for you." It was Joswee.

Slowly Asya turned her head and looked up at the man. An ugly man with that split nose. She closed her eyes without answering. It was too great an effort to speak. Everything was ugly.

Joswee sat down beside Asya. "You cannot go on like this," he stated simply.

Asya took several breaths before she found enough energy to answer. "I . . . intend to rot and decay . . . like Cher Château."

"You are acting very foolish," his voice reprimanded.

Asya felt the man's big hands on her shoulders as he pulled her up to a sitting position. "Wake up." He gave her a vigorous shake. "Your *grand-mère* has babied you long enough. It's time somebody talked business to you."

Resentment at the man's audacity welled up in Asya's breast, bringing vitality along with it. Her head shot up in defiance. "Take your dirty hands off me. I'm no nigger chit for you to order about."

"I'm glad to hear it," he said tersely. "Nigger chits don't talk like you. They got more manners."

"Then go talk to them and let me alone."

"I would if I had my way, but Negu is upset about you. I'm doing it for her sake, not yours."

Asya gave a nasty laugh. "Who would have thought it! You and that ugly old witch."

Joswee's big hand slapped across her face.

Disbelieving, Asya touched her smarting cheek. "You—you struck me."

"And I'll do it again if you ever speak insultingly of your *grand-mère*."

Asya got to her feet. She glared up at the giant of a man. Coldly defiant, she spoke in measured tones: "I'll say whatever I want about her or anybody else and you'll not stop me. Because our blood is the same color does not give you the right to order me about."

No sooner had she spoken than the man before her became a wild animal. His eyes popped open until she thought they would come striking out at her like two musket balls. His lips curled back, baring powerful teeth made fanglike by the black caverns left by those he had lost. Suddenly Asya was frightened. This time she had gone too far.

Grabbing Asya by the waist, Joswee held her high above his head and began to shake her wildly. Then, opening his hands, he let her fall down upon the rubble of broken marble where she lay too scared to cry out against the pain of her fall.

Like an ogre of wrath, Joswee stood over Asya, and she would not have been surprised had flames come pouring from his nostrils. "You! You!" He raised a big foot and placed it on her stomach as though she were but an ant to be crushed. "You fresh little mongrel pup. Whatever made you think you were so important? You owe everything to Negu. If it hadn't been for her you would still be a nameless orphan rotting away without a franc of your own. Who do you think forced M. Drapeaux to sign papers making you his legal heir? It was Negu." His voice rose up, exploding the answer into Asya's ears. "Negu. Do you hear? Negu."

Removing his foot from her body, Joswee reached

down and, pulling Asya by her hair, stood her on her feet. Putting his face next to hers he hissed, "Do you think your father gave a damn about his black bastard over in France? He sent your mother there to be rid of the two of you. You were born of a black girl, and your birth was of no more interest to M. Drapeaux than that of a bitch dropping its pup in the gutter. And that gives you the right to put on airs, does it?" He pulled her hair tighter. "Does it?" Asya could feel his breath on her face. "Answer me."

"*Non. Non,*" Asya whispered, trying not to move her head.

"You didn't earn Cher Château. You were lucky to have Negu save it for you. When the other plantations around here were burnt during the revolution, Cher Château stood. Do you know why?" He shook Asya's head with his hand still tightly gripping her hair. "Do you know why?"

Not giving her a chance to answer, Joswee roared on, "It was because Negu put up the Nagshead. Only a priestess can hang up a Nagshead to scare off the revolutionaries, and your *grand-mère* did it. She wanted you to have Cher Château. You always made fun of voodooism. You thought that because stupid niggers who can't read and write believed in it, it must be a joke. Why aren't you laughing now if it's such a joke?"

Pulling her by the hair, Joswee raised her up until Asya's toes barely touched the ground. "Laugh, Asya. Laugh. It's funny. Laugh at the big joke." He threw back his head and laughed harshly.

Asya started to cry.

"What?" the big man asked in mock surprise. "Do I see tears? You, who always stuck your nose high in the air, can cry the same as poor people? You who can sass your old black *grand-mère* can cry?"

"You're hurting me," Asya blubbered. "Let me go."

"So I'm hurting her," he shouted with sarcasm. "I'm

483

hurting her, she says. She, who never had a pain, now whimpers because I'm pulling her hair."

Letting go of her hair, Joswee knocked Asya to her knees. She put her hands over her face and sobbed. Joswee grabbed her wrists.

"Look at me," he roared. "Look at me while I tell you about pain. Big pain. It's other folks' pain, so maybe you're not interested, but, by God, you'd better listen or I'll bash your face in." In fear, Asya raised her eyes to the shouting man who towered over her.

"All this time, you've been lying around moaning because your house is burnt and all your pretty clothes are gone. Not once have you bothered to ask about the other people who lived there. Did you ever think about Cilla or her husband or her papa or her mama? You called her your sister and not once have you asked about her. If the voodooists had roasted you and eaten you that night, you would have been lucky to have died like a pig. That would have been a merciful death as to what happened to the others. Ask me. Ask me where they are." Joswee grabbed her by the shoulders and, stooping down, yelled into her face. "Can you think about someone else long enough to ask where they are?"

Asya nodded, and Joswee removed his hands as though she were dirt.

"I'll tell you. I'll tell you about them," he spat out, "and I hope you get sick in the belly when you hear."

Joswee stepped back, and his voice was heavy with disdain. "It was because it was your house, it was because they served you that they died. Watusi. You hired him away from the emperor. He and Cilla would still be together had you not dangled your money bags in front of his face and brought him here. After the fire, we came to look for him. He was so butchered that we couldn't tell if we had gathered up all his parts. The ones we didn't find are still in here somewhere, and the rats will take care of those. If you listen,

484

maybe you can hear them chewing on a piece of Watusi's bone."

Asya let out a long wail, and her body shuddered. The tall man reached down and, grabbing her by the ears, pulled her to her feet. "Shut up and listen!" he ordered. "Can you hear? Can you hear the rats?"

"*Oui. Oui.*" Asya sobbed, certain she heard the gnawing of a thousand rats.

"But Cilla. No, they didn't get her bones to nibble," Joswee shouted into Asya's face. "*Non.* She still lives."

Asya's heart gave a quick skip, and she looked expectantly at Joswee.

"But, not the Cilla we know," he went on. "The Cilla we know is dead forever." His voice lowered. "The one who lives has no mind. She spends her time wandering through the woods looking for her dead child. Yes, her baby died that night. But Cilla thinks it's lost somewhere and calling out to her."

His voice was gruff again. "But, you!" He tightened his hold on Asya's ears and shook her head vigorously. "You have tears for no one but yourself. You cry, because your body is wrapped in a nigger's cast-off dress, and your head rests at night in a nigger shack. Is that so bad? Evadne and Nassy, if they were alive, would be glad to have a shack to lay down in. But because they served you at Cher Château, they are dead. Killed. The barn door the voodooists danced on that night was the lid of their coffin. Did you know that they were under that barn door? Under that barn door being mashed flat like a crêpe by the weight of the dancers?"

Joswee put his big hands around Asya's waist and began to squeeze slowly. "Did you ever think how it is to have the breath and blood pushed out of you? A heavy door pressed against your head. Harder and harder until the skull cracks like an eggshell. And you with no breath to cry out against its pain."

Joswee's split-nosed black face spread across the world before her and Asya felt herself swooning from lack of air. The raging man relaxed his hands about her waist, and let her drop to the ground.

"Are you hiding your misery in a faint? Have we a coward here?" he taunted. "Do you think unconsciousness came so quickly and so mercifully to your cook and butler?"

As she lay on the ground, whimpering, the rough voice of the man above her lashed into her ears. "You are alive and well and you have love. Your *grand-mère* holds out her hand to offer help, and all you give in return is sass. You look upon her as an ugly black witch and not once have you seen into her heart. Do you think she was always old and disfigured? Was Cher Château always charred and broken as it is today? Was it not once beautiful and alive? So was Negu. The most beautiful girl in Haiti. Black or Creole. The deformity on her face is but a badge of her love." His voice gathered momentum. "*Oui*, love, I said," and he put his bare foot under Asya's stomach and rolled her over on her back.

"She dared to love a black man and for that her white owner scarred her face. You think Negu ugly? I don't. I think her beautiful, because I was that lover."

Asya blinked up at him in amazement.

"Don't look so surprised," he snarled. "Because we are old, does it mean we never knew youth and passion? *Oui*," he roared, "the white man coveted Negu. He paid for her caresses, but she loved me and for that we both paid. I was nailed to the barn. Did you hear me? I was nailed to a barn. Stripped naked. They cut off my ears. Did you ever see a man without ears? Look!"

With a quick movement, Joswee whipped off his red turban. His head was bald, but Asya's eyes went straight to the scarred apertures where the earlobes had once been. Without any protuberance on the side, Joswee's head resembled a death skull. A macabre black death skull with livid eyes and snarling mouth.

Asya shuddered and turned away. Death, in the person of Joswee, stood alive before her.

Asya felt the man's rough hands on her shoulders as they glommed down upon her and lifted her to her feet. "Look! I said, look!" His hand grasped her chin and jerked her head up so that Asya faced him. "Take a good look," he hissed. "You are favored to see a man without ears. Not everyone can see a man without ears. How do I look?"

Asya stared wide-eyed, afraid to answer.

The man's nails clawed into her chin as he shook it. "Answer me. How do I look?"

Asya's lips trembled. "Aw—awful," she managed to whisper.

"Now, shall I let down my pants and show you what else they cut off to make sure I would never love Negu again?" his voice whipped.

Asya shook her head. *"Non. Non."* Tears streamed down her cheeks.

"Ah," he mocked. "So you cry? Is it for me or for yourself?" He released her chin but Asya did not take her eyes from his face although the death skull before her wavered through the tears.

In disgust, Joswee smacked the back of his hand against Asya's stomach, knocking her backward against a fallen beam which jutted out from the wreckage of the marble stairs. She laid her head against the scorched wood and gave herself over to tears.

"I've had enough of your self-pity," Joswee sneered. "If you come back to Negu, treat her with respect, or I'll throw you out. And don't think your good white friends will take you in. They're afraid. *Oui,*" he emphasized, *"afraid!* You are taboo with the emperor and no one will touch you. Only your black *grand-mère* dares help you, because she loves you. From before you were born, she has done for you. She has given more than her life to you."

Joswee stopped speaking, and his silence made Asya look up at him. He was gazing at her with compassion in his eyes. He said hushedly as in prayer, "Go to her, Asya. Go to Negu. She needs you. She has suffered enough."

The big man turned and walked slowly down the flagstone driveway which had once led to Cher Château and on into the woods. Asya sat on the rubble where he had pushed her, but she did not cry anymore. She could not. She had scraped the bottom of her barrel of misery and there was no more left for mourning. Asya rested her head against the fallen beam. She was tired. More tired than she had known it was possible to be. She felt whipped and now the whipping was finished.

Asya looked at the wreckage about her. One house. One girl struck down. She sighed. In all this world, just one house. One girl. That was all.

Nearby, something red and shining caught her eye. It was Joswee's turban lying forgotten in the ashes. Forcing herself to her feet, she walked over to it and picked it up. She would return it to the high priest. She was going back to Negu.

Chapter Thirty-five

Asya and Negu now slept together in the same bed. This arrangement had not happened immediately. When Asya returned from Cher Château the day Joswee had heaped his venom upon her, she found the high priest, his head wrapped in a nondescript rag, sitting on the doorsill of Peter's shack. Without a word, Asya dropped the red turban upon his lap and went inside. Negu was bent over the rough table, wrapping a banana leaf about a china chocolate pot. It was a primitive version of a tea cozy. Negu neither looked up nor spoke. The china pot seemed incongruous in this crude environment, and Asya vaguely wondered how it had come there, but she did not ask. It was not important. There was a low stool on the floor at the foot of the bed and Asya wearily sat down.

She noted that there were three gourds set upon the table, and knew she was expected. She should have been cross that these two old people had foreseen she would return to them, but somehow that was not important either. Negu called something to the man on the doorstep, and in a short while Joswee came inside with a steaming black kettle from which a savory aroma arose and filled the room.

Without feeling, without appetite, Asya watched Negu take three wooden plates and spoons from a shelf. She then ladled some of the contents of the hot pot onto the plates and set them out upon the table. She lit a candle, for night had come. Negu and Joswee pulled a bench up to the table and sat down. They looked toward her and waited. For a moment, Asya remained on the stool, recalling that the Creole does not sit at the table with the black servant, but then, she also remembered, without emotion, that she too was now black and this was her family. Asya arose, picked up the stool, and joined Joswee and Negu. What Asya ate, she did not know. All she knew was that one could eat as well with a wooden spoon as with one of silver. After a gourd of hot chocolate, Asya lay down upon the bed and fell off to a dreamless sleep.

The next morning, Asya awakened, feeling more rested than she had been since the night Cher Château was burned. She rose and walked to the open doorway. The world had long since been up. The goat, tethered under a nearby tree, had more than half consumed a japonica bush within its reach. The animal paused in its gustatory routine and frowned at Asya, as if in reprimand for her late rising. Then it vigorously resumed the devastation of the bush and its red flowers. The brown hens scratched away in the dirt, clucking out their exasperation over finding the pickings so meager. Swarms of flies circled in the sunshine and droned out their satisfaction with the flotsam scattered about the dusty yard. All nature, Asya mused, goes about its business, knowing what to do. Only I am lost.

As the days went by, each the same as the one before, Asya submitted herself to this new way of living. She was neither depressed nor gay. Neither hopeless nor hopeful. Each morning she awoke and somehow time drifted along until she fell asleep again at night. She did not think of her former life at all, or of the possibility of seeing Etienne. Though, in the back of her mind, always was the hope that someday he would come for her.

One day Asya mentioned to Negu that she was going to walk into Cap Henri to visit her banker.

"I wouldn't do that if I were you," the old woman cautioned. "It's a long walk to find you have no money."

"I always had money in the bank," Asya answered languidly. The bank seemed to belong to another world. Maybe the bank was burnt too.

"Not anymore." Negu's voice sounded heavy. "Henri Christophe has it."

The old Asya might have seethed at this information, but the new one asked simply, "How could he? It was in the bank."

"He's the emperor, isn't he? He said you're dead and everything goes to him. So he took it."

Maybe I am dead, Asya thought, for the news stirred no reaction in her. The picture was complete. Everything was gone.

But Asya knew she was not dead. This was but a period of anguish, a time of waiting. For what, she did not know and she was content not to concern herself with the problem. She would rest, grow strong, and sometime soon she might think clearly again. But not now. She was too tired.

There were only a few changes in Asya's daily pattern of living. The first came one night when she watched Negu spread out a straw mat on the floor and lay herself upon it. Always before this the old woman had waited until Asya had curled up in bed. Then she had blown out the candle and stretched out herself. "Do you mind taking care of the candle tonight?" Negu asked, and for the first time Asya detected a tiredness in her grandmother's voice.

"I suppose not," Asya sighed. Her voice echoed the lethargy of her body.

Asya stared down at Negu. Shrunken. Skinny. Withered. Nothing more than bones poking out in a faded dress. A fighter, Joswee had said. A fighter. Is that what happens to people who fight? Well, she herself was through fighting. Maybe sometime, some year when she could think, she might fight again. But not now.

A breeze came in through the doorless entryway. The light from the candle fell across the arm of the old woman on the floor. It was a thin arm, and from where she sat, Asya could see a big vein bulging out like a long black worm. The bony wrist, the wrinkled, clawlike hand looked too feeble to change the world anymore.

A strange thought entered Asya's mind. At least, it seemed strange to her for she had not been having any thoughts for a long, long time. "Negu," she said, "you take the bed. I'll sleep on the floor."

Negu did not answer immediately, and Asya wondered if she was already asleep. However, when the old woman spoke, it was with great effort, as though her voice were far away and it took time to find it and drag it back. "This is fine. *Bonne nuit.*"

Asya shrugged. She did not feel like arguing. She arose from her stool and, taking the candle, walked toward the bed. As she did, the light fell on her arm. The skin was firm and unwrinkled. Not like the gnarled black wrist of the now shadowed figure on the floor. In a pleased mood, Asya sat upon the bed and raised the candle toward her lips to blow out the flame. Something was different. It was the mattress. It was softer. Asya bounced on it. Negu must have filled it with more straw during the day. She glanced toward her grandmother as she lay on the thin mat. Hers was a fleshless old body, hard with bones. Nothing to cushion them as they rested on the floor.

Asya got to her feet and, still holding the candle, walked over to where Negu lay. "Get up, Negu. You take the bed."

Negu did not stir.

Asya kept her voice low as she announced matter-of-factly, "Grandmothers do not sleep on floors."

Slowly, Negu stood up. For a moment the dark eyes rested upon the girl. *"Merci,"* she said tenderly, and walking over to the bed, lay herself upon it.

The first night, Asya could not sleep. The floor was hard and she kept hearing steps outside the shack and thought about pigs or goats or snakes which might come in through the open doorway. However, the next night she fell asleep immediately, too tired to notice the hardness of the floor or think about outside noises.

But during the night, something awakened her. It was a low, persistent sound which she began to hear while still asleep. A steady gnawing, chewing, like someone surreptitiously sneaking food in the dark. Asya rolled over to look in the direction from which it came, and the noise stopped. All at once, something ran over her. She could feel the warmth of its body and the pressure of its small feet as it scampered across her stomach. Its hairlike whiskers brushed her arm. As it hurried away, the animal was silhouetted in the doorway by the moonlight. Asya saw that it was the size of a cat, but its head was tiny and it had a long thin tail. Asya sat up and screamed. It was a rat!

Asya screamed and screamed. She rubbed her hands across her stomach trying to wipe away the touch of those filthy feet.

"What is it, *ma cherie?* What is it?" Negu's arms were about Asya, holding the shaking girl against her breast.

"It was a rat!" Asya's voice rose hysterically. "It was a rat! It was on my stomach. Its whiskers touched my arm! A rat!"

Negu pulled Asya to her feet. "Come," she soothed. "Come to bed. It is better there. I will sleep on the floor."

Asya let Negu have her way, but when the older woman started to walk away, Asya clung to her hand. "No, no. You can't sleep on the floor. The rats will get you."

"I am used to them," Negu said in a comforting voice. "I am not afraid."

"No! No!" Asya shouted. "You sleep with me in the bed. See," she said, as she moved over, "there is enough room for two. We will sleep here together."

"*Non. Non.* I can't sleep with you."

493

"And why not?" Asya demanded. "You are my *grand-mère,* aren't you?"

For a moment Negu did not speak. Then she said in a very soft voice, *"Oui,* little granddaughter," and gently lay down beside Asya.

For the rest of the night, Asya slept fitfully. Once when she awakened, she found Negu's arm around her waist. It made her feel loved. Asya could not remember when anyone had put an arm about her. It was a nice feeling.

After that night, Asya was more aware of being alive. She took an interest in the new world in which she found herself. She wanted to help Negu, but now being more conscious of the woman as her grandmother, Asya felt a shyness. Yet, she liked being with Negu, for she exuded a serenity, a confidence that, in time, all would be well again. As far as assisting in any of the chores of keeping house, Asya was no help. She could never wring a chicken's neck and pick its feathers, nor skin a hare. Milking the goat looked easy until Asya approached the animal, and it turned its head to give her a mean stare as if daring her to touch it.

However, she liked fishing. It gave her the feeling of doing something useful but not laborious. Joswee taught her. He showed her what kind of vine to select for a line and brought her a sharp hook from somewhere. Asya never asked from where anything came. Joswee seemed to have a secret inexhaustible source for anything needed. If he stole it, so much the better. Asya had no compunction about breaking the commandments if it added to her comfort. She remembered bitterly how much had been stolen from her.

Asya liked wandering about the woods, finding various streams, and bringing her catch back for Negu to cook. At first, she had been squeamish about cleaning the fish, but Joswee maintained that a good fisherman also cleans the fish he catches. So Asya learned to clean

494

the fish and found, to her surprise, that it was not a task she abhorred.

One day, Joswee came from that mysterious place where he spent his days and whispered to Negu. Asya knew they were talking about her, for their faces were serious as they looked in her direction.

"Is your grandchild becoming a problem?" Asya called over blithely. She was not worried. She had no problems. Those two could take care of everything.

The two old people came over to the table where Asya was sitting, busily rolling dough balls in preparation for a fishing excursion.

"I don't think you should go fishing alone anymore," Joswee said, a worried look on his face.

"Why not?" Asya was unconcerned. "Is there some wild animal loose in the woods?"

"You could say that." Negu nodded her head. "A two-legged kind."

"Oh, those," Asya poohed. "They've already gotten me. I'm not important anymore." She continued rolling the dough balls.

"It's Prophète," Joswee said. "He doesn't like the idea of you being alive."

"Does he begrudge me my fishing line and dough balls? If so, I will make him some. He will not have to send his men to steal them."

Joswee smiled. "It's not that simple. Prophète is a killer."

"And what satisfaction would my death give him?"

"The satisfaction that you're not alive anymore," the houngan said with bitterness. "He wanted to kill you and steal Cher Château. Something happened. His plans went wrong, and he failed."

"My death won't bring back Cher Château."

"Killers don't reason," Negu explained. "They only kill."

Asya straightened. "I didn't know I was so important a person anymore as to win the attention of the captain of the emperor's guard," she said facetiously. "What do you suggest I do?"

"You must stop wandering about the woods alone," Joswee ordered.

"But these are my lands I wander around," Asya insisted.

"And if one of his men kills you here on your own land, who will know?" Joswee asked.

At those words, Asya saw herself as no more than a tiny toad which unconcernedly hops about the weeds until it is crushed by a careless foot. The other toads keep hopping and the weeds keep growing, and no one notices the loss of one little creature. Like the toad, she would not be missed.

Asya did not relish being killed like a toad. She wanted to hop through the weeds as she pleased and sit on whichever river bank she chose. Asya looked up at Joswee. "I like walking wherever I please. It is all I have to do for now. Isn't there some way we can stop Prophète's men from sneaking in?"

Joswee shook his head. "The Nagshead is down. Anyone will come in now."

"Well, then, let's put up another one." Asya turned her attention back to the dough balls.

The two old people were silent. Then Negu said, "*Oui*, I think it time we put up another Nagshead."

Joswee rubbed his chin in thought. "Where shall we get it this time?"

"The Lord giveth and the Lord taketh," Asya said. "I wish I could play God and take back one of those thoroughbreds I gave the emperor for a gift. But," she sighed, "I don't know how to go about stealing from an emperor."

"Umm. I have an idea," Joswee laughed mysteriously. "The emperor is going to lose one of his horses."

Asya looked up at the man's smug face. "How? How will you do it and not get caught?"

"Never mind, *petite femme,* never mind." Joswee

wagged a finger playfully in front of her nose. "The whole country will suspect that the head of the emperor's horse hangs at your gatepost, and no one will be brave enough to do a thing about it."

A faint flicker of excitement stirred in Asya's breast. The first she had known in this new lifetime. "Good," she said. "I wish it could be the emperor's head."

"Let's not be hasty," the high priest chuckled. "One head at a time."

"But how will you do it?" Asya asked. At last, something exciting was breaking the monotony of the daily routine.

"I'll send a honey dipper to steal the horse. No one would stop a honey dipper." Still laughing, Joswee strolled away and disappeared among the trees.

Asya was perplexed. How could a honey dipper, a man who cleaned outhouses, steal an emperor's horse? She asked Negu, "Why wouldn't a guard stop a honey dipper?"

"Because they are Joswee's honey dippers," Negu announced. Her tone implied that this was sufficient reason.

Asya was still mystified. "Are his so sacred that no one dares to touch them?"

The old woman gave her a knowing look. "You might say so. Joswee's men only work at night."

Asya shivered. She recalled having once heard that the honey dippers were zombies. If anyone saw one, he should run away for, it was said, if a zombie touched you, you too, would become a zombie. That was only talk, Asya told herself. She did not believe in the legend of the walking dead.

A few days later, Joswee came to the doorway of the shack and announced, "The Nagshead is back."

Aside from the fact that it was now safe for her to walk over her land, Asya was pleased with the return of the Nagshead. To her, it was the symbol of the beginning of the restoration of her home. One day, Cher Château would be rebuilt.

One day, Asya noticed red flowers blooming among the weeds a short distance from the ruins of her home. She strolled over to take a look. Sadly, it dawned on her that this had once been an old-fashioned flower garden, one where flowers of every color had grown. Only the red had survived the killing weeds. The flowers had bloomed along the path to the chapel, but the path was now overgrown. The chapel! Not once since that awful night when her world had been burned, had Asya thought of the chapel. Was it possible that it had escaped the marauders? As she made her way through the weeds, she felt a tingle of excitement. If the chapel still stood, that would at least be a beginning in the re-building of her plantation. Asya's feet felt lighter as she hurried along. There, up ahead, were the eucalyptus trees, and immediately behind them should be the chapel. Then Asya saw the cross on the steeple, standing out against the sky like a standard waving aloft its encouragement. A feeling of exultation welled up in her breast and she ran forward. Her chapel had not been taken from her! She still owned something after all!

But when Asya came to the trees and had a better view, her heart fell. Through the gaping holes which had once been windows, she saw that the interior of the chapel had been burned. It looked black and gutted. The heavy door must have been hacked from its hinges, for large splinters of wood still jutted from the door frame. Asya looked toward the cemetery beside the church. It too had been desecrated. The black iron fence which had enclosed the graves lay smashed down upon the ground, and the headstones of the dead had either been uprooted completely or stood leaning sideways at crazy angles.

Why such senseless destruction, Asya asked. Why? What possible threat could God's house and the dead be to the living? Why had they done it? The chapel, after all, was but a sign of God on earth, and the graveyard of God in the hereafter. To burn Cher

Château had been man stealing from man, but to destroy the chapel was to steal from God. Their effrontery overwhelmed Asya. What would the sisters of the Sacre-Coeur have said?

With a heavy heart, Asya went through the doorway and into the chapel. Everything was blackened. The desecrators had gathered the pews in a pile in the middle of the stone floor and set them afire. They now lay in a mound of ashes or charred wood. The flames had been high enough to burn through the ceiling, leaving only a skeleton of blistered timbers where once a roof had covered the chapel.

Asya picked her way up to the main altar. The crucifix above it was blistered, but the figure of the crucified Christ had been burnt away. Only a hand still hung loosely from its nail. The golden candlesticks were gone, and the statue of St. Geneviève was toppled over and lay smashed upon the blackened floor. Smashed, Asya thought, like my hopes of ever seeing Etienne Grenier again. Why has he not come to me?

She sighed. I am used to knowing only loss. Strange how one can get accustomed to anything. After a while it does not hurt anymore.

Asya turned toward the side altar of the Blessed Mother. To her surprise, the statue, although blackened by smoke and covered with soot, stood undamaged on its pedestal. The serene face of Mary looking out over the wreckage of the chapel was a message of hope to Asya. All will be well, it said. I shall always be here to help.

All at once, Asya was tired. She sat down on the steps of the main altar, her eyes still on the face of the Virgin. She did not feel alone. God, she guessed, was here, but He always seemed so far away. She was thankful the statue of His mother was here. But she was so dirty. I could expect more help from Heaven if I cleaned up God's Mother, thought Asya.

She found some dried weeds outside the chapel, and after tying them together with a vine to form a small whisk broom, Asya brushed the black ash from the statue. Then she stepped back to inspect her work.

"There," she said aloud to the image of Mary. "You look better. You're standing up there above all this rubble as though you've just been resurrected."

Then her glance fell upon the debris about the steps of the side altar. Well, she thought, if I'm ever going to rebuild Cher Château, I may as well start by cleaning a corner of the chapel.

With her makeshift broom, Asya cleared away the mess of ash and broken plaster which had accumulated about the side altar. As she swept the steps, she noticed how beautiful they were. The risers were made of stone carved into lovely roses. There was something familiar about those roses. And then Asya remembered. The chalice! The chalice! All this time, she had forgotten it! Was it still there?

Dropping to her knees, Asya hastily tried to unscrew one rose after the other. It must be here. It had to be here. But she had forgotten which rose Abbé Brille had removed. Or was it two roses? Asya picked up the broom of weeds and hastily swept the rest of the altar steps, raising a cloud of swirling dust as she did so. Her impatience made her cross. This served her right. She had been such a glutton about owning the chalice that she had paid no heed to the Abbé's instructions on how to get it out of its place of concealment.

When she had thoroughly cleaned the steps, Asya flung the broom aside and contemplated the risers. She tried to recollect the exact scene when the Abbé had first shown her the chapel so long ago. Asya remembered it was the steps on the wall side. Of that she was positive. It was not the bottom riser. She must try all the ones above it. So hard did Asya work to turn each carved rose that by the time she found the first one which unscrewed, her fingers were already bleeding from the rough stone. There was a second rose beside the first. She was remembering now. Her hands were trembling with excitement by the time Asya had both caps removed from the iron stakes which acted as handles to lift out that part of the step beyond which the chalice lay.

"*Mon Dieu,* give me strength," Asya prayed. "Don't let it be stuck."

The section of the step lifted out easily, and there was the silver box shining in the dark recess. Breathing heavily from the effort to control a giddy impulse to shout, Asya slowly pulled out the silver chest. She opened the lid. The chalice was there. Her days of privation were over.

Chapter Thirty-six

Asya concealed the chalice in large banana leaves and carried it back from the chapel. When she showed it to Negu, the black woman was as delighted as her granddaughter.

"It's beautiful. The most beautiful thing I have ever seen." The Negress was breathless with admiration. "How did M. Drapeaux hide it from me?"

"After this, you won't be so smug about knowing everything that happens around here," Asya teased. "You're not God yet." As she spoke, Asya's eyes could not turn away from the treasure in the silver box, which now rested on the rough wooden table in Peter's shack.

"I wish I was God so I could tell you what to do with it."

Without looking up, Asya said simply, "I know what to do with it. Sell it and use the money to rebuild Cher Château."

"Where will you sell it?"

"Here's the address of the agent." Asya reached into the box and produced the envelope. "See," she pulled out a sheet of paper. "Abbè Brille showed me. It's written here where to write. I'll write right away. I'll use the Jamaica address. That will be faster."

Asya put her hands to her cheeks and said in dismay, "I forgot. We have no paper nor quill." Then after a moment's thought: "Joswee can get me some. If he can get fancy chocolate pots and emperors' horses, he surely can steal me something to write on."

Negu's head shot up. "Poof! Hold your tongue," she cautioned. "Joswee does not steal. A houngan is no thief. He is but a wise man who knows where necessities can be found."

Asya saw the slight sparkle of mischief in the old woman's eyes. On impulse, she threw her arms about the woman's wrinkled neck and her voice sang with excitement as she said, "Oh, Negu. You make a wonderful grandmother! You get me everything I want." She stepped back, and with her arms still about Negu's neck, she said, "You and Joswee make a sweet, conniving old couple."

A pleased look spread across Negu's face, and Asya wondered how she had ever thought her cold and hateful. The scar did not make her ugly. It was simply Negu's badge of honor.

"You will get me the paper?" she coaxed. "You will, won't you, Negu?"

Tenderly, the woman took the face of the girl between her hands and kissed her lovingly on the forehead. "You know I will get you anything you want," she said softly. "I am happy when you are happy. But—" Negu crossed her arms on her breast and lowered her head in an attitude of thought "—we must think this whole matter over very carefully. It isn't quite that simple."

"What isn't?" Asya was perplexed. "I write the letter. Joswee posts it, and quick like that," she snapped her fingers, "we have a buyer. Oh, all those gourds!" Her voice trilled, and she did a few lively steps of the gallapade around the table. "Millions of them. Millions! Cher Château, you will soon be back, more beautiful than ever. And you and I, Grand-mère—" The term of endearment slipped out, and somehow to Asya, it was right. The girl caught the old woman by the wrists and pulled her into the dance. "We shall live there happily forever after!"

It was wonderful to be alive again. To be strong. To be rich! To have a challenge! The blood was running wild in Asya's body, and as it coursed through her limbs and her heart, it wiped away the weight of the void which had been there so long. "We are rich! We are rich!" Asya shouted out her song, as she danced Negu about the shack. "None are so rich as we!"

Having given vent to her first burst of enthusiasm, Asya stopped by the silver box. Clapping her hands in delight, she said, "Isn't it beautiful? Isn't it beautiful? When I look at it, it's not the chalice I see. It's Cher Château all back together again. Its flowers and its fields and its parties and its people. And you, Negu, you my *grand-mère*, will never have to wring the neck of another chicken again. You will be dressed in fine silks—"

"Could I have fine linens?" Negu interrupted with a small chuckle. "I think they will be cooler for an old woman."

"Whatever you wish," Asya answered expansively. "Each night we shall eat from golden plates set on fine lace cloths instead of from a splintery old table like this wreck." She gave the table a disdainful push, and it rocked at her touch.

"We'll have a thousand candles in silver candlesticks instead of one crooked candle stuck in a dried-up gourd."

"Sounds wasteful," Negu murmured, but her head was nodding approval and she smiled her twisted grin. For the moment she, too, was caught up in the dream. But her smile vanished, and placing her hands upon Asya's shoulders, Negu said in a sober voice, "Let us not plan what we shall do with the results of our labors before we figure how we shall labor for those results."

Asya laughed. "You sound like Mère Denise. The trouble is, she was always right, but she surely could dampen a girl's spirits." Her face became serious. "I will rebuild Cher Château. Nothing will stop me now."

"That is what we must think about. Asya, what is to keep Prophète from coming again to steal Cher Château?"

504

"The Nagshead."

"I am not talking about his entering the grounds to steal it. There are other ways he might have to get what he wants. And if he cannot get Cher Château for himself, what is to prevent him from seeing that you don't get it either?"

"What do you mean?" Asya asked impatiently.

"He could kill the people who bring in the supplies to rebuild, or, at least, have his men attack them and dump everything over the road."

"I will get my own guards. I will have the money," she said stubbornly.

"There are ways of removing your guards. Their relatives could be beaten up and their homes burned if they persisted in working for you. You know how our people are here. They take care of relatives. Cousins, aunts, in-laws. All are one big family and the responsibility belongs to all. No, Asya," Negu shook her head, "you would have trouble getting anyone to work for you."

Asya did not answer. Her lips were pressed tightly together. She was angry.

"Suppose, let's suppose, you do get the plantation rebuilt," Negu said. "You are allowed to go ahead and do all the hard work. Restore Cher Château, plant your crops. They will laugh behind your back all the way, for to them you are but a pig being fattened for market."

"How?"

"Who will buy your crops, Asya? Who will take them to market? Prophète, either with the emperor's consent or without it, will see that you have no buyer."

"The foreign merchants will not listen to Prophète or Christophe." Asya tossed her head. "The Yankees, the English are not afraid. They are businessmen who are interested in a good deal, and I shall make the best deals in the Caribbean."

"Oh, and will these Yankees and English come out to Cher Château and drive the carts themselves down to the wharf?" Negù asked pointedly. "Will they, on their businessmen's white backs, carry the loads onto the ships, that is, if they get back to the ships alive?"

Asya's face was stormy, but it did not keep Negu from talking. "If no one buys your crops, they will rot on your land, and you will have no money coming in to support Cher Château. No gourds to pay your workers and your guards. Think, Asya. What good will it do you to rebuild if you will have only a war on your hands and in the end you lose anyway?"

Asya sank upon the bench by the table. "I shall never lose Cher Château again," she said in a deliberate voice. Placing her elbows on the table, she leaned her chin upon her fisted hand and announced, "I must think this out."

Negu closed the lid of the silver chest. "You will think better without so much beauty to distract your thoughts." Quietly she walked over to where a string of purple onions hung from a wooden peg on the wall and cut a few from the strand. Then she sat on the doorsill, and the only noise in the shack was the sound of her knife peeling away the skins.

After a while, Asya's voice came across the room to Negu. "Is there anyway to get rid of Prophète?"

"Do you think that a man who guards the emperor is careless about his own safety?" came the woman's flat answer. "Furthermore," she added, "if anything should happen to Prophète, Christophe will take the plantation for himself."

"But why should he? We have always been friends. I bought the books for the schools. I paid for protection. Why should he take what is mine?"

"Because what is yours he can use. Money! If you can give away all those gourds for schoolbooks and still have so much wealth left, then Christophe wants what makes you rich. That is your plantation."

Asya remembered the red eyes of the emperor at their first meeting at the opera in Cap François. His hard voice as he ordered Count de Marmalade from the ballroom at Sans Souci. Negu was right. The emperor Christophe was a fierce enemy.

Asya frowned. "Do you honestly think Christophe is as money-hungry and power-mad as you are leading me to believe?"

"Did he come to help you out after the fire?" Negu snapped. "No, he made no inquiries. He announced you dead and took your money. Not even so much as a low requiem Mass for his good patroness of the schools."

Negu set the bowl of onions and the knife on the earthen floor and stood up. "I'll tell you," she went on in a firm voice. "I'll tell you what kind of a devil calls himself the protector of his people, the builder of Haiti. It's a butcher. A butcher!" She spat out the word like it burned her tongue. "Each day, he sneaks through the fields with a spyglass to see if all his good citizens are up and working. If he sees one, just one, sit for a moment in the shade of a tree or pause to wipe the sweat from his face, he shoots him dead.

"If the roosters on the farms about San Souci get too noisy on the mornings his head aches after the heavy drinking parties the night before, he orders his army out to shoot them. Some empire!" Negu swept out an arm. "Some empire! Our enemies are roosters and the emperor must send out the soldiers at the peoples' expense to slay them. And the young girls!" Her voice rose. "What's happening to our young girls? Do you know," her face came close to Asya's, "do you know that any man in the emperor's pay—office worker, soldier, or chef, yes, even the peeler of his onions—can step through any door in the land and shout, 'The young girl. I want the young girl in the house!' And if the father refuses, he is shot in the face. I know these stories are true, for people come to the houngan every day for a wanga to keep away the evil men. We are being governed by a crazy man who forgets he was once a slave. He has a money bag for a heart, and the mind of

507

a devil!" Negu's voice ended in a shout, and her eyes blazed.

Asya sat with pursed lips. She would be neither intimidated nor discouraged, she told herself. Aloud, she asked, "Is there no way to win him over?"

Negu said nothing. Her silence was heavy with disapproval. Asya had the feeling she had asked the wrong question.

The old woman spoke in a venomous tone: "*Oui*. With your body. Is that what you want?"

Asya shot to her feet, but Negu pushed her back down upon the bench. "Listen to me. With all your pretense of sophistication you are still but a convent babe. When Christophe is through with his women, he does not throw them out in the street. He is proud that there are no prostitutes pandering in the gutters of his country. He takes them up to the dungeon at La Ferrière and buries them in the lye pits where their bodies are eaten away and nothing is left as evidence of their once having lived."

Asya shuddered. She remembered his big, round, red-streaked eyeballs. She would vomit if ever they came close to her face. Asya shook her head to wipe away the image. "Does no one fight him back?" she asked in a small voice.

"Not for long," Negu stated coldly. "Those at court whom he has made into useless puppet noblemen know better than to annoy him. They pay big bribes for the privilege of enjoying his friendship. A more democratic term is taxes," she said with sarcasm. "Where do you think they get their money?"

"From their plantations?"

"That's right. And from their workers."

"I don't understand."

"Their workers are not paid. Oh, sure, they are told they make so many gourds a week, but then they must pay big taxes for the privilege of working in this glorious land. Unfortunately, the taxes seem to amount to about the same as the income. So, the worker makes nothing, and he can't eat on nothing, so he slowly starves."

"Then he should quit and find another job," Asya said with a righteous toss of her head.

"That's the point." Negu's voice was like a knife. "He can't. No one else is permitted to hire him. Everyone is told what the government wishes him to work at, and that is where he must work. All for the glory of Haiti! Hurrah!" she shouted.

"But—but," Asya was overwhelmed, "but the Haitian is back where he started. Back to slavery."

"That's right," Negu agreed, "but this time with a tougher master than the French."

"Does no one fight back?"

"How can anyone? No one can escape him. Even the merchants in town, the men who add so much to the prosperity of a city, must pay protection to Prophète's guards or to the tax collector or to someone. If anyone refuses to pay up, he is beaten or his wife is killed or his home is burned. Even the merchants from foreign lands must pay or they soon discover there are no porters for unloading their wares from the ships. Poisonous snakes appear mysteriously in their files and black ink is spilled over their contracts."

Asya was quiet while her mind slowly disgested this startling information. After a while, she asked, "Does no one run away? I should think that as long as there is nothing left to run away from, everyone must want to leave the country."

"They have tried, but—" Negu shrugged "—what good is that when you are killed before you can cross the border into South Haiti."

Asya's eyes popped wide. "Are you telling me," she asked in a doubtful tone, "that the Haitians are prisoners in their own country? No one is free to move out?"

"No one is free here to do anything but work and pay and pay and pay and then die."

"I shall not be a slave, and I shall not die, and I shall not hide here in the woods forever," Asya announced in a loud voice.

"And just what do you have in mind to do that the other slaves have not tried in this wonderful land of freedom?" Negu's voice was edged with sarcasm.

Suddenly Asya giggled. "Really I don't know," she said in a small voice, "but—" She paused a moment and cocked her head: "I'll think of something. I am definitely not going to sit here and wither away the years until I'm a dried-up old woman who has nothing to do but drool over a fortune big enough to equip an army."

"It'll take an army to budge that monster off the throne of Haiti."

Something clicked in Asya's mind. Her eyes half closed as she tried to recall what she had once heard. "Negu," she said slowly, "I never paid much attention to politics, but didn't Christophe at one time have a war with the southern part of Haiti? Didn't he try to take it over also?"

"*Oui*, the old hog! He thought he could gobble up the whole land. M. Petion and he were elected to govern Haiti together, but that was not good enough for His Majesty. M. Petion was in the south and Christophe in the north. Henri wanted the whole island. Even Spanish St. Domingue, united with us as in the time of Toussaint L'Ouverture. However, the Spanish would have nothing to do with Christophe and remained independent. But Christophe was determined to take over from M. Petion. He and his followers, all hot-headed with the nationalistic spirit, and rum too, I might add, marched down to take South Haiti. But Petion is an educated man, and a dedicated man. Dedicated to his country, and he wanted no dictator taking over.

"Christophe had the supplies, but Petion had the brains and the determination. Much to our emperor's surprise, he was defeated by the man he thought he could brush aside. Christophe tried again, and got nowhere. He did the smart thing. He gave up and came back north."

"Why doesn't Petion attack Christophe and free his countrymen?" Asya asked. "Surely, he is aware of the injustice going on around here."

"Petion does not have the gourds to equip an army. His is a poor land, and Petion is too much of an idealist to bleed his people for the taxes necessary for a large-scale war."

"Uh-huh." Asya nodded her head. Her face wore a smug look. "Just as I suspected. All Petion needs is money, and that I have."

Negu frowned at Asya. "What are you thinking?"

"You know very well what I'm thinking. I am going to Mr. Petion and give him the money I shall make from the sale of the chalice. Don't worry, Grand-mère." Asya came around the table and gave the old woman a reassuring pat on the back. "Petion and I shall save Haiti," she announced.

"You're talking nonsense," Negu reproved.

"It's nonsense which wild dreams are made of," Asya sang out in a jubilant voice. She grabbed Negu by the shoulders and danced her about the shack. "I'll get us back our Cher Château, Grand-mère, and you won't ever again have to wring the chicken's neck before you eat."

"But—but," Negu stammered as she tried to extricate herself from Asya's hands, "but how are you going to get to Port-au-Prince to meet Petion?"

"A minor detail," Asya said, lightly brushing the question aside. "I haven't quite figured that out yet, but I'll come up with something."

"Now talk sense," Negu said firmly. "If you go along the road, you'll be shot for treason for trying to leave the country. Since it's you, Prophète would make sure you are shot without a reason."

"Then I won't go along the road."

"You've never been outside your plantation in anything but a carriage," Negu stated. "How then do you expect to find your way on foot through two hundred and fifty kilometers of wild mountains? But on the other hand," she said with an indifferent toss of the head, "it might be better to take the main road and be shot quickly rather than die slowly of starvation, or fall into a bog and be smothered."

Asya laughed. "Threats will get you nowhere. I am like M. Petion. I too am determined and brainy and educated. We should make a fine team. Come, say we are a perfect match," she teased.

"But, Asya," Negu persisted, "you don't realize the dangers. How will you arrive at Port-au-Prince? You have to get there first to sell the chalice before you may give Petion the money."

Asya cocked her head. "I shall not worry about it." She spoke in a vibrant, happy voice. "We'll figure out something, won't we, Grand-mère?"

In the end, it was Joswee who offered the solution. "I have a man working for me," he said, "who knows those mountains better than anyone. He could guide Asya to Port-au-Prince through the densest parts, and no one would ever follow them or see them."

"Who is that?" Negu looked skeptical.

"M. Grande Bouche."

"Oh, no." An anxious cry came from Negu. Quickly, however, she regained control of herself. "I mean, M. Grande Bouche has not been in those woods for years. By now, he could have forgotten."

Joswee shook his head. "M. Grande Bouche cannot forget. He knew his way through the mountains as well as his hand knew the path from the table to his mouth. He will take her there safely," he assured.

Asya did not meet M. Grande Bouche until just before dawn the day they were to start off. As usual, the morning was heavy with mist and when he appeared in the doorway of the shack with Joswee, he resembled a ghost from the grave. He was thin and bony, like a corpse. His baggy pants were held up by a rope about his waist, and his voluminous shirt hung loosely from his shoulders. The sparse white hair stuck up from his head like dried grass. But it was his eyes that really startled Asya. They were large gray eyes, which stared straight ahead without seeming to see. Only once before had Asya seen eyes like that. It was when one of the mothers had died at the hospital and the nuns had not yet gotten around to closing the lids. Asya shivered. M. Grande Bouche had the eyes of a dead man.

"But—can he see?" she stammered.

"Sure. That's just the way he looks," Joswee explained easily.

"But why do you call him M. Grande Bouche? M. Windbag? He's so very quiet."

Joswee shrugged. "There's no accounting for a man's name. Maybe he came from a family of talkers."

"He surely is all talked out now," Asya said. "He hasn't said a word."

"He can't talk," Joswee stated simply, "but fortunately he hears and will obey whatever you tell him. He knows he's to take you through the mountains to Port-au-Prince, and you are to come to no harm. M. Grande Bouche does only what he is told. If you are to arrive there safely, and that is his job, he will get you there safely."

"He doesn't look very alert," Asya whispered to Negu, "and he gives me the creeps, but as long as he knows the way, he doesn't have to be handsome too. At least, you won't have to be concerned about any romance along the way," Asya giggled.

Then she put her arms about the old woman's neck and said, "Don't worry about me. I shall be very careful and not do anything foolish. I am grown up now, and I mean to have Cher Château back for you and me. Adieu, Grand-mère. You are the most wonderful grandmother a silly girl could have. I love you." Asya kissed the old woman on her scarred cheek and then followed M. Grande Bouche out into the misty morning.

For Asya, the weeks which followed were a voyage through no-man's-land. Jungle and rocks and swamps and wet feet and mosquitoes and then jungle and rocks and swamps and wet feet and mosquitoes all over again. In the beginning, M. Grande Bouche traveled only during the morning hours, before the wind blew away the mist and cleared the air. Then they hid in caves or, sometimes, M. Grande Bouche would hack a small clearing in the dense jungle with his machete, and after they had crawled in, he would build the tangled mass of branches and leaves back up again so that no one could see where they hid.

Those first few days, so little distance was covered that Asya began to think M. Windbag was a lazy fellow who preferred sitting in the woods to reaching Port-au-Prince.

Once, when the day was especially lovely and the jungle was fragrant with the perfume of its flowers which grew bold and beautiful in the warm dampness, Asya said to him: "Let's keep moving. We can travel farther when there is no mist. Why do we always hide as soon as it is clear?"

M. Grande Bouche sat staring ahead with those eerie eyes, giving no sign that he heard her voice. So, as always, they waited for the dawn and traveled only in the mist.

During one of those misty dawns, Asya learned to trust in the wisdom of M. Windbag's odd time schedule. They had just started out when there was a sudden rustling ahead and a gruff voice called, "Who is dere?"

M. Windbag reached back and quickly knocked Asya to the ground.

"Who is dere, I say? Yuh tell me!"

M. Windbag dropped the load he was carrying, and with his machete in hand stood motionless, waiting for the owner of the voice to approach.

"Can't you talk none? Who are you?" A little uncertainty had crept into the words, and Asya had a feeling the unknown voice was losing its bravado. She hoped so, for her own heart was pounding hard enough to shake the ground she was lying on.

Asya and M. Grande Bouche watched the figure of a man come toward them through the mist. He walked up to M. Grande Bouche and snapped, " 'Ow cum yuh don't talk? Whatcha—" Suddenly his voice trailed away. He craned his head forward as he tried to peer into the face of Asya's motionless guide. The he let out a bloodcurdling scream, "*Bon Dieu,* it's a zombie! It's a zombie!"

With that, he whirled about and streaked off through the mist, his screams trailing behind, "Don' touch me! Don' touch me. Ah don' wanna die."

Asya took in a deep breath and let it out again with relief. So my guide is a zombie, she thought. Am I glad he is on my side!

After about two weeks or two months or two forevers—Asya was not sure of time anymore—M. Grande Bouche guided their little safari during the more pleasant hours of the day. One morning, when the sun had warmed away the night's chill and the breeze had brushed against her face, causing Asya to feel alive and strong and ambitious to be doing something about changing the destiny of Haiti, they came over the brow of a mountain, and before them, miles below, lay the sea.

Slowly, M. Grande Bouche raised his arm and pointed off in the distance. At first, Asya could see nothing but land and water, but the way M. Windbag maintained his statuelike pose, she had better see something or they would be rooted to this spot until she did. After a close scrutiny of the scene below, Asya could just make out a town at the water's edge.

"It must be Port-au-Prince!" Asya shouted. "It is, isn't it? We're almost there!"

The man's arm came down slowly, so slowly that

Asya expected to hear it creak. She was right. It was Port-au-Prince.

Asya wanted to run and shout, so happy was she to be almost at her destination, but M. Windbag continued to plod along at the same steady pace he had set when they had commenced the trip. That's the trouble with being a zombie, thought Asya. No enthusiasm.

To keep her mind off the excitement of her approaching destination, Asya studied M. Windbag's feet as she followed behind him. The rocks along the path were sharp, but he tramped over them as though he had been born with the hoofs of an animal. M. Grande Bouche was a white man. How had he come by such tough feet? She herself was thankful that Negu had given her a pair of leather thongs to wear. Asya did not want her feet to grow horny. They would scare a man if one ever crawled into bed with her. That is, if she ever married. Maybe she would never marry.

Asya's thoughts flew to Etienne. Would she ever see him again? And if she did, would he want her? Would he want a black woman for his wife? If he loved her, where was he? Why had he not come to help? Surely he must know about Cher Château. Maybe they told him she was dead. Maybe by now he was married to someone else.

So intent was Asya on her thoughts that she did not notice the sky until a crash of thunder caused her to look up, expecting to see black clouds spreading across the sun. Lightning cut across the heavens, knifing white jagged gashes in the blackness. Being so high up in the mountains, Asya felt a mad enemy was concealed behind the clouds from where he hurled out his bolts of lightning, aimed for her head, and each time they came she involuntarily ducked in an effort to escape the blazing daggers.

The rains came fast and heavy, and M. Windbag found a shelter for himself and Asya beneath a large overhanging boulder. With each crash of thunder, Asya feared it was the sound of the rock severing itself from its hold above them. But the rock hung protectively over them, as the storm put out the light in the heavens and pounded the earth to sleep for the night.

The next morning, when Asya and M. Grande Bouche crawled from their shelter under the rock, the earth was still soaked. The sun shone big and red, like God's warm hand trying to sop the wetness from the trees and mountainside. The birds were badgering Heaven with shrill chirps.

"Don't be so impatient," Asya called up to the twittering creatures in the trees. "God will get around to sponging up your wet little perches. He has the whole world to dry up. Wait your turn."

And suddenly, it happened. Asya had been happy, delighting in the lovely morning. There was a rumbling, and before her ears could communicate the sounds to her brain, Asya was shoved by some strong hand down over the side of the mountain, where she rolled and bounced like a dislodged stone until she came to stop in a briar bush.

For several moments, she lay still, afraid to move her bruised body lest the sharp thorns, which pinioned it, sink deeper into her flesh. Carefully, Asya moved one hand and pulled away the pricking branches, extricating herself as she did so. She stood up. Her knees were bloody, but they worked. Once on her feet, Asya ignored her aching body. She had the feeling something was wrong on top of the hill. She must get back up, and quickly. Selecting a place where there were stumps of trees and deeply imbedded rocks for footholds, Asya laboriously made her way back up the hillside. A pall of dust hung over the place where she had stood only a few moments ago. The birds were strangely silent. The quiet was so loud that all life seemed to have gone from the earth.

"M. Grande Bouche! Where are you? M. Grande Bouche! Where did you go?" And then a light breeze blew away the dust, and she saw him. But only part of him. His legs. They protruded out from under a great rock which had crashed down upon the upper part of his body, imbedding it into the earth.

"M. Grande Bouche!" Asya cried out, not believing what she saw.

"Are you alive? Answer me!"

Tears spilled down her cheeks. "Answer me. Don't leave me. Answer me," she shouted with some vague notion of her words penetrating through to the still man's brain.

Asya put her hands against the rock and tried to push, but even as she did, she knew it was futile. Yet, she had to keep trying. With all her strength, Asya pushed until her side hurt and she fell to the ground, sobbing in helpless despair. "M. Grande Bouche. Poor M. Grande Bouche. You are gone. Gone."

When she had wept her tears away, Asya tenderly laid a hand on M. Grande Bouche's leg. She had never touched a dead man, and it made her feel so alone. Left behind. "You saved my life," she whispered as in prayer. "You didn't know me, but you saved my life. It was you who pushed me out of the way, for where you lie was where I stood. I am grateful, and now, you will never know that I am."

After a while, Asya dried her tears and stood up. She gazed down at M. Grande Bouche's legs, so thin as to be scarcely perceptible in the voluminous breeches. She could not leave him lying there, his legs exposed to the elements. She looked about and found some large leaves, which she brushed clean and wrapped tenderly about the man's legs. Then she covered them with earth. "You poor little man," she said sadly as she worked, "not even a pillow for your head. Only stone to protect your face from the dirt."

Suddenly she stood up. "No, M. Grande Bouche, I will not let this be your burial place for all eternity," Asya said in a clear voice. "I promise you, I shall return. When Cher Château is rebuilt, I shall bury you in the cemetery there. You will have golden candlesticks at your requiem and a marble marker for your grave. It is fitting that you should sleep with the Drapeauxes since you gave your life that this last one might live."

Then Asya walked over to the hanging rock under which she had spent the night and dragged out the sack containing the chalice in its silver box. It was heavy, and she thought of M. Windbag's bony arms which had carried the bundle up and down the mountains and through the jungle for so many weeks. She was ashamed that not once had she offered to help. Asya flung the sack over her shoulder, as M. Windbag had done, but she found it an awkward, lopsided way to carry something.

Suddenly she remembered how the Haitian women carried their produce in big baskets as they walked to market. She too was a Haitian woman. Asya placed the sack on top of her head, and started for Port-au-Prince.

Part Three

Chapter Thirty-seven

From the railing of the ship, Etienne Grenier watched the Haitian shoreline flow closer and the mountains grow taller. It was three years since he had left Cap Henri, and his return was not the happy occasion he had expected to look forward to. His mission to the United States had been hopeless. The Southern senators bluntly refused to sanction any diplomatic relations with a black nation, and they had been powerful enough to persuade the Congress of the United States to refuse to recognize the independent country of Haiti.

But his failure in the diplomatic field was not the only reason for M. Grenier's depression. He was concerned about Asya. In all this time, not once had he heard from her. She knew he loved her. He had told her so. And in the note he had sent her from the States, he asked her to marry him. Not a word in reply in all this time. He had posted subsequent letters of love, of anxiety for her welfare, and also of anger over her indifference. Finally, he stopped writing. Now, he was coming back to Haiti, and Etienne wondered.

The ship tied up at dock. There were no curious onlookers standing about, as in other countries, to eye the returning traveler. Christophe permitted no idleness. All must work. It was a cold return. It made Etienne feel that his departure had not been noticed, for there was no one to welcome him back. He walked down the gangplank of the ship and up the steps to the wharf. He looked around for some conveyance to take him to his home, but there was none. There were only the dock workers who indifferently emptied the ship's hold. A man, carrying a bundle of straw hats over his shoulder, was meandering among the workmen, trying to sell them his wares.

As Etienne stood there, momentarily wondering what to do next, the vendor shuffled up to him.

"A hat, monsieur? The sun, she is very hot," the man said as he dropped the hats in a pile on top of Etienne's shoes.

"Well, I'll be damned," Etienne exploded, caught by surprise. "Do you always bury your customers in hats?"

"I have a message for you," the man said in a quiet, unruffled way as though Etienne had merely asked him for the time of day. "Negu, she says for you to come right 'way. See nobody else." Casually he picked up a straw hat and holding it at arm's length, nodded his head in obvious approval. "See her first." Etienne took the cue and feigned interest in the merchandise while he asked, "Where is she? At Cher Château?"

"Oh, no!" the vagrant merchant answered quickly. Too quickly. Horror had crept into his voice, and for a moment he was nervous and dropped the hat he was holding up for Etienne's inspection. Etienne stooped down and selected another from the pile of hats surrounding his feet. "Where is she?" he asked.

"At your house," the man answered, his tone once again that of the itinerant huckster. "She says come at once. See no one. Talk to nobody. Very, very 'portant."

Etienne removed the black hat he had bought in the States and handed it to the man while he put on the straw hat he had been holding in his hand. "How much?" he asked as he reached into his pocket.

The vendor raised his head and studied the sky with his big brown eyes, as though the price were written up there. "Dere's a horse," he drawled, "tied up by de back of de harnass shop at de edge of de swamp. Take it. Ride quick to your house. Fast as dat horse kin pick up his feet an' put 'em down agin."

"I know it's a nice hat," Etienne spoke in a businesslike voice while a laborer, carrying a sack of grain on his back, plodded by, "but a gourd is too much."

The vendor's attention was now held by the foreign hat in his hand. Almost caressingly, he rubbed his hand over its crown. "Dat's pretty," he said admiringly. "Dat's soft." He looked speculatively up at Etienne. "I make you bargain. Good bargain for you. Dis hat of yours no good here. Too hot. I give you good straw hat. Cool for in Haiti. Fine hat. I keeps dis no-good black hat. Yuh git off lucky."

Etienne nodded. "Agreed."

Quickly, almost as though he must hurry before Etienne changed his mind, the stranger placed the high black hat on top of his kinky head, scooped up his wares, and scooted away.

Etienne had made a bad deal, but he did not care. The message the hat-seller had brought gnawed at his breast, and he quickened his step as he headed for the harness shop near the swamp.

Etienne Grenier was a veritable volcano, seething with an explosive force of destruction. He was on his way to kill Henri Christophe and he could not contain his anger until he met up with the emperor face to face. He would beat him with his bare hands. Pummel him until he was as shapeless as a snake flattened under the wheel of a loaded cart. Negu had told him what had happened. From no one else would he believe such savagery was possible in this modern age in a civilized country. But Negu had told him everything that had happened that awful last night at Cher Château. He would kill Henri and then, like Samson, tear down the palace in his rage. His anger was strong enough to pull out the pillars, one by one, and he would laugh so loud as to be heard from Milot all the way back to Cap Henri as the ceilings came down to squash out the lives of the murderers who had not raised a hand to stop the torture and pillage that night. "Asya! Asya!" his heart cried out. With only a stubborn little chin and her courage to combat a savage horde. He could have wept over the feebleness of her pathetic defense, but his desire to kill was stronger than his pity.

Etienne dug the heel of his shoe into the flank of the horse, but the movement served only to relieve his own stymied feelings. The horse was doing its best, and no amount of prodding was going to add more speed to its lagging legs. The gates of Sans Souci came into view, and when the guard stepped out to inspect the visitor to the palace, Etienne knocked him to the ground, shouting out as he rode on through, "Get the hell out of my way! Can't you see it's Grenier with news for the emperor? Big news," he hissed through clenched teeth.

Etienne rode his horse up the wide circular outside steps, through the door of Sans Souci, and into the marble entrance hall. Only then did he slip from the saddle and, to the amazement of the bug-eyed palace hangers-on, leaped up the stairs to the emperor's office on the next floor. He flung open the door. Christophe was sitting with his feet atop his desk. Beside him a Negro with red hair read from a newspaper.

The emperor jumped to his feet. "Grenier!" A big smile spread over his face. "This is an unexpected surprise." He thrust his hand across the desk in a gesture of welcome, but Etienne ignored the extended hand. Instead, he glared at the aide and barked, "Get out!"

Like a frightened rabbit, the man gave one leap and was gone. Deliberately, quietly, Etienne closed the door of the office. Then he turned to the emperor, who, his smile slipping away, was now regarding him with an uneasy scowl.

Etienne spoke slowly, his words cold and measured. "Before I kill you, your explanation of the burning of Cher Château."

"Cher Château?" Henri asked in a quivering voice. "I—I don't know what you're talking about."

"Quit stalling!" Etienne's eyes were as cold as his voice.

"Are you talking about the Drapeaux plantation? Oh, that," he laughed uneasily and sat down. "I had nothing to do with it. Nothing at all. It was Prophète."

Etienne said nothing. He glared down at the man in the chair and only the little play of muscle under his ears betrayed the anger he felt.

Henri gave Etienne a furtive look as he spoke in a hesitant voice. "You know how Prophète is. Drinks a little too much. Plays a little too rough." He shrugged a shoulder. "That's the way it is. But he's a good boy. Does his job well. The empire needs him." The emperor gave a sheepish smile and leaned back uneasily in his chair.

"Go on," came the voice of steel. "This is your trial."

Henri sat up. He tugged at his lapels and the feeling of the coat about him must have offered some security, for when he answered, his voice held more assurance. "I don't know why you hold me responsible for the conduct of one of my officials. Why don't you ask Prophète about it?"

"You're the emperor, aren't you?"

"Naturally. But I cannot take the blame for all the crimes of everyone on the island."

"You take the taxes from everyone."

"Of course."

"Then you owe your taxpayers protection."

"I have a chief of police. That is his job."

"Why didn't he arrest Prophète?"

"Because no one brought any charges."

Etienne exploded. "Who the hell was left to do it? Did you expect a dead man to bring charges? Was he to gather up the parts of his body and drag them down to the gendarme?" He was shouting now. "Did you expect a girl whose mind is crazed to file a complaint?"

In his anger, Etienne lunged out, and grabbing Henri by the scruff of his neck, he pulled him from the chair and flung him across the desk. With all his strength, his fingers tightened about the neck of the emperor until he thought it would break in his hands. Abruptly, he released his hold and flung his victim onto the floor.

"Choking is too good a death for you," Etienne shouted, hate in his voice. "A slow death is what you deserve. I'm going to beat you. I'm going to beat you until your guts run over the floor and the walls are splattered with your brains. I'll smash your damn bones until the flesh falls away and then I'll throw them out the window for the dogs to chew to dust."

Etienne leaned over the desk and shouted to the man on the floor in a voice hoarse with hate, "Get up, you damned coward! Get up and take your beating!"

Christophe laboriously pushed himself up on his knees and, leaning his body against the desk, panted noisily for breath. Etienne railed, "Get up on your imperial feet so I can push your damned arrogant face back down onto the floor."

The emperor rested his forehead against the desk and moaned.

Etienne sneered, "Look at the brave ruler of his people. The mighty one who hides behind the stone walls of a fort and the knives of his army of murderers. The great Henri who cannot stand up and fight one unarmed man."

Christophe's head slipped off the desk and he slumped back down upon the floor.

"Get up off your black ass," Etienne barked, "before I kick the shit out of it. Get up and fight!"

With much effort the emperor raised his face above the desk. His eyes were half closed, and the lids quivered as he looked up at Etienne through little red-rimmed slits. His neck had swollen out to the jaws, and his chin was wet with the saliva which trickled out the side of his mouth.

"And when I'm through with you," Etienne bellowed, "do you know what I'm going to do? Do you know what's going to happen to your little paper empire?" he shouted with more vigor. "I'm going to do everything in my power to turn it over to Petion. North and South Haiti will be one land again. The people will dance on the dust of your royal bones and hope you are in Hell, for they hate you. I will be your enemy forever and not rest until your fellow butchers are burning in Hell along with you. You are not a leader of your country. You are an animal who devours it. For that I damn you!"

Christophe's mouth twisted into a snarl. He placed one big hand on his desk and with great effort pulled himself to his feet. Slowly he brought up the other hand. In it was a pistol.

The two men faced each other in heavy silence. Christophe spoke first. "Who's damning whom?" His voice was arrogant.

Etienne said nothing. In his anger, he had forgotten the cunning of a trapped man.

"You'll never live to damn anyone except the executioner." Christophe's words were deliberate and resonant. Like the gong of a tower clock. He was again the emperor. His head held high. His chin thrust out in hauteur. "And the executioner is used to being damned."

With the back of his free hand, Henri Christophe wiped the saliva from his chin and in a gesture of disdain flung the wetness into Etienne's face. "That's my thanks to you." The emperor laughed in derision, but the hand on the gun remained steady. "You have served your purpose and you are now a nuisance.

"But," Christophe raised his high brows and cocked his head at a jaunty angle. He was obviously enjoying turning tables on his would-be assassin. "But we must not be too hasty in sending an old friend off to the devil. We must arrange for a fitting departure. A long lingering farewell. You are entitled to a proper gun salute as befits your rank and work here in Haiti. I shall speak to your favorite official about it. Prophète will be most happy to oblige."

The emperor quietly contemplated the man before him, giving the impression of mulling over various fiendish methods of extermination. Christophe chuckled. "I have it," he announced with obvious satisfaction. "A twenty-one-gun salute is the proper honor for so great a man. One shot for each thumb. One for each ear. One for each wrist. One for each elbow. One for each knee. One could dispose of the nose. But then, it takes two for the jaw. One to remove the upper teeth and one for the lower. Oh, but then," he shrugged a shoulder in dismissal of the project, "why should I bother my head as to how Prophète will carry out the honor we are planning for you? Let him plan the details as to which parts of you will receive our farewell blessing. The twenty-first salute will be reserved for your heart. You see, we really are not butchers after all. We could not leave you pining away for a merciful last shot. You will receive the full honor."

"What is this great honor which must be given at gunpoint?" came a cool voice from behind Etienne. Without turning, he knew that the empress, Mme. Christophe, had come into the office.

"We have a traitor here. Our trusted friend," the emperor spoke with sarcasm, "has come to kill me." He shook his head reprovingly. "M. Grenier should know by now that no one kills Henri Christophe."

Etienne was unprepared for Mme. Christophe's next words. The empress gave a short, derisive laugh and sneered, "So, our friend is showing his true colors at last." She walked around the desk and stood at her husband's side. "Pretending to want to help us," she continued in the same cutting tone, "when all the time he was plotting your murder. Was I the next to be slaughtered, Etienne? Did I too stand in your way? Was that why you professed to be in love with me? The better to kill me and your emperor?"

Etienne was speechless. Had she lost her mind?

Mme. Christophe looked up at her husband. "I am glad you are going to kill this man. I never trusted him and his blabberings of democracy. I'm fed up to here," she placed the back of her hand under her chin, "right up to here, with his crazy talk of what's good for Haiti. You, my dear husband," and she patted Henri's cheek, "know more about running an empire than this stupid book-learned bag of air. Glad to be rid of him."

"You surprise me, Marie Louise," Henri said, at the same time keeping his eyes on Etienne. "I thought you two were more than friends."

"Henri!" It was a hurt little cry. "I have always been faithful to you. I merely tolerated this political Messiah because I thought you needed him."

"Good. Will you call the guard?"

"Gladly." The empress started for the door and stopped. With a worried look, she studied the emperor for a moment. "Are you all right?" she asked.

"Of course," he snapped, obviously annoyed by her solicitude.

But the empress was not put off. She walked toward her husband and touched his swollen neck lightly with her fingers. "Dear, dear Henri. You have been hurt. Hurt badly. I cannot leave you here alone with this awful man. You might faint. Your throat is growing so big that it could cut off your breath and you could not even call out for help."

At her words, some of the emperor's fortitude left him. Etienne saw the gun hand waver. "You are ill," the empress said to her husband. "Here, let me hold the gun." She took it from his hand, keeping it pointed at Etienne. "Sit down," she continued in a soothing tone. "Sit down and rest a moment. I can't leave you in this weakened condition."

Christophe dropped his long figure into the desk chair. Carefully, he felt his neck and moaned. Mme. Christophe, with a firm hand on the pistol, faced Etienne. Then she backed away until she stood behind the

531

chair in which Christophe was sitting. Slowly, the empress placed the butt of the pistol against the back of her husband's head.

"Go, Etienne," she commanded. Her voice was low and terse. "You are free."

"What!" The figure in the chair started to move forward, but before he could do so, Mme. Christophe clutched his hair and pressed his head back against the point of the gun. "Don't move," she cautioned, "or I shall kill you."

The man in the chair stiffened. "You bitch!"

"Look who's talking." The empress gave a hollow laugh. "How many of your sluts lie eaten away up in the lime pit at La Ferrière? Do you think an emperor is above gossip? Did you think I would not hear?"

"And you are no better than the rest of the sluts. All the time letting Etienne, posing as my best friend, make love to you. You, my wife. Can you deny it?"

"You'll never know." Mme. Christophe sounded amused. She looked at Etienne. "Go. Go fast. Go at once."

But he did not move. "*Non*. Henri will kill you. I can't leave you with this madman."

Etienne walked to the other side of the desk and held out his hand toward the empress. "Give me the gun. I will kill him."

"*Non*." Her voice was firm as she pushed Etienne aside with her free hand. "Let history take its course. It is not for one person to deny the people the pleasure of killing their tyrant. It is a fitting punishment that he should live in fear, day by day, never knowing when death will come for him."

"But I can't go, leaving you here unprotected."

"I am not afraid of death," she said calmly. "That is why no harm will come to me.

"But you," she paused a moment and looked up at him, her eyes clear and determined, "you must go now. Escape while you can. It is what I want, Etienne. It is truly what I want," she insisted. Her eyes returned to the prisoner in the chair. "I shall always be grateful for having known you."

The empress took a deep breath and said in a soft voice, "*Merci, merci*, Count Grenier. This tavernkeeper's daughter will never forget. Always you honored me as a lady." She held her head high, but a sad little smile played around her lips.

"The finest," he said gently. Bending, he kissed her on the cheek.

For a fleeting moment her eyes looked up at him, and he saw the urgency in them. "Go at once," she ordered. "I will keep him here for an hour. You will have that much time before the alarm goes out for you. Etienne, Etienne," she begged, "fly like the Devil is after you, for indeed he will be."

Etienne looked down at her. The most courageous woman he had ever met. He reached for the hand without the gun and kissed it. Then he stepped back and bowed. "Adieu, my Empress."

He hurried from the room, closing the door quietly behind him.

With long strides, Etienne hurried along the hall and down the marble steps of the palace. At the bottom he saw the red-haired Negro who had been reading to the emperor, slouching against the wall and laughing with some men Etienne vaguely remembered as political leeches.

The emperor's aide jumped to attention when Etienne said in what he hoped was a casual tone, "The emperor does not wish to be disturbed until he sends for you. He is with the empress." Etienne gave a quick glance about. "Where is my horse?" he asked. "I had left it here."

The men burst into laughter as though his question were a joke. "Well," the red-haired man answered while his cronies clucked their amusement, "well, it's like dis. De palace steward, he don' like no horses pickin' up and puttin' down dem feet on his clean marble floor. And dat horse of yours put more—" he became convulsed with laughter, but finally managed to finish "—put more down dan jist his feet. De steward sure am bustin' mad." He was laughing so hard that tears were running out of his eyes.

"What did he do with my horse?" Any other time, Etienne might have seen the humor of the situation. "Where is it?"

"In de stable," someone answered.

Luckily, Etienne knew the palace well. He dashed off toward the stable, taking a route which led him through the kitchen. In the confusion of dinner preparations and the wide-eyed stares of the chefs, Etienne felt safe from any pursuer.

But he was worried. The horse which he had ridden to the palace was slow at best, and now, after the rigorous workout he had already been given, the animal was useless. He could probably walk faster.

A thought came to Etienne, and even as he hurried toward the stables he smiled to himself. The irony of what was in his mind pleased him. The thoroughbred. The one left from the pair he had brought from Mexico and Asya had given to the emperor. That was his escape horse. It would please Negu. She had told Etienne about the new nag's head. Now both animals would serve the emperor's enemy.

At the stable Etienne had no trouble. He was known. "Business for the emperor," he said. "And hurry."

The thoroughbred was saddled and Etienne rode out of the stone courtyard and onto the Plain du Nord. He headed for Thomasico, the emperor's garrison at St. Marc near Petion's territory. Already Etienne had a plan. It formulated so quickly that he wondered if it had not been in the back of his mind all along.

Chapter Thirty-eight

M. Petion did not wish Asya to ride along with the soldiers up into the mountains, and when she asked why not, he simply answered, "Because you are a young woman. Is that not reason enough?"

"I'm twenty-four, going on twenty-five. How old does one have to be before she can ride with the army?" she asked with a pretense of guilelessness.

"A lady is never old enough," he reproved in his quiet fatherly voice. "You're being sassy now, and you know it." There was a sparkle in his sunken eyes.

Asya ran up to the chair where he sat and tucked the blanket about his legs. It had not really come loose, but she felt better doing something for the man. The sparkle in his eye tugged at her heart. How full of life he must once have been. Asya knelt at his side and took his hand in hers. It was a big-boned hand with long fingers. The flesh had wasted away and it felt hard and cold as she held it against her cheek. Petion had been a big man. Strong. Virile. She wished she could have known him then. What a magnificent leader for Haiti! A man who had a heart for his people. His people. They were her people now, too, Asya thought.

She looked up into Petion's face. The whiteness of his hair made his sallow skin look tan. A dull tan. Almost as though whatever color it had once been had wearied and faded. She too was a mulatto. Black and white. When she grew old, would her two bloods grow tired and blend in this same drab tan also?

"I am proud of my black blood," Asya told him, following her train of thought. "There was a time when I wanted to die rather than live with it flowing through my heart. That was before I knew that Negroes are people too. With hearts and dreams. And aches."

"You must be proud of both bloods, Asya." M. Petion spoke in the voice of a father instructing a daughter.

"Oh, I am. I am. I was born being glad I was white. It was only that I had to learn to be grateful for being black too." She looked at him admiringly. "What do you value most that you inherited from your Negro blood?"

Petion gave a thoughtful smile. "Of all the gifts I received from the black race, the one I enjoy most is the optimism it bequeathed me. It is not an optimism that grows in my mind and then argues to assure me. It is something that just naturally is in my being. It is a spirit that, when I am confronted with failure or discouragement, sings a happy beat through my veins, rattles my heart with a merry shake, and dances a jig in my feet. It chants, 'All will be well. All will be well.' "

"I have the same song in me too," Asya said playfully. "Do you know what the words say?"

"Non."

."They sing, 'Ride with the soldiers. Go to the mountains. Meet Le Brigand. All will be well. All will be well.' "

M. Petion wagged a reproving finger. "You have tricked me. Tricked me with my own words," he said. A smile spread across his emaciated face. M. Petion was happy and relaxed.

Asya was up on her knees beside him again, her hands on the arm of his chair. "M. Petion, do let me go with the men." She was serious, all coquetry gone. "I am stifled. I can no longer stay in my house and wait and wonder and do nothing."

"Already you have given much to the republic," he

reminded her. "All your wealth you have put at our disposal. Is *that* nothing?"

"That's only money. That's the easy part. Others are having the excitement of using it, making things happen. Look at Le Brigand!" she exclaimed, referring to the renegade leader who had holed up in the mountains to fight Christophe. She had heard stories of the fearless bandit, and was privately longing to meet him.

"You want to go to war and fire a musket with the men? Is that what you want?"

"*Non. Non.* I want to ride with the supplies up to the mountains. I won't go near the fighting. All I want to do is be close by and find out how the revolution is going. Else I won't know for months who deserted at Thomassique. Who followed the strange brigand into the mountains. Who *is* this guerrilla who has come to our defense, and now is in danger of being wiped out if we do not send supplies. If I stay home, I shall know nothing and I shall suffocate," she announced.

M. Petion looked at Asya with a suspicious eye. "Is there one man in particular you would like some information about?"

The unexpectedness of his question made Asya sit back on her heels, her arms limp at her sides. She felt herself blushing and put her hands up to her cheeks.

Petion gave a soft chuckle. "That's all right, my dear. Your face has answered for you. So," he wore a happy look as he nodded his head in approval, "there is a young man. The old woman of twenty-four is but a girl after all."

"And I may go?" Asya asked, grinning up at him.

"*Oui. Bonne chance.* I am not so old that I would come between lovers."

Asya's heart fluttered at the word. Lovers. He had told her that he loved her. But how long ago had that been? How could she tell this kind man that to be loved by Etienne was but the wishful yearning of her heart?

With the blessing of M. Petion, and in the company
of his private chaplain, Abbé Gregoire, Asya rode with
the soldiers up the long road from Port-au-Prince to
Bouza and from there headed into the mountain wil-
derness. The president had insisted the priest go along.
"Those poor men in that ragged army, trapped up
there in the mountains, have not had an opportunity to
make their Easter duty. Only God Himself knows how
long it has been since they have enjoyed the
sacraments."

Asya had an idea it was not the men and their un-
shriven souls about which M. Petion was concerned.
The president was old-fashioned enough to think she
needed a chaperone and yet sharp enough not to discuss the matter with her. Thinking about her need for
protection brought a smile to Asya's lips. Who would
want to make advances to her, dressed as she was?
Even the water boy looked better.

Asya had "borrowed" some faded green pants from
her gardener, and since he was inclined to grow a
paunch, it was necessary to secure them by tying a red
scarf about her waist. After a few days on the journey,
Abbé Gregoire handed her a rope with the captain's
orders to replace the red scarf. Its bright color was too
easily spotted by the enemy.

The white blouse was her own. Its high-buttoned
collar made it seem a modest garment at the time Asya
had selected it, but during the long rides, she grew hot
and took to leaving it open at the neck. This relief was
short-lived, for, as her watchful chaperone was quick
to point out, her attire was not very proper and she
ought to button her collar. Her large-brimmed straw hat
was disreputable, but she cherished it. Asya had rolled
her hair into a ball on top of her head, and the only
hat which would fit was that of her cook, a large ro-
tund woman with a head to match her girth. The hat
always hung on a peg beside the kitchen entrance,
handy for donning against the sun when the woman
went to the iron market or out to the garden for

herbs. The broken straw stuck out at crazy angles in so many places that it looked as though an untidy bird had built its nest atop her head. But it served its purpose, as it doggedly repulsed all efforts of the gusty winds in the high mountains to dislodge its grip upon her hair.

Each day, the army of reinforcements rode until the sun set. Asya had no idea how far they had gone, or where she was. After a while, all the mountains looked the same. To her it was like riding in the middle of the sea with waves of rocks and trees instead of water.

Early one morning as she was ready to mount her horse, Abbé Gregoire came to Asya to announce that she was not to ride with the men that day. They were approaching their destination, and fighting was expected. The soldiers were going on to the aid of the trapped brigand, but the supplies, other than those needed for the skirmish, would be left here at a safe distance.

"Well!" Asya was indignant. She was being shoved out of the excitement. "I didn't come all this way to sit on the sidelines and keep an eye on the provisions."

"That won't be necessary," the abbé said seriously. "The captain has assigned a guard to keep watch. You will be safe."

"Me? Am I the only one left behind?"

"*Non. Non.* The cook will stay too." He started to hurry away.

"But what about you?" Asya ran after him. "Aren't you staying here with us too?"

Abbé Gregoire paused long enough to turn around and give Asya a withering look. "*Bon Mère!* I am a man of God. My place is on the battlefield with the injured and the dying." With that, his sandaled feet whisked him after the column of soldiers heading toward a clearing where the horses waited.

As the days passed, Asya thought of herself as the impedimenta referred to in Caesar's wars, which she had studied in Latin class. Never in her wildest dreams could she have foreseen herself in this role. Yet, here she was. She tried to make conversation with the cook, but he had a well-guarded jug, whose contents he imbibed frequently. It was obvious that he did not mind being classified impedimenta.

Such thoughts were silly, of course. She was really occupying herself with these lighter reflections to keep her mind off graver matters. There was M. Petion. Would she ever see him again? This past year she had watched him slip toward death. It was his stomach. When he ate, the pain went up his back, across the top of his head, and down into his eyes. She had often seen him like this, his arms held stiffly out from his sides, his fists clenched as though he would squeeze out the hell within. Physician after physician had come to him. The houngans had taken their turns. Some said he might overcome it, but most shook their heads.

And yet, M. Petion worked on, attacking the duties of his office with the vigor of a well man.

"Why don't you rest after one of those spells?" Asya once asked him.

"Why should I? I didn't die, did I?" He was amused that she should ask. "As long as I'm still alive, I may as well work."

Asya would always be grateful to M. Petion. When she received the payment for the Chalice of Casals and had offered the full amount to him for his fight against North Haiti and Christophe, he had refused. "If I take this money, you will have nothing, Asya. You must invest it and give only the interest for our cause. Someday, you will return to your home and you will need the principal for a fresh start."

"But—but I don't know anything about investments." She had felt so ignorant.

"I'll take you to a banker. You can trust him," Petion assured her. "Whatever he advises will be safe."

Remembering, Asya smiled. She had later reported to Petion that she had bought a rum factory, and he remarked that it was a very lucrative business. What she had not told him about was her other investment, the major source of her large donations to the cause. A man of his ideals would not have approved.

Suddenly Asya felt lonely. In her musings, she had been sitting on the wild grass, her back against a tree, but now she ran back toward the cook and the guard and the impedimenta. If she talked to someone, perhaps she would not cry.

Asya lost count of the number of days she waited. At last a subaltern came to escort her to Le Brigand's hideout far up in the mountains. She was heady with anticipation. The long time of impatience and boredom was wiped out as though it had been endured in another era.

Asya and her companions and, of course, the impedimenta, rode uphill for two days and finally came out upon a plateau, carved millennia ago by the winds and the rains from the top of the mountain. It was a large area, as large as a town square, with trees and giant rocks breaking the bleakness. At one end, a waterfall ran down from a mountain above. Up here, a group of rebels could hold off an attacking force forever if it had the supplies. A thrill went through Asya's body. She had made those supplies possible.

"Where is Le Brigand?" Asya turned to the subaltern, whose name she had never asked. "I want to meet him."

He pointed toward the side of the mountain to a thicket of ivy, which grew down over a straight wall of rock. Asya was puzzled and opened her mouth to ask what he meant when she saw a hand protrude from the ivy and thrust it aside like a curtain of coarse green strands. A man stepped out, a soldier with a face so weather-beaten that Asya could not tell if he was white or Negro. His rumpled uniform was as nondescript as his face, giving the effect that he was an extension of landscape.

This must be the guerrilla of the mountain. She ran toward him. "Are you Le Brigand?"

If she had been a St. Bernard with a cask about her neck, the soldier could not have looked more surprised. His eyes blinked with his stupefaction. He shook his head. *"Non,"* the voice stumbled. "He's—" The voice died, and the man could only point with a wavering thumb toward the ivy from where he had come.

Asya was annoyed. Had he never seen a woman in pants? "I want to see Le Brigand," she announced in what sounded to her ears like a tone of haughtiness, but she did not care.

With that same look of disbelief, the soldier, his eyes still on Asya, tilted his head and called back through the ivy in a voice which was no more than a croak, "He-she wants to see you."

"Who the devil is he-she? A Chinaman?" someone boomed out from behind the ivy curtain.

Asya's heart leaped in her breast. Was it possible? Had she suspected all along? Pushing aside the soldier, or rather knocking him over, Asya shot through the green vines, into a cave beyond. And there he was! Seated at a table of rough boards, his head bent over a sheaf of papers which he was holding up close to the flame of a candle that flickered from the lip of a jug at his elbow. Even with the beard, Asya knew it was he. She stood still, saying nothing. Looking and adoring. The shape of his head. The light and shadow caressing his cheek. His hair bleached to a white gold from too much sun.

Without taking his eyes from the papers he was studying, the man at the table asked, "What do you want, he-she?"

There was that same amusement in his voice. Remembering, love for him surging through her whole body, stifling her, Asya could scarcely breathe. She could not speak.

When she did not answer, and there was only silence, Etienne Grenier, Le Brigand looked up. The papers slid from his hands. He stared at her, his eyes open wide in shock. Asya's heart was pounding so

542

fiercely against her chest that her strength was slipping away. In this all-encompassing weakness, her eyes could not retain their tears, and in their wetness, the face of her beloved swam before her. Asya saw him leap to his feet, and as her knees buckled, Etienne's arms came around her and she sank against him.

Asya sobbed. The warmth, the wonder of him. No struggle. It was all over. Only the ecstasy was left. The ecstasy of resting her head on his breast. The ecstasy of his hand holding her head tightly against him. His voice saying over and over again in a hushed, gentle way, "Asya. Asya. I have found you."

There was so much she wanted to tell him, but her voice was lost. She did not miss it, for tears are the words of the heart. She lay against him until her eyes stopped their weeping, and her heart, limp from its ordeal, had curled up and snuggled itself deep in her breast—or was it in his? Asya felt Etienne's hand under her chin, tilting back her head until he looked into her eyes and she into his.

"I love you." He said it quietly; his eyes were serious and clear, speaking from his heart. His head came down and their lips met. They clung to each other, wedded by the warmth, the yearning which flowed between them. Her whole physical being throbbed to become part of him, at the same time crying out, demanding he be a part of her.

Etienne picked Asya up in his arms and carried her to—somewhere. She did not know, for they floated high above the world. When he laid her down, never taking his arms from about her, and she felt the weight of him upon her, Asya's body flowed to him, demanding him, claiming him, yielding, drowning itself in the deep, deep sea of the wondrous warmth which was Etienne.

Asya awakened the next morning to bright sunlight streaming in through a high aperture in the side of the cave. Its golden rays shone down upon her face and she shut her eyes again so that she might bask in its caress. She lay very still so as not to disturb the blissful state which permeated her whole being. She was being created again, born into a happy world where she could love and be loved. Never would she have to fight again. Never would she be lonely.

Slowly, Asya opened her eyes and let them rest on the ceiling of the cave. The rocks pointed down in jagged spears or disappeared into black recesses in the mountain above, as though fashioned by a clumsy mason with no pattern in mind. Languidly, Asya turned her glance to the opening in the cave which framed the patch of blue sky. This was her little cell of heaven in the mountains. She was like that monk of Vienna the soeurs had told her about. The one who had spent his life in a hole in the rocks, with only a small window, carved out of the stone, through which to look down upon the earth. At the time she had thought it a harsh way to spend a life, but she was wrong. Life in a cell was glorious. No wonder the monk did not leave. He had his God to keep him company, and she her lover.

Asya stretched out her arms, and the bedcover fell back. She was naked. It was an exciting sensation. She threw back the rough blanket so that the length of her body might feel the warmth from the sun. She laughed because she was so happy that some sound must come from her throat.

"And what amuses *ma cherie,* my sleepyhead, so late in the morning?" came a voice from somewhere in the cave. His dear voice.

"Oh," Asya gasped, at the same time pulling the cover up over her body. "I thought I was alone.

"You were until now. I came in to see if you were ever going to awaken." He sat down beside her. Leaning over, he kissed her on the forehead, his lips light, caressing. They touched along her nose and around her mouth, gentle brushings of the wings of love. He kissed her throat, making her tingle with the touch of him,

544

and then he laid his head against her breast. "How beautiful you are, Asya."

Tenderly she stroked his hair. Only then was she aware of the change in his appearance. "Why, Etienne," she smiled. "You've shaved your beard. "Was that for me?"

"And only now do you notice it." Etienne looked up at her and shook his head in playful disapproval. "Asya, on *what* have you been keeping your thoughts?"

Asya blushed. She knew she was blushing, for she could feel the blood rushing up into her cheeks.

"Don't answer. I know," he teased. "Your red face gives you away, and I love you for it."

"I guess I'll always be a naive schoolgirl," Asya pouted.

"I guess so." His eyes sparkled with humor.

"But I don't want to be. You discourage me when you agree with me. I like to think of myself as a femme fatale."

Etienne threw back his head and laughed. "You'll never be a femme fatale. You might be able to strut about like a well-bred lady for a little while, but when you want to spout off, you'll always become your natural self again—your natural, ornery self." Etienne reached out and tousled her hair. "And I love you for it," he said softly.

"I'm glad." Asya ran her hand lovingly along his cheek. "You know, I'm happy you shaved your beard."

"Why?" he asked.

"Because it will be easier to pick you out from all the other men up here in the wilds." With that, Asya ducked her head under the cover and rolled over on her stomach.

"Coward." Etienne gave her a loving swat on the tail.

Asya giggled again.

"Femmes fatales don't giggle," Etienne told her.

Asya pulled the edge of the blanket away just far

enough to peer out with one eye from behind strands of her tangled hair.

"Look at you. What kind of a bride will you make?" Etienne chided. "Have you no pride in your appearance on your own wedding day?"

Asya sat up, clutching the blanket tightly about herself. "What are you talking about? You haven't asked me to marry you."

"I'm asking you now," Etienne announced. "*Non,* I'm telling you. We're being married this afternoon."

Slowly Asya got to her feet, the blanket still wrapped around her. She stood before him and was quiet, saying nothing, biting her lower lip. He stared down at her, bewilderment on his face.

"Don't you love me, Asya?" he asked.

She nodded. Tears started to roll down her cheeks. "You can't marry me," Asya sobbed. "I'm black."

"That's nothing. Take a bath."

Asya let out a wail. "I am serious, Etienne. I have Negro blood in me."

Tenderly, he folded her into his arms. "I know, Asya. Negu told me. Don't you see, I love *you,* whatever it is that you happen to be." He laid his cheek against the top of her head. "Don't cry, darling," he comforted. "I don't care what kind of blood runs through your veins, so long as it flows, keeping you warm and loving, and yielding as you were last night. Love is of the heart, not the blood."

"But what about our children? They'll be all mixed up. Black and white. What kind of a legacy will we be giving them?"

Etienne laughed softly. "If they pick up the conniving ingenuity of their great-grandmother, Negu, and the combativeness and spirit of their mother, what else do our *petits enfants* need?" He shook his head in admiration. "A glorious heritage!"

Asya managed a weak smile. "And what, monsieur, will you contribute toward our glorious progeny?"

"Support." He took her face between his hands and

kissed her on the tip of her nose. "Now, go make yourself into the most beautiful bride that ever was. You have until this afternoon."

And beautiful she was. Her only shirt, buttoned modestly to the chin, and the too-big breeches, once more held up by the bright red scarf, were Asya's wedding gown. Her long black hair, gathered loosely at the neck with vines of orchids, hung unpinned down her back. In her hands, Asya carried a bouquet of wild, white poinsettias. Her wedding ring was a circlet fashioned from the golden feathers of a hummingbird.

The wedding ceremony itself could not have been more beautiful if it had been performed in the most fashionable locale. The side of the mountain served as the altar. An altar of stone. It rose majestically high above the earth like a finger pointing to God, beckoning Him to notice the mortals at its feet. The walls of the cathedral were the trees, and its floor was their leaves and needles, dropped by the boughs overhead into a rich mosaic of browns and greens. The candlelight was the golden sunlight filtering through the trees. The birds formed the choir, singing from their lofts in the treetops. The organ music was made by the water cascading down over the rocks of the mountain. And the dome of the church was the blue sky, hung with white clouds of angel's wings.

The guests had been invited, and they had all come, dressed in their worn uniforms and shaggy beards, watching from among the trees like little brown gnomes who had crawled up from the earth to witness the wedding of two of their woodland friends.

Chapter Thirty-nine

Mère Brigitte waited in her office for the arrival of Sophia, Queen of Prussia. She was looking forward with relish to this meeting—confrontation was perhaps a better word—and the nun made no attempt to control the excitement she was feeling. It was not often an abbess called a queen to account, especially one who had donated so liberally to the order of the Sacre-Coeur. Mère Brigitte had never called anyone to account before. Perhaps that was the reason she savored the prospect of the role she was about to play.

It had been a long climb up to the position Mère Brigitte now held as head of Sacre-Coeur Hospital. As she looked back upon it now, the way to the top had been lonely, dreary and, at times, hopeless. That she had been selected as mother superior of the hospital had come as a surprise to Mère Brigitte. Nothing nice, as far back as she could remember, had ever happened to her. True, she had worked hard at the hospital simply because that was the way she was raised. "You must do your best, and God will reward; He sees all," had been among the platitudes urged upon her during her growing-up years, but Mère Brigitte never dreamed that God or anyone else would ever seek her out for one of life's awards.

To enter the monastic order had not been Mère Brigitte's choice. It was thrust upon her. Ordained by Heaven, her parents and aunts had called it. Born the fifth daughter of the Marquis and Marchioness de Rainilly, Annette, as she was christened, was referred

548

to by her relatives as "the little bird." Annette thought it was because she liked to run and hop and jump. Her feet had invisible wings, for they never wanted to be still. She loved motion for itself.

Then she found out why they called her "the little bird." One day some relatives called and were having chocolate in the garden. Annette wandered among them, seeing how many sweetmeats she could filch from their plates, when a hawk flew down and landed on top of the table where the plates of cakes were standing. One of the maids screamed and tried to shoo it away, but the bird held ground and refused to budge. Annette was used to hawks. They were only birds, but this one was an ugly one. He was larger than any she had seen, and he stuck his beak out as though daring anyone to order him off the white tablecloth into which he had dug his sharp claws. Annette was fascinated and went closer to get a better look. She held out a *Prager Kuchen,* and the bird snatched it from her fingers, giving her a nasty look which seemed to say it was about time it got some service.

Someone giggled behind Annette, and she heard a voice say, "Seeing them together, one wonders which is hawk and which is child."

The bird took off, and, at the same time, Annette ran into the house, sobbing to herself. "I hate aunts. I hate all relatives."

Once inside, she stood on a chair and looked at her beaklike nose in the salon mirror. Fresh tears broke out. She *did* look like that ugly hawk. "Even a bird does not want to look like me. I'm ugly."

Whether ordained by God or by her relatives, Annette was packed off to the convent the day after her Confirmation. She was eager to go after overhearing one of the relatives at her Confirmation Day feast remark, "It's well the convent is taking that girl. With her looks, she'd never get a husband." At least, Annette told herself, there would be no aunts at Sacre-Coeur Hospital.

Annette liked the convent. Dressed exactly the same as the other nuns, her ugliness was less noticeable. When she sat in the chapel during Vespers or Holy Mass, Annette's eyes liked to wander over the rows of robed women of the Sacre-Coeur and muse how everyone was identical. A happiness came into her heart. This was the way God regarded the souls of all mankind everywhere. Identical. Of equal value. Even ugly little girls with noses like hawks. He loved them all, and saw them all the same.

After years of training, Annette, now Soeur Brigitte, was placed in charge of the nursery. She was delighted. It was not the service she rendered that gladdened Soeur Brigitte's heart. It was the warmth and cuddliness of the babies themselves which she loved. Her heart, for most of her life, had been a cold, damp room, but now, when she held a baby in her arms and crooned a little song in his ear, he kindled a glow within. Babies did not say unkind words nor give orders nor make one combative. They were little souls just sent from God, still wrapped in His love, and if you held them close, you could feel His blessing of peace, which every new baby brings from Heaven as a gift.

Only once was Soeur Brigitte called from the nursery. That had been years ago when Mère Denise and Mère Magdelaine had gone to Rome, and she was made acting mother superior during their absence. She had not liked the temporary honor, as the other nuns seemed to regard it, for she had been called upon to make decisions, and decisions frightened her at that time. She herself thought she had done well in her brief term as head of the hospital, but when Mère Denise and Mère Magdelaine returned from Rome, they were most upset that she had permitted Asya Drapeaux to leave for Haiti. Soeur Brigitte had seen no wrong in it. The solicitor was a *bona fide* gentleman of the law, and his papers, with their bright seals, clearly requested Asya's immediate departure for Haiti, if she was to claim her inheritance. Surely everyone knew that someday, she must leave the hospital. Soeur Brigitte was merely obeying the law. It was as simple as that.

Certainly she had loved Asya as much as the rest of them. The girl had been but a toddler when Soeur Brigitte was first assigned to the nursery. At first, Soeur Brigitte was afraid of the little girl. She appeared so big beside the newborn infants. But soon Asya became a great help to Soeur Brigitte. She knew where everything was kept and was a specialist in the job, in which she claimed priority, of swabbing the poor little seats, when they became irritated, with egg white mixed with olive oil.

Asya must be a young woman by now, she mused. About twenty-five. Probably married with her own batch of babies whose little behinds needed rubbing with egg white and olive oil. She wondered if Asya remembered the homemade Sacre-Coeur panacea for sore bottoms.

Mère Brigitte shook her head to wipe out the reflections of the past. This pending meeting with the Queen of Prussia was a serious matter. A woman, a spoiled, indulged woman, had by her own indifference, or cowardice, changed the destiny of a human life. That was for God to do, and she, Mère Brigitte, meant to help God put that life back on its intended course.

The matter had come to her attention shortly after Mère Brigitte assumed her new office. It was the duty of the mother superior to keep the files on the births and deaths of the babies born in the hospital, and no one—*no one*—but she was permitted to touch these files.

One afternoon Mère Brigitte was examining some of the older files to learn how her predecessor had recorded the personal data of the hospital patients. And then she found it! Found the sham which had been perpetrated upon a little girl. A little girl who had once been a baby like the babies of her own she must now be cuddling! It was all there in the files!

Asya Drapeaux had been born out of wedlock to Sophia, then Duchess of Hesse, and Orlando D'Azio of Cádiz, Spain. She was not the child of Celeste and André Drapeaux. That baby had died at birth!

Who had done this? Who had falsified the hospital records? Who had switched the babies? Surely not Mère Magdelaine. Perhaps, the child's mother, Queen Sophia herself! No, she could not even entertain such a thought. But the Queen had certainly expressed an unusual interest in the Order of the Sacre-Coeur. Mère Brigitte stiffened in anger. Why, her munificent gifts of buildings and furnishings had been nothing but bribery! Her regular visits to the hospital, ostensibly in the name of charity, were actually to see her daughter. Why, she had been nothing but a fraud!

There was a tap on the door. A nun in a white habit, identical to that of the mother superior and all the other members of the order, high or low, announced that the queen had arrived.

"*Bon jour,* Mère Brigitte," said the queen as she stepped into the office.

The nun looked at her visitor, saying nothing for the moment. In her mind, Mère Brigitte had told herself that the queen was a spineless, simpering old woman, overly touted by the members of the Sacre-Coeur, who, like a bunch of children, were blinded by the gifts she gave them. But in front of her stood lovely Queen Sophia, still golden and beautiful as ever. Her soft voice, the regal way she held her head, her slow, lovely smile, bespoke breeding and innate graciousness.

As she looked at the repose of that face and into the queen's clear, gray eyes, Mère Brigitte knew a twinge of bitterness. Age and sin had left no ugly mark upon this woman. There are always some souls, she thought, God makes special.

"Congratulations, Mère Brigitte," Sophia broke the silence, "on your election to head of the hospital. My best wishes for you are that you enjoy your duties as much as your last two predecessors, Mère Magdelaine and Mère Denise." She held out her hand to the nun.

Mère Brigitte barely touched it. Motioning to a chair, she said coldly, "Do be seated, your Majesty."

With a righteous air, Mère Brigitte sat down behind her desk, her symbol of authority giving her every right to preside over this inquisition. She wet her lips in what seemed a natural preamble to the easy issuance of words, folded her arms across her bosom, and looked at the summoned visitor, who, by now, was regarding Mère Brigitte with a quizzical eye.

"It is precisely because of my predecessors that I have asked you to come," the superior announced. "There is much to be done, and the sooner the better, so I shall not indulge in useless banalities while you wonder why I have sent for you."

The queen made no comment, but her eyes brightened with interest.

"I have been going over the past files of the hospital," Mère Brigitte paused a brief moment, "as is my duty as mother superior. I find a great injustice has been done to one of the babies born in our care. I learned that Asya Drapeaux is your daughter and not the child of a mulatto and a Creole from Haiti. That child and mother died the day of the birth."

Not so much as a flicker passed over Queen Sophia's face. She was attentive and interested as though listening to the tale of some unknown person.

"Is this so?" Mère Brigitte asked accusingly.

"*Oui*," Sophia answered in the same lovely soft voice she might have used to comment upon the beauty of the weather. "Asya is my daughter. That is right."

Mère Brigitte stared in amazement at the woman across the desk from her. "You do not deny it, then?"

"*Non.*"

"There is no mistake in the files?"

"*Non.*"

"Am I to understand that Mère Magdelaine went along with the idea to misrepresent the child's identity?"

Sophia sighed, as one does before the start of a difficult, unpleasant task. "It was Mère Magdelaine's idea to switch babies. The mulatto infant had died, and my brother came to the hospital to kill my baby. Why lose two lives? It was Mère Magdelaine's quick thinking which saved Asya."

Mère Brigitte scoffed, "Come, now, you expect me to believe such dramatics? Why should your brother wish to kill his own niece?"

The queen leaned forward and, with a twinkle in her eyes, whispered, "Because he thought he was God."

The mother superior of the Order of the Sacre-Coeur scowled across at her visitor. Was she trying to imply that she too was meddling with God's work. "Why did Mère Magdelaine not order him out?"

"My brother had leprosy and planned to contaminate the whole hospital with the disease if she did not give him the baby. You did not know my brother. He would have done so, too."

"Nonsense! Leprosy is not contagious in a temperate climate such as ours."

Sophia bowed her head in a gesture of shame, but when she spoke her voice betrayed her attitude as but a sham. "How stupid of us women. Too bad you were not there, Mother. You could have enlightened our ignorance."

Mère Brigitte bristled. The situation was not going to her liking. "I shall no longer question your story," she said testily, "but I cannot understand why this fraud was permitted to continue after your brother had gone."

The visitor raised her head and stared innocently at her inquisitor. "What *should* I have done?" she asked. "I was to marry the King of Prussia. Do you think he wanted a child along with his bride?"

"Of course not!" Mère Brigitte snapped. "I merely wish to point out that your child should have been allowed to assume her proper identity after the crisis with your brother was over."

Sophia gave a bitter laugh. "Where my brother was

concerned, there was always a crisis." She sobered. "We could not endanger Asya's life by running the risk of Actah's learning she was still alive. We felt my child safer living under another's name."

"And who are we?"

"Mère Magdelaine and I."

"Are you saying that Mère Magdelaine sanctioned this lie, this sin? That one member of our order would dare to hide the truth?"

"*Non.* Not one member of the order, but two. Do not forget that Mère Denise, when she became superior, also went along with the little ruse."

Mère Brigitte was indignant. "Do not think that, by giving it another name, you can disguise evil."

Sophia gave the nun a patient smile, and her poise was as unshaken as when she had first entered the office. "Mère Brigitte, you must try to understand. If you had been there the night my brother came, you would be more tolerant of the situation. The world cannot be ruled by absolute right and absolute wrong. There are times when that which is wrong is seen in a different light, and it becomes right. As yet, you are new in your office as head of the Sacre-Coeur Order. You will find many times that you cannot go by the ordained rules. Instead, you will have to use mercy and leniency, as your wisdom decides."

Mère Brigitte shot to her feet, hot words at the tip of her tongue. But she kept her mouth shut. She must not say anything lest she lose her grip on dignity. Slowly, she sat down.

Choosing her words carefully, the nun said in a vindictive tone, "You are the sinner, and yet you dare to talk to me of right and wrong."

The queen raised her chin. "I do not look upon myself as a sinner. I loved Asya's father. I gave birth to a wonderful child. Where is the sin?"

"In duping the Drapeaux family," Mère Brigitte shot out viciously, "into thinking their child was alive."

"That makes them more fortunate. They will never

know they lost their own child. This keeps everyone happy."

"What kind of a mother are you?" the woman at the desk accused. "To deny her own baby. To sit here and calmly speak of her as though she meant nothing to you."

"I don't deny her. I just don't own up to her. What good would I be to her if she knew who I was? If the world knew? She would be bitter and hate me for what the world would do to her. There is no place for a bastard in society."

"But," Mère Brigitte snapped back, "even if this deception *was* all for Asya's good, why then was the Drapeaux money accepted for the education of a child which had died at birth? Was that not stealing?"

"*Non.* It was worth whatever M. Drapeaux sent the Order of the Sacre-Coeur for the joy of believing his baby still lived. He knew no sorrow and, in the end, his family got the child for whom they had paid all those years. And I—I am the one who does without, and I would not change it, for I know Asya is happy." For the first time the queen's voice betrayed some emotion.

"You have heard from her then?"

"Not directly. My nephew is in Haiti. He helps the emperor there with international affairs. He tells me that Asya has the loveliest plantation in the country. Is beautiful and rich. Could I have given her all that, had I admitted to being her mother? Could I have guaranteed her safety? This way, I know she is safe. I pray for her, believing my prayers will be answered. I trust her to God. Who better to look after her?"

"No other," the mother superior agreed, "in light of what you have told me. However," her voice took on a note of stubborn authority, "I think Asya should now be told the truth of her parentage. She is old enough to be discreet and keep the matter to herself. But tell her we must."

"You sound so very, very determined to upset a young girl's life. Why?"

"Asya, as the daughter of Celeste, is a mulatto. As your daughter, your Majesty, she is a Caucasian. I think Asya should be aware of her true blood."

Sophia looked at the nun in amazement. "How does that make a difference? Asya has made a new life for herself in Haiti. If she is happy, is that not all that matters?"

"There are certain facts in life we must face, your Majesty," Mère Brigitte announced, "and we cannot run from them on the premise that it might upset 'happiness.' I strongly feel it would be a great sin for me to continue this deception of Asya's background. For the world, it need not know. But Asya must know. It is God's will. That is the way I see it."

"Asya was adopted by M. Drapeaux," Sophia said in an icy voice. "As his legal daughter, she was evidently accepted without question. The subject of her background may never have come up, or if it has, by now it is probably settled to the satisfaction of all concerned. What enjoyment can you possibly derive from stirring up a turbulence in someone's life?"

"I am not stirring up a turbulence," Mère Brigitte hammered out each word. "I am merely presenting the truth. Is the truth wrong?"

The visitor did not answer. She sat there and shook her head while her eyes gave the mother superior a pitying look.

Mère Brigitte was nettled. "I am sorry," she said, "that you cannot understand my position. But I am the mother superior and I have a duty to perform. And—" she gave her desk a definite pat with the flat of her hand to emphasize the point she was about to make "—and perform it I shall! It is the principle of the thing!"

Sophia stood up quickly. "In that case," she said, "our conference is concluded," and took a step toward the door.

"*Non. Non.*" Mère Brigitte held up a hand. "Don't go yet. I need Asya's address in Cap Henri."

"You expect me to give it to you?" Sophia asked.

"Whether you give the address to me or not will not alter matters. It will only simplify them. I can always write to Rome and get the name of the bishop or a priest assigned to Cap Henri and post the letter for Asya in his care. So why not go along with God's will and let me have the address?"

The queen gave the abbess a sly look. Her eyes twinkled and she said coyly, "*Non*. You will have to get it on your own. It's the principle of the thing." Then she raised her head defiantly and swished from the room.

The Abbé Corneille Brille was preparing to say Mass. He had many things on his mind, the least of which was the note he had received only the day before from the mother superior of the Hospital of the Sacre-Coeur in Chalon-Sur-Marne, France. The letter she had enclosed for forwarding to Asya was, according to Mère Brigitte, of the utmost importance and she expected him to make certain that it reached Mlle. Drapeaux's hands. As soon as Ookie arrived, Abbé Brille would dispatch him with the letter to the dock. There was a ship in now, a Portuguese sail, which was leaving sometime today for Port-au-Prince. The priest knew the captain. He could be counted on to see that the letter reached its destination.

Abbé Brille did know the exact whereabouts of Asya Drapeaux. In fact, everyone in the imperial palace knew that she was somewhere in South Haiti, plotting against the emperor. Her hostile actions against Christophe had been reported back to him. Although Petion was now dead over a year, Asya had joined forces with General Boyer, his successor, and Henri Christophe saw her hand, her financial hand, behind every one of his military's setbacks at Fort Thomassique. The townsfolk seemed unaware of the painful thorn in the side of their emperor, or if they knew, they feigned ignorance, having accepted the story that Asya had died the night her plantation was mysteriously burned.

But Abbé Brille had no time for the war between Asya and the emperor. He had a funeral this morning. One of his flock had been murdered. Shot down yesterday by the gendarme in the marketplace. The man had been a farmer, a chicken farmer, who brought his fowl to the market for selling. A police officer had selected the best two hens for himself, and when the farmer held out his hand for a gourd, the price agreed upon, the gendarme had laughed, so the bystanders reported, and said something about its being pay enough for the honor of selling to the police. The man called it stealing and demanded his money. Whereupon the champion of the law raised his musket and coldly shot him in the throat. A life exchanged for two hens!

Ookie, his most dependable altar boy, came early, as usual, and when Abbé Brille handed him the letter, with the exhortation to hurry back for the funeral, Ookie slipped out of his sandals and dashed away in his bare feet.

In no time at all, Ookie delivered the letter to the captain and was running back toward the cathedral when a hand grabbed him by the scruff of his neck. "Whoa, boy! Whoa!"

Ookie gingerly turned his head and looked into the face of the police chief of Cap Henri.

"What you done wrong, boy?" the man yelled, shaking Ookie at the same time.

"Nothing. Nothing. I'm on my way to Mass. I gotta serve."

"You lie. No boy runs fast to git to Mass. He runs to git away. To git out. What you done that you're runnin' from so's not to git caught?"

"I tell you, it's the truth. I have to serve."

"Then why you so late? Good boys git to church early for serving. I served when I was a boy. I know." He still held Ookie by the shirt, as though he were loath to part with his quarry.

559

"Because Abbé Brille sent me to the wharf." The boy squirmed but the restraining hand remained firm.

"What for? He don't git no Mass wine down there."

"I had a letter. He wanted me to give the letter to the captain on a ship."

"You lie! You lie!"

"*Non. Non.* You can ask the abbé. It's the truth."

"Naw. I ain't gonna ask no priest nothin'. They're always tryin' to git you in church. Not me."

"Then you just have to believe me. I carried a letter for the abbé."

"Was there a name on the letter?"

"*Oui. Oui,*" the boy answered quickly.

"Oh, so you was readin' the abbé's mail," the policeman accused.

"That's all I read. The name on the outside."

"You can't read," the man said in derision. "Boys can't read. How do I know you're not just makin' up a name?"

That was a maddening thing to say to the smartest student in his class. Ookie would show him. "I can write the name that was on that letter. You'll have to believe I can read then."

"Ain't got no paper," was the dismissing answer.

"Then I'll write it right here in the street." With that, Ookie dropped to his knees and with his index finger wrote in the dirt:

> *Mlle. Asya Drapeaux*
> *c/o Gen. Boyer*
> *Port-au-Prince*

The police chief pursed his lips while he studied the writing at his feet. He had never learned to read, but he was not about to divulge this fact to a smart kid. "That's only writin'. If you're so smart, read what you wrote."

Ookie read, "Mlle. Asya Drapeaux, care of General Boyer, Port-au-Prince."

The gendarme stiffened. The only part of him that moved was his eyes which blinked wildly as his mind groped to comprehend the meaning of what he had heard. "You sure? You sure you read that right?" he asked as he laid a heavy hand on the boy's shoulder. "You sure?"

"Of course I'm sure. I wrote it, didn't I? I can read what I write."

The policeman stopped his blinking and speculatively eyed the boy before him. It was a long time since he had received any recognition from the palace. The gendarme had an idea they might just be interested in what this skinny urchin had to say.

"Come," the police chief slithered up close to Ookie and put an arm about his shoulders. "Come with me," he said in an oily voice. "We'll ride up to the palace and show the emperor how well you can read."

Up at the palace, Ookie proudly did his writing-and-reading act for a tall, handsome soldier in a brilliant red uniform of the Dahomey guard. His name was Prophète. Then the emperor came, and Ookie did it all over again. He explained how he had come by the letter and when he had finished, the emperor snapped at the police chief, "Did you stop the ship in the harbor? Did you arrest the captain?"

The gendarme wilted. Ookie noticed how he trembled. "*Non*, your Majesty. I just came right to you. Fast."

"You fool!" the emperor shouted. "You fool. When you don't use your head around me, you don't keep it long!"

Some soldiers came in and dragged the now screaming police chief from the room. Ookie was frightened, for, long after the door had closed, he could hear the cries from somewhere far off in the distance.

"So, it is that fat pig of a priest who spies upon us!" the emperor spat. Then his eyes fell upon Ookie as though he were seeing him for the first time. "Get out of here!" he shouted, at the same time raising his foot and giving the school's prize student a resounding kick in the behind. "Get the hell out of here!"

It was twenty-five kilometers from Sans Souci to the cathedral at Cap Henri, and although he ran and walked and twice got a lift on a cart, Ookie did not get back to the city until early the next morning. While he was bewildered as to the turn of events, the boy remembered it was his week to serve Mass, and he made his way toward the church. Much as he had hurried, Ookie was late. Abbé Brille had started with only one altar boy and was reading the Canon of the Mass when Ookie arrived.

Quickly donning his cassock and surplice, he hurried out to take his accustomed place on the right side of the altar steps. Consecration was about to begin, and Ookie reached for the bell. At that moment, noises came from the sacristy. Rough, unfamiliar noises made by coarse men. Suddenly, two halberd-carrying soldiers in red uniforms rushed out into the sanctuary and up the altar steps toward the priest who stood with the chalice in his upraised hands.

The first soldier, before the eyes of the horrified churchgoers, made a mighty sweep with the halberd and severed the head of the abbé from his body. As the priest slowly sank to the floor, the second soldier crashed his halberd into the tabernacle door. It happened so swiftly that Ookie was amazed to find himself still ringing the sanctuary bell for the Consecration, while the priest's blood flowed down the altar steps.

Chapter Forty

Angels are usually depicted with golden hair, but despite her ebony locks, Asya was feeling exactly like an angel. She was certain a halo shone about her head, and she had the urge to reach up with her scarf and burnish it to a greater brilliance. For today she was an obedient wife. Today was the day she would dispose of her lucrative investment. Etienne would be pleased the next time he came down from the mountains to learn she had carried out his wishes. Orders were more like it. Etienne had been very angry. Asya laughed now to herself, as she recalled how his eyes had flashed with indignation; but at the time, she was scared.

"My wife, a dope smuggler!" he had flung at her in disbelief. "If you had not told me yourself, I could not have believed it!"

"You shouldn't have asked me," Asya countered in a frightened voice.

"I am your husband. Shouldn't I be aware of what everyone else knows?" Asya had never seen Etienne so cold.

"Nobody else knows," she explained. "Only M. Défilée at the bank, the old blabbermouth. I don't know why he had to tell you. That was my private business."

"Oh," he asked sarcastically, "are husbands then to be kept ignorant of any nefarious business their wives happen to be trafficking in?"

Asya bit her lip. "I really didn't think it mattered. I

563

would have told you had I thought you wanted to know."

"You planned to tell me only after I found out for myself."

Asya pouted. "Is being a smuggler so bad?"

Etienne snorted in disgust. "Quit acting. Who put you up to this ugly business?"

Asya hesitated. "M. Petion." She almost whispered the name.

"M. Petion?" he shouted. "M. Petion was a saint. He would never have steered you into this messy business."

"Well, in a way," Asya wrinkled her brow, "he did. He told me to invest the money I received from the chalice so that I would always have an income, and he sent me to M. Défilée for advice."

"M. Défilée advised you to go into the dope-smuggling business?" Etienne's words snapped out like a whip that was already lashing the recalcitrant banker.

"He not only advised me, he went in along with me." As she spoke, Asya gave her husband a wary look. "We were partners."

"Were? Are you no longer partners?"

"*Non.* I bought him out."

"*Mon Dieu!*" Etienne's hands flew to the top of his head as though he had been hit there. "Do you mean that you have been dealing personally with these smuggling rats?"

"Oh, *non.* The captain of my ship takes care—of—those—a—a—those business deals necessary in the disposal of the cargo."

"My wife," Etienne said as his eyes scathingly lashed her from toes to head, "my wife trafficking with a waterfront rat!"

"But Captain Middleton is a very fine gentleman. He's not one of those coarse, ragged fellows that you see hanging around the docks. He is married and has five children and a beautiful house at a place in the States called Martha's Vineyard. *Mon amour,* anyone who comes from a town with such a Biblical-sounding name has to be a good man."

Etienne snorted. "All I can say is that it sounds like a very good front for the nefarious work he does."

"Really, it isn't at all like that. Captain Middleton is a whaling captain. He sails to the other side of the world to get his whales. Sometimes, he has to go as far away as Australia. Since he is almost at China—well, he goes a little farther and stops off there to pick up the opium. After all, it's practically on his way."

"I ought to spank you." He took a step toward her.

"*Non. Non.*" Asya backed away. "Don't be cross with me. After all, I didn't take the money for myself. I gave it to M. Petion, and now to General Boyer so we can win the war against Christophe. He needs the money, Etienne. He needs it badly for all that equipment and rifles." She flung her arms about her husband's neck. "Tell me you love me, and quit shouting at me. You frighten me so."

Asya felt his hand under her chin, and he raised her face so that he could look into it. For what seemed like a long time, Etienne studied her with those green-brown eyes of his, now cold and unfathomable. Her heart thumped against her breast so wildly that Asya felt faint, and, closing her eyes, she leaned against Etienne. "I am sorry I made you angry," she said, sobbing as she spoke, "I am sorry because I love you."

His arms went around her, caressing, possessive arms. The rigidity went from his body. She relaxed against him, knowing he loved her too.

Asya promised to sell the ship to Captain Middleton when next he came into port. For a long time he had been waiting to buy her out, and she knew he would be pleased. It pleased Etienne too.

And so, it was settled. After that, it was Etienne's money that financed the army of South Haiti. He went to Jamaica and made arrangements with his own banker to pay for the war against Christophe, and he took Asya with him. They were gone three months, and when they returned to Port-au-Prince, Asya was pregnant. The knowledge of his impending fatherhood stimulated Etienne's determination to overthrow Christophe's empire, for he wanted his first child born in a free land. When her husband left for his camp in the mountains after tenderly kissing her farewell, Asya knew that the long journey back to Cher Château was truly underway.

Now, it was almost time to keep her appointment at the banking house, for this was the day Captain Middleton received title to the ship. When Asya heard running feet, she assumed the houseboy had come to inform her that the carriage was waiting to take her down the hill into town. But instead, it was General Boyer's messenger with a letter for her. In the five years she lived in Port-au-Prince, Asya had never received a letter. A letter was an exciting occurrence, and, quickly breaking the seal, she sat down at the escritoire and read:

Hospice de Sacre-Coeur
May 20, 1820

Dear Mlle. Asya Drapeaux,

It has been many years since you left the hospital of the Sacre-Coeur, and if you recall, I was the acting superior during Mère Magdelaine's stay in Rome at the time of your departure for Haiti. At the demise of Mère Denise, my immediate predecessor, I was elected permanent mother superior.

Mère Denise, dead! Asya's heart fell. Nervously, she read on.

In my present honorable capacity, I am permitted to examine the files which record all births and deaths which take place here in the hospital, and while doing so, I learned that you were grossly misinformed as to your parentage.

According to our records, you are not the adopted daughter of M. André Drapeaux of Haiti, born out of wedlock to Celeste, a mulatto woman, also from Haiti, but the child of Sophia, Duchess of Hesse, whom you knew as Queen of Prussia, and a Spaniard, Orlando D'Azio. However, I am sorry to have to tell you that your parents were not married, and our records show you illegitimate.

For what reason this fraud was perpetrated upon you and the kindly Drapeaux family is not quite clear in my mind, but after a recent conference with Queen Sophia I was informed that she wished this hoax continued.

However, I am a religious woman whose life is pledged to truth, and I could not proudly wear my habit as a member of the Order of the Sacre-Coeur if I did not divulge to you the correct facts surrounding your birth. As I explained to your mother, the world need not be told, but you, as her daughter, should know. I am sure you can be counted upon to handle this information in a discreet manner.

As to the Drapeaux family, I shall not write to acquaint them of the death of their own beloved infant at the time of her birth. I shall leave that to your own good judgment as to the best way to inform them that they have been victims of a cruel deception. I feel I should not interfere into whatever love and respect have grown between you and your supposed family. You can best resolve this unpleasant situation.

I shall pray, my dear child, for the Lord to bless you and wipe away any bitterness this letter might enkindle in your heart for those who wronged you so long ago. In your charity, forgive them, remembering only that their actions were guided by their love for you.

Yours in Christ,

Mère Brigitte, S.S.C.

Asya's first reaction was to throw back her head and laugh, as she flung the letter from her. "Now they tell me," she said aloud to herself. "Now, when I am happy and no longer need a mother, I find I have one." She leaned back in her chair and stared scornfully at the letter where it had landed on the floor under the settee. You useless piece of paper, she thought, you are encroaching on my snug little world, and I want none of you. You are an outsider, and you cannot come in.

That meddlesome old nun! Why did she have to be so righteous? She should have saved herself the trouble, because Asya was not the least interested in the knowledge that she was the daughter of Queen Sophia. What had Sophia ever done for her that she should be called Mother? Playing the lady bountiful by building wings on the hospital in order to safeguard her secret. Bribery, that was what it was. If she loved her daughter, Queen Sophia should have adopted her. André Drapeaux thought highly enough of his daughter, bastard that she was, to take legal steps to adopt her. A little twinge of envy for that other dead baby born long ago on the same day as she herself touched Asya's breast. The mulatto's child was wanted. She was not.

And now, having lived as that mulatto's child for twenty-nine years, how could she suddenly wrench herself from one identity and become someone entirely different? She had her own family. Negu was that family. Negu had stood by her when Asya needed her. She had saved her life. She had tended her when she was sick, when she was obnoxious, when she was rude, and when she was nothing. Only a grandmother gave that much love.

A warm yearning to be with Negu came over Asya. She wanted to lay her cheek against that dear old scarred face and put her arms about the bony body and tell her she loved her. Would always love her. Never would she inform Negu that the efforts of a lifetime had been spent on somebody else's unwanted child. Asya must protect Negu, for although they were not related by blood, they were relatives by heart.

A shadow fell across the floor, and Asya looked up to see Etienne stepping through the open door.

"Darling!" She leaped to her feet and was across the floor and in his arms, kissing him hard on the mouth before he could say a word.

Abruptly a thought occurred to her and she stepped back. "Etienne, what are you doing home so soon? You said you would be gone weeks this time."

Etienne laughed. He pulled her to himself and, folding his arms around her, held her head to his breast. He rested his cheek against her hair and said, "What kind of a sweetheart is this who demands an account of my actions before she is properly kissed?"

"Oh, Etienne. It's only that I missed you so much. It's a wonderful surprise to have you here. I am happy you're back."

"If you're that happy to see me, then stop talking and kiss me."

"But I—" She never finished. Etienne kissed her.

They sat on the settee. Rather, Etienne sat on the settee and she on his lap, snuggling against him, a contented glow within.

"Since you were so surprised to see me," Etienne asked, "what mischief am I interrupting that you had planned for today?"

Asya sat up and clapped her hands together in delight. "Etienne," she said with excitement in her voice, "today's the day. The day I sell the ship to Captain Middleton. I am doing just as you told me. You see, I am an obedient wife after all." She looked to him for approbation.

He tweaked her ear affectionately. "Yes, after *all!*"

"Don't do that!" She drew back and teasingly wagged a finger at him in admonishment. "Do you want our baby to have big ears because you pulled her mother's before she was born?"

"So, we're to have a girl!" He folded his arms across his chest and stared imperiously at Asya. "What, young lady, makes you think you'll have a daughter?"

"One of the women in church told me. She said I walk like I am going to have a girl."

"How's that?"

Asya thought a minute and answered slowly. "I really don't know. She said you can tell from the back."

Etienne threw back his head and laughed so hard that Asya had to put her arms about his neck to keep from slipping off his lap. "That's a sneaky way to prophesy," he finally commented, as he pulled her closer to him. Then he sobered. "Asya," he said, "I am glad I got here before you sold the ship. We need it for one more trip."

Asya's eyes twinkled. "You mean Captain Middleton can go to China one more time?"

Etienne put his hands on her shoulders and turned her so he could look straight into her face. His voice was reprimanding, but his eyes were amused when he said, "Asya, sometimes I think there's a bit of the devil in you."

Asya tilted her head and gave him a sly look. "You could be right at that." Her voice grew serious. "Just where *do* you want Captain Middleton to take the ship?"

"To Cap Henri."

Asya looked at her husband oddly. "But—but it isn't a battleship. It can't storm the harbor."

"Asya," he said as he put his hand against the back of her head and pushed it down on his shoulder, "listen quietly. There is something I have to tell you." He stopped as though trying to select his words. "You remember Abbé Brille, don't you?"

570

She nodded.

"He is dead."

Asya gasped. She tried to speak, but Etienne gently laid his hand against her cheek and pressed her head back against his shoulder. She knew he had more to tell.

"He was killed. Killed while saying Mass. I am not sure why, but the story I've been able to gather is that Christophe ordered him killed as a spy."

Asya's head shot up. "He was no spy. He couldn't have spied for one person against another. He loved everybody." Tears came to her eyes. "Poor Abbé Brille. He won't be happy in Heaven without his flock to look after. And his people? What will they do without him, Etienne?"

"Revolt. They've gone wild. They are wrecking and burning Cap Henri and have marched out to Sans Souci to kill Christophe, but his palace guard is shooting them down as they approach the gates. The army is deserting. At Fort Thomassique they killed the captain and sent his head to Christophe.

Asya spoke sadly: "They never should have killed Abbé Brille. He was a man of peace. While he lived, the people did not rebel, for he taught them to hope. Christophe is a fool," Asya denounced. "He has taken away the people's hope. Now they have nothing left but despair and revolution."

"And, in revolution, they slaughter their own."

"What are we going to do about it, Etienne?"

"We?"

"Yes, *we*," she repeated, jumping to her feet. "That's our country now, Etienne, and it needs our help. I haven't spent my money for nothing. I'm a woman, and women want their money's worth."

Etienne stood up, his face sober. "I am leaving now. My men and I are joining with the rebels at Thomassique and going down into Cap Henri. General Boyer will take his South Haitian army across the mountains and back us up. Boyer, as the military commander, will unite north and south into one country again. Asya, it is the end of the empire!"

"You make it all sound so simple," Asya said as she turned her back and slowly walked away from him. She was worried about her husband's safety and did not want him to see her face. Asya took a deep breath to clear her throat, for she feared she might burst into tears. "What—what is it you wish Captain Middleton to do with the ship?" she turned around to inquire.

Etienne reached inside his jacket and brought out some papers. "Give these to him. They are lists of supplies we shall need back at Cap Henri. The ship's chandler should know where to find them."

Asya gave a quick glance at the papers he handed her. "What are all these for?" she asked in amazement. "How can you win a war with goats and seedlings and chickens?" Quickly she riffled through the lists. "And mattresses and cook pots and bolts of calico. Jugs and machetes and shovels. Oh, Etienne, what an odd cargo to fight a war with!"

Etienne took her hands in his and, watching her face, said in a happy, almost exultant voice, "Ma cherie, these are the ingredients for rebuilding Cher Château. There is nothing left back there but the land, and we must plant our roots deep, deep into it if our efforts are to last. A war is won, not in killing, but in living again. Abbé Brille's people need work and they will have it at Cher Château. I can see it all now, Asya." Etienne placed his cheek against hers and put his arms around her shoulders. "The pink-plastered walls of Cher Château rising up. The white balconies. The fields alive again. Flowers everywhere, and our children shouting and laughing, as they annoy the gardener when they trample them down."

"And Negu." Asya was caught up in his enthusiasm. "She will have a purple dress with a white lace fichu and sit at our table and complain, as a grandmother is supposed to, that we're raising our children all wrong."

Their parting was quick. Etienne took Asya's face in

his hands, kissed her hard on the lips. Then, as silently as he had come, he was gone through the open door.

Asya did not go to the door to watch as he rode off, but stood in the room where he kissed her good-bye. She did not want to remember him riding down the road away from her, but as he had been in this room—alive, talking, teasing. Above all, here.

Already Asya felt a depression clawing at her heart, but she determined to ignore it. If she kept herself busy, very busy, perhaps it might go away. She must be about the business that her husband had entrusted to her. She looked down at the lists he had given her, still in her hands. A tiny ray of excitement flickered in her breast. She was holding the beginning, not just a dream or a hope, but the actual concrete beginning of Cher Château.

Asya picked up her bonnet where it lay on the table and walked over to the mirror to put it on. As she tied the ribbons under her chin, she saw, reflected in the looking glass, the letter from Mère Brigitte, lying forgotten under the settee. She dismissed it with a wrinkle of her nose and, whirling around, hurried out to the piazza to await the carriage to carry her down to the bank. Such a useless little letter. Someday, she might mention its contents to Etienne, but for the present it was of no importance. Perhaps the housemaid would find it and burn it with the rest of the trash.

No spirit was wilder,
No passion greater
In vengeance or
in love

Tarifa

by *Elizabeth Tebbets Taylor*

She was a beguiling child, a bewitching temptress.
Many men worshipped her, many loved her,
some even tried to tame her. But only one man
could possess her. Bart Kinkaid, a daring sea
captain saw past her dark desires to the burning
within. Like ships in a tempest-tossed sea, their
love soared beyond the boundaries of time itself.

A Dell Book $2.5o

*A tumultuous drama
of misplaced love
and betrayal*

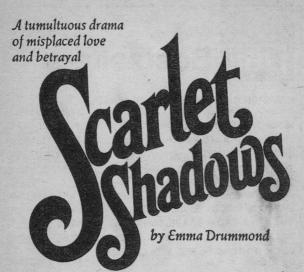

Scarlet Shadows

by Emma Drummond

Sweet, innocent, beautiful Victoria Castledon loved her dashing
and aristocratic husband, Charles Sanford. Or at least she thought
she did, until she met the notorious Captain Esterly. He alone
could awaken Victoria to the flaming desires within her, and she
would not be happy until she yielded to love's sweet torment . . .

From London to Constantinople Victoria pursues Captain Esterly
only to find out that this man she so desperately loves is her
husband's brother. Her scandalous desire blazed across continents
—setting brother against brother, husband against husband, lover
against lover . . .

A DELL BOOK $2.25

234-2977

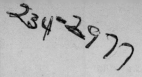

Dell Bestsellers